August 21ˢᵗ, 2010

by

Bill Ashley

Enjoy the book!

W Ashley

First published in Great Britain in 2006

The right of William John Ashley to be identified as author
of this work has been asserted by him in accordance with
the Copyright, Designs and Patents Act 1988

Published by Rubicon Books
www.rubicon-books.com

ISBN: 1-903172-67-5

Cover image: NGC7293, Helix Nebula in Aquarius, taken by
Dr George Greaney using an Optical Guidance Systems 14.5" f/7.9
Ritchey-Chretien telescope

Forethought:

About 20 years ago, I heard a talk given by the late Reverend David Sheppard, former Anglican Bishop of Liverpool, entitled 'Samson's Hair is Growing Again'. In it, he said he'd been asked the question, "If God came down to Earth today and we asked Him what He wanted of us, what do you think He'd say?" In response, David Sheppard had answered, "I think God would say He wanted us to get back to a time when we had little but Him." Those words made a powerful impression on me when I first heard them and they still reverberate in my mind today.

Acknowledgements:

I would like to thank:
- my partner, Jill, for her unwavering support throughout this project and her faith in me to complete it
- my parents, in particular my Dad, for their doggedness in reading, correcting and re-reading the manuscript in various drafts
- John and Philippa White, their daughter Judith and her husband James, Philippa's mother Jessie, my solicitor, John Garner, my accountant, Alan Harrison, Liz Mack at Stray's Books in Newark and umpteen other critical readers for their invaluable feedback on the manuscript
- my guide and mentor, Molly Burkett, of Barny Books, her business partner Jayne Thompson and many other people whose support I value

My special thanks go to:
- Dr Jay Melosh, Professor of Theoretical Geophysics in the Department of Planetary Sciences at the University of Arizona, Tucson, whose team has published a model on their website for calculating the effects of planetary impacts which I used in creating the story and who generously agreed to appear in person in the book
- Dr George Greaney of Las Vegas, Nevada, for his kind permission to use the image of NGC7293 taken from his website at: www.astroimages.com

I am indebted to a host of contributors to the Internet too numerous to mention and Wikipedia – the free encyclopedia – in particular, which I turned to repeatedly for information on virtually every aspect of the book.

I would also like to thank:
- Professor Sir Ian Kershaw for his kind permission to use a brief extract from his book, 'Making Friends with Hitler: Lord Londonderry and Britain's Road to War' published by Allen Lane.
- B Feldman & Co Ltd, London WC2H 0QY for their kind permission to use a brief extract from the popular song "We're in the Money" words by Al Dubin and music by Harry Warren © 1933 M Witmark & Sons, USA

Dedication:

This book is dedicated to Keith Moser, who not only released me from the ties that bound me to my former life, which hampered me from getting on with this book, but who also polarised my thoughts about religion with one simple comment he made to my parents, which galvanized me into writing it now.

Keith is a practicing Christian. On discovering that my parents were likewise practicing Christians, he was a little taken aback and said, "All this time, I thought you were agnostics. If I'd known you were Christians, I'd have gotten to know you sooner." That comment, made casually in conversation and no doubt made in all innocence, epitomises for me everything that is wrong with organised religion; it represents the visible – and, consequently, fairly harmless – tip of a huge iceberg of religious intolerance; unfortunately, the ninety percent that's submerged below the surface, which cannot be seen, is hidden in men's hearts and runs from mild dislike and distrust of people whose beliefs are different, to the blackest hatred of them.

Introduction:

I am an agnostic: I believe that nothing is or ever will be known of the existence or nature of God.

That doesn't mean to say that I believe there is no God (if that was the case then I would be an atheist and there would be an end to it – I would not have been inspired to write this book). But ask yourself: If there is no God, what gives substance to the World we live in, to our Solar system, our Galaxy, the Universe, and the void beyond? What is existence? When did it start? When will it end? What more evidence do we need of a Creator than Creation itself, of which we are an almost infinitesimally small part?

I am also a Deist: I believe in God. For me, that's where religion starts and that's where it ends. But I don't believe in God as the conclusion of a logical argument, or because the alternative is either too monstrous, or frightening, or defiant, to contemplate. I simply *feel* the presence of God. I believe that everything exists in the mind of God. However, I also believe that we are as nothing in the face of God; God looks benignly on the vilest of humanity whilst allowing the least vile of us – believers and non-believers alike – to suffer the most terrible and appalling fates? [As I write this, the official death toll from the December 26, 2004 tsunami, caused by a magnitude 9.0 undersea earthquake off the coast of Sumatra, in Indonesia, has just topped

150,000 human victims and continues to rise.] God *must be* aware we exist but how much interest God takes in us, individually or collectively, I cannot guess at. This may be a frightening thought but if we ignore it and the spectre of death and what lies beyond, we can enjoy life.

What really frightens me is how men have hijacked God in the name of religion and use the fear of God and the threat of God's retribution as a stick to beat simple people with, to bend them to its will and beliefs, to make them conform, and to observe its rituals – in short, to enslave them. Whilst God should bring *all* people together, the divisiveness and intolerance of organised religions keeps us apart and breeds distrust, hatred and hostility. Yet if all religions insist there is only *one* God – *their* God – isn't each religion seeing *the same* God from a *slightly different* perspective? So why are men driven to such extremes by these slight differences that they would kill each other to defend their particular faith? And in claiming to know and speak for God aren't religions being supremely arrogant, for who can know God? However, I don't believe that we will be punished for our arrogance by the wrath of God but by God's indifference to our fate. If nothing else, I hope this book makes you think about that.

Part 1: The Power of Nightmares

Chapter 1

(Saturday 31 July 2010, about 21:30 Pacific time)

"Jack, is that you?"

"Martha, you know I'm tied up right now. You'll have to be quick! What is it?"

"It's Billy. He's disappeared again. I've looked everywhere and I can't find him. Jack, I'm worried. I haven't seen him since yesterday morning. I left it as long as I could before calling you. I'm sorry but I'm at my wits' end…"

"Have you looked in the loft? In the old treehouse?"

"Yes! I've even been up on Drover's Hill where we found him last time but he wasn't there. I've had Margaret and Beth out looking. We can't find him anywhere. Please come home, I need your help."

"Martha, I can't. I told you this is an emergency. You'll have to deal with it yourself. Call the police… although what they'll make of it after last time, I don't know."

"And what do you call this if it isn't an emergency? Billy's your son for God's sake. I can't believe you don't care about him. He's twelve years old. He's autistic. He can't communicate. Anything might have happened to him. What's wrong with you? Don't you love him? Don't you care?"

"You don't need to remind me about my own son… and, of course, I care… but I'm sorry, Martha, I can't come. Get Nick and Claudette to help. I've got to go now."

"I never thought you'd abandon your own son. I can't take Nicky and Claudette out of school. It's their finals this year. Don't you want them to get good grades? Jack… Jack… Are you there?" There was no reply. Martha screamed into the phone, "You selfish bastard!" but the breath caught in her throat. Then the tears started streaming down her cheeks. Her hands shook with rage as she put the handset down clumsily.

—•—

Jack sat on the corner of the desk, his hand on the receiver and stared at the floor. He felt lower than he'd ever felt in his life. He'd never dismissed his wife like that before. It hurt him to realise that he'd turned his back on her for the first time in their twenty-four years of marriage at a time when she needed him so desperately. But before he had any time for remorse the door burst open and his assistant, David Johnson, came in.

"Jack, hurry up! The Director's going ape. He wants you in the Control Room right now! The drive card for the polar axis motor's fritzed and it's got to be changed. We've got less than an hour to get it back up and working again before the target comes into our field of view. The maintenance crew's on its way with a spare amplifier. We've got to meet them there."

"That's all we need!" Jack jumped up from the desk and immediately pushed thoughts of Martha and Billy to the back of his mind. He pushed past his dishevelled assistant and walked briskly down the corridor, his long legs taking huge strides as David struggled to keep up with Jack and brief him at the same time.

"The telescope's stuck. We can't drive it into position. Arthur and his Control Room boys are trying to wind it by hand as close as they can to the next anticipated sighting until the drive's fixed. I've been giving them a hand but it's hard work trying to turn three hundred tons of telepscope using nothing but a small crank handle. I'm jiggered!"

Jack shot over his shoulder, "Go and get cleaned up then join me upstairs. We need tonight's sighting. It's imperative! You're no good to me in that state. You've been on the go for three days without a break, so get a bite and some coffee... And bring me one too, I need it. I'll be in the Control Room."

Saying this, Jack peeled off and went up the stairs, taking the steps two-at-a-time without breaking his pace.

As Jack was about to enter the Control Room, Dan Ackland, the Director of the Observatory, came out and almost collided with him. "Jack, where in God's name have you been? It's like Hell with the lid off in there and you go AWOL! I presume you know the 'scope's out of action. I want it back up in thirty minutes or we'll miss this sighting. It's vital, so get to it for Christ's sake!"

—•—

Martha sat on the arm of the chair. Her chest heaved and she was racked with sobs. Margaret came over and put her arm around Martha's shoulders. "He'll be alright. Billy's not going to be far away. We'll find him. He'll probably come back when he's hungry, so don't you worry."

When she'd calmed down, Martha said, "I wish I could share your optimism, Maggie. Billy would go for days without eating if I didn't put his food in front of him. He might even starve himself to death... I don't know, we never tried it. Even then, food doesn't seem to matter to him. He never goes looking for it. He just eats when he's given food because it's what we programmed him to do from an early age. The only up-side is he eats what he's given. He has what we have and never complains, never wants anything different. It's a blessing in that respect."

Beth came from the kitchen. She'd been talking to her husband.

"Roger's going to put the kids to bed. I said I'd stay here with you until Billy's back." Martha started to protest but Beth cut her short saying, "It's what friends are for. If he needs me, he'll call and I'll pop home. We need to concentrate on finding Billy. When's Jack coming home?"

"He's not. He's staying at the Observatory. There's some kind of emergency going on up there. When he left yesterday morning… no, two days ago now… he told me there was something happening. He wouldn't tell me what, just that he'd be tied up for a while and might not be home the following morning. I've never seen him looking so concerned or preoccupied about anything. It must be serious because he's never spoken to me like that before, even when there's been trouble."

Before she could stop herself Margaret blurted out, "Let's hope it's not that pretty little research student of his… the one with the blonde hair and pneumatic breasts… that's got him all tied up." All three laughed, more to relieve the tension of the moment than because it was genuinely funny.

Beth asked Martha, "What are we going to do now? Should we split up and take different directions to cover more ground or go together and cover each area more thoroughly?"

Martha sat and thought for a moment, then said, "I think it's time to call Bill Finn over at the Sheriff's office and get some help. We can't cover the ground fast enough with just the three of us."

Margaret said, "Do you think the Sheriff would come over again after last time? He was mighty upset to think we'd dragged him and his dog team out just to find a small boy moongazing on Drover's Hill. Shouldn't we give it one more go then call him in the morning if we've had no success?"

They could see how tired and worried Martha was. "No" she said, "I think we should recognise that we've run out of places to search…" then added, more to herself than the others, "It's odd but the last three times he's disappeared we've found him somewhere high up, each time higher than before and each time he seemed strangely calm. I was wondering whether that's significant… But there's nowhere higher than Drover's Hill around here so I can't think where he might be."

Beth asked, "Do you think we're looking in the wrong place altogether? Do you think Billy might have gone down to the beach? You know how much he loves the ocean. Mind you, it's a long way for a little boy to travel alone and on foot."

"I don't know… No, I doubt it. The last couple of times we went down to the sea for a swim, Billy got very agitated. The first time this year, at the end of June, he just stood staring and pointing out to sea, rocking backwards and forwards and moaning. He was clearly very disturbed and wouldn't go near the water. The last time we went, on the Fourth of July for a picnic, Billy wouldn't even get out of the car. When Jack tried lifting him out to carry him to the beach, Billy just clung to the door and screamed. I've never seen him that worked up. It was as though he was terrified of something. It really shook me up. It really shook Jack, too. Eventually, we had to give up and go elsewhere. In fact, we ended up on Drover's Hill and Billy seemed very much calmer and happier. He even went to sleep with his head in my lap which is also strange because you know how restless he can be and it's been getting worse recently."

Martha picked up the phone and called the Sheriff's office. "Bill, hi, it's Martha Culver here. I'm real sorry to trouble you at this time of the evening but I need your help. Billy's disappeared again. He's been gone now since yesterday morning and I'm getting very worried about him. I've searched the house and gardens. I've been out with Beth and Margeret and we've looked everywhere... even up on Drover's Hill... but he's nowhere to be found."

"Martha, don't worry, we'll find him. He can't have gone far. I'll be with you in twenty minutes. Meanwhile, have a look in his room and round the house to see if there's anything out of place that might give us a clue to his whereabouts."

—•—

(Saturday 31 July 2010, late evening into the early hours of Sunday 1 August 2010, Pacific time)

"Well Jack, there it is. Exactly where we predicted it would be... and exactly where we *didn't* want it to be. The latest laser measurements confirm its speed at about a hundred thousand miles per hour. Based on its position and trajectory that puts its distance at just over fifty million miles away from the point where it'll cross our path... in twenty-one days time. In fact, it should be crossing the orbit of Mars as we speak... Let's hope we pass like ships in the night... otherwise, God help us."

"Thanks, Arthur. It's a pity Mars isn't in its path, to draw the asteroid into itself or deflect it... Have we been able to get any more information yet about its make-up or solidity?"

"All our readings simply confirm a solid nickel-iron mass, roughly spherical but slightly irregular in shape, with traces of other elements... some fairly commonplace, such as cobalt and tungsten, others fairly rare, such as iridium, platinum and gold. It's tumbling, of course, which makes it more difficult to determine its size precisely. To the best of our measuring capability, it's about twelve to twelve-point-two miles in diameter. Assuming it's solid... and we've no reason to assume otherwise... that's a weight of about thirty to thirty-three trillion tons."

"Well, that's consistent with the weight we calculated based on Jupiter's influence on its speed and trajectory. It's ironic but before its brief encounter with Jove, it was just another lump of debris moseying harmlessly through space. Now, after Jupiter's slingshot effect has accelerated it and hurled it in our direction, it's become *truly* a weapon of mass destruction. What's even more ironic is that it could be debris from the core of a planet similar to our own... maybe one that's been destroyed in a collision with another planet or some even more violent event... Dave, can you run the latest data and update the computer projection of its path for the midnight briefing? We need to know how close this mother's going to come to hitting us."

David re-appeared a few minutes later carrying a bundle of papers and computer-generated drawings. The asteroid had re-appeared from behind Jupiter and its course had altered towards Earth. The Observatory had been following its progress through the heavens. Three weeks ago – at about one hundred million miles out – it came into clear view for the first time. Only then did the possibility that it might come close to Earth become a reality. From the first calculations based on their initial measurements, the possibility of a collision had never been more than a million-to-one chance. Now, for the first time since assuming responsibility for plotting and reporting its course, David Johnson looked careworn and pale. With these latest measurements of the asteroid's trajectory more accurate than ever before, the cone around the Earth showing the plane of uncertainty through which it would pass relative to Earth's orbit had shrunken considerably – and alarmingly so – and had become tightly centered on the Earth itself.

Jack knew it was bad news before David laid the drawings out on the table. David prepared himself by clearing his throat and swallowing hard, something he hadn't done before at one of these briefings. It was almost as if he was too nervous to start speaking for fear of what fate his words might portend. He braced himself and said, "Based on the latest measurements from today's sighting of asteroid 2010 AS241 and extrapolating its path from its progress over the last few weeks, the plane of uncertainty has decreased to about ten Earth diameters... Unfortunately, these latest measurements also center the plane bang on Earth... No pun intended. Our latest calculations show there's at least a one-in-a-hundred chance of it colliding with Earth, greater still when the increasing influence of gravity is taken into account as we get nearer to each other."

11

As he sat there, Jack Culver saw in his mind's eye an image of the Earth seen from afar against the black backdrop of space, drawing the asteroid inexorably in towards itself, culminating in the most awesome – and awful – fireball and it left no room in his mind for any other thought.

Everyone in the room sat in silence until the Director said, "Jack, I'm not casting doubts on you or your team's abilities but as Director of Astronomy, I presume you've checked out calibration of the 'scope and re-checked it… There's no chance that our measurements are out?"

"No, Dan, no chance… *unfortunately*. The measurements are as true as the equipment's capable of. Today's readings are probably more reliable than some of the earlier ones because the object's nearer and the sky's been very clear recently. We'll check it again, of course. As of yet, we can't say precisely what time the crossing event will happen, which determines the outcome of everything but a PU of ten centered on Earth is far too close for comfort."

"We have no option but to inform the President of this potential disaster. We have to continue tracking it and refining our projections. Jack, keep your team focussed on S241. I need one hundred percent commitment until we know for certain whether or not it's going to hit Earth and, if it is, precisely when and where. Do I have that?"

"Yes Sir."

"And let's just hope it doesn't…"

—•—

(Saturday 31 July 2010, late evening Pacific time)

Beth answered the door. "Good evening, Bill. Come in. How's Shirley? I hope her arthritis isn't troubling her too much."

"Oh, she's fine, thanks Beth. Actually, this warm spell we've been having is keeping it at bay, thank goodness. You know how she suffers when it's cold and damp… Now, where's Martha?"

Margaret appeared from the kitchen carrying a coffee pot and cup. "She's having another look in Billy's room. She'll be down in a minute. How about a coffee, Bill? Freshly brewed." He held his hand up but before he could decline, Martha came in. "Thank you for coming over, Bill. I'm glad to see you."

"I don't suppose our stray's turned up yet… When did you last see him, Martha?"

"Yesterday morning, at about eight-thirty. I had some chores to do in the basement… laundry, ironing and the like. I left Billy watching the news. Normally, he doesn't watch much TV but he'll watch it if there's something interesting or informative on. He seemed quite engrossed so I assumed he'd be okay on his own for a while. I must have got lost in what I was doing because by the time I came back upstairs it was about eleven o'clock and he'd gone."

"What was he watching? Could it have been something that frightened him... scared him into hiding or running away?"

"No, I don't think so. If I remember rightly it was an article about this unseasonal migration of whales and dolphins out of the Pacific... You know, the one scientists think is a sign of unusually bad weather to come. Jack's sister, Ellen, is a marine biologist down in San Diego. She's been monitoring it for a few weeks. She was here last weekend, on her way up to Vancouver Island to study the orcas and she was discussing it over dinner. Billy seemed very interested. He was listening intently. I noticed that he even looked at her whilst she was speaking, which is something he almost never does. Whether he was taking any notice of the other unpleasant stuff in the news... terrorist attacks, the Middle East, Israel and so on... I couldn't say but I don't think so."

"So you don't think he got scared and went off and hid some place and perhaps got locked in a cupboard or outhouse? Have you called out to him?"

"I've looked every place around the house. It's no use shouting him because he wouldn't answer. He'd probably come if you gave him a direct instruction and he heard it and he may rattle the door if it was stuck, to let you know where he was..."

The Sheriff continued, "Unless, of course, he was injured and couldn't do so. Do you have any reason to think he may be injured? Is he on medication and could've forgotten to take it and maybe fallen into a coma?"

"No, he's not on any medication... and I've no reason to think he's hurt. Why should I?"

"I'm just exploring every avenue, Martha. Well, I can't see him going very far. He doesn't have the necessary faculties for running away, does he? I mean, he is a very... er... simple little boy, no offence intended Ma'am."

"None taken, Sheriff but you couldn't be more wrong when you describe him as simple... far from it. Billy's a very complex and complicated little boy. He has autism, yes, which makes communication with him extremely difficult... well nigh impossible. He never discusses everyday thoughts or feelings... maybe he doesn't have any. He never shows any sign of affection and never craves any attention. He'll let you give him a hug, although he usually remains absolutely rigid but he never looks for human contact. Never once in his life has he come to me for a hug... And he's surprisingly strong for his size. It probably comes from holding the same rigid posture, sometimes for hours on end... If he doesn't want a hug he can push you off and break free from your clutches with ease. And if you try to keep a hold of him he'd struggle until you let him go but he'd never attack you... or at least not in my

13

experience. It's just a struggle you'd never win... The only person he ever seems remotely comfortable with is his older sister, Claudette and even then he only sits on her knee occasionally. Usually if she tries to cuddle him he either stiffens up or gets off. Oh! And his grandmother, Jack's mother but he doesn't see her very often. She's very patient with him and they have a strong affinity for each other... Certainly a closer bond than I have with Billy... But he's not mentally retarded if that's what you were implying. The doctors describe him as an autistic savant simply because there's no more appropriate pigeonhole to put him in. How his mind actually works, nobody knows but he's far from stupid. In fact, his mind seems to work furiously... and non-stop."

At that point, Margaret said, "Bill, are you sure you wouldn't like a coffee?" and Bill agreed he would. "Milk, no sugar, please Margaret... Thank you... So, Martha, do you have any idea what might have happened to Billy. You were looking in his room... Is there anything there that might give us a clue as to where he is?"

Martha said to the Sheriff, "Please drink your coffee first Bill, then we'll go to Billy's room... Yes... Now I've looked around it more closely there are things missing, things I didn't see before when I was just looking for Billy."

"Such as what?"

"Well, his backpack is gone... and some of his clothes... oddly enough, mostly winter clothes... a couple of books... a pair of binoculars... and the last three hundred dollars from his moneybox... I know because he recorded the withdrawal in his cashbook... It also looks as though he tried moving his telescope but gave up. It's much too heavy for him to carry far..." After a brief pause, Martha continued, "You look shocked, Sheriff. What at? The fact that Billy has his own money... or a telescope... or that he's actually got the wherewithall to run away from home..." The Sheriff didn't reply but drained his cup and followed Martha as she started up the stairs, with Beth bringing up the rear. Margaret went back to the kitchen to wash the pots and put them away; she'd already seen Billy's room.

Martha pushed open the door. Beth and the Sheriff stood side-by-side in the doorway, too surprised to say anything. Martha said, "This is mostly Billy's work, Sheriff. Now do you begin to understand what I was saying downstairs?" The room was long and narrow, with the neatly made bed against the opposite wall. The long wall facing the door, with the exception of a small alcove for the bed and one end wall were entirely taken up with shelves completely filled with books. At the far end of the room French doors opened out onto a balcony that looked down towards the moonlit Pacific Ocean, about six miles away. Standing on the carpet inside the doors was Billy's magnificent telescope pointing just above the horizon. On closer

14

examination, it was obvious from the deep indentations in the carpet that someone had moved it recently.

"Does Billy use this?" asked the Sheriff, admiring the telescope.

"Yes, with Jack. They spend hours up here together when Jack's not at work. When he is, Billy spends hours at it on his own. I usually have to tell him it's bedtime, otherwise he'd be here 'til sun up. It's an excellent place because there are no major conurbations between here and the ocean… in fact, between here and Japan… so there's next to no light pollution."

"Does Billy know what he's looking at?" asked the Sheriff.

"It's difficult to say. According to Jack, Billy has a photographic memory. He only has to see a constellation once and he remembers it in every last minute detail but I don't know whether he truly comprehends what he sees."

"That's remarkable", observed the Sheriff lost for words.

Martha continued, "This was our dressing room, our bedroom's next door. When it became obvious Billy wasn't… like other children we converted it into his room so he'd be close to us in case he needed us in the night… You can come in…" said Martha, beckoning to Beth. "It's not as though it's a crime scene" she added, with a hint of sarcasm.

Beth said, "It must be delightful having a son… *no, any child…* who's so neat and tidy. I could scream sometimes when I see the state of Laura-Anne's room. It drives me crazy."

Bill Finn went to the bookshelves and took down a book at random from a section entitled 'Math' and thumbed through it. "The Importance of Prime Numbers in Non-Cyclic Functions. What in Heaven's name does a twelve year old boy make of this?"

Martha said, "I don't know, Sheriff. I don't even know if he understands any of it but he picked it out himself. He's chosen most of these himself."

Suddenly, as the Sheriff turned a page, a sheaf of papers fell out and floated down to the floor. The three of them stooped down to pick up the sheets and Martha read the title in Billy's distinct handwriting, 'Riemann's Hypothesis – a Proof' and asked herself, 'And what's Riemann's Hypothesis when it's at home?' She studied the blizzard of hieroglyphics for a moment but they meant nothing to her, so she laid the sheets carefully between the open pages of the book. The Sheriff clumsily laid the sheets he'd collected on top of the rest. Knowing how particular Billy was about his things, Martha took the book from him and rearranged them tidily. Her attention was arrested momentarily when she noticed the bold capital letters at the bottom of the last page, 'Q.E.D' – 'quod erat demonstrandum', usually used at the conclusion of a formal proof to convey that it demonstrates the truth of its claim, that much she knew – and Martha wondered briefly just what it was that Billy had proved. When Martha had returned the book to the shelf, she continued, "One day, Jack overheard Billy sitting on his bed quietly chanting out numbers.

15

He'd already been at it for hours..." at which she started snapping her fingers like the slow beat of a metronome. "By this time he was into seven figures. At the time it didn't mean anything to Jack but he was so intrigued, he taped it. Later, he sat listening to it. It took him a couple of hours to work out that what Billy was doing was counting up in prime numbers... And Jack's a *magna cum laude* in astrophysics... When he realised what Billy was doing, he was astonished. Jack checked all of Billy's maths books for tables of prime numbers, to see if he'd memorised them but he couldn't find one in any of his books. Billy was working them out in his head... correctly and without missing any... at a rate a computer could hardly keep pace with. I can't remember why he stopped... Maybe we called him down for dinner or something... Maybe he didn't stop... Maybe he's still doing it as a background task somewhere in some deep recess of his mind..." After a brief pause, Martha went on, "Billy's obsessed with numbers... counting things... measuring things... timing things... God knows whether he has any real concept of time but he insists on having the best, most accurate watch money can buy and even then he's always looking for something better. It's the only personal item of any value he's ever asked for. Jack and I got him the latest model for his birthday when we were in Dubai recently. We were on the way back from a conference at which Jack had given a paper... We couldn't get a watch like it at home anywhere. It hadn't been released here... It's so sophisticated it automatically adjusts itself to the time signal from the atomic clock at the National Standards Institute in Boulder, Colorado. We spent ages choosing it. It's Billy's most prized possession... after his telescope, that is. I don't think it's left his wrist since we gave it to him."

The Sheriff said, "If Billy's such a techno-fr... er... techno-wizard, I assume he's also got the latest cellphone... If he's got it with him, the phone company should be able to locate him..." but Martha replied a little acerbically, "You assume too much, Sheriff. What use is a cellphone to a boy who can't communicate... who never normally goes anywhere on his own?" Seeing the look of bewilderment on the Sheriff's face, Martha observed dryly, "So my son's something of a mystery to you too, Sheriff... Just as he is to me."

Bill Finn continued looking along the shelves. "Earth History and Natural Sciences; Our Solar System; Space and the Universe; maps of the World. This is a veritable library. It's remarkable! Did Billy do all this by himself?"

"No, Billy just organised the books into logical groups. Jack printed the titles and put them up."

"There's a section here for road atlases of the USA. Are there any missing?"

"I don't think so, just let me check... No, Sheriff, they're all here."

"In which case, if he's gone of his own volition he can't be planning to go far."

"Oh Billy wouldn't need a map. He knows every city, town and village in the continental USA, the distance between them and the number of every road connecting them off by heart. He sits for hours studying every map he can get his hands on. He memorises them all. If we go anywhere in the car, you can ask him how to get there and he'll tell you the number of every road, the total distance from home to destination and the distance still to go, to the nearest mile. He actually watches the mile markers as we go along. It's uncanny. Last Fall, we drove to Jack's parents' holiday home in up-state New York for Thanksgiving... They have a cabin in the Adirondacks... Billy sat in the front while Jack drove... Funnily enough, it's one of the few things Billy and I have in common... We both hate flying... Every time Jack asked him which town was coming up next and how far it was, Billy just glanced at the odometer and told him then went back to looking out the window... After the holiday, Billy stayed on for a few days. He was so happy up there... Then his grandmother came to stay with us for a couple of weeks. They rode the Greyhound all the way back. It took them four days... Mabel knows Billy loves the bus. When they got back, Mabel said Billy'd told her exactly where they were at various stages of the journey. What's so remarkable about that was that Billy told her without being asked. Usually, he's not that forthcoming..." Martha finished by saying, "Billy's not totally helpless on his own, Sheriff. He's not without resources... but he's just not very worldly and that makes him vulnerable."

"I see things a bit more clearly, Martha. He's an extraordinary little boy. But where does that leave us? What does it tell us about where he might have gone?"

Chapter 2

(Saturday 31 July 2010, mid-morning Eastern time at the White House)

The President slapped the table hard with the flat of his hand. "I'm sick of all this goddam in-fighting between the agencies. We are the National Security Council, for God's sake... We're all supposed to be here to uphold and protect the interests of the United States of America and her people and all you do is snipe at each other and try to shift the blame for your failures onto one another. It's time you all worked together openly and shared your information freely and stopped worrying about who gets the kudos. Stop trying to score points at each other's expense. While you're doing that the bad guys are slipping between the cracks..." So saying, the President took a deep breath then continued, "So you're saying the CIA received intelligence last week about a possible sale of plutonium to al-Qaeda... Just when did you intend tabling this information?" He glared at Travis Johnston who was clearly uncomfortable at being put on the spot, which he demonstrated by sliding his finger inside his shirt collar and easing it away from his neck then swallowing hard. The President asked, "Where did they get the stuff from? Who would sell it to them?"

Travis Johnston, Head of the CIA's Counter-Terrorist Operations, raised his head and said, "Last week, it was an unsubstantiated report which I received *after* the last NSC meeting. I was waiting for confirmation from my field agents, which I received *yesterday*, before I told the other agencies..." The President thought Travis Johnston was covering his back and was about to launch into him again but let it drop when he continued, "It came from one of our agents in Chechnya, which is a clearing house for terrorist deals. The Chechens are still sore that America wouldn't intervene with the Russians on their behalf, to try to persuade Russia to stop persecuting the Muslims. Of course, Russia gave the Chechens what they wanted... eventually, after enough blood had been shed... At the time, we weren't *for* them, so in their eyes we were *against* them. So now *we're* their enemy. The plutonium, I understand, is from old nuclear subs being de-commissioned in Murmansk or somewhere on the Kola Peninsula. It's weapons-grade material from nuclear warheads. The word on the street is that it's being bought by the Russian Mafia who are using Chechen runners to transport it across Russia and down through Kazakhstan, Afghanistan and Iran to the Arabian Sea, then by boat to Yemen where it's being delivered to al-Qaeda..." After a brief pause, he continued, "The Mafia are absolutely ruthless and greedy enough to do such a thing, yes... but I'm not so sure it is them. I've recently received other intelligence suggesting this is the work of a group of old-style, hard-line Communists in or near Government who want to see the collapse of capitalism

18

and who're using Muslim extremists to try to bring it about. Of course, that would provide them with perfect cover... Who'd believe that God-fearing Muslims would do the bidding of godless Communists? The rumour has some credence. I can't believe the Russians are so careless they'd let anyone steal their plutonium and smuggle it out of their military bases. After all, its extremely valuable. We've offered to outbid all other takers for any plutonium and uranium they want to dispose of. Surely, if they want top dollar badly enough they'll make certain it's kept safe and secure until they can deliver it to us... which suggests to me they've had a change in ideology. They're selling it to Muslim terrorists... *they may even be giving it to them...* on the basis and with the full knowledge that they'll use it against America".

Everyone round the table sat in silence for a few moments, taking in the significance of the message. It was difficult enough fighting a bunch of faceless religious fanatics who were ready to die for their beliefs, made far more difficult because they were well financed and highly trained terrorists backed by rogue states or wealthy individuals. If their old enemy was covertly sponsoring terrorist acts against the West – and, worse still, doing so as a matter of state policy – while presenting a friendly public face to the world, such sinister duplicity, if proven, would have far-reaching consequences. It could even provoke full-scale war. Just who was the enemy? The President asked, "Has anyone heard similar rumours that might give this one legs?" Heads shook around the table. There were a few quiet 'No, Sirs'. He waited for a positive response but when none came he said, "Then I'd ask you to keep watch for firm evidence of this rumour becoming reality, Mr Johnston and report back to us when you have more solid information..."

Turning back to Alan Davies, FBI Executive Director for Counter-Terrorism, the President said, "So, Mr Davies, please elaborate on this latest threat."

"Yes, Sir. Yesterday, the NSA *overheard* a telephone conversation carried out on cellphones between two suspected terrorists, one of whom was already under surveillance in Wilmington, Delaware at the time and the other was actually here in DC... This was confirmed by the phone company." He switched on a portable recorder and two voices, speaking in Arabic, issued forth which quickly became over-dubbed in English for the benefit of the listeners. The audience listened attentively. After it had been played twice over, Alan Davies said, "Before we come to the contents of the message and what we think it means, I can tell you that it was between one Mansour Al Rashid..." at this, two photographs appeared on the monitors, "...seen here on the left, who's been living here in the USA, in the town of Newark, near Wilmington, as a naturalized American since March, two-thousand-two... and on the right, Mohammad Faisal Quereshi who has known links to al-Qaeda... We have intelligence that Quereshi recently joined an extremist splinter group called 'Metraqat Allah', which translates as 'The Hammer of God'. Al Rashid was originally from Iraq but was living in exile in Lebanon as a political refugee from Saddam Hussein's Ba'ath regime prior to coming to the United States... That's where he met his wife. She's Lebanese... He applied for asylum, claiming that Saddam had threatened to have him assassinated for continuing to spread anti-Ba'athist propaganda..."

The President cut in, "A perfect ruse for getting into the States... Now he turns on the country that's given him refuge. I presume this must be part of an elaborate long-term plan to infiltrate terrorists into the very heart of American society..."

Alan Davies continued, "Yes, Sir. We believe Al Rashid is a 'sleeper' planted here after the attack on the World Trade Center, to be activated as needed for another job. He's kept his head down and become a good American... and a fairly successful businessman selling marine insurance. He has an office in Wilmington and he's recently opened a second office here in downtown DC, in the business quarter. He's taken a suite on the top floor of a highrise just off Connecticut Avenue, within half a mile of the White House... We'd had no previous intelligence linking him to any terrorist group but his neighbours recently reported him to us as a suspected terrorist. They became suspicious when they noticed his wife and children were no longer living there and because there's been a lot of coming and going late at night. He told a neighbour they'd gone back to see family in Lebanon but they've been gone nearly two months... That's one helluva long duty visit... He's a Muslim known to pray at home and at work. He regularly visits a mosque in Phili and, less often, another mosque in Baltimore which is where we think he meets his controller. He also visited Mecca on pilgrimage last year... He's definitely one to watch."

The President said, half-jokingly but with a hint of irony, "So that's what it takes to get on the FBI's most wanted list these days. I'd better watch out when the First Lady takes the kids to see her mother and I have a few of the guys over for a Saturday night poker game before going to church Sunday..." Then added, with some feeling, "What's happening to America that neighbours spend more time spying on each other than getting on with their own lives? What in God's name is the country coming to?"

Either ignoring the irony or simply failing to register it, Alan Davies said, "It shows how effective the neighbourhood watch schemes set up under the last administration are... They must be, this one's potentially netted two big fish." The President couldn't argue with that but he still felt a vague sense of despair about the whole sorry state of affairs.

The President asked, "So what does their conversation tell us about the next threat?"

Alan Davies started expounding the FBI's interpretation of what had been said, some of which could only be put into context using intelligence gathered from other, related sources. "That al-Qaeda is planning an attack is now absolutely certain. The evidence from various sources is overwhelming. I won't go into these... they were adequately covered at the last meeting. Firstly, we believe the next attack will take place on September eleven which is a Saturday. This is based on the reference Quereshi makes to 'God striking his next blow at the black heart of the Infidels on the tenth anniversary of Him smiting down the twin pillars of evil...' an oblique reference, we believe, to the Twin Towers... Secondly, we believe the next attack will be here in Washington because of his reference to 'the heart of the Infidels'. Assuming we're the Infidels... that is, the 'not faithfuls' or non-believers, then Washington is probably the heart..."

The President interrupted, "I understand Islam uses a different calendar based on lunar cycles, so their anniversary may not be the same as ours... We aren't going to find it's next week by any chance and they've wrong-footed us?"

"No, Sir. We've already thought of that one... The Hijri date... that is, the date in the Islamic calendar equivalent to September eleven, two-thousand-and-one was twenty-third Jumada Al-Akhirah, in the Hijri year fourteen-twenty-two. This year, twenty-third Jumada fell on June fifth, which has already gone, so we're safe there."

"I guess we should be thankful for small mercies...", said the President. He pondered a moment longer, then asked, "What form is this attack likely to take? Do we know?"

"Not exactly, Sir but the intelligence suggests some kind of dirty bomb detonated within or above the city. This may be where Al Rashid's new office on Connecticut comes in... It puts ground zero high above the city and within easy striking distance of the White House, Capitol and many other Government buildings... even the Pentagon. We've also had supporting intelligence about the plutonium. From this, we originally thought al-Qaeda might be planning to make a thermonuclear bomb which, of course, would have wiped Washington off the face of the Earth. But, quite frankly, that didn't make sense. Taking into account the information the CIA have received, which suggests the material was only shipped to Yemen recently, along with information from our own sources, our experts think it's unlikely they're planning a nuclear bomb. It's far too complicated, time consuming and expensive to put together the necessary resources and build such a bomb in time for September eleven. It's also not something that can easily be done by the layman... It takes real expertise. If you haven't designed, built and tested one before, you'd also need a trial run to make sure you've got it right. No, our experts think the most likely scenario is that they're planning to use the plutonium to build a dirty bomb... that is, a conventional blast bomb surrounded by plutonium that'll disperse it over a wide area. That's where Quereshi's reference to the mills of God grinding exceeding small comes in. It's from Longfellow..." and here he quoted, "Though the mills of God grind slowly, yet they grind exceeding small... Rather odd, I thought, for a Muslim terrorist to be quoting an American poet but there you have it... He may have been educated in America or lived here under a different name. We don't know, our intelligence on Quereshi is fairly limited. However, it does suggest they're pulverising the plutonium into a powder so it contaminates the widest possible area... And where better to do that from than the fifteenth storey of a tower block?"

The President exclaimed, "My God! It's diabolical. It would cost a fortune to clean up the city and in the meantime it'd bring the process of government to a standstill."

Alan Davies responded, "Plutonium is extremely toxic, one of the most poisonous substances known to man. There's no level at which humans can tolerate breathing it in or ingesting it, however small the dose. It's also very persistent... Weapons-grade plutonium-239 has a half-life of twenty-four thousand years... It could take a quarter of a million years for the radiation to decay to a safe level. Our experts think it may be impossible to effectively de-contaminate the city. Washington may become a no-go area... We might never get the city back..."

At that moment, Alison Ord, the President's principal aide stood and asked to be excused, saying that she had to take an urgent call. As she left the conference room, the President stood and said, "I suggest we take this opportunity to pause for a moment, ladies and gentlemen... This is a good time to take a comfort break. I'll ask for coffee to be brought in..." There were murmurs and nods of assent. The meeting had already been going on solidly for two hours and looked as though it could continue a lot longer.

Coffee was brought in and everyone gratefully helped themselves. Three small groups had formed, one including General Landsbergh, Chairman of the Joint Chiefs of Staff of the United States Armed Forces and Colonel Reinhardt, head of the Pentagon's Strategic Planning Department and adviser to the Army's Counter-Insurgency Unit who had commanded an armoured brigade in Iraq for two years, helping to suppress Iraqi rebels. He'd witnessed many atrocities at first hand, in one of which he himself had been severely injured. His Adjutant and seven soldiers had been killed when the armored personnel carrier in which they'd been riding had been destroyed by a car bomb detonated outside a Baghdad school in the predominantly Shi'ite slum district of Sadr City. Twenty-four children and two teachers had also been killed and scores of others injured in the blast. The bomb had been planted by extremist Sunni rebels opposed to the interim government which was heavily Shi'ite in its make-up.

Representatives from the FBI, the CIA and the Department of Homeland Security stood together in another huddle. They all felt that their futures as autonomous organisations depended upon greater success, which would only be achieved through increased cooperation with each other and who, as a consequence, were discussing how best they could work together to nip this threat in the bud before it materialised.

Once coffees had been drunk everyone went back to their places, ready for the meeting to resume. They sat discussing the morning's developments. After a couple of minutes, Travis Johnston started to wonder what was delaying the President. It was very unusual for him to be absent for more than the briefest period; normally, he set a brisk pace for meetings to get them over with as soon as all important issues had been addressed. As everyone round the table was starting to notice the President's absence, Alison Ord walked in and said, "The President sends his apologies. He's been detained on a phone call. He'll be back shortly."

The President walked in and went back to his seat. He said nothing for a moment but looked very troubled. He collected himself then said, "I have just received some terrible and very sad news. I've been on the phone to the US Ambassador in Israel. Apparently, a Palestinian terrorist group launched an attack on the Israeli Prime Minister's home. His wife and two children have been killed. He's in hospital. His condition is critical. Twelve people including bodyguards and staff are dead, seventeen more have been wounded. Israel is on full alert... This may be the spark that sets off the Middle East powder keg. God help us all if it does. I've asked that the Israelis do nothing for the time being until we can properly assess the situation. Whether we can keep them in check and for how long, I don't know... General Landsbergh, you should know I've been on to General Corfield at the Pentagon and appraised him of the situation. He's stepping up satellite surveillance and putting our forces in the region on the highest state of readiness. I've also informed the Head of the CIA. I've told them to keep lines to the White House open. We may have to abandon our meeting if we're needed more urgently elsewhere. In the meantime, I suggest we proceed from where we left off. Mr Davies, please continue."

"Yes, Sir. I don't know whether Quereshi's use of the quotation from Longfellow also implies that the milling process is going slower than anticipated, so they're behind schedule but he mentions that the goods are late and shipment is delayed... 'The goods will be shipped one week later'. From this and other intelligence, we believe that the bomb is being built in Yemen then sent here by sea but we don't yet know when that will be. Al Rashid is involved in marine insurance. It's good cover. It means he can make detailed enquiries about sailing times, cargo, etcetera, without raising suspicion. He also owns a forty foot ocean-going cruiser which he berths down at the boat club in Annapolis. Here our intelligence starts getting a bit sketchy... If the bomb is being landed by ship, it'll probably come into the country in a container and be landed at either New York or Norfolk, Virginia and be consigned through to one of the container terminals at Phili, Baltimore, or Washington, where it'll be unloaded. We consider this route unlikely because containers are subject to random inspection... it might be discovered... and there are sophisticated radiation detectors at all ports of entry... Effectively shielding such a bomb so it couldn't be picked up would be very difficult. Alternatively, it could be unloaded out at sea onto Al Rashid's boat and brought into any one of dozens of marinas or boatyards up and down the Chesapeake or Delaware Bays. This would be my favorite..." Alan Davies stopped to ponder for a moment then thought out loud, "I suppose he could even bring it right up the Potomac into the heart of DC. If there was any risk of him being apprehended, he could detonate it on the boat... You know how willing these looneytunes are to blow themselves to Kingdom come."

The President said, "Well, you need to re-double your detection efforts to find out exactly how this bomb's getting here and where it's destined for..." then after a moment's thought, "I'm interested in his finances. Surely, an office on Connecticut is very costly? I've heard membership of the Annapolis Boat Club takes serious money. Is his business doing so well he can afford all this? You know what a tough time the insurance industry's been having since the Twin Towers. You need to look deeper into this guy's background."

"We're doing that, Sir. The IRS reckons his business is profitable but not sufficient to pay for a second office at such an expensive address... and he should be overstretching his own personal means to afford the boat *and* club membership but his bank account's still fairly healthy. We believe he's being financed from outside... which in itself suggests he's been planted here for nefarious purposes... so he can put on an affluent front in order to be better accepted and be able to move more freely in the right circles. Unfortunately, we can't approach his accountant for more information. He's also a Muslim. We don't know if he's active but there is a danger he might warn Al Rashid he's under investigation and blow the whole deal."

The President reflected for a while then said, "I don't know... This is too pat. My gut instinct tells me we're being set up. Most of the evidence you've amassed so far is based on verbal reports... hearsay and supposition... and a few tenuous links to past events. There's no tangible proof... no photographs, no ship's manifests and the like... on which to base your conclusions. Could this be a foil to throw us off the scent and distract our attention away from the real event? Don't forget... we got virtually no intelligence warning us of last year's attack on the Mall of America..."

"No, Sir, we don't. We think this is the real event. It may be that they've become a bit sloppy or a bit too cocky... thinking they're invincible... or maybe we got lucky. If it hadn't been for Al Rashid's family going away... and him having such observant and patriotic neighbours... we wouldn't have been carrying out surveillance on him in the first place."

On the Saturday before Christmas – the busiest shopping day of the year – al-Qaeda had attacked the Mall of America, in Bloomington, Minnesota, releasing Sarin nerve agent through the Mall's ventilation system. The Mall had been packed with Christmas shoppers. The terrorists had used young Muslim recruits, boys of fifteen or sixteen, to carry the bottles of Sarin into the Mall in their backpacks to avoid suspicion. The terrorists took over the HVAC services rooms housing the massive ventilation fans while their fellow terrorists used cars and trucks to block the exits then machine-gunned the fleeing crowds to prevent them from getting out. In all, twenty-three thousand, one hundred and fifty-one men women and children had died, including two of the Muslim boys acting as mules who must have been so appalled to see hundreds of dead and dying people that they panicked and took off their gasmasks in disbelief at the sheer horror of it all and had succumbed themselves; their apparently unintentional acts of self-destruction had been captured on CCTV. Many of the dead had been killed by the Sarin but many more were crushed in the stampede to get away from it. A further twenty-seven-and-a-half thousand people were injured to a greater or lesser degree, the worst affected being reduced to physical wrecks by the Sarin, racked with coughing spasms, fighting for breath, gasping, wheezing, drooling, twitching, shaking, sweating, blind, unable to control their bladder or bowels or do anything for themselves for up to a month after their exposure to the nerve agent. There had been no warning and no intelligence even hinting at an attack. Within thirty minutes of the attack, the FBI and the Minnesota National Guard's NBC response unit had sealed off the entire building. It had taken a further eight hours to evacuate everyone still alive, far too late to help many of the dying. The emergency services and hospitals in the Minneapolis – Saint Paul's area had been completely swamped by the disaster and some of the less severely ill patients had to be transferred to other hospitals as far afield as Chicago and Saint Louis. The effect on America had been shocking and profound, not least because the attacks were becoming more frequent and each successive attack more damaging – and therefore more successful – than the last. Many people were now living in a permanent state of fear and rapidly losing confidence in the Government's ability to do anything to combat these terrible attacks within their own borders. All of the terrorists with the exception of the two young boys had managed to get away from the Mall. Two of them had subsequently been cornered and shot dead at Milwaukee railway station, waiting to board a rush-hour train to Chicago but not before eighteen innocent bystanders had been killed and another thirty-seven wounded by grenades and gunfire, some of it 'friendly' fire from local police and FBI. The terrorists had strafed the crowded platform, to create mayhem, probably hoping they would be able to escape under cover of the resulting chaos.

In the forensic investigation that followed, the scientists found that the Sarin had been injected into the ventilation systems downstream of the inlet filters and chemical sensors, using hardened steel nozzles cleverly fashioned from fuel injectors to pierce the ducting. It had been released without detection so there was no warning. The fans continued running, filling the atrium with Sarin. They also recovered one of the canisters which a terrorist had dropped in his hurry to leave. On examination, they found that the Sarin had been carried as a binary system and mixed from two precursor chemicals immediately prior to being discharged into the airstream, then atomised to create an aerosol of tiny droplets that rained down on the unsuspecting victims which maximised its potency. The equipment was well engineered and incorporated some highly innovative features which told the scientists that al-Qaeda had access to some very skilled and sophisticated resources. Being heavier than air, the toxic vapor had settled in the Mall which had to be closed for three months for decontamination. Every item of stock, plus all furniture, carpets and other fittings had been removed and incinerated and the refurbishment and re-stocking had taken a further month. Of the five hundred and twenty-nine stores, seventy-eight had shut permanently – in the case of thirty-three owner-managed stores because the owners had either died in the attack or been too traumatised to return to work. The fourteen movie theaters also remained shut. The heaviest casualties had been suffered in these closed environments, in some instances with virtually hundred percent fatality. However, four months after the Mall had re-opened, customer numbers still remained far below most stores' breakeven level. Most of the victims who survived the Sarin attack had fully recovered from its physical effects but many still suffered from panic attacks and nightmares. Some had never set foot outside their homes since the day they returned from hospital. Almost seven-and-a-half months after the attack, the most seriously injured were those who had been shot or crushed, some of whom would be disabled for life.

The President asked, "Why do you think the bomb's being assembled in Yemen, rather than here?" Alan Davies responded smartly, "For various reasons, Sir... Firstly, handling plutonium needs fairly sophisticated equipment if you're going to avoid contaminating and killing the people processing the materials and assembling the bomb. You couldn't easily set that up in a basement in your average American suburb without attracting someone's attention... Secondly, the Yemenis will have plenty of martyrs willing to die for the cause... It wouldn't matter if a few of them working on the bomb did become contaminated and died. They'd just drive the bodies out into the desert and bury them in some convenient wadi. Here, it'd be far more difficult to dispose of a corpse without questions being asked, particularly if it was highly radioactive... And the last thing they'd want to do is jeopardise their highly trained attack cell immediately before an operation... Thirdly, there are radiation detectors in all our cities. Less sensitive than those at the ports admittedly but still highly effective. It would mean that the radioactive materials would have to be very well shielded to avoid detection... and it's when you're handling the plutonium powder that you're most likely to spill or scatter it. Even if they only carried a trace of it out into the street, it may give the game away. Once it's incorporated in a bomb it's properly packaged and shielded, so it minimises the chance of detection... And, of course, there's less pressure on them there because there's no risk of detection, so they have more time and resources to build a better, more sophisticated bomb..." Alan Davies concluded confidently, "Yes, we're sure that's what they're doing."

Everyone round the table remained quiet. Eventually, the President asked, "Why sell the plutonium from a warhead? That means dismantling it, which would risk exposure to radiation. Why not just sell the complete warhead, lock stock and barrel? It'd be so much easier for all concerned and far more effective than a dirty bomb... however dirty."

Alan Davies seemed flustered for a moment, as though he should already have considered this possibility and hadn't but then he rallied and said, "It would be far more difficult to steal the whole thing... Firstly, the missiles carrying the warheads are removed from the submarines at their military bases where they're *supposed to be* dismantled under strict supervision and the electronic triggers destroyed so that they can't be detonated, rendering them useless as bombs. These bases should be controlled by the Russian military. However, the plutonium is then sent to civilian re-processing facilities for conversion into reactor fuel. This is where the security gets a bit lax. We believe the plutonium is being stolen, either during shipment or from the re-processing plant. After all, it'd be obvious that a warhead had gone missing which should set alarm bells ringing around the world. Finagling a few kilograms of plutonium would be much easier and it may not be missed for ages, if at all, by which time the thieves could have covered their tracks fairly comprehensively..." Alan Davies petered out without giving a second reason why this possibility shouldn't be seriously considered.

The President said, "I'm yet to be convinced... Clearly, you still have a lot of sleuthing to do on this one. In the meantime, we need to be vigilant on every front. I want all agencies to give this threat top priority and report back to me immediately there's any news. Now, to the second item on today's agenda... How to deal with the terrorist threat in the broader sense and what can be done to deter or defeat terrorism? We have three reports... But first, I suggest we break off to freshen up. We'll resume in five minutes..." and with this, the President excused himself and hurried out of the meeting.

As he stood at the urinal trying to pass water, the intense pain from his inflamed prostate gland was excruciating. He thought to himself, 'Thank you, God! As if I didn't have enough on my plate at the moment... now You send this to torment me. Please... just let me take a leak in comfort... *Christ! That hurts! It's like pissing razorblades...* I can't put off getting my Johnson fixed much longer, however busy I am...'

—•—

The small boy stood outside the Ladies' restroom with his back to the entrance. He walked carefully without stepping on the joints between the paving slabs and counted three slabs from the door, then turned to his left and counted thirteen slabs along and stood in the exact center of the slab, facing the lockers that were standing against the opposite wall. He checked that the same lockers – numbers seventy-nine above and one-hundred and twenty-seven below – were still there; reassuringly enough, they were. He then quickly scanned the long rows of lockers, smaller ones on top and bigger ones beneath and counted three-hundred-and-thirty-one in all – all present and correct and precisely as it should be. His grandmother always visited the restroom before getting on the bus, even though the bus had a very comfortable if rather cramped little lavatory. He stood in precisely the same spot he stood in every time he waited for her to finish in the toilet whenever they travelled by bus. He looked up and scanned the ceiling tiles and counted how many there were and how many had lamps set into them. He noted that there were seven more lamps out now than the last time he'd travelled. She would normally be out by now. Then, starting to become somewhat irritated, he turned round and compulsively began counting the bricks in the wall. His counting was interrupted by the two vending machines that were standing, a little apart either side of a concrete pillar, against the wall between the doors to the Ladies' and Men's restrooms. He was startled when he noticed a pair of eyes staring at him from the shadows, which made him jump with fright.

Billy stood quietly in the dark alcove between the vending machines, watching the small boy. He had seen the old lady enter the bus station with the boy skipping along beside her, talking up to her continuously as they walked along, followed by a taxi driver carrying her suitcase. As they arrived at the ticket booth, the cabbie put her case down beside her and the old lady thrust a ten dollar bill into his outstretched hand. The cabbie dipped forward slightly from the waist, said something to the old lady that Billy couldn't hear and turned to leave. Billy had been loitering by the kiosk, pretending to read a comic book when the old lady had bought two return tickets for Cheyenne, Wyoming. By concentrating hard, his sharp ears had overheard the clerk tell her that they would be changing buses in Salt Lake City. He'd asked the old lady if that was okay and she'd said it was. He told her which bus she wanted and where to catch it and, in a slightly imperious voice, the old lady had said, "Thank you, young man. I know! I should do. I've been travelling this route since you were in short pants."

The boy recovered his equilibrium and stared back at Billy. Eventually, he plucked up courage and went over and introduced himself. "Hello, my name's George. What's yours?"

"Billy"

"I'm going to Laramie. That's in Wyoming. Where are you going?"

"Cheyenne"

"Hey, that's only fifty miles beyond Laramie…"

"Forty-seven miles east on I-80 to exit 362 then two miles north on US-85."

"I'm travelling with my Gramma. Is your Gramma looking after you?"

"No"

"Your mom?"

"Yes"

"Where is she then?"

When no answer was forthcoming, George tried another tack. "Is she in the restroom?"

"No"

"Is she on the bus?"

"Yes"

"*Wow!* She lets you get off the bus and back on again alone… *How cool is that!* She must be a great mom. Gramma wouldn't let me do that. She says I'm so daft I'd get on the wrong bus and end up in Chippewa Falls, wherever that is…"

"Wisconsin" then, after a moment's hesitation, an unaccustomed twinge of curiosity got the better of Billy and he asked, "Why Chippewa Falls?"

"Dunno… Maybe Gramma just likes the name… Hey, would you like to ride with me? I'd like someone to ride with. Gramma's always telling me to be quiet. She says I get on her nerves with my ceaseless prattling… You could ask your mom if we could ride together when you get back on board… Please,

29

Billy... Please..." After a brief pause with no response, George gave Billy an imploring look and finished off with a plaintive little, "Will you?"

Not recognising the pleading note in George's voice, Billy simply answered, "Yes". George danced round in circles and laughed with delight.

By the time the old lady emerged from the restroom George was in full flight, excitedly telling Billy all about his home and the special school he attended and his favorite books and films and games and toys. When the old lady saw that he wasn't in his usual place but was talking to a stranger who was half-hidden behind the Coke dispenser, she called out, "George!" in a sharp tone. At the sound of her voice, George flinched and spun round. "Come here!" she commanded brusquely. George took hold of Billy's hand and gingerly lead him out. When the old lady saw that it was only another child, her demeanour softened slightly and she said sternly, "Who's this, George?"

By way of introduction, George said, "Gramma, this is Billy. He's on our bus... with his Mom... They're going to Cheyenne... I asked him if he'd like to ride with me... Is that alright Gramma? Is it?"

"Well... I guess it's okay with me if it's okay with Billy's mother..." Then the old lady said "Hello Billy, I'm pleased to make your acquaintance" and reached out to shake Billy's hand. Billy stood unspeaking, looking down at the floor, until the old lady slowly lowered her hand again.

With his heart in his mouth for fear his grandmother would take umbrage at being snubbed and forbid them to sit together, George said timidly, "He's very shy, Grandma... He doesn't mean to be rude..."

The old lady contemplated Billy. Something about him touched her heart and she said, in a softer voice than George had heard her use in a long while, "Anyway Billy, it's very nice to meet you..." then, in a more business-like tone, "Come along boys, don't dilly-dally, the bus is waiting. Let's join the queue or it'll go without us... and it's a heck of a long walk to Cheyenne."

"One-thousand-one-hundred-and-sixty-three miles" said Billy.

"Well then, young man, all the more reason not to miss it" said George's grandmother, smiling inwardly to herself as she shepherded the two boys and gently propelled them towards the bus.

The two boys clambered up the stairs, George leading Billy by the hand, closely followed by George's grandmother. The driver barely noticed the boys in his hurry to greet the old lady and stow her case. "Nice to see you again, Mrs Col'houn, lovely day... Let me take your luggage... Welcome aboard..." he said, helping her up the step. He was always very respectful; Mrs Colquhoun was always a generous tipper.

"Yes, Frederick, thank you. It is a lovely day. Not too hot and with a gentle breeze that makes everything bearable... And it's very nice to see you again... Do you anticipate any problems en route?"

"No Ma'am, it should be a smooth journey... Good weather conditions reported and no roadworks... Enjoy your trip, Ma'am."

"Thank you Frederick" With that Mrs Colquhoun went to her accustomed window seat near the middle of the bus. George had already staked their claim and Billy had walked to the rear of the bus and had come back. George was eager to see him. "What did your Mom say? Can you sit with me?"

"Yes"

"*That's great!* I'll go and say thank you..."

At first, Billy seemed flustered but then gathered himself and said emphatically, "No!" then rather more hesitantly, "Please don't... She's going to sleep... She's tired." George instantly dismissed any thought of disturbing Billy's mother and maneuvred Billy into the window seat immediately behind his grandmother and sat down next to him. By the time the bus pulled out of the terminal, George was again in full spate.

Mrs Colquhoun sat listening to George's steady outpourings as he told Billy all about his adventures. She'd heard most of them innumerable times before and was secretly relieved not to have to listen to yet another re-run of them. Much as his childish repetitiveness irked her, she disliked herself for not being more patient with the grandson whom she loved more dearly than life itself.

As the bus turned out onto the highway and settled to its cruising speed, Mrs Colquhoun was aware of George's unbroken chatter; she also noticed that Billy had not uttered a single word. As she put on her reading glasses and took a novel out of her capacious handbag, she mused over the comparison between chalk and cheese and began to read. Gradually, as she became engrossed in her book, she registered George's babble less and less; assisted by the throbbing of the engine and the hum of the tires on the road, it simply became part of the background noise. She was enjoying the ride and the opportunity to indulge in her favorite pastime. The sun was shrouded by a thin veil of high cloud which tamed some of its usual ferocity at this time of year and it warmed her. Lulled by the constant drone of the bus and the gentle rocking as it rode over the undulations in the road, her book slowly settled into her lap, her head sank down until her chin rested on her ample bosom, her spectacles slid to the end of her nose, her eyelids flickered a few times then closed and, by and by, she fell into a deep sleep.

—•—

The President sat down, feeling far more comfortable and without further ado said, "So... how to stop the terrorists... Mrs Marshall, would you lead off, please?"

Niara Marshall, Head of the Department of Homeland Security, said, "Certainly, Mr President. You should all have a copy..." holding up a quarter-inch thick document. Everyone nodded that they had one. "This report was prepared in conjunction with the FBI and CIA. It covers three main areas... One! Measures to improve detection and surveillance of terrorists to reduce their success... Two! Greater cooperation with foreign banks, in particular European and Swiss banks, to monitor the flow of funds to terrorists in the hope of identifying their financiers and cutting off their funds... Three! Tighter immigration controls to stop Muslim terrorists entering the country under cover of the asylum process and closer monitoring of the Muslim community that's already established here..." Niara Marshall talked steadily for fifteen minutes, summarising the three main planks of their proposal. The first contained no new initiatives that would increase effectiveness; it simply proposed increasing spending on additional operatives and resources to be able to cover the ground more thoroughly. When the second proposal was stripped of its padding it amounted to little more than a thinly veiled threat to coerce European banks into cooperating by threatening that US banks would withhold information from European intelligence services on a tit-for-tat basis, unless the Europeans changed their policy. However, this would hurt European countries far less than it would America – because of their non-interventionist stance in respect of Islamic nations they suffered far less Muslim terrorism. The third proposal took longer for Niara Marshall to present because it was politically sensitive and she chose her words and the tone in which she delivered them carefully; it advocated barring all Muslim immigrants and asylum seekers entry into the country purely on the basis of their religion, irrespective of their intentions or the dangers from which they were trying to escape.

The President responded tersely, "Mrs Marshall, expenditure on security has increased every year for the last ten years. We're getting worse value-for-money now than ever before... Detection rates are falling... The terrorists' strike rate is rising... and here you are asking for a further eleven percent budget increase. How do you think I'll get this through Congress? Moreover, it'll take time to recruit and train new agents. What, six months... a year for them to be ready for active service? We haven't got the luxury of time. We need more radical solutions *now*! So, please, go away and think about that and be prepared to present more hard-hitting proposals at the next meeting... As for the Europeans, I'm fed up trying to get them to march in step with us. Even the Brits are starting to break rank, what with terrorist bombings at home weakening their resolve and political pressure from Europe to take a softer

32

position on Iraq and the Middle East... I agree in principle with your second proposal. I'll have our Ambassadors approach the Europeans again, particularly France and Germany. We'll try persuading them of the need for greater cooperation on banking, intelligence and so forth but it may prove fruitless. They make all the right noises but don't deliver on their promises. I have the feeling we're being suckered..." There were general murmurings of agreement, particularly by the delegation from the Pentagon. The President continued, "Your third proposal has to be given serious consideration... If we're letting in people whose sole intent is to attack America from inside, it must be stopped. If a few innocent bystanders get caught in the fall-out from such a policy then so be it. In my opinion, it's now a necessity... Of course, discriminating against someone on the grounds of their religion is a human rights minefield. The lawyers'll see it as their invitation to a turkey shoot... And it may necessitate a change in the Constitution... but I don't think our Founding Fathers could have foreseen this possibility... I don't think they'd object much... It may take time to put the required legislation in place but I don't think we have much choice."

At this, Alison Ord spoke up, "Excuse me, Mrs Marshall but how are you you going to single out terrorists simply by asking them whether they're Muslims? You might as well ask them whether they're terrorists..."

Niara Marshall patiently explained how Immigration would investigate the background of everyone entering the country, particularly from the Middle East and that, yes, they would be asked about their religion. If there was any doubt that they had answered truthfully, they'd be asked to take a lie detector test.

"You mean you'd exclude anyone who admitted to being a Muslim and be suspicious of everyone else? That's an awful lot of lie detector tests..." Alison Ord said.

Slightly disingenuously, Niara Marshall responded, "Surely, devout Muslims wouldn't deny their faith... and if they did, it'd show when they took a polygraph test."

George Horowitz, the President's senior adviser on national affairs, spoke up, "A Muslim terrorist would have no problem denying his religion. He'd put his hand on his heart and look you in the eye and tell you he was a Christian... or even a Jew for that matter... if it'd let him complete his mission... and he'd do it without skipping a heartbeat. He wouldn't see it as a mortal sin and break down in tears, even if you grilled him. He'd know that Ibrahim... or Abraham... the patriarch of Islam... and coincidentally of Judaism and Christianity as well... denied his beloved wife, Sarah, to avoid being killed by the Pharaoh when they entered Egypt. He would see a strong parallel here... He'd already have been pardoned for this deception before he'd committed it because it would be in the cause of *Jihad*."

At this, Travis Johnston butted in, "But the Egyptians didn't have the polygraph…"

"That's true… All I'm saying is, don't become too reliant on modern technology… We're steeped to the eyeballs in it… we've spent *literally billions* of dollars on it, yet so far the terrorists have been able to get through… in the main with impunity. Also, many of them are from other areas of the World with large Muslim populations… Indonesia, black Africa, even Caucasian countries… They may not be Arabs, but as Muslims and as terrorists they're every bit as committed. How are you going to identify suspect Muslims before you start interrogating them? They won't all come here wearing dishcloths on their heads just for our convenience. Segregating them isn't going to be easy. And don't forget… today, there are more than six million Muslims living here in the USA. What do we do about them when we're denying their relatives entry for the purpose of making legitimate visits? What you're proposing is 'Fortress America'… but a fortress with a strong, well defended front door and many unguarded back doors… Rather than keeping the enemy out, we're more likely to become prisoners trapped inside with the enemy free to circulate in our midst. It's one of the penalties of living in such an open society…"

At this point, the President intervened. "Let's move on. Mrs Marshall's third proposal is worthy of consideration… George, let's get the view of the Legislature before we proceed… Thank you, Mrs Marshall. Now, moving on… General Landsbergh, we come to your report…"

As Colonel Reinhardt got up to give each of the delegates a document marked 'Top Secret' in bold red letters, the General proceeded. "Thank you, Sir. Ladies and Gentlemen, America has suffered more than enough at the hands of Muslims. Over seventy-five thousand US citizens… innocent men, women and children… have been killed by Muslim terrorists within our own borders… That's more than the number of combatants lost in the Vietnam war. A further four and a half thousand have died outside our borders while going about their legitimate business. Over ten thousand US servicemen and women have been killed policing Afghanistan, Iraq and other Muslim countries in defense of democracy… theirs and ours… and still their religious leaders steadfastly refuse to give democracy any real chance to get a proper foothold. Moreover, the American people are losing confidence in our ability to defend them at home and abroad. The terrorists' stated intentions are the destruction of America and the extermination of Christians and Jews alike… The latest attack on Israel this very day clearly demonstrates their evil intent. They're waging an undeclared and covert war against America and our allies… The cowardly perpetrators are sniping at us from behind cover, giving us nothing to shoot back at… The terrorism is rooted in Islamic fundamentalism… So… the Pentagon proposes that America strikes back…

with ultimate force… to destroy Islam and terrorism once and for all…" The General paused. The atmosphere in the room bristled as every one round the table received the message and tried to grapple with its implications. Before anyone could query what he meant, the General continued, "Turning to the report, briefly, our proposals are summarised on page two…" Everybody dutifully opened the document at the specified page but no one could read it. They could only sit staring, their eyes rivetted on General Landsbergh. "Firstly, the detention and subsequent deportation of all Muslims currently living in the USA. Secondly, the destruction of all Muslim holy sites around the World, including all mosques and other places of worship, starting with Mecca and Medina, which will deny them any focus for their religion. It'll also send an unambiguous message… one they can't mistake… that we mean business. Finally, the suppression of all Muslims that stand in our way or raise arms against us… If necessary when we've finished Islam won't exist, not even in the heart of a single, solitary, ragged-arsed peasant tending his flea-bitten goats on some God-forsaken hillside in the remotest outpost of Islam. Within a couple of generations, Islam won't even be a memory. The Earth will be cleansed of its scourge…"

The meeting sat in stunned silence, too intimidated by the sheer enormity of the military option to say anything. Once it had sunk in, Alison Ord looked at General Landsbergh and said, "There are over one point two *billion* Muslims in the World. At least a billion of them are old enough to pick up a gun or any other weapon they can lay their hands on. Attacking Mecca would be like poking a stick in a hornets' nest. They'd go berserk. It would unleash hatred and fury like nothing we'd ever witnessed before. We'd have a much bigger problem on our hands than we have now. Their leaders would incite them to rise up *en masse*…"

At this, the General said emphatically in a level voice that was cold and hard as steel, "Yes… and when they show their heads above the parapet, we'll blow 'em clean off!" It was delivered with such malevolence, such hostility, that a chill ran through Alison Ord. She turned to the President and said, "This is monstrous. It's obscene! How can we consider it? How can we even be discussing it? It's genocide. It makes us no better than the terrorists… No! It makes us worse… Far worse! As a Christian nation we shouldn't even be contemplating such an *inhuman* course of action. I, for one, am not prepared to be part of an administration that would even entertain such thoughts…" and so saying, she collected her papers and got up to leave. The President said, "Alison, please sit down. We're simply considering all options, however unpalatable. Don't forget… we're the innocent victims of terrorism here. If we don't consider all options, it may leave us vulnerable to attack on the one flank we failed to defend…"

Siding more with Alison Ord than did any of the others, George Horowitz leaned over and gently put his hand on her arm, trying to restrain her but she snatched it away saying, "That's horseshit and you know it... Sir."

As she turned to leave, the President said, with a hard edge to his voice, "Miss Ord, please leave your papers... And don't forget, you're sworn to secrecy. You must reveal *nothing* of what's been discussed here today. Absolutely nothing! Do you understand?" Alison Ord left her papers on the table and marched out without acknowledging the President's last question, barely able to breathe for the fear and anger welling up inside her, feeling as though an enormous weight had been put down on her chest. She could hardly begin to comprehend what she'd just witnessed but she felt completely overwhelmed by it.

Sounding a little uncertain of himself, the President sighed and said to nobody in particular, "Please excuse my aide. This... er... whole terrorist situation's tough on us all..." then, feeling resigned to continuing but wishing he could avoid it at any cost, "Would you like to expand on the military option, General Landsbergh?"

"Thank you, Sir. Yes, I would... The first thing we recommend is putting all Muslims, citizens and visitors alike, in detention centers then deporting them to their country of birth or their father's country of birth if they were born here. This should be done as a matter of the greatest urgency, as soon as legislation can be passed... or using existing anti-terrorist legislation if it fits our needs better... Of course, in extremis... in a dire emergency... and then only as a last resort, martial law could always be imposed..." The President looked hard at General Landsbergh who stared back with a neutral gaze. He felt very uneasy that the comment contained an implicit threat, however vague. The General swiftly continued, "It's obvious these people can't be trusted. Just look at the current situation with Al Rashid. Who'd have suspected him of all people, a man on the run from tyranny, to be plotting against the very nation that gave him sanctuary? God knows how many more of these subversives are living in our midst but we can't afford to sit on our hands until we find out the hard way. The time has come to eliminate the problem... *Now!*"

George Horowitz said, "General, you have to understand, these people are Muslims first and foremost, irrespective of race, nationality or anything else. Their first allegiance is to *Islam*... After all, it means *submission*... to the One and Only God. All Muslims would feel obliged to answer the call if it came, so I suggest..."

At this, General Landsbergh cut in abruptly, "That's precisely what I'm driving at... There are six million ticking bombs in the heart of American society just waiting for some mad Mullah to push the button... and BOOM!

They explode in our faces. Well, Sir, we're not going to sit and wait for that to happen. '*Action this Day*' has always been my motto and I propose we act now, before it's too late." George Horowitz waited patiently for the General to finish, then said, "What I was going to suggest is that we do nothing to alienate the Muslim community... worldwide. Islam is essentially a peaceful religion. The Koran advocates tolerance and respect towards all people, irrespective of their beliefs. We can't simply treat them all like cattle because of the acts of a handful of extremists, however horrific their acts may be..."

"Oh can't we, Mr Horowitz? Just ask the families of the ninety thousand dead Americans about how peace-loving Islam is... Look at the Iran – Iraq war for Christ's sake... They love each other so much, they killed a million fellow believers... Look at Saddam Hussein, good Muslim that he was... killed over three hundred thousand of his own people... innocent men, women and children... Don't tell me they couldn't kill innocent Americans, Mr Horowitz, because they have and we all know they could *and they will*, unless we kill them first!" The General stopped his tirade as abruptly as he'd launched it and sat quietly for a moment. He was very red in the face and had clearly been on the verge of rage. When he'd calmed, he said, "I now come to our second proposal... The destruction of Islam..."

As the General started talking, the President's thoughts drifted off. 'How in God's name did we ever come to be so far at odds with our fellow man that we'd consider wiping him out... rubbing him out so completely as to leave no trace... And yet if al-Qaeda strikes another blow only half as successful as the last one, it might be taken out of my hands altogether... It might be impossible to restrain the military, particularly if the people are behind them... They'd obviously think I'd failed... Well, I would've failed... I'm way down in the polls. They're starting to lose faith in me... Christ knows, I'm starting to lose faith in myself... I don't feel as though I'm in control of things... Then God only knows what'll happen... If they're all like Landsbergh, what then? How will it end? I need a victory to re-assert my authority... A resounding victory for democratically elected government over religious fundamentalism that'll restore people's confidence and put a stop to this madness... How to achieve it? How? How?' The President's attention snapped back to the meeting as he heard the General saying, "...the question is whether or not we warn Islamic nations that if we suffer another terrorist attack we'll destroy their holy sites... and if we're pushed to it, yes, we'll engage them in war... then rely on them to muzzle the terrorists. In other words, to use the threat of massive retaliation as a deterrent, to persuade them to neutralise the terrorists themselves..."

Travis Johnston interrupted, "Don't forget, General, forewarned is forearmed. Is it a good idea to alert them to our strategy? Do they alert us to theirs? What are the alternatives?"

At this, the President snapped, "Whatever the alternatives are, launching a retaliatory strike on a holy place isn't one of them. If we did, we'd become outcasts. The rest of the world would treat us like pariahs and rightly so... It might even precipitate a world war..."

Whether out of courtesy or because he was sizing him up, the General waited a few moments before asking, "May I continue, Mr President?", at which the President curtly nodded.

"Lastly, we come to the suppression of Muslims that rise up and threaten us or any of our interests worldwide... Hopefully, they'll be so stunned and terrified by our first show of power that they won't have the courage to rise up. However, if they do, the Pentagon proposes that we don't commit ground troops in the first instance. Wherever they rise up in sufficient numbers and threaten the stability of a region, we use long-range weapons to destroy them. If we have assets in the target area, we withdraw our people to a safe distance then use neutron bombs to de-populate the area but leave the assets intact. Whatever we do must be swift, decisive and result in as few US casualties as possible. The American people won't want our body-count building up. They'll only back our actions if it effectively crushes Islam and puts a stop to the killing without too much suffering on our part..."

The President was about to jump in but George Horowitz beat him to it. "Do you really think the American people would stand behind us if we vaporized thousands of innocent people? Somehow I don't think so."

The General responded tersely, "That may be your opinion, Mr Horowitz but it's not one I share..."

George Horowitz countered, "On a purely practical note, General... Mecca is in Saudi Arabia. The Saudis are *supposed to be* our friends. They also supply a fifth of our oil. We're dependent on that relationship continuing. Attack Mecca and they'd stop the flow of oil *instantly*. So would all other Arab nations. America would grind to a halt within weeks..."

At this, the General cut in, "Saudi Arabia is a country of twenty-five million people, predominantly Sunni Muslims. They're widely infected with virulent anti-Westernism promoted by ultra-traditional Wahhabi clerics who vilify and demonise Jews and Christians and incite terrorism. It's where most of the terrorism in the world is spawned... We're there at the invitation of the Saudi royal family who control the country. They're only our friends and want us there because they rely on us for their wealth and power but they're only about six thousand strong... and you've already told us they're Muslims first and foremost... Alone, they couldn't turn back the tide of a fundamentalist revolution like the one that deposed the Shah in Iran... And come the revolution there's no certainty about the loyalties of the Saudi National Guard... The country's in turmoil and it's getting worse. They're managing to keep the lid on it now with our help. Revolution is just around the corner, then where would we be? What's more, their oil is starting to run out. Their reserves have topped out and will only decline from now on. That's why we've been steadily reducing our dependency on Saudi oil. That's why for the last decade we've been establishing oil industries in other areas of the World. Why do you think we've spent so much money and committed so many troops... yes... and suffered so many casualties... entrenching our position in Iraq? Because Iraq is sitting on a quarter of the World's oil reserves and it's within *our* control... At present, we have huge forces stationed in the Persian Gulf, Red Sea and Indian Ocean. In the event of a war, we could crush the Saudi National Guard just like that..." snapping his fingers with a sudden crack, "...and take over the oilfields of the Arabian peninsula as well if we choose to do so..."

While this exchange was going on the President sat quietly wondering if, under more benign circumstances, the General could be made to undergo exhaustive tests to determine whether he was insane with a view to having him removed from office. However, it was clear that this was not the view of one deranged man but represented the strategic thinking of the US military's high command developed over a number of years in response to the rising tide of Islamic terrorism.

Both the President and his adviser were uncomfortably aware of the disadvantage of being in elected government – these people had had years to put down deep roots in secure positions, to develop their strategies and to influence powerful men and gain their support, whereas they were both here at the whim of the electorate. Their positions were temporary and their hold on power was tenuous at best. They could be removed as easily if they failed to steer just the right course, and they would be judged more harshly over their handling of the accursed problem of terrorism than over any other issue. The President said, "You've clearly put a lot of effort into this, General. And you obviously know that pursuing this course of action would effectively put America on a war footing... In fact, it could result in outright war. Militarily, we've never been better prepared or had more resources available for fighting a war... and *probably* for the first time in our history, the people are pressing us to take the fight to the enemy. Still, we need to think very carefully about where that might lead us and humanity before we take even the first step down this road because it could lead to Armageddon... Now we come to our last report, from the government. George..."

Already feeling on the defensive, George Horowitz started talking as his report was passed round the table. "We've been struggling with vicious Islamic terrorism now for a decade. I needn't elaborate on the grim statistics of the dead and injured. We're all acutely aware of them. It's ruined many more lives. People are living in dread, waiting for the next attack. It's cost this country *countless billions* of dollars in detection, in prevention and... when we fail to prevent an attack, in re-building... and the cost continues to soar... We're all paying for terrorism. For some it's a far higher price than for others. It's undermining people's confidence in our ability to defend ourselves and ultimately in government, in the security services and the armed forces. On balance, we're all net losers. In real terms, no one benefits... Oh yes, you might all have fairly secure, highly paid jobs but at what cost? Fighting terrorism is the *ultimate* waste of money and we can't even begin to quantify the lost opportunity costs of tying up such enormous resources in the fight against terrorism. The money we spend on it could be put to far better uses... healthcare, education, research, developing trade, the pursuit of peace... and we could free up so many people whose efforts could go into helping improve the world we live in..." Even though, when he'd started he'd had the feeling that his words would be futile and would fall on deaf ears, he believed passionately in what he was saying and started warming to it. He continued, "We also have to look at what motivates the terrorists. It's not wealth or fame or glamour. They're not doing it for themselves. They're driven by religious belief. They're doing it *for Islam*. They're not deterred by failure or afraid of the consequences. Don't forget, they've been promised eternity in Paradise as the reward for dying in the cause of *Jihad*... And the main reason... They think America's presence in Saudi Arabia is defiling their holiest places... They also resent the powerful influence we exert in the region. Their hatred of us... for that's undoubtedly what it is... is also magnified by the profound differences between us... Our open, democratic, forward-looking, technologically-based, secular, consumer society... Their closed, often backward-looking societies controlled by religious authority... or countries like Saudi Arabia which are torn between the two cultures. I'm not saying either one or the other is right, just that we're very different... We might not approve of their treatment of women, for instance, particularly in the most... er... *traditional* of Muslim societies... On the other hand, they may not approve of our headlong rush into modernism. In fact, looking at the cesspits of vice, corruption, violence, crime and drug-fuelled squalor that some of our inner cities have become, we might even *benefit* from the order that comes from their strict religious discipline... Lastly, we're fighting a losing battle against the terrorists. They're still getting through despite our enormous effort and expenditure... In short, our anti-terrorism policy isn't working and we need to face the fact. We're struggling *precisely because* of the differences... They're lone individuals or small groups operating autonomously. They can blend into the crowd... it's like looking for one particular grain of sand on a beach... whereas our military forces are still largely geared to fighting big set-piece battles against mechanised armies... How can you shoot at your enemy when he's just one face in a sea of faces? So… the White House is advocating a very different approach… that we engage with the terrorists, possibly directly, possibly via mediators, to try to defuse this situation or at least take some of the heat out of it… to understand their grievances and try to meet them part way…"

The General snorted derisively. "I could smell that coming a mile off and it's exactly the kind of touchy-feely tree-hugging hippie shit I'd expect from some mealy-mouthed politician. The situation's gone *way too far* for words. It calls for action… decisive action… and here's you wanting to sit down *now* and jaw-jaw with these bastards. It's far too late for that! Why didn't you do that *before* the Mall of America attack? Or the two-thousand-eight Super Bowl? Phoenix still hasn't recovered from that one yet. God knows if it ever will… Why didn't you talk to them *ten years ago*, before the World Trade Center? If you'd been able to sort this out before now you should've done so? I'll tell you why you didn't… Because you couldn't! You couldn't then and you can't now. Talking never resolved a damned thing. At the end of the day someone has to take *action*… every time… and that sure as hell ain't politicians. Where are you when the shot and shell are flying? I'll tell you where… Buried deep in some bunker way behind the front line, safe from the shrapnel…" By this time, the General was clearly livid.

George Horowitz could no longer restrain himself and fired back. "I think it's worth trying before we commit irrevocably to a course of action that would *inevitably* have far-reaching and long-lasting consequences that would change history. Don't you think I understand the suffering… on both sides… and want to see an end to it? Speaking as a Jew I understand suffering as well as anyone. I lost *all* my grandparents in the Holocaust…" George Horowitz hesitated, feeling that he had revealed too much and immediately the General jumped in.

"Mr Horowitz, your people may have suffered but you don't have a monopoly on it. Americans are suffering equally ghastly fates today. It doesn't make any difference whether you're poisoned in a gas chamber at Auschwitz or in a shopping mall in Minnesota, the result's the same… If it hadn't been for decisive British, Russian and American action… note the word *'action'*… that cost *millions* of allied lives, the Nazis would never have been defeated and your people would have been exterminated… And don't forget… during the nineteen-thirties, the British tried appeasement. They even put off re-arming in the hope it would avoid war but all to no avail. It was doomed to failure from the start. But, as a consequence, it nearly cost them the war… And why? Politicians! Incompetent, misguided, arrogant politicians who refused to wake up and smell the shit on their own doorstep, even though the stench of it was impossible to ignore… Naive, idealistic, stupid politicians who thought that aggression could be ameliorated by friendship, who presumed that politics is determined by goodwill, moral objectives, the gentleman's code of honour and the preservation of legal order... In short, politicians who thought they could talk their way out of war... And that was before a single shot had been fired... We've already suffered tens of thousands of casualties of war. How much longer do you propose we wait before retaliating? How many more American lives are to be sacrificed whilst you pander to your egos and indulge in a vain attempt to talk this problem to death?" However passionately George Horowitz felt about his policy he could see that the General was equally vehement as he continued, "And let me just add three more things... Firstly, the British appeasers didn't give a damn about Hitler's rabid anti-Semitism. It didn't even register in their thinking. The salvation of the Jews was purely happenstance... a fortunate by-product of the war fought to defeat Fascism... Had it not been fought, Hitler would still have exterminated the Jews anyway, totally unopposed. Do you think Britain would have gone to war just to save your sorry asses, especially when you did so little to save them yourselves, despite all the warnings? The Jews suffered as they did because of *inaction*. Most of them buried their heads and hoped the threat would simply evaporate... And by comparison the Nazi's was a cold, clinical, dispassionate hatred that was pursued discretely... in secret almost... which pales into insignificance compared to the seathing, impassioned hatred whipped up in public displays of mass hysteria by the most vociferous Muslims today... What do you think they'd be capable of?" The gruesome implications were obvious so, without waiting for anyone to proffer an opinion, the General continued, "Secondly, what do you think'll happen in Saudi Arabia if we cave in to the terrorists and pull our troops out? I'll tell you... It'll implode! Islamic fundamentalism will storm the country and we'll be far worse off than we are now... It's another form of Fascism and it has to be dealt with just as rigorously... And lastly, who are you going to *"engage"* with?" and the General raised both hands and waggled the two forefingers of each hand, indicating speech marks. "It sounds impressive but what the hell does it mean? Islam doesn't have a Pope or anyone else with absolute authority. It's amorphous with no central ruling body so who are you going to appeal to?"

The President stood, leaning forward slightly with both fists on the table and said, "Gentlemen, this isn't helping us reach a conclusion... Please, General, do us the courtesy of hearing us out, then we can discuss the relative merits of each approach. Whatever we end up with has to be a workable and successful policy. Nobody's going to be rewarded for failure."

"Certainly, Sir but having been put on the spot by Mr Horowitz to answer a direct question, may I be accorded the same privilege and ask him one? After all, it's one that must be answered before this policy could be seriously considered..." at which the President nodded. "Mr Horowitz, we all know that one of the terrorists' central demands... no, *the* central demand... will be for America to withdraw from Saudi Arabia *totally...* If we acquiesce to that demand, we'll have lost our foothold and there'll be no regaining it. Pray tell us... what'll prevent a fundamentalist revolution? And once it happens... as it surely will... it'll undoubtedly spread like wildfire throughout the rest of the Middle East, destabilizing the whole of the region. Then what fate lies in store for Israel... isolated... alone... surrounded by hostile neighbours?"

George Horowitz knew that Israel was his and America's Achilles heel – everything they did would have repercussions of some kind on the tiny, beleaguered country – and just as keenly, the General knew it was and had no hesitation in exploiting this weakness. George Horowitz stumbled to explain how Israel's future would be guaranteed in any negotiations but his fire had been doused by the General's critical analysis of the situation and his brutal and withering delivery of it. He now felt less sure of the robustness of his proposal than he had when he'd formulated it and, as a consequence, none of what followed sounded convincing – the words 'naive' and 'stupid' kept ringing in his mind. The one thing he couldn't bring himself to do was risk sacrificing his spiritual home for the benefit of the country where he lived.

The President sat listening as George Horowitz summed up his argument in favor of moderation in their approach to terrorism, feeling more depressed than about any other issue he'd had to deal with in his short time in office. The principal reason was because the more he thought about it, the more convinced he was becoming that the military option was likely to be the most positive, most decisive one and, therefore, the least avoidable. After a few moments reflection, the President said, "All three approaches are profoundly different and could lead to very different outcomes. Certainly, I see no merit in simply trying to maintain the *status quo*. It'll just lead to more terrorism and more misery... Which leaves us with the stark choice of either appeasement... or war. It's impossible to decide which way to go on the spur of the moment. The matter needs further consideration. I'd like to read your report in more detail, General and it may raise some questions that need answering..." The General muttered, "I'm at your service, Mr President."

"I hope to reach a decision on our chosen strategy by next month's full NSC meeting. I'll report back to you then... Thank you everyone for all your efforts... and let's keep right on top of this latest terrorist threat..."

As the President rose and started collecting his papers, everybody else filed out led by General Landsbergh walking briskly with an upright military bearing, closely followed by Colonel Reinhardt whose artifical leg swung out slightly as a result of his rolling gait. When they'd gone, the President slumped back down into the comfy leather-upholstered chair and sat staring into the middle distance, deep in thought. George Horowitz had been at the tail end of the column leaving the conference room. After waiting briefly outside the door, he realised the President wasn't following and eased the door ajar. The President was sitting slightly stooped, looking as though the cares of the world were on his shoulders which, he reflected, was precisely the case. He well understood the President's need for a little privacy, few understood it better. He was about to leave but changed his mind. He pushed the door open softly and padded in. As he approached, the President looked up and said, "Come in, George. Sit down... Well, we certainly got more than we bargained for. I know I said I wanted more *radical and hard-hitting solutions...* They don't come much more radical or hard-hitting than war."

George Horowitz sat musing for a minute, then said, "I don't know what you think of the General but I get the impression of a very angry man. Of course, he controls his anger extremely well as you'd expect but it's there all the same. I think it's coloring his judgement of this situation and I can't help feeling it's what's behind the utter cold-blooded savagery of his solution... I wonder what it could be?" The two men continued talking about the different proposals for a while until the President said, "I can't really give it any more thought until I've read the reports, George, so let's adjourn..."

"Certainly, Mr President... but on a more pressing note, Sir, what do we do about Alison Ord?"

"I don't know, George. Would you talk to her? I won't have such dissension or such unprofessional behaviour... On the other hand, I don't want to lose her, she's too good at her job... And I must confess, I had to admire her moxie in speaking out so forcefully against us taking a course of action she believes would be *essentially wrong...*"

—•—

Mrs Colquhoun slowly roused herself. Her head was a little woozy from having slept so soundly for so long. It took her an unaccustomed couple of minutes to fully come round. She looked over her shoulder through the gap between the seats and saw her grandson, slumped over with his head on Billy's shoulder, fast asleep. Although she couldn't quite turn far enough to see Billy's face, she knew from his erect posture and the angle of his head that he was awake and staring out of the window. Having contented herself that everything was peaceful, she picked up her book, turned back to the previous page and, in the gentle evening glow, re-read the last paragraph then resumed from where she'd left off.

As the bus glided along I-84, George had continued talking steadily. It passed Hood River, Mosier, The Dalles, Rufus, Arlington, Boardman and Stanfield with barely a break save to catch his breath and take little sips of juice from his sport bottle. By the time the bus approached Pendleton, the flow had ebbed measurably. As they were passing through the Umatilla Indian Reservation, George's head had started to loll and his chatter had gradually tapered off to nothing.

As they'd left Portland, George had started telling Billy about his favorite fictional character, Harry Potter. He told Billy that he had all the Harry Potter books at home and had read each of them many times over. He'd also seen all the films at least twice; his favorite scenes were of Harry on his flying broomstick playing Quidditch and of the flying Ford Anglia, both of which George thought would be terrific ways of travelling even though in reality he was terrified of flying. He'd asked Billy if he liked Harry Potter too but, after some coaxing, he'd learnt that Billy had never read any of the books or even seen the films. George had given Billy a detailed and accurate account of the plot of each book, remarkably missing out none of the main characters or events. All the while, Billy had had his head half-turned away from George and had been staring out of the window. Whether Billy had been listening to him or not, George had been quite content at having a passive audience. After he'd exhausted the topic of Harry Potter, George told Billy about his school. He had been unabashed about telling Billy that he went to a special school for children with learning difficulties because he had a problem concentrating on his lessons. "I can't sit quiet for more than a few minutes before I start having these weird thoughts… Gramma says I'm a real daydreamer, always away with the fairies… But it's not really like that…" Then, in a quiet voice, George confided, "I keep having this horrible, scary dream, over and over. I dream that I see this bright light in the sky and I feel this fiery burning all over me and then I hear a loud bang… Then everywhere's dark. I can't find Gramma or my Mom and Dad. I keep calling them but they don't answer… I don't know what it is but I know it's bad and it frightens me. I don't like it, Billy…" and then, a little forlornly, he added, "I wish I was at Hogwarts, with Harry and Ron and Hermione. I wish I could do magic like them so I could make good things happen and keep bad things from happening…" George sat quietly for a moment, then said, "I told my Mom about my dreams… We'd watched a program on TV about the atom bombs that America dropped on Japan in the Second World War… They dropped two… The first one was called Little Boy then they dropped his big brother, Fat Boy…"

Without looking at George, Billy said by way of correction, "Fat Man".

"Yes, Fat Man, that was it… But now my Mom won't let me watch TV… not unless she's checked out the programs first. She says it was the pictures of the bombs going off that upset me… but it wasn't. I told her I was having those dreams before we watched that program but she wouldn't listen… It's not fair… Does your Mom stop you from watching TV, Billy? Does she?" This time, Billy didn't respond but went on staring out of the window. He registered that they were passing a sign for the Boardman Bombing Range. Wondering if Billy was starting to tire of his chatter, George had continued talking for a little while longer but the excitement had gone out of his voice and the sparkle had disappeared from his eyes and he seemed to have nothing more to say that had any joy in it. Before too much longer he had stopped talking altogether.

As the bus sped along the Old Oregon Trail Highway where it separated the small town of Island City from its larger neighbour, La Grande, Billy noticed that the old lady was beginning to stir. By the time they had reached North Powder, staying stock-still and pretending not to be paying her any attention, he watched out of the corner of his eye as she peered over the seatback to check on her grandson. By the time they were passing Baker, he noted that the old lady was deeply engrossed in her book.

As the bus passed Huntington, Billy noticed that the old lady had started fidgeting. Easing George's head from his shoulder, then laying it down gently on the armrest, Billy slipped out of his seat and quietly made his way towards the rear of the bus.

Mrs Colquhoun saw the sign coming up, saying, 'You are now leaving Oregon and entering Idaho' and in smaller letters underneath, 'The Beaver State bids you farewell. Please come back soon. Welcome to the Potato State.' She was pleased with herself. Once again, through a combination of sensible preparation, modest fluid intake and strength of willpower, she had managed to control her bladder until the bus had crossed the State line; the scatty, thoughtless women who were constantly drinking, then nipping to the toilet themselves or chivvying their spoilt, whining brats, many of whom stumbled clumsily down the aisle jogging people's elbows and disturbing their tranquility, did irritate her so, which is why she always chose to ride in the window seat. As she got up, Mrs Colquhoun saw that Billy was no longer in his seat. George continued to sleep soundly and she noticed that Billy had thoughtfully folded George's jacket and put it under his head as a pillow. As she made her way to the rear of the bus, she noticed Billy sitting beside a small, drab-looking woman with dark crescents under her sunken eyes who was fast asleep. Her head was tipped back slightly, supported by an inflatable neck collar. Her mouth had dropped open and a silvery bead of saliva dribbled from the corner of her lips. She saw that Billy was reading but as she approached he put his book down, took out a clean, neatly-folded handkerchief and carefully wiped the trace of drool from the woman's chin. Mrs Colquhoun could not bear to watch Billy, not out of disgust for what she had just witnessed but because she was so deeply moved by the intense privacy of his act of kindness, so she continued on her way to the toilet without acknowledging him. On her return from the toilet, Billy still had his back turned to the aisle so she chose not to disturb him but, as she passed him, she saw that his small hand covered the back of the sleeping woman's hand which lay on the armrest.

It was dark as the bus pulled into the terminal in Boise. Mrs Colquhoun stretched, then turned to the two boys behind her. Although she had neither seen nor heard Billy return she knew that he had because she'd heard George talking to him for the last half-hour. Addressing George, she said, "Would you like a bite to eat before we set off again?"

George nodded enthusiastically. "Yes please, Gramma... And can Billy come too?"

Mrs Colquhoun looked a little concerned and said, "What about Billy's mother? She might want Billy to eat with her..."

"Oh no, that's alright, Gramma. He told me his Mom's already had a snack a while back and now she's gone back to sleep again... Can he come too, Gramma? Please..." The old lady turned a benevolent gaze on Billy and said, "Would you like that, Billy? My treat."

Billy stared at the back of the seat in front. With a small nod of his head but without looking up, he silently mouthed, "Yes..." then, after a moment's hesitation, "...please".

As they alighted from the bus, Mrs Colquhoun had a few words with the driver and slipped a twenty dollar bill into his hand. "Thank you, Frederick. A pleasant journey... even more so than usual. I look forward to seeing you on the return leg?" Frederick touched the peak of his cap and said, "Thank you, Mrs Col'houn... and no doubt you will. I hope you enjoy your onward journey... Aleisha's the relief on the next leg so you're in good hands." With that, Mrs Colquhoun followed the two boys across the concourse.

Mrs Colquhoun sat in the dark, thinking about how different the two boys were superficially and yet, looking a little deeper, how strangely alike they were in certain respects. Both, she reflected, would probably have very great difficulty making any real headway in the brutally materialistic, fast-paced, brash and commercialised world they lived in today. She was thankful that she had sufficient money to be able to insulate George from the harsh reality of it, if that's what it took. But what of Billy's chances? His poor mother looked as though she didn't have two cents to rub together. How would he manage to project himself onto the world stage, afflicted as he was by such crippling shyness? It had taken a tortuous process of questioning with simple, monosyllabic "Yes" or "No" answers, just to elicit from Billy what he had wanted to eat. George had persevered, seemingly unphased by the procedure, which also struck her as unusual when she reflected how impatient he could

47

be. She had been surprised when, after rejecting a long list of alternatives, Billy had chosen a plain cheese sandwich which, coincidentally, had been her own choice and a drink of tap water. She was pleased that George had also been swayed by Billy's choice into having a cheese sandwich. Normally, he would hanker for a burger. She always felt mean asking him what he wanted then telling him that he couldn't have it. She hated the thought of George eating greasy junk food but his look of disappointment at her refusal to allow him his own choice always tugged at her heart. As the bus continued toward Salt Lake City, Mrs Colquhoun gradually slipped into a doze.

As the bus approached Rupert it hit a bump in the road and the gentle jolt jogged Mrs Colquhoun into wakefulness. No longer feeling tired, she sat looking out of the window into the blackness. The headlamps illuminated a large roadsign informing drivers that they had the choice of continuing south on I-84 to Salt Lake City or heading east on I-86 to Pocatello and Idaho Falls and beyond that to Grand Teton and Yellowstone National Parks. Thinking back to a wonderful sightseeing trip she and her sister had been taken on as children by their parents, she thought, 'I know, I'll suggest to our Jessie that we take George up to see Old Faithful... He'll be fascinated... Everyone should see it at least once in their life... Why not? We've got three weeks to kill... It'll be a nice outing for him... For us all, come to that...' For a while, she reminisced about their childhood. Before they had crossed the State line into Utah, Mrs Colquhoun had nodded off again.

—•—

As soon as the President sat down at his desk, he noticed the envelope propped discretely against his desk lamp and knew immediately from the beautiful, flowing penstrokes who it was from and what it contained. With a sinking heart, he unfolded the letter and read Alison Ord's resignation. He was very touched by the apology she proffered, not for her conduct in the meeting but for failing him. He read on, 'This afternoon, before taking my leave, I called an old friend in the Personnel Department at the Pentagon. She told me that, back in 2002, a Captain Andrew Landsbergh, aged 27, serving with the US Marine Corps had been killed in action, in Afghanistan, by Muslim rebels whilst trying to protect a party of medics carrying out emergency treatment on a seriously injured child. Whether or not it's true, there was some talk at the time that the child had been shot by the rebels on purpose and left in the street as bait to draw in the Marines. Andrew Landsbergh was General Landsbergh's son. Nine months later, unable to come to terms with her grief at the loss of her only child, Mrs Landsbergh took her own life. I tell you this because it may help explain his bitterness and his antipathy towards Muslims...' The

President groaned as he imagined the anguish the General must have suffered and wondered to what extent it might have influenced his attitude.

As he sat pondering, George Horowitz knocked and came in to give the President the news about Alison Ord's departure. Without a word, the President handed him the letter. As he read it, he said, "It probably explains a lot but how does it *help* us?" As he handed the letter back, he added "To paraphrase Josef Stalin… the death of one man is a tragedy, the death of a *billion* is merely a statistic."

Chapter 3

"With all due respect, Mr President, the gentlemen from the US Geological Survey have been waiting to meet with you since yesterday afternoon... May I remind you that it was you who asked to see them, Sir."

"With all due respect, Mr Kaufmann, may I remind you that we're at war here. I've been tied up with the NSC all day, trying to decide how best to deal with this latest terrorist threat. We've had intelligence that al-Qaeda are planning to detonate a dirty bomb... a *very* dirty bomb... in a major American city... maybe even here in Washington, on September eleven. That gives us less than six weeks to neutralise the threat. I don't have time to worry about a volcano that may erupt some time in the next ten thousand years... if ever... Need I say more?"

"No, Sir... If you'll excuse me..." Paul Kaufmann, the President's former second aide recently promoted, tucked the report he'd been given by the scientists from the United States Geological Survey under his arm and turned to leave but the President said, "I'm sorry, Paul. I'm feeling very tired. I guess it's making me crankier than usual. Ask them to stay one more night. I'll try and see them tomorrow... How is the situation at Yellowstone?"

"Worrying, Mr. President. They have no doubt it'll erupt. The evidence is starting to become overwhelming. When it does, it'll be a major catastrophe. The question is... When? We must have an action plan or it could be seen as a dereliction of duty on our part, especially if the unimaginable happens..."

"You don't have to remind me about our duty, Mr Kaufmann. I stood for President because I wanted to serve my country. Unfortunately, it seems that between terrorists on the one hand and now this damn volcano on the other, my presidency isn't being given much chance to shine." Then, after a few moments thought, "How serious a threat is this volcano if it blows?"

"The scientists we met with yesterday judge it to be a massive threat, possibly an extinction level event. If it does blow, everything in a four or five hundred mile radius will be wiped out in a couple of hours. The ash could settle over an area up to two thousand miles diameter. That's from the west coast to the Mexican border and the farming states of the mid-west. It would be tens, maybe even hundreds of feet thick near ground zero going down to a couple of inches deep at the periphery. They estimate three to five million people would be killed by the initial blast. Almost everyone in the fallout zone would die of asphyxiation or lung damage caused by the dust which is extremely abrasive. Tens of millions of people could die within a few weeks. Obviously, our economy would be wrecked and every link in the food chain would be broken... but that's not all. They also warned that millions of tons of dust would be blasted into the upper atmosphere where it would be carried round the globe by winds, leading to global cooling… What's referred to as a 'volcanic winter'. That would result in much of the vegetation dying off and the subsequent loss of many of the complex lifeforms on Earth, us being one of them."

The President sat deep in thought for a few minutes. "If this threat is real it eclipses the worst, most destructive acts a few terrorists could perpetrate. If it isn't and I divert a significant proportion of our efforts into dealing with it while the terrorists get away with *literally murder*, that's my Presidency finished. If it did blow, my Presidency may be finished anyway." He thought for a moment. "What certainty is there that Yellowstone will erupt?"

"The scientists say there's been three major eruptions in the last two million years. According to them, the next one's ten thousand years overdue. The geological record doesn't lie… Or so they say. They're convinced it's coming. It's just a matter of time…"

"Right, I want to meet them first thing tomorrow morning, eight o'clock in my office. Keep the diary open, cancel any meetings I've got scheduled or defer them until we're done. I want them to re-run this for my benefit."

"Certainly, Mr President."

The President bid his aide goodnight and went to his private quarters.

(Sunday 1 August 2010, 07:55 Eastern time)

At seven fifty-five, Paul Kaufmann tapped gently on the door of the President's office and walked in. "Your visitors from the US Geological Survey have arrived, Sir."

"Thank you Paul. Show them in. I have to make a quick call to housekeeping. I want to order a bouquet of flowers for the First Lady. It's her birthday tomorrow. Did you know that?"

"Yes, Sir, I knew that." He'd actually been out the day before and bought her a small but tasteful gift, a token of his respect and admiration for her. He wondered to himself why the President always referred to his wife as 'The First Lady' and never by name. Then he thought, 'Still, why should I worry. At least they're devoted to each other and his attention is never distracted by other women. He's a real man of business whose focus never wavers from affairs of state, except when he's relaxing with his family and at such times you'd never know he was leader of the most powerful nation on Earth.' Paul Kaufmann enjoyed working for him tremendously and had enormous respect for his unstinting dedication to the job, his innate sense of decency and responsibility and the geniality he normally radiated.

51

As the President picked up the handset, Paul Kaufmann said, "Before we start, I must remind you there's a delegation coming in from JPL later today. This latest near-Earth object sighting..."

"I hadn't forgotten about them."

"They'll probably be here early afternoon. Should I put them off until after we've concluded with the USGS guys?"

"Are the two things related?"

"No, Sir. Not as far as I know."

"Then they'll have to wait their turn. One natural disaster at a time is quite enough..." the President quipped.

Shortly after four o'clock that morning, Paul Kaufmann had taken a call from the Director of the Jet Propulsion Laboratory in Pasadena, California, asking to speak to the President on a matter of great urgency. Paul Kaufmann had asked for a brief summary which he'd relayed to the President who then spoke directly to the person at the other end of the phone. From the one-sided conversation, he already knew the President regarded the matter seriously enough to request a personal meeting.

At two minutes to eight, Paul Kaufmann ushered in the representatives from the United States Geological Survey. "Please sit down. Let me introduce Graham Tandy and Bairstow Eves of the US Geological Survey. Mr Tandy was recently appointed Scientist-in-Charge at the YVO... that is, the Yellowstone Volcano Observatory. Mr Eves is Senior Scientist responsible for collection and interpretation of data from the site... Larry you already know from yesterday's meeting... and this is Ellen Livvy, one of Larry's colleagues at FEMA who joined us recently. Unfortunately, Ellen couldn't make yesterday's meeting... And this is George Horowitz, the President's advisor on national affairs." George Horowitz leaned forwards and offered his huge, bear-like paw. The three men shook hands over the table. Graham Tandy had the distinct impression that George Horowitz thought he should be somewhere more important.

The President finished on the phone and came over and shook hands with the two visitors, "Good morning..."

"Graham Tandy, Sir" standing to shake the President's hand.

"Mr Tandy... and Mr Eves, I presume... I'm sorry to have detained you."

The President sat down between Ellen Livvy and Larry Myers who were White House staff responsible for liaising with the Federal Emergency Management Agency.

"I'm aware of the report your predecessor submitted to mine, Mr Tandy but I haven't read it in detail, so I'd be grateful if you'd tell me exactly what the situation is at Yellowstone... from the beginning."

Graham Tandy started speaking slowly in measured tones. "Certainly, Sir... Yellowstone National Park sits atop a super volcano, so called because of its enormous size. It's far bigger than most other volcanoes on Earth. Instead of forming the usual cone-shaped mountain as with most volcanoes it's actually in a shallow depression which is so big it can only be seen from the air. We know from the geological record that it's erupted at regular intervals of six hundred and thirty thousand years or thereabouts." At this, Graham Tandy took out a map of the United States showing the fallout zones and put it on the table. "Just over two million years ago, Yellowstone erupted in what is known as the Huckleberry Ridge eruption, depositing about two thousand, five hundred cubic kilometers of rock and ash... that's about six or seven *trillion* tons... over an area stretching from the Pacific coast in the west to the Texas-Louisiana border in the east and south into the Gulf of Mexico, as shown here..." he said, pointing to the map. "By comparison, the nineteen-eighty eruption of Mount Saint Helens produced about one cubic kilometer of debris spread over an area about thirty kilometers or twenty miles in diameter... It's a frightening thought, isn't it?" Graham Tandy paused for a moment to allow the statistics to sink in before continuing. "Excuse me, Sir. Before I go on, do you mind me talking in metric units?"

"Not at all, Mr Tandy, I'm familiar with both systems. Remind me... Is it about one-and-a-half kilometers to the mile?"

"One-point-six..."

"Thank you. Please go on."

"The last major eruption, about six hundred and forty thousand years ago, which is called the Lava Creek eruption, discharged about a thousand cubic kilometers of debris over a slightly smaller area, from way out in the Pacific to Kansas City in the east and the Mexican border in the south... The distribution of ash depends on wind direction. You'll notice that, in both eruptions, there's not much spread northward into Canada, possibly because the prevailing wind was from the north-west. This left a caldera or large crater about sixty-five kilometers by forty-five... or forty miles by thirty. There was a minor eruption about seventy thousand years ago but that was far less explosive so most of the lava that escaped filled the caldera left by the last major eruption and gave us, more or less, the landscape we see today."

"Does this give us any indication of the size of eruption we might expect today?"

"Not necessarily. The eruption one point three million years ago produced less than three hundred cubic kilometers of debris... small by comparison but still sufficient to devastate a huge area and severely disrupt Earth's climate, ecosystems and agriculture... at least in the Northern Hemisphere."

"So we understand it better, please explain... *briefly*... what causes a volcano."

"Yes, Sir... Volcanoes form over hotspots in the Earth's crust caused by an upwelling of magma... that is, molten rock from the mantle... which melts the overlying crust sufficient to weaken it such that the magma breaks through the surface due to the internal pressure..."

Graham Tandy paused momentarily but the President murmured, "Please go on."

"The type of eruption and type of cone or caldera that forms depend largely on the type and quantity of magma. At one end of the scale there's basaltic magma which is very fluid. After the initial bang as it breaks through the surface, these volcanoes often erupt gradually producing those awesome rivers of lava that flow for miles down the flanks of volcanoes but are usually the least threatening. These are called effusive eruptions. As a result, they generally form shallow cones or shield volcanoes as they're called because of their characteristic shape. Magma also contains a lot of dissolved gases, such as carbon dioxide and sulfur dioxide, as well as super-heated water. By the time it reaches the surface, basaltic magma generally contains very little of either because the gas rises up through the magma and can escape relatively easily... which is why you see those spectacular pictures of lava pools belching great bubbles of gas... but the magma usually just oozes out when it reaches the surface. Even then, such volcanoes do occasionally catch out unwary populations living around them." After a brief respite to catch his breath and collect himself, Graham Tandy continued, "At the other end of the scale are volcanoes like Yellowstone that erupt mainly rhyolitic magma which is extremely viscous. Rhyolitic magmas entrain huge amounts of gas and super-heated water because it can't easily escape. Under Yellowstone there's a huge magma chamber which for the last six hundred thousand years... with the exception of one small eruption... has been accumulating boiling magma at a temperature of nine hundred to a thousand degrees Celsius, which is steadily melting the overlying crust. The water in it remains liquid only because of the colossal pressure contained under the capping rock. This makes Yellowstone particularly dangerous because when eventually the surface fails releasing the pressure, the water will turn to steam... suddenly and very violently... and will be discharged in a massive explosive eruption that will be heard around the World. This will take with it huge amounts of volcanic gas, rock and tephra... that is, ash and dust... some of which will reach the upper atmosphere."

"Thank you, Mr Tandy. That provides me... er... us... with an excellent insight into the danger. Now then..."

"Excuse me, Sir but with all due respect, it's not over yet. The worst is yet to come."

"I'm sorry, Mr Tandy. Please finish."

"Once the initial out-gassing has reduced pressure in the magma chamber sufficiently, which could take two or three days, the roof will collapse under its own weight into the magma chamber. This will be accompanied by enormous and devastating earthquakes and a ring of volcanic eruptions around the caldera, followed by massive pyroclastic flows... that is, ground-hugging clouds of ash, pumice, rock and volcanic gases at temperatures in excess of five hundred degrees Celsius... that will travel at speeds up to four or five hundred miles an hour in every direction, covering a vast area. Nothing in its path will survive this blast. Even after the main eruption there are likely to be further, smaller earthquakes and eruptions for tens... possibly even hundreds of years."

"So why is the situation suddenly so urgent it needs to be brought to my attention now, Mr Tandy?"

"Because it's deteriorated since my predecessor's report to the previous administration, Sir... Perhaps I could ask Mr Eves to enlighten you. He's far more familiar with things on the ground at Yellowstone than I am."

"Please tell us, Mr Eves."

Bairstow Eves was less seasoned than his older colleague and obviously less at ease making presentations, being more used to fieldwork where he seldom met anyone, never mind having to talk for any length of time. He started with some difficulty, "Er... to give you a little of the background, Mr President... About... er... eighty-seven years ago, the Park was surveyed... in nineteen-twenty-three, to be precise... In the mid-seventies, it was noticed that Yellowstone Lake was starting to run off into the forest at its southern shore. Re-surveying the park, it was found that the northern end of the lake... in fact, the entire center of the park... had risen by about thirty inches in just over fifty years..." Here he paused to take a sip of water to moisten his dry mouth and help calm his nerves, then continued. "From a NASA survey of the park carried out in the sixties, geologists had become aware that Yellowstone was a previously little-known type of volcano which they termed a 'super volcano'. At that time, it appeared to be dormant. However, they soon realised that the up-lift could only be caused by a rising column of magma, suggesting the volcano was indeed active. Given this evidence plus the widespread geothermal activity and increasing frequency and severity of the tremors, the Geological Survey decided to set up a seismic monitoring program... to keep an eye on things, as it were."

The President asked, "And what evidence of an impending disaster have you uncovered?"

Being more comfortable dealing with facts and figures, Bairstow Eves started to relax and found he could approach the subject with greater enthusiasm. "Well, firstly, we've observed that the center of the park has continued rising but at an increasing rate..." At this, he spread various charts and graphs out on the table in front of the President and continued steadily building the evidence. For an hour, Bairstow Eves talked knowledgeably and convincingly about increased seismic activity, a steady reduction in the thickness of the magma chamber roof, increased hydrothermal activity with increasing numbers of geysers and mudpots, more new fumaroles venting steam and sulfurous gases, increases in ground temperature killing off vegetation over wider and wider areas, more areas of the park being closed to the public because of the increased dangers from scalding streams and much, much more. As he turned over the last few sheets of the copious evidence he had amassed, he said, "Finally, for my money, the two most compelling pieces of evidence for a forthcoming eruption are as follows... Firstly, based on the latest seismic measurements of the thickness of the magma chamber roof at its thinnest point, the magma is now only about three-point-six kilometers below the surface... Bear in mind Mount Saint Helens blew when the magma had reached half a kilometer from the surface but that was over a tiny area by comparison... The roof is far too thin for safety. The stresses in it must be enormous... And secondly... and probably the most frightening of all for me, particularly when I'm out in the field... is the fact that over the last fifty years or so, three huge domes have developed..." and here he tapped the map with his forefinger, "...here in the Mallard Lake region in the south-east of the park, here at Sour Creek in the north-west and under Yellowstone Lake itself. Fissures have recently started appearing in the ground over and around these domes. Whilst the cracks are only superficial at the moment... perhaps five to ten feet deep and a couple of inches wide... they pose no immediate threat but if they continue propagating downwards, they'll eventually break through the dome and vent the pressure in the magma chamber which will trigger the eruption."

"Thank you, Mr Eves. And what are the implications if it erupts?"

"There's no question of '*if*' Mr President. Yellowstone *will* erupt..." Graham Tandy said emphatically, "It's simply a matter of *when*."

The President's face was drawn. Paul Kaufmann thought he looked even more tired than he had the previous evening. "Your predecessor's best estimate of when it would blow is some time in the next ten thousand years, Mr Tandy, which might be... er... *safe* in geological terms but it's of no use to this Administration. I can't sell to Congress the need to divert resources away from other much-needed areas and onto Yellowstone based on such a vague prediction. They simply wouldn't buy it. You need to be more specific. So... the sixty-four thousand dollar question, gentlemen, is... *when* will Yellowstone erupt?"

Graham Tandy said, "I'm afraid we can't give you a specific date, Sir but based on our observations, I'd say ten years... a hundred at most. Of course, it could begin before this meeting's over. It's now only a matter of time..." at which Bairstow Eves nodded to show he was in full agreement. "My gut instinct tells me it's already gone critical. The ground won't take much more deformation before it fails catastrophically. One severe earthquake could do it then all hell's let loose." That was the chilling prediction the President had been waiting for.

Graham Tandy took a deep breath and continued, "We've talked about the immediate local devastation... that is, within a radius of five hundred miles. That area will be totally devastated and uninhabitable for thousands of years, as effectively as if a massive nuclear bomb had been detonated there... Of course, it'd take the equivalent of five-hundred-thousand to a million megaton-sized bombs exploding simultaneously to come anywhere near the force of this eruption..." After a brief pause, during which everyone grappled with the mental imagery, he continued, "In respect of the long term consequences, it's not so easy to say categorically because we have limited experience to base it on. It's more speculation... The first noticeable effect... noticeable that is from way outside the blast zone... would be a giant eruption column spewing billions of tons of dust into the upper atmosphere, which would be carried around the World by jetstreams... strong winds at high altitudes... turning the skies dark and overcast, possibly for years. The dust would reflect much of the sunlight back into space, which would result in *significant* global cooling... perhaps by as much as five degrees Celsius... That would translate to summer temperatures in the USA cooler by about twenty degrees, which would seriously harm plants' growth cycles. Along with the dust, millions of tons of sulfur dioxide and hydrogen chloride would be discharged which would precipitate as acid rain. The combined effect of acid rain, choking dust and increasing cold would be to kill off most of the vegetation on land... After the initial eruption and subsequent earthquakes had subsided, the Earth would slide into what's known as a 'volcanic winter'... It might even trigger the next Ice Age... Most, if not all complex life on Earth... that is, anything more complex than bacteria, viruses, fungi, moulds, lichens, some of the hardier insects, possibly creatures that live on and around deep sea hydrothermal vents and maybe certain types of fish... would perish..." Here he paused again then said, with a harder edge to his voice than he'd used so far, "When it happens, it will *truly* be an extinction level event."

Thinking of her little girl, Ellen Livvy spoke for the first time since the meeting had begun, "And the fate of mankind... What's that likely to be?"

Graham Tandy continued, "About seventy-four thousand years ago, Toba, on the Indonesian island of Sumatra, erupted discharging about two thousand, eight hundred cubic kilometers of debris... even bigger than Yellowstone... Interestingly enough, at roughly the same time that geologists were investigating the Toba eruption... and purely by coincidence, I might add... genetecists studying mitochondrial DNA discovered that, between seventy and eighty thousand years ago, the human population fell from more than ten million beings... and probably nearer to fifty million... to fewer than five thousand.... Possibly as few as two thousand people survived worldwide. Humans were pushed to the very brink of extinction. The most likely cause for this is thought to be the eruption of Toba. What saved us, why we were spared, I couldn't guess. It was possibly our adaptability, our inventiveness... Who knows? Maybe our time simply hadn't come."

The meeting sat in silence until the President asked quietly, "Can you get evidence that confirms or denies your estimate of the timescale?"

"Yes, Sir. We could probably come up with a more reliable estimate once we've collected more data and performed more tests but at the moment we've topped out on our budget. Ideally, we need at least one of NASA's InSAR satellites... that is, satellites used for surveying the surface topography of the Earth very accurately... to be dedicated to Yellowstone, as well as all the computing power to go with it for processing the data. That'll tell us where the ground's swelling and at what rate which will allow us to position our ground sensors in the right places to get the other data we need. But I can't swing that, it's way beyond my budget... and my clout."

"Don't worry, Mr Tandy, it's not beyond mine. George, after the meeting, please get on to NASA and make sure these gentlemen get everything they need without delay."

George Horowitz nodded and said, "Yes, Sir."

Everyone sat in silence. The President said quietly, "The million dollar question is... how do we prevent it?"

Again, Graham Tandy spoke up, "We can't. This involves immense forces that shape the planet... that drive its internal engine. It's unstoppable. There's no technology... at least, none I'm aware of... that could prevent this eruption."

The President shot back, "But we can't sit back and wait for it to wipe us out. There must be things we can do to help protect ourselves... to contain the eruption and limit the devastation."

Larry Myers, who was a planner by nature as well as by profession, said, "The first and most obvious thing is to inform people of the facts then put in place a systematic program of voluntary evacuation starting with the area immediately around Yellowstone. Logistically, it's a mammoth task. It could take years to move and re-settle everyone and the longer it went on without an eruption, the more likely it is that folk would doubt what they'd been told and start migrating back into the danger zone."

Bairstow Eves chipped in, "The other problem is where do they go? Because, in the ensuing volcanic winter, nowhere will be hospitable... at least nowhere in the Northern Hemisphere and, if the eruption's big enough, possibly nowhere in the Southern Hemisphere either."

"You paint a bleak and depressing picture, gentlemen but I refuse to give up hope altogether. We're homo sapiens... *wise man*. We're nothing if not resourceful... How do you think we came this far? You say we survived the eruption of Toba seventy-four thousand years ago. I say we can survive this one, so long as we're determined to get through it. So, I want us to consider for a moment what we can do, if anything, to mitigate the effects of this eruption... *when* it happens. You say the main eruption will be triggered by a sudden release of pressure under the dome... Is that correct?"

"Basically, yes, Mr President."

"So is drilling down into the magma chamber to get a *controlled* release of pressure an option? I believe we have the drilling technology to go that deep."

Not wanting to deliver a completely negative message, Graham Tandy cautiously conceded, "If it was possible... *maybe*... We'd have to develop drilling and pressure control equipment capable of handling the high temperatures, as well as the corrosive and abrasive conditions. That could take years... And the gas is dissolved in molten rock, so separating it to vent it off won't be easy. But if we *could* release the pressure slowly it *might* help. Of course, the pressure will continue to be replenished from below but if we could maintain equilibrium just below the critical pressure at which the overlying rock fractures, it may buy us time to consider what further action we might take."

The President looked more positive than he had since the beginning of the meeting, possibly because he felt he was back on the offensive. "And how about quenching the magma by pumping water into the magma chamber? Would that work?"

"I couldn't say, Mr President, I doubt that water could be pumped in at sufficient rate to cool the magma... Don't forget, there's at least ten thousand cubic kilometers of it in the magma chamber... that's about thirty-five *trillion* tons... at a temperature of about a thousand degrees Celsius. That's a lot of heat to dissipate... and it's continuously being fed from underneath. It might even initiate an eruption..."

"Okay, so that may be a non-starter. What else could we try?" The meeting sat in silence, none of the other participants having the faintest idea what to suggest or were just too stunned by the magnitude of the whole thing to think at all.

After a while, the President said, "You say Yellowstone is in a depression. How about damming up the caldera and flooding it to create a huge lake? You don't seem to hear of sub-sea eruptions causing nearly so much devastation as volcanoes on land. It might not prevent an eruption but it might help quench it when it did occur. Could it help reduce the amount of ash discharged into the atmosphere? The cost would be astronomical, I know... and the timescale... but if it would help save mankind from extinction, the whole of humanity should want to get behind this project. Do you see what I'm driving at? However we tackle this volcano, it'll be a mammoth task but we won't give in without a fight…"

Graham Tandy sat quietly for a moment, then said, "It's an interesting thought. There's evidence to suggest the caldera may actually have been a lake at one time which drained when the Grand Canyon of the Yellowstone River formed. It might help… how much, I don't know… but it would take tens, maybe hundreds of years to fill up given the inflows available today… and that would only be after all the outlets had been dammed up. Still, it could be worth considering…"

George Horowitz suddenly sat forward and said, "I know this one probably comes at you from left-field, Mr Tandy but could an eruption be triggered by, say, a thermonuclear device detonated in the vicinity?"

Graham Tandy was clearly taken aback by the question. "That's difficult to say…" then after a few moments thought, "Possibly, if it was big enough to excavate enough material from the cap to weaken it sufficiently… or to fracture it. But it would probably have to be buried at least half a mile deep to have such an effect. I'd be surprised if the shockwave from a bomb detonated in the air above the surface would generate sufficient downward pressure to crack the cap… but I don't know, I'm guessing now. I'm not an expert in such matters…" then added, "But why would you consider doing such a thing?"

"I'm thinking about this from all angles, Mr Tandy."

Paul Kaufmann knew exactly why George Horowitz had asked the question and it prompted another worrying thought. As casually as he could, he asked, "Could an eruption possibly be triggered by any other external event? For instance, a large meteor hitting the Earth… or something of similar magnitude."

Graham Tandy said, "Given the frequency with which such events occur, we'd be extremely unlucky if that did happen but yes… anything that generates huge shockwaves, such as an earthquake or meteor impact, could trigger an eruption."

By now, everyone in the meeting, including the scientists who had been living with the growing awareness of impending disaster and who'd been the bearers of the bad news were too weary to continue discussing the harsh details. The President said, "Does anyone have any more questions or points they'd like to raise… No. Then to conclude… I want you, George, to head up a dedicated team, including Ellen and Larry from the White House and these gentlemen from the US Geological Survey, to continue monitoring Yellowstone. Pull in any additional resources you think are necessary. I'm not concerned about the costs. I'll get those approved later when we know what they are. I want three things from you… Firstly, your most reliable prediction of when it will erupt and any indication of possible magnitude... failing that, we must assume the worst... Secondly, detailed proposals as to how we manage the situation now in terms of public awareness, re-location, evacuation procedure and so on and, after an eruption, in terms of survival strategy for the greatest number of people. Thirdly, viable suggestions as to what can be done... irrespective of cost... to contain an eruption and limit the damage. Is that understood?"

In unison, they all said, "Yes, Sir."

"And are you all willing to undertake this?"

"Yes, Sir."

"Finally, I cannot impress on you too strongly the need to keep this under wraps... at least until we've decided on a way forward... and that goes for anyone else you bring into the team. For the time being, the official line is we're just stepping up our level of vigilance. You can guess at the widespread panic this would cause if it was leaked in an uncontrolled fashion. Is that understood?"

"Yes, Sir."

"George, I want regular monthly briefings, please... And I'm to be informed *immediately* of any developments. Fine! It's lunchtime and a good point to break, so I suggest we draw the meeting to a close. Thank you everybody."

They all stood. George Horowitz said, "Excuse me, Sir..." then turned to the team, "I'd like a briefing in my office now, to firm up our action plan." Whilst the President said farewell to his visitors, Paul Kaufmann slipped out of the office. He returned almost immediately, as George Horowitz was shepherding the visitors out of the President's office. When they'd gone, he said to the President, "The visitors from JPL will land at Dulles at about two... Washington National's been closed due to a bomb scare... so they'll be here by about two-thirty, Sir. I've sent a car for them."

"Thank you, Paul. George said your briefing should be finished by two at the latest. I want you both in here to meet the JPL guys as soon as they arrive. Let's try and put that one to bed pronto..."

"Yes, Sir. There's just one more thing... I know Ellen Livvy's flying home this afternoon for her grandmother's funeral tomorrow morning, so she'll be out... She's already postponed her flight once to be at today's meeting. FEMA don't have anyone who can attend this afternoon's meeting. They're swamped with this latest 'quake in California. It's taken most of their available resources... Immediately he's finished with George, Larry's supposed to be flying out to California to help coordinate rescue efforts there... and to support the VP in representing the Administration... Do you want me to ask one or other of them to change their plans, so they can sit in on this next meeting?"

After a moment's reflection, the President said, "No, I don't think so, Paul. Let's get a measure of the situation. We can brief them later. In the meantime, you need to get to your meeting and I have an NSC briefing on the latest security report. So, if you'll excuse me…"

In the early hours of Wednesday morning, July twenty-eight, an earthquake had struck a twenty mile section inland from the west coast between Long Beach and Costa Mesa, in a broad swathe about five miles wide. It had peaked at magnitude 7.0 causing widespread damage to roads, homes and communities, wreaking havoc. In an attempt to show solidarity with the local inhabitants and demonstrate to the whole of America that this Administration could be relied upon for support when it was required, the White House had despatched the Vice President with the instruction that he was to reassure the locals they would receive all the help they needed for a full recovery. The Vice President and his wife had flown out the following day on Air Force Two. He was to maintain a presence until the crisis had passed and everyone was satisfied their needs would be met in full.

Chapter 4

(Sunday 1 August 2010, shortly after 05:00 Pacific / 08:00 Eastern)

Dan Ackland and Jack Culver sat opposite Wayne Harland, the Director of the Space Center at the Jet Propulsion Laboratory. The pilot had already been given clearance for take-off ahead of all other traffic out of Pasadena International Airport and, as soon as the door had been closed, the Learjet taxied out to the runway, took off and headed east for Washington DC. JPL was the center responsible for co-ordinating space watching on the West Coast and Hawaii and Wayne Harland was the man who ultimately had to make the decision about whether a near-Earth intrusion warranted informing the President. Within fifteen minutes of receiving Dan Ackland's phone call in the early hours of the morning and reviewing the data that had been e-mailed to him, Wayne Harland had picked up the phone to make the one call he'd hoped he would never have to make.

"It's good to meet you at last, Jack. Dan's told me a lot about you. Thanks for coming out so promptly. It's an ungodly hour to be up and about, I know and I'm sure you'd both rather be tucked up in your beds at home but the White House want us there immediately. That's why I sent the plane for you straight away."

Dan said, "Don't worry, we were up anyway. I managed to grab an hour's shut-eye on the way down here so I don't feel too ragged." Jack said nothing but reflected that he hadn't had a wink of sleep on the way here – he'd spent the entire flight worrying about his son.

"I called Mauna Kea last night, after we spoke and had them re-assign Keck II to S241. Jim Murray, who's Director of Operations down there, should've been in touch... Has he?" When Jack realised that Wayne Harland was addressing him, he jerked to attention and confirmed that, yes, he had and that his assistant had already down-loaded all the necessary information on S241's trajectory to the W. M. Keck Observatory on Hawaii to enable them to locate it tonight.

Wayne Harland continued, "Unfortunately, Keck I is out of service. I told them to get it fixed a.s.a.p. but it won't be ready in time to make tonight's sighting. I also asked the President's office whether we could approach the European Space Observatory, at Cerro Paranal, to see if they could provide us with another sighting using the VLT but apparently the President wouldn't hear of it. It seems they want to keep this under wraps until we know exactly what it is we're dealing with... which also gives them more time to decide how they want to play things if the worst comes to the worst."

Dan Ackland interjected, "Not much time… We need all the data we can possibly get and we need it *now*! This is a potential doomsday scenario, for Christ's sake. Don't they realise the magnitude of the situation? The more information we get, the sooner we'll know for sure whether we're going to have to confront our own destiny. Measurements from the Very Large Telescope could help cut days off that process…"

"It's no use getting het up, Dan. I tried persuading them of the seriousness of the situation but the White House won't share anything with the Europeans. It's this whole stupid climate of suspicion and mistrust that's developed between us because of their stance on terrorism, in particular how we deal with these Islamic fundamentalist lunatics… Still, if S241 does hit us, it'll hardly matter. There won't be any Muslims left to bother us… There won't be any us…"

The three of them continued discussing the situation for a while, until there was nothing more that could usefully be said. Dan Ackland dozed off. Wayne Harland went back to the galley and made a pot of coffee for everyone and took two cups to the cockpit for the pilot and co-pilot. Whilst he was gone, Jack called home using the plane's in-flight cellular phone. Claudette answered. He could tell immediately by the tremor in her voice that she'd been crying. His throat tightened and his mouth went dry. He hardly dared ask, "Claudette, how's Billy? Is he alright?"

"We don't know Dad, we haven't found him. Where are you? We need you *here… Now!* Mom's nearly frantic with worry."

"Put your mother on. Let me speak to her."

"Mom's not here. She's out with the Sheriff and the neighbours looking for Billy. Nicky and I just got in from college about ten minutes ago. He's having a shower. I called this morning early. I don't know why. I woke up in the night with this feeling of dread. I was having this horrible dream. I *knew* something was wrong and I just had to call home. Mom told me that Billy'd been gone for two days. I had to get back to help look for him…" And then, somewhat hesitantly, Claudette continued, "She thinks Billy may have *run away*. She says his backpack's gone along with some of his things from his room." At first, Jack was too astonished to say anything. He sat in silence, absorbing what his daughter had said but then, as he reflected on it, his surprise receded. After all, nobody knew better his son's extraordinary talents – Jack had witnessed them at first hand. But this – he would never have expected it. Where would he go? *And why*? Billy knew nowhere but home. And how would he cope? As his mind ranged over such questions, his thoughts were interrupted by Claudette.

"Dad, where are you? Why don't you come home?"

Jack Culver said, "I'm sorry Claudette but I can't. I'm on my way to Washington for a meeting with the President. We should be back later today but I may not get home tonight. Tomorrow, maybe. In the meantime, you'll have to continue the search for Billy yourselves. Tell your mom I'll try and call her as soon as I can but I'm on a very hectic schedule. You know I love you and you're all in my thoughts..." and he thought to himself, 'And I hope and pray no harm comes to Billy or they'll never forgive me for not being there... I'll never forgive myself.'

"Why are you going to the White House, Dad?"

"I'm sorry, honey, I can't discuss it now. I have to go. Tell Mom I'll be home as soon as I can. Bye bye, darling."

"Bye Dad. I love you..." and with that the connection was severed. Claudette stood listening to the tone for a few seconds. She knew something was very wrong. The tears welled up in her eyes then rolled down her cheeks and, for some inexplicable reason, she felt very afraid.

Jack Culver sat back in his seat and shut his eyes. His thoughts were of his family. Martha, his wife, her slim figure, her lovely wavy chestnut brown hair and her pretty face with the most beautiful green eyes he'd ever seen. When they'd met at their graduation ball, he'd been completely smitten by the lovely biochemistry student. He really had fallen in love with her on their first meeting. Although he didn't know it at the time, Martha had been struck equally forcefully by him but she had played harder to get, having been taken to the ball by a very dishy but rather self-loving medical student. It had taken a concerted campaign on his part, waged over three months at a distance of six hundred miles, to win her over but the sustained effort had paid off and within three years they were married. Thereafter, they'd had lots of fun for the first seven years, with regular holidays both at home and in Europe. Jack was from a modestly wealthy family and they were sufficiently well off to be able to escape whenever the opportunity had arisen, which is why Martha had never ceased to be impressed by the fact that Jack was so fascinated by his job that he spent such long hours at work when he could easily afford not to work at all. Then the twins, Nicky and Claudette, had come along, as alike as two peas in a pod when they were born. As small children, Jack had loved to cuddle them, in particular Claudette who had secretly been his favorite and still was, although he would never say so openly, not even to his wife. He thought back to drying them after their baths, gently towelling their little bodies dry then touching their velvety skins, stroking them like cats, which he thought was the most sensuous pleasure he'd ever experienced. He had enjoyed watching them growing up, Nicky becoming tall and athletic like him and Claudette remaining petite like Martha's mother and grandmother and even prettier than Martha but sensitive also, like his mother, in a way that Martha wasn't. Billy had followed on five years later, after Martha had suffered a miscarriage and a heart-breaking still birth. Jack had never before been quite so aware of how deeply he loved Martha until he saw her grieving for their dead baby girl. Billy, Jack only ever remembered as being a calm baby, always still and watchful but also very happy and contented. His sister had doted on him and had played with him endlessly and he never once complained. Jack saw relatively little of Billy in his early years because, at that time, he'd been very heavily involved in the building of the new observatory where he was now Director of Astronomy and in designing and commissioning its new optical telescope. Consequently, Jack saw less of his youngest son as he was growing up than he had of his first two children. Possibly because of this Jack had noticed, from about the age of nine months, that Billy's development was markedly different from that of the twins. He was becoming progressively more introvert and irascible when he was distracted by everyday activities such as washing, dressing and eating. The older he grew, the less he liked being picked up and would become more difficult if you tried to play with him. It seemed as though he was retreating into a world of his own. It wasn't until he had undergone a barrage of tests that, at the age of two, Billy's doctors confirmed their diagnosis of autism. Martha had struggled with feelings of guilt and disappointment over having given birth to her imperfect son but Jack found that he only loved his son the more for being different and had grown to admire him for leading such a self-contained life on his own lonely little planet.

"Jack... Jack! Wake up! We're on the ground..." Dan Ackland shook Jack's arm firmly as the Learjet taxied to a halt. "Get your things together, there's a car on the apron waiting to take us to the White House." Jack was quickly wide awake. He'd slept well considering the reason they were here. Feeling better than he had when he boarded, Jack picked up his briefcase and followed the others off the plane and to the waiting limousine.

—•—

"Right, Mr Davies, tell us what you have to report."

"There've been some interesting developments, Mr President. Yesterday, Al Rashid's wife returned home with the children. She brought his mother back to stay with them. It seems she'd come from Iraq to visit her in-laws in Lebanon, presumably to see her grandkids. At first, it didn't make sense to us but it did make us wonder if he's done it now to try to create an air of normality... maybe to distract our attention away from his other activities... because he suspects we may have got wind of their little plot... Of course, if they assume we'll think like Westerners, the obvious conclusion for them to draw would be one of *'Surely this guy wouldn't expose his family to such a risky situation... Maybe we're way off beam here... Maybe he's not a bad guy after all, so let's scale down our surveillance on him and focus on a more likely candidate...'* A bluff, if you will... But he is a terrorist, after all, whether his wife knows it or not... Whether she knows about the bomb or whether she's a willing party to it, who knows? He's not likely to worry about her safety... or the kids'... or his mother's... At the end of the day, they're all expendable... If it succeeds, they're all going to bask in reflected glory... and if it blows up in their faces... well... I guess he's told himself they're all going to join him in paradise... unwittingly or not... So, we must assume it's business as usual as far as Al Rashid's concerned..."

The President butted in, "That's an awfully convoluted explanation, Mr Davies... And an awful lot of assumptions. Far too many for my liking. Expand the word *'assume'*, Mr Davies. It could make an *'ass'* out of *'you'* and *'me'*... To me, this feels even more like a decoy than it did before... I think we're being blind-sided by these crafty bastards..."

"In fairness, Sir, we've been through exactly the same thought processes ourselves. We've checked and re-checked our intelligence but we're still convinced this is real... And not solely based on this alone. There's more..."

"So let's hear it."

"Well, firstly, Al Rashid called his secretary today... a Mrs Bilhal, another Muslim... to tell her that he was extending his vacation by another week... It seems he'd already made arrangements to have next week off work, starting tomorrow, Monday the second... but he told her that he's now decided to have the following week off as well... starting Monday ninth... and that she should re-arrange his diary accordingly... Something to do with his mother's surprise visit... Our guess... because that's what it is at the moment, without corroborating intelligence... is that he was having the time off to take delivery of the bomb and get it planted but, because it's been delayed a week, he needs more time off... And secondly, he also called the marina to let them know he'd be taking his boat, 'Nesmat al-Rabiya'... which is Arabic for 'Spring Breeze'... out for two weeks, not one as he'd originally entered in the log. He could be going down to the Ocean, possibly to rendezvous with a ship to collect something. Maybe the bomb... Furthermore, one of our agents went to the marina to make discrete enquires about Al Rashid's boat. Apparently, it went into the boatyard for a refit recently. Amongst the other things they did was to install a large removable sunroof in the deck over the main cabin and reinforce the hull below the waterline in that area so it could take a heavy load directly beneath the aperture. According to the yard's manager, both very difficult and expensive modifications and, he thought, strange requests. Apparently, Al Rashid tried explaining away the opening by saying that his wife and daughters weren't allowed to sunbathe on the deck... something to do with their religion... but they could sunbathe down below, in the cabin, where they'd be out of sight. He thought it sounded a bit quaint but plausible... but of course, it didn't explain the reinforcement. Our agent, who's a boating enthusiast himself, saw Al Rashid's boat and says that such modifications wouldn't enhance the value of the boat. In fact, they're more likely to detract from it... But he did say it would certainly make an excellent hold for stowing a large, heavy object, such as a bomb... It all fits, Sir, it really does..."

"It all sounds a bit flimsy to me, Mr Davies. Surely, a detached observer seeing this from a slightly different perspective could put a purely innocent interpretation on most if not all the facts we've amassed so far... Couldn't they?"

"Possibly, Sir... but they wouldn't have the wealth of experience... gut instinct, if you like... and the background information we have, all of which tells me we have an on-going hostile situation on our hands, Mr President."

The President sighed and asked rhetorically, "I really don't know, Mr Davies... Why do we see things so differently? Is it because it's in your nature to be suspicious of people, whereas it's in mine to trust them... unless and until proven otherwise?"

Trying to maintain a neutral tone, Alan Davies said quietly, "With all due respect, Mr President, I can't afford the luxury of waiting for events to prove me right because... more often than not... by the time they do, innocent people are dead."

After sitting deep in thought for a while, the President said, "Please explain this to me, Mr Davies... Yesterday, you thought the bomb hadn't been shipped yet. In fact, your interpretation of Al Rashid's telephone conversation suggested that it's still at least a week away from completion... Surely a ship would take what... three... maybe four weeks to sail from the Middle East? If that is the case... that it hasn't been shipped yet... how can Al Rashid be collecting it within the next two weeks?"

"I appreciate that, Sir but that was only our best guess. We don't *know*. It could be on the water even now. It's all smoke and mirrors with these guys. They don't telegraph ahead to let us know what they're doing. They do their best to confuse us with misinformation and coded messages we can't easily decipher. They give us very few dots... some of which turn out to be false... and we have to try and join them to form a coherent picture. It's not easy but we're doing our best with very limited information to second-guess these bastards before they perpetrate another atrocity against America."

Seeing that Alan Davies was clearly feeling stressed and starting to get worked up, the President said in a somewhat placatory tone, "I understand, Mr Davies and I sympathise with your predicament. I'm just as anxious as you are to stop these terrorists but I'm also concerned that we're being distracted by a sideshow and missing the main event."

Alan Davies calmed a little. He retorted quietly, "With all due respect, Mr President, I'd hardly call shutting down Washington permanently with a dirty bomb a *sideshow*... As shows go, how much bigger do they come?"

Travis Johnston said, "May I intercede, Mr President?" Without waiting for the President's consent, he promptly went on, "Apropos the timing... We recently received sound intelligence about arms shipments from Yemen to Muslim guerillas in Guyana and Surinam in South America. We learnt that the arms were being flown to Senegal which is on the coast of West Africa and from there by ship out of Dakar. There's no shortage of willing supporters to help speed the arms on their way. The vast majority of the Senegalese population, over ninety percent, are Muslims. If the bomb were to follow a similar route, it would cut the sea passage to somewhere like Norfolk to a week... ten days max... The bomb could be here by the time Al Rashid's vacation is over."

The President sat brooding until at last he said, "So... Let's *assume* you're right, Mr Davies... Where does that leave us?"

Feeling buoyed up by Travis Johnston's substantiation of his theory and relieved that the President's attention was now squarely focussed on the issue, Alan Davies rallied and said, "Well... Assuming Al Rashid is going to collect the bomb personally, it's probably safe to say he'd originally intended rendezvousing with it by Friday August sixth latest... possibly sooner... so it would've been in place by the time he'd resumed work on Monday ninth... Now it's delayed a week, we assume they're aiming to collect it by Friday the thirteenth..."

'An auspicious date' the President thought to himself but left it unsaid.

"...with a view to having it in place before he returns to work Monday sixteenth... Of course, they may put it in temporary storage until nearer the date then move it to its final resting place just before September eleven..."

"Why not simply detonate it immediately, once it's in place? Why wait? It only increases the risk of it being discovered in the meantime."

"Well Sir, we did consider that possibility but we're fairly confident they'll wait until September eleven..."

"Why?"

"Islam's holiest month... Ramadan... starts Wednesday August eleventh. This is the month when Muslims fast during daylight hours and offer up special prayers to their God. It's sacred. They're not even supposed to think bad thoughts about fellow believers during Ramadan, never mind blow them to smithereens. Islam considers the slaying of fellow believers to be a sin at any time but killing a fellow believer during Ramadan would be an absolute no-no... And, of course, there's no guarantee the bomb wouldn't kill

Muslims… Just think of the World Trade Center and every attack since then. In each one, Muslims have lost their lives along with all the other victims. However, we've checked and there's no record of an attack during Ramadan…" and then, after a slight pause, "Ramadan ends September ninth, two days before D-day. We think it's unlikely they'll launch an attack during Ramadan, unless they're cornered and have no option but to detonate the bomb sooner than intended. September tenth is the first of Shawwal, on which they start three days of celebrations with Eid ul-Fitr… the Festival of Breaking Fast… which is also a special holiday. So, if you were a Muslim, the second of Shawwal would be a very good day to carry out your attack. You'd have gotten all your religious ceremonies out of the way and you could do it without the spectre of damnation haunting you…"

The President abruptly interrupted Alan Davies' flow. "But if delivery had been on time, the bomb would've been here before Ramadan… Do you think they originally planned an August attack? And if that was the case, what assurance do we have that they won't simply defer their plans by a week and carry out the attack during Ramadan?"

Alan Davies sat forlornly thinking about it then said meekly, "None, Sir."

"Then my instruction to you… to *all* our security services is, 'Remain vigilant… Identify the threat… Determine that it's real... Immediately it's been verified, neutralise it… without hesitation! If necessary, use ultimate force'… but…" and here the President leaned forward, scanning each one round the table in turn, looking them in the eye with a cold, hard stare. For the first time, the President spoke with real malice in his voice, "…*under no circumstances whatsoever are you to let those ungodly bastards unleash this thing on the streets of the Capital*… Is that understood?" Everyone round the table responded affirmatively and in unison, "Yes, Sir!"

As the meeting broke up, the President remained seated. When everyone had gone, he closed his eyes and let his chin slump down on his chest. He looked washed out and felt exhausted; in fact, unusual for him, he felt positively ill. After sitting like this for a couple of minutes, he got up wearily and went over to the beautifully tooled globe that stood discretely against the wall of his office, which cunningly disguised a drinks cabinet. He hinged back the Northern Hemisphere, took out a bottle of twenty-one year old, single malt Scotch whisky and, for the first time in his tenure, poured himself a stiff measure. As he sat sipping the fiery liquid, he flushed a little. Gradually, the color returned to his cheeks and he began to feel better. As he was draining the last finger of whisky at one gulp, Paul Kaufmann knocked and walked in. "Yes, Paul… and what can I do you for?" the President asked with excessive jocularity.

Paul Kaufmann eyed the empty tumbler suspiciously but made no comment. He said, "The party from JPL will be here in five minutes. Should I show them in straight away, Sir?"

Breezily, the President replied, "Yes, Paul. Whatever the tune, we've got to face the music and dance. I'm not going anywhere so wheel 'em in as soon as they're ready..."

Paul Kaufmann went out again, feeling a vague sense of unease he'd never experienced before in the President's company.

—•—

"Let me get this right... You say you first saw this asteroid... S241... when it was *five hundred million miles out... Beyond Jupiter...* That must be like seeing a dime at the far end of Constitution Avenue... That's one helluva telescope you have there, Mr Culver."

"Well, to be strictly correct, Sir, we didn't actually see it at that point. We simply inferred its presence because it obscured our view of more distant stars as it passed in front of them. We were actually looking for Cepheid variables... that is, stars which vary in brightness over a period of time... They're particularly useful as markers for measuring astronomical distances. The computer simply picked out stars that varied in brightness... to nothing, as it so happened... as the asteroid crossed their faces. It was my assistant, David Johnson, who first joined the dots and noticed they formed a path..."

Struck by the irony of an amusing thought, the President nearly choked as he stifled a laugh. Everyone round the table mistakenly thought he'd hiccuped, especially when he finished a little sheepishly by saying, "Excuse me", with the exception of Jack Culver who guessed exactly what it was that had tickled him so much. Ignoring the interruption and without waiting for the President to regain his composure, he continued "At that time, S241's trajectory was pretty much tangential to Jupiter's orbit. In fact, at one point we expected it to collide with Jupiter. We lost it for a while and thought it might've gone in on the far side where we couldn't see the impact... Of course, we realised it hadn't when there was no impact wound. We picked it up again quite by accident a few weeks later, after it'd re-appeared from behind Jupiter. By then, of course, its trajectory had altered substantially. That was three months ago. It wasn't until three *weeks* ago that we actually *saw* it for the first time, at about a hundred million miles out. But you're right, Mr President, it is one helluva telescope. Ten years ago, we'd have had trouble seeing it ten million miles away..." After a moment's hesitation, Jack added, "Oh... and for what it's worth... from here in Washington, it would have been more like seeing a penny in Detroit... at night... backlit by someone striking a match in Green

Bay, Wisconsin..." then, by way of clarification, "I know. I worked it out on the way in from the airport..."

Wayne Harland said, "I wondered what you were doing with that map..."

The President couldn't help but laugh out loud, struck by the absurdity of what Jack Culver had said and everyone round the table joined in. When the laughter had subsided, Jack finished off matter-of-factly by saying, "That was then. I also worked out that, as of today, it's just north of Frederick, Maryland, heading straight down I-70 towards the Capital..." which immediately dispelled the air of levity and cast a somber mood over the group.

The President said drily, "Well, let's hope it stays on I-70 to Baltimore. If it takes two-seventy, let me know and I'm out of here..." but this time, there was no hilarity.

George Horowitz asked, "What level of risk does it pose, Mr Culver?"

"Based on our most recent sightings, Earth is directly in S241's flightpath. Our latest projections indicate it'll cross Earth's orbit in twenty-one days time... on August twenty-first... We currently estimate that the plane through which it'll pass relative to Earth's orbit... what we call the *plane of uncertainty*... is roughly ten Earth diameters or about eighty thousand miles across which suggests there's *at least* a one-in-a-hundred chance of it hitting Earth... In other words, it'll come within forty-thousand miles of us, which is the cosmic equivalent of a bullet grazing your temple. The more worrying factor is that, with each new set of data, the plane of uncertainty is becoming increasingly centered on Earth itself which increases the probability of a collision, but to what odds I couldn't say offhand... safe to say they're not very encouraging..."

George Horowitz interrupted, "Excuse me, Mr Culver but I'm a bit confused. Would you mind explaining, for my benefit, why there's so much *uncertainty* about the *degree of uncertainty*... and just how much reliance we can put on your figures."

"Yes, Sir, I'd be happy to oblige... First, you must bear in mind that all our measurements are subject to a tolerance... a tiny error. Consecutive sightings allow us to plot a path through space. We can project that path forward, ahead of the actual object, which is what we've done to arrive at *this*..." said Jack Culver, pointing to the drawing laid out on the table. "Because each reading is subject to an error, the points we've measured may not fall precisely on the true flightpath. They may only be fractionally out but they're out. So the computer fits the best possible curve... or centerline... through the points we've already got, to create a theoretical flightpath, then it considers all the slight errors and discrepancies and puts a tube around the centerline defining the worst-case deviation from the true path... It takes a computer to do it because there's so much data and the calculations are so complex it would be impossible to do by hand. But in this case, the reality is even more difficult than the theory… Firstly, if this thing was crossing our line of sight it would trace a broad arc in the sky, giving us big angles to measure and the errors would be less significant… Of course, we'd also be less concerned about it if it was… However, it's coming almost straight at us *along* our line of sight, so there's very little difference in angle between subsequent sightings making the measurement errors more significant… Secondly, like every object in the Solar system… indeed, in the Universe… it's being acted on by the gravity of every other object, however remote. The bigger and closer the object, the greater its gravitational pull… Of course, it was Jupiter that catapulted it in our direction in the first place but now Jupiter's influence is diminishing… It's increasingly coming within the maw of the Sun… and the Earth… All these factors and more must be… *and have been*… taken into account in generating this projected flightpath, Mr Horowitz. The really scary thing is, as you can see from subsequent plots, the tube is getting narrower and its centerline is becoming more tightly focussed on Earth… You'd better believe we're in its cross-hairs…"

"Please don't think I'm questioning your professionalism, Mr Culver but I wanted to gauge how confident you were in your own prediction… It's clear you're convinced this is a serious threat…"

Jack Culver said emphatically, "Believe me, Mr Horowitz if it hadn't been, there's something far more urgent I should have… *and would have been doing*… at home right now."

There was an uneasy silence until the President asked, "When *will* you know for sure whether S241's going to hit Earth, Mr Culver?"

"August twenty-second, Mr President… No, Sir, I'm not being cute. We can go on taking measurements and updating our charts but we won't be absolutely certain until the very last few days. Even then, we only need some overcast… a spell of cloudy nights two weeks from now and we'll be *literally* blind. This thing could go sailing by in the darkness and the vast majority of people on this planet, with the exception of the six of us round this table and a handful of astronomers back at the Observatory, would be blissfully ignorant of it. And perhaps, if you asked them, many of them would probably say they'd rather they were unaware of the impending danger until it'd passed… and some folks maybe not even then…"

"Well, ultimately that's my decision, Mr Culver but I'm grateful to you for being so candid… If you don't know *whether* it'll hit, I don't suppose you have any idea about time and place?"

"No, Sir. It'd be a fluke if today's projection was correct, simply because every one we've done so far has varied a little from previous ones. Of course, recent projections are becoming more tightly grouped than earlier ones but ideally we need it to be much closer before we can give you a reliable prediction... And it's pointless speculating about *where* until we know *when* it'll hit us... to the minute almost..."

"Why so precisely, Mr Culver?"

"Well, Sir, timing's everything! The Earth's travelling through space at a little over sixty-six thousand miles per hour... That's about eleven-hundred miles per minute... The Earth's about seven-thousand, nine-hundred miles in diameter... Every seven minutes or thereabouts, it travels a distance equal to its own diameter... In effect, the Earth presents itself as a target for just over seven minutes then it's gone, neatly side-stepping any inbound near-Earth object. That period's extended a little because of the influence of Earth's gravity on NEOs but with S241 barrelling along at a hundred thousand miles per hour, Earth's gravity won't have long to influence it hugely... And the surface speed at the Equator is just over a thousand miles per hour. So if the point of impact was there, it'd be moving at about seventeen miles per minute... Of course, if S241 does hit us, being seventeen miles from ground zero wouldn't save you... *possibly not even seventeen hundred miles...*"

"So what can you tell us about the potential effects of this asteroid hitting Earth, Mr Culver?"

"Well... the resultant damage could vary enormously, dependent upon where and how it strikes... Whether it comes down on land or in the sea and whether it comes in normal to the surface or obliquely..." said Jack Culver, striking the up-turned palm of one hand a glancing blow with the flat of the other so that it made a sharp, smacking sound, "...but if it happens, however it happens the result will be devastating. Of course, we know the kinetic energy of the asteroid itself and as soon as we know its angle of entry and its point of impact we can estimate the total impact energy... because, of course, it's not just running into us, we're also colliding with it. Whatever the value, it'll be massive... the equivalent of six billion megatons or more... That's at least seventy-five thousand times the total combined energy of all the nuclear weapons existent on Earth..."

"I suppose you did the sums for that cheerful little tidbit on the way in from the airport, as well..." the President observed wryly.

Jack answered flatly, "Yes, Sir. As it happens, I did..." then immediately continued, "Anyway, from that, I plugged the figures into a software model for determining the effects of Earth impacts devised by a friend of mine... a Professor of Geophysics who's a recognised authority in the field of Planetary Sciences... in fact, his model's become the *de facto* standard for such calculations... and worked out roughly how serious the impact damage would be... How much harm it actually does would also depend upon whether the point of impact is in a remote, empty region or a densely-populated area... But again, we may not know that until shortly before it struck..."

The President interrupted, "But what's the likely magnitude of the disaster, Mr Culver? What will the scale of this event be if it happens?"

"Catastrophic, Mr President. Utterly unimaginable devastation. I'm not an expert in such things... you really need a geophysicist for that... but a direct hit by S241 would probably obliterate a small continent like Europe."

"What! Surely you're exaggerating, Mr Culver... Aren't you?"

"No, Sir, I'm not. Consider what happened sixty-five million years ago when a rocky asteroid hit the Yucatan Peninsula, at Chicxulub, in Mexico, which is widely thought to be the event that brought about the demise of the dinosaurs. Various estimates put that one at between nine and eleven miles in diameter... that's roughly between a half and three-quarters the size... or a third to a sixth the mass of S241... It made a crater about one hundred and twenty miles in diameter and thirty miles deep. The first evidence of that disaster was discovered in Umbria, in Italy, by a geologist who was curious about a certain quarter-inch thick layer in the geological strata at the KT boundary... that is, the boundary between the Cretacious and Tertiary periods... Bearing in mind Italy's about six thousand miles from the impact site... That layer was the fall-out from the Chicxulub asteroid which vaporized on impact and it can be found in varying thicknesses all over the World... It truly was a Global event... Then there's the Manson crater, in Iowa... That precedes Chicxulub by about nine million years. It's the biggest impact crater in mainland USA but it's only about twenty miles across and three miles deep. A mere flesh wound by comparison. That was caused by a rock about one-and-a-half miles in diameter, weighing in at ten-to-twenty billion tons... S241 weighs over thirty *trillion* tons..."

"Yes, Mr Culver but the significant thing about both of those events is they're ancient. They happened way back in prehistoric times. Are such things likely to happen today?"

"Well, Sir, you may know Barringer Crater... better known as Meteor Crater... in Arizona..."

"I don't actually *know* it but I've seen pictures of it... It's impressive!"

"That happened within the last fifty thousand years. It was caused by a mere pebble comparatively speaking... an iron asteroid a hundred and fifty *feet* in diameter weighing three-hundred-thousand tons and travelling at only forty-thousand miles an hour... but it still left a crater three-quarters of a mile in diameter... Then there was a rocky asteroid of a similar size that exploded over the Tunguska River in Siberia, in nineteen-o-eight, which flattened an area of forest the size of Rhode Island. That was only *a hundred years ago*. Fortunately, the area was so inhospitable that few people lived there and so inaccessible that the first expedition couldn't get to it until twenty years after the event... Just because events of this magnitude haven't happened in living memory doesn't mean they haven't happened... or won't happen again. We estimate there are upwards of seventy-five *million* asteroids bigger than thirty feet in diameter that could threaten Earth and more than a thousand bigger than three thousand feet... The biggest, Ceres, is about six hundred miles wide. Imagine what damage that could do... And that's before we even start counting the number of comets... It's estimated that on average the Earth suffers a Manson-scale event every million years or so and a Chicxulub-scale event every fifty-to-a-hundred million years... Within the last decade, there've been at least a dozen near misses that I know of... and by that I mean within a hundred thousand miles of Earth... by asteroids as large as your average family house. Any one of those would've taken out an entire city the size of New York. Most of those we only saw after they'd passed by... *and they're only the ones we saw...* So why should we have trouble believing this one poses a real threat?" Jack looked around the group, waiting for some comment but when none came he continued, "Coming back to S241 for a moment... I did a rough approximation using the software model and cross-checked it against data from other impact sites. As an absolute minimum, I estimate S241 would release sixteen times the energy of the Chicxulub asteroid, which would create an initial impact crater a hundred and fifty miles in diameter, by forty-five... maybe fifty miles deep. After the rim has finished collapsing into the bowl, the final crater would be more like three hundred miles in diameter. The impact zone, in which the devastation would be *total*, may be ten times that diameter. The aftermath... Global catastrophe..."

The group sat in silence reflecting on what Jack Culver had told them. Each of them felt utterly helpless and very uneasy, distracted by concern for their own and their family's safety but they tried burying it beneath their concerns for the wider world and what could be done – if anything – to soften the blow if it came. With a sinking feeling in the pit of his stomach – because intuitively he thought he already knew the answer – the President tentatively asked, "So what can be done to destroy it... or divert it?"

Eventually, Wayne Harland broke the silence. "Nothing, Mr President..." It was the response he'd half expected but it still came as a body blow.

"Nothing!" he exploded. "Nothing! What about our arsenal of atomic bombs? Our ballistic missiles for delivering them? Can't we send some up to deflect it?" Wayne Harland chose his words carefully, with precision, so as to give no false hope.

"No, Mr President, it's *impossible.* There's *nothing* we can do to alter the outcome *one iota.* We don't have the necessary technology and, even if we had, it would be far too late to deploy it now. I can go into a long-winded explanation of why it's not possible if you like but take my word for it, it's not. The die's cast and whatever will be is at the mercy of God."

With a weary sigh, the President said, "I have to decide what to tell the people and when... That is *if* there's anything to tell them... What can we tell them for their own safety? We need to tell them how to survive this."

Jack Culver spoke up. "For those people at ground zero out to a radius of twelve... maybe fifteen hundred miles, there'll be no chance. Obviously, *no one* will survive in the area of the impact crater itself and probably not in the area immediately surrounding it because that's where much of the ejecta heaved up by the asteroid will be deposited. They'll be buried alive if they survive the initial impact. Beyond that, in the impact zone, everything standing will be levelled by the air blast and flying debris, possibly out to a radius of fifteen hundred... maybe even two thousand miles. The only way anyone in that area might conceivably survive the initial blast is by being underground in a hardened shelter... Of course, it doesn't end there... In fact, it doesn't even begin there... As the asteroid hits the atmosphere, it'll compress the column of air in front of it. Even though it'll only be a couple of seconds from the moment it first enters the outer atmosphere to the moment of impact, it'll heat the air to sixty or seventy thousand degrees. That's ten or twelve times hotter than the surface of the Sun. If it comes down on land, everything combustible in the immediate vicinity of the impact zone will ignite instantaneously and, as the wavefront radiates outward, it'll set light to anything flammable for hundreds of miles. This'll deplete the air of oxygen, which'll suffocate most living creatures. The blast may also blow a huge amount of the atmosphere out into space which wouldn't help either. On the other hand, if it comes down in the open ocean, it'll displace the water down to the ocean floor, creating an enormous wave that'll radiate outwards and inundate any landmass it arrives at... Of course, it's with the impact itself that things *really* turn nasty... The asteroid will partially vaporize, partially melt, along with the underlying crust itself. It'll generate a huge amount of thermal radiation that'll ignite anything combustible for hundreds of miles around within seconds. It'll also blast out vast quantities of molten rock in blocks up to the size of houses that'll travel hundreds of miles, setting everything alight wherever they land. It'll also generate a blizzard of dust that'll spread around the World, carried by the winds, choking everything and killing vegetation... Because S241's so *vast*, the impact's bound to trigger massive earthquakes and volcanic eruptions around the globe which will only add to the atmospheric pall that descends... The frightening thing about Chicxulub wasn't just the fact that debris from the impact was found in a single, unbroken layer *all over the World* that settled very shortly after the event but *on top of that* is a layer of soot and ash, suggesting that much of the Earth's surface subsequently burned... Where the hell do you go under those conditions?"

"*There's nowhere to go when you're already in Hell*" Dan Ackland noted sourly.

Jack Culver continued, "The geological record shows that Earth's climate plunged into a profound cold spell that lasted ten thousand years as a result of Chicxulub... Of course, this period saw the extinction of the dinosaurs..."

"Ah yes, Mr Culver... but if I remember my natural history, it also saw the rise of mammals..." the President interjected, "So how did they survive to become the dominant species? That's what we need to focus on, Gentlemen. We need to do what our ancestors did but do it more efficiently. And don't forget, we have the twin advantages of being intelligent *and* forewarned. Gentlemen, we have twenty-one days to prepare for the worst. So... Where to begin? But before we do, I need a pit stop if you'll excuse me, everyone... In the meantime, Paul, perhaps you could rustle up some drinks. I've got a thirst like a sun-struck buffalo. I'll be back in a minute" On that note the President went out, seeming far more chipper than he had been throughout the whole meeting.

—•—

(Sunday 1 August 2010, about 1.30pm Mountain / 3.30pm Eastern)

Billy sat on a bench in the bus station idly swinging his legs. He looked like any other boy waiting for someone. Occasionally, he scanned the concourse as though he was looking for his rendezvous but, each time, he stole a surreptitious glance at the departures board. One of the transportation police had already cruised past twice. When he'd passed Billy, the policeman had taken a good look at him. Billy felt uncomfortably that, next time, the policeman might stop and ask him what he was doing, so as he approached for a third time Billy got up and sauntered off to the restroom as casually as he could. The Sun had been overhead for the last hour or more and Billy had watched the heat rising off the tarmac, causing the air to shimmer. Even with the haze in the sky, it was searingly hot and Billy was glad to retreat into the cool of the toilet cubicle, away from prying eyes.

The bus had arrived in Salt Lake City in the early morning as the city was starting to come to life. The old lady had awoken as the bus passed Roy and had sat quietly, vaguely aware of her grandson's gentle snoring, enjoying the beautiful view over Great Salt Lake and Antelope Island in the soft morning light as it cruised south on I-15 past Farmington, Centerville and Bountiful.

As the bus entered the city limits, Billy had been unable to resist the urge of nature any longer. He picked up his backpack, left his seat and went to the little lavatory at the rear of the bus. He sat in the quiet compartment, rocking and swaying with the bus as it left the Interstate and negotiated the city streets, until it came to rest in the terminal and the driver had shut down the throbbing engine. When he'd finished and washed his hands, he cautiously opened the door and glimpsed furtively up the stairwell. To his alarm, he saw the old lady standing in the aisle talking to the woman he'd been sitting with the previous evening. Fortunately for him, Mrs Colquhoun hadn't noticed Billy emerging from the toilet, so he turned and slipped unobtrusively out of the rear door.

Mrs Colquhoun had waited until most of the other passengers had alighted before getting out of her seat. As she stood, intending to shake her grandson awake, she had glanced down the bus and caught sight of Billy's mother trying to smooth her crumpled skirt. She left George and went back down the aisle. "Hello. I'm pleased to make your acquaintance, at last. My name is Katherine Col'houn, although my friends call me Katie... We haven't met but I wanted to thank you for letting Billy ride with my grandson... You can't begin to guess at what a blessing it's been that George has had a friend to travel with... And someone so patient and kind as your son... It's been a rare treat for us both, believe you me, Mrs... er..." Seeing the quizzical expression that had spread over the woman's tired face, Mrs Colquhoun ground to a halt. After a moment's hesitation, the woman said, "Holland... Muriel Holland... I'm sorry but you must be mistaken. I don't have a son called Billy. My son's name was Wesley but he's dead. He died July twenty-ninth last year. He was killed in a hit-and-run accident on the sidewalk outside our house. It was Wesley's tenth birthday. He was trying out his new bike... The last thing his Dad said to him before he went down the drive was 'Be careful!' The police found the driver, slumped over the wheel of his car, blind drunk..." After a brief pause, Muriel Holland continued, "His Dad saw it all. Of course, he blames himself. Between them, the guilt and the grief have as good as killed him... He won't talk to me about it... He won't talk to our Pastor... He won't talk to anyone... I'm at my wits' end... I stayed at home for the first anniversary but I couldn't stand it any longer. I had to get away so I'm going to see my sister in Cheyenne. It'll be the first time I've seen her since the funeral." Mrs Colquhoun said, "I'm so sorry, Mrs Holland but... I thought..." The two women sat down together and Katie Colquhoun gave Muriel Holland an abbreviated version of the events she'd witnessed. As she recounted how Billy had sat by her side, holding her hand, plump tears welled up in Muriel Holland's eyes and rolled down her cheeks. Katherine Colquhoun reached into her handbag and pulled out a tissue and handed it to Mrs Holland. As she dabbed the tears from her face, she said, "It's funny but I dreamt my Wesley was back with me. We were riding the bus together... And I felt a strange peace come over me. A peace I haven't felt since he was taken from me..." The two women talked for a little while longer, Katherine Colquhoun listening attentively and finding that she could sympathise effortlessly with the woman. Before they parted, the two women hugged each other tightly and Katherine

Colquhoun felt the slight, bony frame of Muriel Holland give a little as some of her burden of grief transferred itself to the older woman. For the first time, Muriel Holland felt that a tiny scab had started forming over the horrific wound on her heart.

Katherine Colquhoun walked back down the aisle to where George was still asleep. As she looked down at him, a wave of tenderness washed over her. She took hold of his arm and gently massaged it, all the while crooning softly in his ear, "Wake up you sleepy head, it's time to get out of bed..." over and over, until the little boy began to stir. As he stretched and yawned, he looked round sleepily, then asked, "Where's Billy, Gramma?" His grandmother thought momentarily, then improvising said, "He's had to go somewhere with his mother... He said he hopes to see you later... Now come along George, chop-chop. We have to change buses." Wide awake now and looking a little panic-stricken, George sat bolt upright and said, "I hope so too, Gramma..." then, "What do you mean he's had to go somewhere... Where's Billy had to go, Gramma?"

George stood dejectedly on the platform, his head hung down as his grandmother checked that their case had been transferred to the next bus. The driver assured her that it had been. As Mrs Colquhoun thanked her, she took her hand and pressed a twenty dollar bill into it, then squeezed it gently and held it lightly between her own strong hands. "And how's the family, dear?" The driver thanked her for the tip and said, "Oh... just fine, thanks, Mrs Col'houn... Clyde's growin' bigger'n stronger ev'ry day. He's a'ready tall as his daddy... He's still very keen on sport'n he's talkin' 'bout tryin' for a sports scholarship to college next year. He wants to play pro' basketball... And Jemma's doin' real well in school. Straight 'A's all the way down the line..." Aleisha hesitated, so Mrs Colquhoun asked, "And how's little Alex?"

"Oh, y'know, she's holdin' her own. She has her good days'n bad days but the Lord's seen fit to spare her so far, so we must be thankful for small mercies... I guess... Momma's lookin' after her, which let's me continue workin'. She's bin a rock. If it hadn't bin for her, I don't know where I'd have found the strength to carry on, I really don't..." The thought that she must be starting to sound sorry for herself crossed Aleisha's mind and she faltered. Katherine Colquhoun could see that Aleisha was finding discussing her sick daughter emotionally draining, so she changed the subject. "Oh! Aleisha... I meant to mention... I suspect you've had a stowaway on this trip... A little boy called Billy... He joined us in Portland..." Aleisha said, "Okay, Mrs Col'houn. If you give me the details, I'll report it to the office... But you'll have to be quick, your connection's leavin' shortly..." At that moment, the shrill warble of Aleisha's cellphone rudely interrupted the old lady's revelation. Aleisha dipped into her pocket and pulled out her phone. Flipping it open, she put the phone to her ear. "Hello Momma... Yes... How is she?" Katherine Colquhoun noticed the look of panic flood over the woman's face. "Okay, I'll see if I can fly back. If not, I'll catch a ride home on the next bus out. I'll be there just as soon as I can. Tell her Mommy's comin'... I'll let you know when I'm on my way. Bye Momma." Aleisha snapped her phone shut and apologised, "I'm sorry, Mrs Col'houn but I must go. Alex's had another turn. Real bad this time. They've rushed her into hospital again." Katherine Colquhoun saw the fear in Aleisha's eyes and, as she let go of her hand, said, "You go, dear, with God's speed. I'll be thinking of you" and with that, Aleisha was running down the platform towards the Transport Manager's office.

Billy peered round the concrete column, watching George and his grandmother board the bus. George had scanned the terminal, hoping that Billy would re-appear. They'd waited until the very last moment, as the bus was about to pull away from the platform before boarding. Even then, the old lady had had to propel her grandson bodily up the steps. As she'd made her way down the aisle, Katherine Colquhoun had had to cling to the handrails as the bus rolled and jerked whilst weaving through the terminal and out into the street and she'd had to brace herself against the seats on a couple of occasions, to prevent herself from falling over. Once, as the bus had lumbered round a tight corner, she'd bumped heavily into an unshaven young man who was settling himself down to take a nap. She'd apologised profusely but the student had simply helped her regain her balance and said courteously, "No problem Ma'am. No harm done." Billy watched the bus's tail lights disappear out of the terminal then came out from behind the pillar and sat down on a bench and studied the overhead departures board.

Mrs Colquhoun finally eased herself down in her seat, feeling hot and flustered. George slipped silently into the seat beside her. It took Katherine Colquhoun a couple of minutes to settle herself down and regain her normal composure. She glanced down at her grandson and saw that he was sitting hunched over, his hands clasped between his thighs. Before she could ask him if he was alright, she noticed a teardrop fall onto his bare arm. She reached over and, putting her hand under his chin, gently lifted his head up so she could look at him. The tears were streaming down his face. Somewhat disingenuously, she asked the little boy, "Whatever's the matter, George?" George simply replied, "I miss Billy, Gramma." In a kindly tone, his grandmother said, "I know you do, darling..." Katherine Colquhoun put her arm around her grandson's shoulder and hugged him to her. George turned and snuggled his face into her side. She could feel the little boy's body racked with sobs. She leaned over and delicately kissed the fair crown of his small head repeatedly, rocking him gently to comfort him, until eventually he fell asleep in her arm. Katherine Colquhoun sat for a while thinking what an extraordinary effect Billy had had on her grandson in such a short time. When she was satisfied that George was soundly asleep, she reached into her handbag and took out her novel. She lightly gripped the yellow silk, embroidered bookmark her sister had given her as a birthday present and opened the book at the page where she'd previously left off. In it, she found a small piece of notepaper with neat, rounded handwriting on it. To her surprise, she read, 'not stop laramie. not go back. keep go east. billy'

—•—

"So, Gentlemen, what advice do we give people?" asked the President on returning to his seat. Whilst he'd been absent, the five of them had been discussing what people could do to try to ensure their own survival. Their conclusions had been, dishearteningly, very little but they were determined to be upbeat rather than defeatist. Wayne Harland started cautiously, "Well... if it happens, there'll be two distinctly separate phases... the first being the impact and its immediate aftermath... the second being the longer-term consequences... For anyone within a couple of thousand miles of ground zero, the *only* way to survive the blast is to be underground in a shelter, protected from it. Anyone caught above ground, even at the farthest extremities of the blast zone, is liable to be killed by the initial shockwave or cut to ribbons by flying debris... And it'll be no use being out in the open to watch the spectacle, thinking you can nip down to the shelter before the blast hits you. The impact will cause a blinding flash, brighter than a thousand suns, which would totally disorientate onlookers, followed by a massive fireball that'll sit on the horizon for maybe an hour or more emitting vast amounts of thermal radiation, setting light to everything combustible for hundreds of miles around... Also from the impact, a shockwave will radiate out at enormous velocity, destroying *everything* in its path... Following this a few seconds to a few minutes later, will come a vast, roiling wall of darkness stretching to the Heavens, advancing at many thousands of miles per hour... much faster than the speed of sound... Anyone venturing out after the initial shockwave has passed would see a bewildering veil of turmoil approaching silently then be instantly consigned to oblivion... The heat from the initial blast will cause widespread fires but molten rock blown up into space will continue raining down for hours afterwards, setting everything alight... Without a doubt, it'd be wise to hunker down in your shelter at least two hours before the anticipated time of impact... in case we'd gotten our calculations wrong... and remain there for at least twelve hours after or until the all-clear is broadcast over radio and television once the danger's passed... *If it does happen*, I'd recommend staying down below for *at least* twenty-four hours after the impact... Of course, if it comes down on the North American continent or anywhere nearby, it'll be down to individuals' own judgement as to how they act thereafter. It'll be every man for himself because all forms of government, communication, law, order... in fact, *all* systems of regulation and control... you name it... *everything* will have broken down..." Jumping in his seat as though he'd been stung, the President thundered, "I won't have any of that loose talk outside this room...", pointing a menacing finger at Wayne Harland, "...*under no circumstances must such opinions be voiced outside these four walls*. It'll be hard enough riding out the storm *without inviting subversion as well*. Do you understand? Do you *all* understand?"

To a man they replied, "Yes, Sir" and Wayne Harland added, "I'm sorry, Mr President but that's likely to be the result if S241 *does* hit the USA... leastways that's how *we* see the situation..." indicating with a sweep of his hand everyone around the table. He continued, "Anyway, Sir, I think we all understand the need to bridle our tongues and downplay this situation. One way or another, there'll be enough drama when we announce it. We don't want to make things any more difficult than they're already going to be..."

"Thank you, Mr Harland. I'd be grateful if you'd remember that... *all of you*... Anyway, I presume that deals with the impact and its immediate aftermath... What's the death toll likely to be?"

"That depends on where it comes down, of course... If it's in a highly populous area such as India or China, it could *easily* be one-and-a-half to two *billion* people... a quarter to a third of the Earth's population... in the first twenty-four hours alone... After that, who knows? Of course, if it were to strike there, it'd be on the opposite side of the globe... At least America would be spared some of the devastation of the initial impact..."

"And what of the long term, Mr Harland?"

"That's more conjecture, Sir... Without question, the impact will cause a massive shockwave through the Earth which would trigger widespread earthquakes and volcanic eruptions around the globe... It may also cause tsunamis to rise up and inundate shorelines for many miles inland... And the enormous disturbance to the ionosphere would probably knock out communications systems worldwide, so it'd be impossible for survivors to find out what's going on elsewhere... The pall cast over the Earth would blot out the Sun for months, maybe years, which would lead to drastic climate changes. We know from Chicxulub that dust and soot in the atmosphere caused disastrous global cooling for a period of ten thousand years. That inevitably reduced vegetation resulting in many of the herbivores dying off and, consequently, the carnivores that predated on them. At a guess, the dinosaurs probably succumbed worldwide because they were cold blooded... lived in the open... had restricted diets... and were invariably large and needed lots of food... Mammals probably survived because they were warm blooded... lived mainly underground... ate a varied diet of berries, seeds, insects, you name it, anything they could find... many were covered in fur... and most were small, so the amount of food they needed would likewise be small and they could survive on the meagre rations that could be scavenged within a fairly restricted radius around their burrows... But there's very little parallel between them and us... We're big... We need a lot of food and we have no experience of foraging for it... or making do with grubs... We live in houses above ground, many of which will have been destroyed... We're totally reliant on all manner of service providers for food, warmth, clothing, health, mobility... all the basic essentials of survival... You name it, we buy it... from someone else who's just one step further up the supply chain than we are... and if S241 does hit Earth... *anywhere*... most links in most supply chains will be smashed, many of them irreparably... Then what?"

As Wayne Harland tailed off, the President echoed, "Then what, Mr Harland?"

"With all due respect Sir, that goes *way beyond* the remit of astronomers. We spend our time looking outwards, trying to understand the Universe we live in. It's down to politicians to take care of things at home. If it's anybody's responsibility... besides our own, that is... our survival is your responsibility, Mr President."

With a weariness born of resignation at accepting his lot, the President said, "Thank you for reminding me of my duties, Mr Harland... lest I should forget them."

They all sat in silence, struggling with a jumble of practical thoughts mixed with powerful fears and emotions, which were confused by conflicting demands on their loyalties. To distract everyone's mind away from the awful reality of S241 for a moment and defuse some of the tension, Paul Kaufmann asked, "As a matter of interest, where did S241 come from?"

At that, Jack Culver said, "We can't be certain. It may have been stooging round in the asteroid belt... that is, the belt between Mars and Jupiter where there *should have been* another rocky planet like Earth or Mars... since the formation of the Solar system four-and-a-half billion years ago... The material may have been prevented from coalescing into a planet proper by Jupiter's massive gravitational influence which caused the proto-planet to break up and just left a bunch of debris meandering round for perpetuity... On the other hand, the planet may have formed only to be smashed to pieces in a collision with a giant asteroid. Certainly, the size, shape, composition and density of S241 are consistent with it coming from the core of a planet... Jupiter simply herded the debris into the asteroid belt... Why this particular asteroid left its orbit, who can say? It may have been perturbed by some freak conjunction of Mars and Jupiter... We simply don't know..."

The President said, "If S241's got our name on it, it's what fate's decreed and I guess there's nothing we can do to change the event... other than pray, maybe..."

"*If* it's got our name on it, you can forget praying because that won't alter its course *one scintilla...*" Dan Ackland cut in curtly, "Our fate... *whatever it turns out to be...* was sealed the instant S241 was nudged out of its orbit. After that, it's all down to Newton's Laws of Motion."

Ignoring him, the President continued, "So... we have to concentrate on changing the outcome of the event. From you, Gentlemen..." addressing the three astronomers, "I need regular daily updates and, at the earliest possible opportunity, your confident expectation that this thing is definitely going to hit Earth... or not... and if it is, exactly where and when... Will you do that?"

"Yes, Sir."

"And one more thing... I want everyone to observe strict confidentiality and report to no one but me or my staff. Is that understood?"

"Yes, Sir."

"Then I'd like to thank you, Gentlemen..." the President concluded hurriedly, "That's all I need for the time being. Is there anything you need?"

"Yes, Sir, there's one more thing... We need all the information we can get on S241 if we're to make an accurate and meaningful prediction, the more the better. We've got the Keck Observatory on Hawaii looking for S241 from tonight but we could still use another opinion... Can we ask other observatories around the World? Specifically, can we ask the European Space Observatory, down in Chile? They have four enormous telescopes that can be linked together to give unprecedented resolving power. It could help speed up the process enormously... After all, if S241 does hit Earth we're all in it together..." then, with a firmer tone, "*This goes way beyond national interests. It affects the whole of mankind...*"

"I don't know, Mr Harland..." the President said distractedly, "Can you let me think about it? I'll give you my answer in a day or two. Is that okay?"

Seeing that the President was starting to become somewhat agitated, Wayne Harland said hesitantly, "Okay, Sir..." thinking that it was anything but okay, "...but the sooner the better, Mr President."

The President stood at the urinal, his prostate gland burning intensely. He'd dismissed his visitors abruptly and rushed to the bathroom. Now he stood in agony, his waters stubbornly refusing to flow. Eventually, after much coaxing, they started, a slow, faltering dribble. The pain was more exquisite than anything he'd suffered so far but, as his pee started to flow more freely, it eased and he began to relax. '*Damn it!*' he thought, 'That wasn't handled very well. I have unfinished business with those guys. They might not have all the answers but they sure as hell understand all the issues involved. I need them to help me identify who to ask about the after-effects... and to transfer the statistics to other experts who can work out just how much damage this thing could do... *Tarnation!* They'll be on their way to the airport now. I can hardly drag 'em back again. They'll think I'm an idiot...'

—•—

As the limousine sped west along I-66 towards the evening sun, the three men sat looking at each other quizically. Eventually, Wayne Harland broke the silence. "Well! That ended a little hastily and not wholly satisfactorily to my mind. Maybe we stunned him into silence..." Feeling tired and depressed, Dan Ackland cut in sarcastically, "Maybe he just couldn't take any more good news." In conclusion, Jack Culver voiced the unkind thought that had been nagging at each of their minds, "Maybe he couldn't wait to get rid of us because he needed another shot of booze." Wayne Harland observed, "Perhaps not. But at least we know what we've got to do so let's get back and do it." The group sat musing quietly over the meeting until Wayne Harland said, "I'm fascinated, Jack. Tell me, did you *really* work out that thing with the penny in Denver or did you just say it for effect?"

"Actually, it was Detroit... And no, I didn't say it for effect... or at least not in the way you're implying. When I talk to people... even the brightest of people... I usually find they don't have the faintest appreciation of astronomical distances. People can't relate to them. A lightyear means nothing to them, never mind a parsec. They have absolutely no conception... So I always try to use similes they can relate to, to give them some sense of how vast space is and how small and insignificant we are by comparison." Wayne Harland sat quietly for a few moments, then said, "Metaphor... I think you mean metaphor..." then, after reflecting a moment longer, "Or would analogy be more accurate?" With a small shrug of his shoulders and shake of his head, he finished off with, "Who knows?" With the finality of driving home a nail, Dan Ackland chipped in bitterly, "Who cares?" Nothing more was said and the remainder of the journey passed in silence.

As the Learjet banked steeply and headed towards Pasadena, Wayne Harland eased back in his seat, snugged down and immediately fell into a doze. The effects of being woken in the middle of the night combined with the triple heart by-pass he'd had last year had conspired together to drain him of his energy. His eyes rolled under their lids and his arms and legs twitched occasionally, bearing witness to the turmoil going on in his head, as a result of which he slept fitfully. Dan Ackland sat watching Jack Culver who was clearly preoccupied with concerns of his own. At first, he thought Jack was worrying about S241 but then he remembered Jack's comment to George Horowitz. He leaned over and touched Jack lightly on the arm. "Is everything alright, Jack? In the meeting you mentioned there's something urgent you should've been doing at home?" Jack told Dan about Billy's disappearance. He briefly recounted his exchange with Martha and his conversation with Claudette and told Dan how guilty he felt about not being there for Martha when she needed him. "Are you *sure* Billy's run away, Jack? It's not beyond the bounds of possibility, I suppose… But, Jack, you're wealthy. Have you considered that your money makes him a potential target for kidnappers?"

"The thought did cross my mind, Dan but Martha thinks all the signs point towards him going of his own accord. And it's been two… no, three days now and there's been no ransom demand. So, no, I don't think so. In fact, it's funny but I have this strange feeling. The more I think about it, the more I'm positive Billy's run away. But why, I don't know…" They continued talking for a while. Jack also mentioned that despite being worried about Billy and feeling guilty at not joining in the search, he felt curiously proud that his son had had the courage to do something so bold. Dan finished off by saying, "Well, Jack, if there's anything I can do to help, don't hesitate to ask. You know how fond I am of Billy…" then added rather shyly, "Well, of all of you."

Martha and Jack had had Dan over to dinner regularly since his wife had died three years previously and Dan had come over to stay each Christmas and Thanksgiving, having no family of his own to go to. Jack knew that the couple had had a child but that the boy had died in infancy over twenty years ago. The four of them had been friends before Jane's illness but not so close as they'd become after it had been diagnosed. They were rare amongst Dan's friends, most of whom had stopped asking him out once Jane had died; in fact, many of whom had stopped asking either of them out long before she'd died if truth be told. They had both been devout church-goers but Jane's long, drawn-out illness, her gradual deterioration to an unpleasant and undignified death with the pain only kept at bay by large doses of morphine and his subsequent loss had shaken Dan's faith and he now found no comfort there.

—•—

After the President had relieved himself, the three men reconvened in the Oval Office. As soon as the President entered his office, Paul Kaufmann noticed how gray and haggard he looked. His immediate thought was 'Good God! He must be suffering… He needs to see his physicians pronto. Ignoring the problem won't make it go away… I'll prompt him after the meeting… If he still persists in being awkward, I'll have a discrete word with the First Lady. She'll brook no nonsense from him, head honcho or not…' then, after studying him a little longer, 'I really don't think he's very well. His eyes are sunken. There are deep shadows under them... He has an apprehensive, almost hunted look about him...' then, after a while, 'Or am I just imagining it? Maybe he isn't sleeping very well... It's probably the pressure of the last few months. It hasn't been easy on him... Still, it hasn't been easy on any of us...' Tapping a deeper reserve of energy, the President said, "Well, let's get to it..." then, with a glimpse of his old humour, "Who can we call on to save the World?" Entering into the spirit of things, Paul Kaufmann replied, "Where's Bruce Willis when you need him..." and George Horowitz rounded off with, "I don't think we need three guesses at that..."

The President spoke more calmly and assertively than he had when he'd been closing the meeting with the astronomers from JPL but Paul Kaufmann was still left with the impression that it had been forced and had taken him a real effort to maintain his grasp on the issues.

They discussed the options and now thought they had a coherent strategy. Firstly, they would inform the Pentagon of the potential disaster and put the Army, National Guard and police on full alert so they could mobilise their forces. Then they would inform the civil defense authorities so that shelters could be prepared and make-shift bunkers built. They had concluded that there was little point in formulating evacuation plans because, until the precise impact area was known, there was no point in fleeing and once it was known – if ever it was known before the event – it would probably be too late to evacuate a large population more than two thousand miles. Finally, when all preparations were under way, the President would inform other national governments then, simultaneously with them, make televised announcements to their peoples, giving everyone the maximum amount of time to prepare as best they could. They still needed to find experts who could determine the extent of the damage and different experts who could advise on how to survive in the hostile environment that would ensue if S241 did hit the Earth. The President summed up and said to Paul Kaufmann, "I want you to draft our plan and let me have sight of it by nine o'clock latest, sooner if possible." Paul Kaufmann replied, "Yes, Sir. It'll be on your desk by nine..." and left the office. When he'd gone, George Horowitz said, "It's ironic... This morning we were being warned of a natural disaster that will *definitely* happen but the experts couldn't be certain *when*... at least, not to within the nearest ten years... This afternoon, we're being warned by *another* group of experts about *another* natural disaster they can time *almost* to the nearest minute but they can't be certain *if* it'll happen... Talk about the fickle hand of fate..."

"More capricious, I'd say", the President grunted in response, acknowledging that he'd heard what George Horowitz had said but hadn't really been paying attention. He was distracted by the chart that the astronomers had left behind at his request, which was laid out on the table. He was browsing over it. The drawing contained a small, wire-frame globe showing the lines of longitude and latitude as if viewed from space high up in the northern latitudes, positioned roughly in the center of the sheet, with the trajectory of S241 surrounded by a tube defining the extreme limits of its flightpath coming in from the bottom right-hand corner. Whereas in the earlier projections they'd been shown the centerline had continued beyond the Earth, in this one which was the latest, it stopped at a point on the surface of the sphere marked by a small cross. He muttered to himself, "Assuming the thick line is the Greenwich meridian, the point of impact is about thirty-five degrees east... and about twenty-five degrees north, just above the Tropic of Cancer. Where's that, I wonder?" He sauntered over to the globe standing by the wall and spun it round gently until he found the UK then followed the meridian down towards the Equator. As his finger traced eastwards over the surface, it crossed North Africa and came to rest in Egypt about four hundred miles south of Cairo, at the northern end of Lake Nasser, not far from the Red Sea coast. "I don't believe it!" he exclaimed. "George, look at this. I'll give those bastards 'The Hammer of God'... What about *that* then?" George Horowitz came over and peered down at the place the President was pointing to. The President said triumphantly, "That can't be more than five hundred miles from Mecca... six at most... and even closer to Medina. If S241 comes down there, it'll wipe them off the face of the Earth and our problems with Muslim terrorists will be solved *at a stroke*. It'll also put paid to the Middle East conflict to boot..."

Noticing that Israel was in similar proximity, George Horowitz thought, 'It'll put paid to the Middle East conflict *because it'll put paid to the Middle East*' but he said, "Don't forget, Mr President, they stressed this was only provisional and could well be revised. Future projections may change dramatically. Let's not bank on it coming down *here...*" tapping the globe with his fingertip. "And don't forget that if it does come down *anywhere on Earth, nowhere will be safe.* Being in the impact zone probably guarantees a quick death but anyone outside it may simply be condemned to a slow one."

The President responded heatedly, "Yes! But don't forget... In the first place, they only gave this thing a one-in-a-hundred chance of hitting Earth at all... If they're just seven minutes out in their estimate, it'll miss Earth altogether and then who'll be any the wiser... But if they're only marginally out, it'll probably come down somewhere in this vicinity... Certainly, they're not going to be so far out that it comes down on the opposite side of the World, now are they? That'd be too ridiculous to laugh at!"

George Horowitz hesitated to contradict him but decided he couldn't remain silent on the matter. "Don't forget, three months ago they reckoned the chances of it hitting Earth were one-in-a-million. By last month, the odds had shortened to one-in-a-thousand. I simply don't think we should withhold this information, Sir... *Just in case...* If for no other reason, I strongly advise you against doing so on humanitarian grounds..." But the President clearly wasn't listening because he was already striding to the phone. "Paul, I want you in my office *right now*. We're going to revise the plan. I want us to delay releasing *any* information to other governments and announcing the threat of S241 until the last possible moment, which gives our people just enough time to find shelter. Even then, I don't want to be too specific about where it'll come down, in case we're wrong or in case it misses Earth altogether... We wouldn't want to look foolish, would we?" Thinking quickly of a plausible reason for the sudden change of strategy, he added, "It'll minimise the pandemonium that's bound to break out after we make the announcement..." He also thought, 'It'll also give those A-rabs no time to prepare for what's coming. They'll be caught out in the open with their pants down. Or, more appropriately...' thinking of the Arab he'd seen in a Riyadh backstreet with his long white robe gathered up round his waist, squatting at the roadside, defecating, '...with their dishdashas hitched up...' at which thought he let out a wicked little laugh.

Part 2: Twenty Days in August

Chapter 5

(Monday 2 August 2010, mid-morning Pacific time)

Martha and Bill Finn sat in the waiting room of the Portland Police Department. "What in Heaven's name's taking them so long? All we want is an officer to come with us down to the bus station so we can ask them a few questions."

"Calm down, Martha. I know you're worried and I can understand how frustrating this must be for you but I have no jurisdiction here. We can't go marching in, demanding their cooperation and expect to get it. Unless I have good reason to believe a crime's been committed... and I don't... yet... we can't presume on these people... If there'd been anything to suggest that Billy'd been abducted or kidnapped, I'd have called in the Feds *straightaway*. They have the clout to get things done *pronto*... But there isn't... and I'm just a small-town sheriff making enquiries about a missing boy. We don't know for sure if he's come this way or this far..." then, after a brief pause, "Martha, it's over a hundred miles to Portland. Is it realistic to think Billy's come this far on his own?"

Feeling that the Sheriff had somehow doubted the truth of her story from the outset, Martha was becoming more than a little exasperated by his constant questioning and she snapped, "How the hell do I know! Until three days ago, Billy was just a small boy... my son, yes... but, quite frankly, something of a stranger to me. How could I have guessed he'd do something like this. I have no more idea what goes on in his head than you do..." then, having blown off a little steam and relieved some of the pressure, she added more calmly, "All I can do is go on what the Controller at the bus station said when we showed him Billy's photo'... That he thought he'd seen a boy who looked like Billy hanging about in the terminal... He thought he must be with someone... He didn't realise Billy was alone which is why he didn't look more closely... There's no evidence of him catching a bus. How could he? He couldn't buy a ticket on his own at his age... But why else would he be at the bus station if he wasn't planning on going somewhere... And if he did, where else would he have gone if it wasn't here? There's not much place else *to go* from our neck of the woods. And we've called at every other town along the way and nobody's seen him getting off there... If he's not here, I have no idea where he might be."

The Sheriff saw that Martha was beginning to get fraught. He sat pondering for a while then said, "You don't suppose Billy was waiting for someone? Could he have gone there to meet someone off the bus, maybe someone you didn't know about?" At that moment, a tubby policeman waddled into the room and apologised for keeping them waiting, which stopped Martha as she was about to let fly at the Sheriff and tell him not to be so stupid. By the time Sergeant McKenna had introduced himself, Martha had regained a little of her composure but she disliked the way the Sheriff then manouvered the Sergeant out of her earshot. The two of them talked in hushed tones for a few minutes until the Sergeant turned to her and said, "Well, Mrs Culver, I've squared things with the General Manager at the bus station. He's assured me that we'll have their full cooperation in finding your son…" then added cryptically, "…if he's there to be found." Martha thanked him as they walked out to the cars. Whilst Sheriff Finn concentrated on following Sergeant McKenna's cruiser through the traffic, Martha sat wondering what the two of them had been discussing so conspiratorially.

The Traffic Controller at their local bus station – affectionately known by the town's children as 'The Fat Controller', for obvious reasons – had called over the driver of the bus that had left for Portland last Friday morning and Martha had shown him Billy's photograph. The driver had peered at it for a while but, just as Martha thought he'd been on the verge of delivering some good news, he'd said, "Friday, you say… That was the day our Church group took a whole bunch of kids to Portland. My wife took Rosie and Jim… that's our grandkids. They came back on the late bus yesterday saying what a great time they'd had… They'd been to the Zoo… and the Children's Museum… and the End of the Oregon Trail Center… and they'd taken a trip on the old sternwheeler riverboat through the Columbia River Gorge…" then, hesitating to look down at the photograph again, said, "No, I'm real sorry lady. It was so busy, I couldn't rightly say whether your boy was on the bus or not…"

On the Sunday morning, whilst Martha and the Sheriff had visited their local bus station and the truck stops and other places that could offer a means of escape from the town, Margaret and Beth had continued searching the town and surrounding area. Around mid-morning, they'd been joined by Nicky and Claudette who'd had the forethought to print a bundle of flyers headed 'Missing Child' containing Billy's photograph and a description of him and giving various telephone numbers to contact in the event that Billy was found. The twins had carried out a hasty door-to-door of every home and other establishment in the small town whilst Margaret and Beth had stopped passers-by in the street to ask whether anybody had seen Billy. However, with the exception of a couple of people who'd thought they may have seen him but weren't actually sure it was him, nobody had any encouraging news. By lunchtime, when they'd exhausted most of the possibilities in the town and its outlying homesteads, they were beginning to feel deflated. Spirits rose a little when they rendezvoused with Martha who reported that Billy may have taken a bus out of town – but, if so, how he'd done it and which one he'd taken she hadn't a clue – in which case she had surmised that the only place he could logically have gone to was Portland. Having no leads – firm or otherwise – worth pursuing, Martha immediately plumped for this one. To her surprise and without her asking, Bill Finn offered to drive her.

Martha went home and packed a few things in an overnight bag. Half an hour later, the Sheriff came by to pick her up and they set off. She had asked the twins to stay home, one to man the phone and to make sure someone was in the house in case Billy should turn up and the other to continue the search. Margaret offered to accompany Martha but she'd declined, saying that she would prefer her to continue scouring the area near home. Beth had gone home to see to her own family but had promised to resume the hunt with Margaret as soon as she'd fed and watered her brood.

The Controller had given Martha a timetable which showed the scheduled stops the bus made at the larger towns it passed through on its way to Portland but he told her that it also stopped on request so the two of them had had to stop at every tiny hamlet in between to ask whether anyone had seen Billy. The trip would have been quicker if Martha hadn't insisted on calling at shops, post offices and gas stations in every place they'd stopped at to drop off a flyer which she'd asked the proprietors to put prominently on display.

—•—

Jack groaned and rolled over. His head ached. When Dan Ackland opened the blinds in his office, the bright light from the noonday sun hurt his eyes. His mouth had a stale, unpleasant, slightly sour taste to it. When he ran his tongue over his teeth they felt sticky and rough. He had been asleep for about five hours but he could willingly have turned over and gone back to sleep. "Come on Jack. Get up! We've got work to do." Last night, he'd needed the coffees to help him stay awake. One of the control room technicians had offered him a couple of his sugar doughnuts, something Jack never normally ate but he felt it would have been churlish to refuse them having mentioned he'd eaten nothing since the previous day, so he'd accepted them gratefully and swilled them down with a large black coffee. Now he regretted having flopped down on the sofa without first cleaning his teeth.

The journey home had been prolonged because their plane had been stuck in Pasadena for a couple of hours due to air traffic control problems. The delay meant they would have been too late getting back to the Observatory in time for the next sighting of S241 so whilst they'd been sitting on the apron

Jack had called David Johnson using the plane's cellphone. David had given Jack the news that, due to high cloud and an unusually high level of airborne particulates – industrial pollution that had originated in China which had been carried to high altitude by unseasonably hot weather then blown across the Pacific Ocean – they had missed tonight's sighting and, worse still, anticipated missing them for the next three, possibly four nights, which was when the National Weather Service had predicted that the prevailing wind would shift again. David had called him back three hours later. As Jack had been about to ask whether Keck II had picked up S241, David Johnson pre-empted him by saying light-heartedly, "I've got some good news and some bad news. Which would you like first?" Being in no mood for jokes, Jack had snapped, "Just give it to me straight!"

"Well, Mauna Kea had some difficulty in locating S241. They found it eventually more than four hundred miles from its expected position. That's a discrepancy of fractionally less than two arc-seconds but it obviously raises the perennial issue of calibration… Who's right? Who's wrong? We're checking it out now and so are they but it'll take us a couple of days to do a complete statistical analysis and until we're able to synchronise both 'scopes precisely, it does raise a slight doubt about the accuracy of our projections…" With uncharacteristic bile born out of fatigue, Jack spat out irritably, "What a balls-up!" David cut in, "Maybe so, Jack but the good news is… I've just re-run the projections, applying an offset to our readings to compensate for the discrepancy on the basis that it's us that's wrong and guess what… S241 comes very close to Earth… mighty close… but just misses it!" David finished on a high note. Jack exploded, "Don't tell me we've just scared the President over a risk that might not even exist…" Trying to temper some of his optimism so that he sounded more like a sober scientist and less like a giddy schoolboy, David added hurriedly, "Of course, the PU remains the same but its trajectory no longer impinges on Earth…" then, with more than a hint of wishful thinking, "Could it be our calibration that's slightly out, Jack?" Jack sat brooding. Unable to think of anything more he could usefully say, David remained silent. After giving it some thought, Jack said, "We've checked it exhaustively. I'd stake my life on it being bang-on…" Without failing to register the double irony in his boss's last comment, David said, "I was afraid that's what you'd say, Jack…"

Dan Ackland had overheard Jack's telephone conversation and had a fair grasp of one end of it. When Jack had replaced the handset, Dan leaned over and asked, "What was that about? As if I couldn't guess…" Jack gave Dan a potted account. He was surprised when Dan remained calm and unruffled; he'd expected him to flare up in his usual manner. He hadn't expected this uncharacteristically mellow response. However, Dan simply commented, "It's a larger discrepancy than I'd have anticipated but first sightings can be notoriously unreliable when you're positioning your 'scope to someone else's coordinates, as well you know Jack. Still, we'd better go though the motions again... But if you're not careful, you can go round this loop so many times you start to doubt your own judgement. For what it's worth, Jack, my money's on us being right and justified in warning the President... even if in twenty days time it turns out we were wrong."

—•—

"There! There! There's Billy!" exclaimed Martha, pointing excitedly at the black-and-white monitor screen.

"I'm sorry, Martha. I don't see him..."

"There look... There... between the news stand and ticket booth. You can't see him properly. You get the odd glimpse of him behind that old lady. I'm sure it's him..." As the old lady moved away from the counter, ticket in hand, she picked up her case then gestured to the small boy who'd been milling about outside the kiosk to follow her and headed off in the direction of the restrooms. Before the next passenger came up to the sales window, the boy peeped out furtively then stepped momentarily into the full view of the camera before moving off in the same direction that the old lady and the little boy had taken. The Sheriff recognised Billy instantly. The look of surprise on his face spoke volumes to Martha who laughed then choked back a little sob of relief. The Sheriff heard her say, "Thank God he's okay" under her breath, then Martha said to the bus station's Security Supervisor, "At least we know he *was* here. I assume he got here by bus but how can we tell if he took another bus out of here... and if so, which one and where to?"

"That's more of a problem, Ma'am. We only have continuous CCTV surveillance on the ticket booth because that's about the only place we have a serious risk of stick-ups... Of course, there are other cameras about the place but they're primarily time-lapse systems mainly covering the concourse so we mightn't see which bus he took... I suggest we start with the ticket clerk... Now, who was on the desk on Saturday morning..." The tall, spare man reached for the phone and after a couple of minutes consultation with the Booking Office replaced the handset and turned to face Martha Culver and the policemen. "They're sending him over now... He might be able to help us..." Within a couple of minutes, a gangly youth with an unfortunate outbreak of acne stuck his head round the door and said, "Good morning, Sir. The office said you wanted a word with me..."

"Yes, come in Simeon... I want you to take a look at this CCTV footage and tell me if you recognise this boy..." The Security Supervisor re-played the film and pointed out Billy.

"I don't know him but I do recall seeing him hanging about. Who is he?" The Supervisor briefly explained then asked whether the boy had approached the booth to buy a ticket. "No but run it again..." The Supervisor re-wound the tape a few frames and pressed 'Play'. "Yes I remember... I don't know why but at the time I got the impression he was with that old lady... the one who's just bought the ticket... yes, she's with the other boy... because he followed them away from the booth and I remember thinking, 'If this kid's with her, why didn't she go for a senior citizen's special summer offer?' You know... the one where they pay for one grandchild and a second one goes free... There's a poster advertising it on the booth right alongside the window... Surely she couldn't have missed it... But when I thought about it, I was pretty sure she'd only asked for one child when I sold her the ticket. I wracked my brains but for the life of me I couldn't convince myself that she'd said two children and I'd just misheard her. Then another customer came up and I forgot about her altogether... until now, that is..."

The Supervisor asked, "The old lady... Do you know her, son?"

"No, Sir. I've only been on the job three weeks. I've never seen her before... But I got the distinct impression she's a regular traveller..."

"Her ticket then... Do you remember where she was going?"

"Ummm..." Simeon went quiet as he thought. He was about to give up in defeat when he said, "No... but I remember which bus it was... I told her she needed to change at Salt Lake City... She was a bit snotty when I told her but I was only trying to be helpful... She said something very condescending like, 'You don't have to tell me, sonny, I know. I've been doing this journey since your were in diapers...' or something to that effect... Where she was going after that I can't remember..."

The Supervisor said to Martha, "I'd like you to watch the footage again, starting maybe half-an-hour prior to this sighting, to see when your son first appears... to five minutes after he walks out of shot... Once we bracket the times he arrived and left the ticket booth, we can run a print-out from the computer and get a record of all the tickets sold during that period... If he was looking for a party to latch onto, maybe he found them... And if I was a betting man, which thank the Lord I'm not, Ma'am, I'd stake good money that he found what he was looking for in the old lady and the boy... Why else would he hang around the booth and then choose to leave at that instant if it wasn't to follow them?"

The group pored over the print-out, trying to tie up precisely which ticket the old lady had bought. After comparing the time on the CCTV footage with the times the ticket sales were recorded, they had narrowed it down to three transactions – one was a single ticket to Spokane, via Olympia, changing in Seattle, for a traveller with a severe disability; the next was an army veteran on a round trip to Reno, via Salem, changing in Sacramento. It was clear that the old lady fitted neither of these profiles. The third was for a senior citizen travelling with one child, to Cheyenne, Wyoming, changing in Salt Lake City. "Bingo! If that's not the one Billy was interested in, I'll eat my hat, Mrs Culver... Now, to find the driver..." The Security Supervisor checked the drivers' log and found that the driver of the bus on the first leg to Boise, Idaho, on Saturday morning was one Frederick Chapel. "Fred's one of our longest-serving and most reliable drivers, Mrs Culver. He has an excellent rapport with most of our frequent travellers... If anyone can help, Fred can..." The Supervisor called the Traffic Manager who checked his roster and told him that Frederick had come in from Boise yesterday afternoon after a stopover on Saturday night and today was his day off; he wouldn't be back on duty until the day after tomorrow. When he relayed the news, he registered the anguished look that flitted across Martha's drawn face. "Don't worry, Mrs Culver. We have a policy whereby we can call in drivers in an emergency. I'd say this was one, wouldn't you? We'll call Fred at home and ask him to come in specially, so you can talk to him. I don't think he'll mind..." As it happened Frederick Chapel did mind, having taken his wife out for a celebratory lunch to mark their fortieth wedding anniversary but when the Security Supervisor explained the situation, he came in willingly. An hour later, the Chapels appeared in the office, him a jolly rotund man with shining skin as rich and brown as chocolate and her equally round with bright button eyes set deep in a pleasing, pudgy face. As they walked into the Security Supervisor's office, her husband holding the door open for her, he looked up and said "Hello Bonnie. Hello Fred... I'm real sorry for interrupting your special day but thank you for coming in." The big, jovial woman smiled and said, "Oh no worries Francis. We was just about to set off for home anyways, so you di'n't spoil nuttin... It bin a wonderful treat, ha'n't it Fred'rick?" Her husband said, "I'm sorry we've bin so long but we were out of town havin' lunch when you got me on ma mobile... We wuz jus' sittin' finishin' off our coffees when you rang... We came straight here on us way home..." Francis Doolittle introduced Martha Culver who thanked the couple. She showed them the picture of Billy. Bountiful Chapel said, "Well, sugar, let's see if Fred here c'n help you find your little angel..."

As he re-wound the tape, Francis Doolittle said, "We think Billy may have tagged along with an old lady... a frequent traveller, by all accounts... and a boy... presumably her grandson... Do you know them, Fred?"

"Why, that's Mrs Col'houn... A real fine lady... She's bin ridin' with us for at least the las' twenty years now... As long as I've bin drivin' for you... And that's her grandson... James... Joseph... No... George, I think... Yes, that's it. George. I've seen him half-a-dozen times afore... Now I think back, there was another boy with 'em. George almost dragged him up the stairs onto

97

the bus... Real quiet sort, kinda shy, di'n't say much... Jus' th'opposite of lil George... I assumed they was travellin' on one o'those special senior citizens deals, so I must admit I didn't check her ticket nun too careful-like... The second chile's discount's on'y shown by a tiny cross in a little biddy box'n I wa'n't wearin' ma readin' glasses at the time..." Francis Doolittle chipped in, "You're not in any trouble, Fred. Even if Billy did travel with them, Mrs Col'houn qualifies for a free second child anyway. It was just a little... er... unconventional way of going about things, that's all..." Fred finished by saying, "...but I'd swear on ma gran'chilluns lives it was your boy, Mrs Culver..." Martha's chest jerked and she felt herself crying with sheer relief, knowing that for the time being at least, Billy was safe. Bountiful Chapel reached out her enormous arms and hugged Martha to her, patting her gently on the back and cooing in her ear, "It's alright, honey, Billy's okay... Hush now... He's okay..."

When Martha had pulled herself together and wiped her eyes, Frederick Chapel said, "Since she lost her husband, Mrs Col'houn goes to see her sister's family a fair bit... I think they all meet there high days and holidays with their littl'uns... If I remember rightly, she buys a ticket to Cheyenne but she don't allus travel through... She often gets off in Laramie... I think her sister has one o' those dude ranches somewhere close by..."

They all sat quietly until Martha said quizzically, "Why would Billy want to go to Cheyenne? That must be all of a thousand miles away and then some... He doesn't know anybody out that way..." Sergeant McKenna asked, "Does he know George... from school perhaps?"

"I don't know. I certainly don't recognise him. Billy attends a special school for learning impaired children so I'd be surprised if George went there too. Leastways, I've never seen him before..." Frederick said, "I'd be mighty surprised if you had, Mrs Culver... Mrs Col'houn lives local, just over the State line yonder in Vancouver. She has a very grand spread between the lake and the Columbia River. I think she once told me her grandson comes from some place back east a'ways... Georgia maybe... or Tennessee... or one o' the Carolinas... He on'y comes to stay with her in the holidays..."

Martha sat deep in thought. Eventually, she said, "Where's Billy going? And how do I catch up with him? He's already so far ahead of me..." Francis Doolittle spoke up. "Perhaps we can help, Mrs Culver. We know which direction he's headed in, Ma'am... East obviously... I can put out an APB to all our terminals east of here, to hold Billy if they see him. I'll just need a copy of that sheet with his photo', so I can circulate it to them..." Martha handed him a copy and he studied it, then said, "We have a 'Home Free' program. It was set up specially for runaways like your boy. If we find him, do you want us to hold him for you to collect or would you like us to put him on the next bus home? No charge, Ma'am. The Company picks up the bill... so to speak… It's all part of the service." Not really thinking clearly, Martha said distractedly, "I don't know, Mr Doolittle. I can't think about that right now. Let's worry about what to do with him once we've found him. You have my contact numbers on the flyer…"

Seeing that Martha was feeling rather desolate, Francis Doolittle didn't press matters further but went to the wallmap and started making a list of all the terminals he thought should be alerted about the missing child. Martha watched him as he pointed to likely destinations he thought Billy might logically head for beyond Cheyenne and where he could be by now, given that he should have arrived in Cheyenne yesterday afternoon. Not wanting to appear disinterested, especially after all these good people had been so helpful and shown such concern, Martha went and stood alongside the Security Supervisor as he scanned the map. Putting his finger on Cheyenne, he said, almost to himself, "Now whereabouts could the young whipsnapper be?" Moving his finger eastward, he muttered under his breath, "Certainly not as far as Cleveland… *not yet*… or Charleston… or Knoxville… but, just conceivably, he could have reached Chicago… Kansas City… Albuquerque… even El Paso…"

Martha butted in, "Why would Billy go to Mexico? He doesn't know the place. He's never been there… Assuming he's getting as far away from here as he can, I can't see him choosing to go there… And if he was going to Mexico, surely it'd be more sensible for him to go this way…" running her finger south down I-5 to Los Angeles and San Diego. "So where would he go?" Just then, a thought struck Martha. "Jack… that's Billy's dad… has a sister who lives in San Diego… Billy showed great interest in her work when she visited us recently… But why would he go to her? She's family… yes… but Billy's never been very close to her. He doesn't know her all that well… And besides, she's not there. She's up in Vancouver Island at the moment studying the whales…" And then she blurted out, "That's it! It's so obvious. Why didn't I think of it before… Jack's parents live near Irondequoit in upper New York State… They have a house on the waterfront overlooking Lake Ontario… Billy gets on extremely well with his grandmother… well, with both of them really but especially with his grandma. That must be where Billy's going. I'd stake my life on it!" Martha let out a hollow little laugh and said, "How could I have been so blind? It's so obvious! Everything points in that direction." The Sheriff, who'd contributed very little to proceedings so far, said nothing but looked very hard at Martha.

The Security Supervisor thanked the ticket clerk and dismissed him. Sergeant McKenna excused himself and left, wishing Martha every success in finding her son. Before the bus driver and his wife left, Bountiful Chapel took both of Martha's hands in her own and reassured her that Billy would be alright, then she'd given Martha another big hug which would have been impossible to resist even if Martha had wanted to and whispered in her ear, "Don't worry, honey. The Good Lord looks after his own..." As she became enveloped in Bonnie's enormous breasts, Martha breathed in the heady mixture of the woman's spicy musk combined with the delicate, flowery scent of her eau de toilette which had been liberally applied earlier in the day. Her husband shook Martha's hand and said, "If you need any more help, Ma'am, please don't be afraid to call on us..." Martha thanked the couple profusely as they left.

When they'd gone, Martha said, "Excuse me, Mr Doolittle. I'm going to call home." The Security Supervisor said, "Of course, Mrs Culver. Please do." Martha took herself off to a quiet corner of the office and took out her cellphone. As soon as Martha told Claudette that Billy had been caught on video tape she heard the girl gasp and knew she was crying tears of relief. Martha interrupted her daughter abruptly, saying, "We haven't found him yet. In fact, we have no idea where he is right now but I think I know where he's going..." Martha gave Claudette a precised account of the afternoon's events, then asked her to call off the searchers and update her father on the latest developments. Martha reflected momentarily that it was the first time she'd thought about her husband all day and a sudden pang of loneliness stabbed at her heart. Martha heard her phone beep three times, warning her that the battery was nearly flat. Claudette was about to ask, 'What next, Mom?' when she heard her mother say, "I'm sorry, Claudette, I have to go. My cell's about to die..." Before Martha could tell Claudette that she loved her, the phone went dead.

To get Martha's attention, the Security Supervisor said, "Mrs Culver... I'm going to send out an alert to all stations on our list of likelies. It'll take me an hour or so. Then we'll have to wait for reports of sightings to come back... We probably won't have anything useful come back tonight because a lot of the day staff will have gone home by now..." Seeing the look of dismay on Martha's face, Francis Doolittle said, "Don't worry! Our people know what to do if they see Billy..." then continued, "You don't want to hang around here, Mrs Culver. What are you going to do? There's a real nice hotel close by if you want to stay over and you're welcome to come in tomorrow morning as early as you like... I'll be here from six... In the meantime, I've got your contact numbers. I'll call you immediately we have some news..."

The Sheriff interrupted the Security Supervisor, addressing him directly, almost as though Martha hadn't been present and he'd had to make up her mind for her in her absence. "We really have to get back. I've neglected my other duties for two days now... and... er... Mrs Culver hasn't got her car with her so she can't go on alone without me..." Then he turned to Martha and said, "How about I take you home? We should be there by eight-thirty... nine at the outside if we set off now." Martha felt as though she was being railroaded – gently maybe but without much say in the matter all the same. Not having given much thought as to the next move she hesitated, then said, "Well... yes... I guess so..."

—•—

Knowing how antsy Jack could get if he was disturbed whilst he was in the middle of a difficult job, Dan Ackland sidled up to him and as casually as he could, asked, "How's it going, Jack?" Without shifting his gaze from the screen, Jack replied, "Oh... pretty much as expected... Repeatability on each axis is within a few ten-thousands of an arc-sec... Absolute accuracy looks spot-on... near as 'Damn it' is to swearing, as old Granny Culver would've said... Of course, we won't know for certain 'til tomorrow evening, when the calibration routine's finished..." and then, with more temper than he usually exhibited over any problem, "Christ! I hate calibrations! Two days of unrelenting tedium interspersed with the odd burst of activity... I know the process is pretty much automated nowadays but... you know me, Dan... I find it difficult to leave things to their own devices at such a critical time... Normally, I'm willing everything to be alright so we can get back down to some serious astronomy. This time, I'd give my eye teeth to find something wrong with the system..."

Dan sat beside Jack and idly looked over the data print-outs whilst Jack punched the computer keyboard, calling up more analytical routines in the hope that one would find an error with the telescope's positioning system. Eventually, Jack sighed and said bluntly, "No... I can't find anything wrong with the 'scope. It's as accurate as ever it was... Any discrepancy must be down to Keck II... or maybe the weather conditions... I really don't think it's down to us..."

The two men sat in silence until Dan asked, "Have you had any further news of Billy?" Jack turned to face his colleague. "Yes. Claudette called earlier and gave me an update. It seems as though Billy has skedaddled after all..." Jack registered the look of surprise on Dan's face. "It's true. Martha saw him at the bus station in Portland... or at least, saw him on CCTV, that is... but that was Saturday morning. That was the last sighting of him... It looks like he's headed east... Martha thinks he's making his way to my parents... They live near Rochester, New York. She's tried calling them, to warn them he might be on his way but there was no answer. I've also tried a couple of times... Ditto... I seem to remember them saying something about a long weekend golfing with friends down in Florida... They never have their mobiles switched on when they're out on the course... Two of the pleasures of being retired, I suppose..."

Lost for a moment, Dan asked, "What are?"

"Golf whenever the fancy takes you and being incommunicado. Leaving your cellphone off... God alone knows how we ever survived before they were invented..."

"What?"

"Cellphones... And golf, come to think of it..." Jack added flippantly. Golf was one of Jack's few passions. Latterly he'd had very few opportunities to play. Dan Ackland stared at Jack Culver for a moment, then said in a low voice, "We're all going to have to learn to survive with a lot less than that if S241 does hit us..."

The two men sat uneasily. There was another ticklish subject Dan wanted to broach with Jack and Jack could sense his discomfort. He knew there was something else. A little hesitantly, Dan asked, "So what's your next move? With Billy, I mean..." Jack sat quietly for a moment, then said, "Well... Martha's informed the bus company and they've alerted the Transportation Police. They're all on the look-out for him... There's no point in me diving off with no idea where to start looking... What would be gained by me tearing around the USA like a headless chicken in a barnyard? I need to follow firm leads, to try to second-guess where he might be so I can intercept him... Or to be there at the other end to meet him once it's clear exactly where he's going... Either way, I'm relying on Martha to do the detective work... And don't underestimate her... She's a first-class analytical scientist... I'm sure she's got the attention to detail necessary to examine the evidence thoroughly and glean from it any important clues that are there. I'd be surprised if she overlooked something significant... And she has the mental acuity to interpret them correctly... If I took off after her now, I'd simply be duplicating her efforts..." After a little more thought, Jack continued, "Billy's not sly by nature... It's not in his nature to be devious or to mislead you in any way... In fact, he's very straightforward. He's never tried deceiving us, or not that we know of... If he thought we were on his tail I doubt he'd try to throw us off the scent by jinking about, leastways not intentionally... Wherever he's going, he'll be going by the shortest, most practical route... in a straight line, if possible... assuming that nothing gets in his way to deflect him from it... And in his mind he'll have gone for a damn good reason... What intrigues me is 'Why?' That's still a mystery but it must have been something very compelling... Something so overwhelming that it's driven him to these lengths... I haven't fathomed out what it is yet..." then, after the briefest pause for reflection, "I only hope he gets there in one piece and doesn't come to any harm along the way..."

After sitting quietly for a few moments, Dan asked, "So when will you be heading off after Billy then, Jack?" Jack knew that, in a roundabout way, this was what Dan had been trying to ask him all along. Jack sat staring at the floor for a long moment before answering. Dan sat looking at him. He could only guess at the struggle that must be going on inside his friend, torn between two conflicting duties which were so diametrically opposed that their positions could never be reconciled. Dan also realised that if fate conspired against him and he made the wrong decision now – whichever decision it turned out to be – Jack would forever live to regret it; on the one hand, he'd be damned if he stayed and, on the other, he'd be damned if he didn't. Jack lifted his head and looked Dan in the eye. "I've already told you I'd stay until we know for sure one way or the other... and I will." Dan sighed with relief. He simply said, "Thank you, Jack", to his friend and got up and went out of the Control Room. As he walked down the corridor towards his office, Dan felt the whole of his insides relax as the tension of uncertainty was eased by knowing that Jack would stick with it to the bitter end. Nobody knew the complex systems of the world's most powerful and sophisticated optical telescope as thoroughly as Jack Culver did. After all, he had been responsible for its design, had overseen its manufacture, assembly and installation, commissioned it, de-bugged it and made it work and if anything went wrong with it at this crucial time, nobody would be better able to diagnose the fault and fix it. He thought, 'Whether he really believes all that preamble about Martha's investigative skills and duplication of effort or not, it was just a pretext to justify staying... To make it easier on himself to come to that decision... and easier on me to go along with it... He could walk out of here any time he likes... But we need him and he knows it... I can't force him to stay... I wouldn't try... and he knows that too... He's had to make an impossible choice... It's a selfless decision and a brave one... I hope neither of us lives to regret it... Martha would never forgive us... either of us... if anything happened to Billy that could've been prevented if only Jack hadn't been stuck here...' then, a little forlornly, 'God knows, I don't think we'd ever forgive ourselves...' Dan closed his office door behind him. He sat down wearily at his desk and leaned forward, putting both elbows on the beautifully tooled leather inset and clasping his hands together in front of him. As his head slumped forward, he shut his eyes and rested the bridge of his nose on his crossed thumbs and his forehead against his interlocked fingers. Without realising he was doing it, Dan Ackland began to pray.

—•—

Martha sat in uneasy silence, brooding over what the Sheriff had just asked her; it wasn't only his line of questioning that had put her on the defensive but the tone in which it had been delivered. In fact, she hadn't felt entirely comfortable since he'd turned up at the house on the Saturday evening. She braced herself and asked, "What are you driving at, Sheriff? How should I know why Billy's taken off like this... It was completely unexpected... But I don't like the inference you're clearly drawing from this situation when you say, '...we might know where Billy's running away to but what's he running away from?' What do you think he's running away from, Sheriff?" It was now Bill Finn's turn to feel uneasy. He could tell Martha's hackles were up. She was extremely indignant.

The Sheriff tried choosing his words tactfully but nothing he said sounded conciliatory. "I have to be very circumspect whenever I'm asked to investigate a missing child, whether it's at the parent's request or anyone else's... I have to take the view that it might not be simply because the child's run away on a whim..." Martha sat trying to make sense of what the Sheriff had said. Eventually the penny dropped and the sheer monstrosity of it was like a slap in the face. "You bastard! You didn't drive me out of the goodness of your heart... or concern for Billy... did you? You came to keep tabs on me... You thought I'd done something to Billy... God knows what... but you didn't want to let me out of your sight... Isn't that the truth of it, Sheriff? Well isn't it?" then, after a moment's pause, "What did you think I'd done? Did you think I'd harmed Billy in some way... maybe even killed him?" When the Sheriff didn't answer but kept on staring at the road ahead, Martha continued, "And now you've seen with your own eyes that Billy's alive, you know your worst suspicions are unfounded... but you still persist in suspecting me of *something*... What is it, Sheriff? Why do *you* think Billy's run away? Is it because you think I've been abusing my own son? Is that it?" Martha ended confrontationally.

The Sheriff replied coldly, "It wouldn't be the first time, Mrs Culver... Let's face it, no child runs away from a happy home... Especially not a child of such... er... limited capacity as your son... And I wouldn't be doing my job if I didn't consider all possibilities..."

Martha sat, smarting at the ambiguity of the Sheriff's last remarks. She remembered back to the last episode when they had found Billy up on Drover's Hill. The dog handler had led them to within a few paces of the summit. The Sheriff's Deputy had been the first to spot somebody standing by the cairn that marked the top and had pointed to the figure and asked, "Is that him?" Martha had recognised Billy's silhouette instantly and had raced ahead of the party shouting "Billy! Billy!" but he'd remained absolutely still with his back to her, staring up at the night sky. As she'd reached Billy, she'd spun him round to face her. Her darkest fear had been dispelled but all the bottled-up anxiety that had been steadily accumulating whilst they'd been searching for him came spewing out and she'd taken hold of Billy's shoulders and shaken him violently, screaming in his face, "Don't you ever do this to me again! Do you hear? Don't you ever Ever EVER scare me like that again…" When all the pent-up fury and emotion had spent itself, her outburst subsided as quickly as it had come on and Martha had fallen around Billy's neck, sobbing, completely overwhelmed with relief. Martha had clung so fiercely to her son that Jack eventually had to peel her arms from around the boy's neck. Throughout the whole scene, Billy had stood ramrod-straight, rigid and unbending, showing no glimmer of emotion, not responding in the slightest to his mother's distress. Knowing how much frustrated love Martha had for Billy, Jack saw in her hysteria only the outpouring of her motherly fears. However, seeing things from another perspective entirely, the Sheriff had registered something very different; whilst he could only begin to guess at the difficulties of dealing with such a disturbed child, he did wonder how frequently the mother took out her frustrations on him in a similar manner.

The remainder of the journey passed in bitter silence. Martha had been so stunned by the Sheriff's suggestions that she'd been unable to express her revulsion but the more she'd brooded on them, the angrier she'd become and the more she resented his intrusion and regretted involving him in the first place. By the time they reached home, Martha's dislike of him had become distilled into pure, unalloyed hatred. When the Sheriff's cruiser pulled up outside the Culver residence, Martha pushed open the door. Without looking at him, she grabbed her bag and grunted a cold, perfunctory, insincere "Thank you" over her shoulder as she swung round to get out of the car. Before she had chance to pull herself up out of the passenger seat, the Sheriff said to her back, "Before you go, Mrs Culver, there's just one more thing… I'd like to see you in my office first thing tomorrow morning… I have some questions… The bus company and Transport Police can continue searching for Billy…"

Before he could finish, Martha snapped her head round and, looking him square in the eye, spat back with undiluted venom, "If you want to question me, you'll have to arrest me and take me in in 'cuffs… otherwise I'm going to find my son and you won't stop me… And if you try, I'll sue you for wrongful arrest… I'll crucify you… We have the financial muscle to bleed you white and believe you me, I'll use it… And if you hold me up for even a second and anything happens to Billy in the meantime, I'll kill you!" Without a backward glance, Martha got out of the car and marched up the drive. As the Sheriff watched her disappearing into the gloom, an icy shiver ran down his spine as he realised that Martha's had been no idle threat; her cold, hard stare had been as predatory and unfeeling as a raptor's gaze.

—•—

"So what am I going to tell the President?" Wayne Harland asked. Dan Ackland thought for a moment, then answered, "Tell him the truth... That the sky's too cloudy for us to get a sighting of S241, so the best prediction we've got so far... *in fact, the only prediction we've got so far...* is our last one... And you can also tell him, quite honestly, that Mauna Kea's only had the one sighting last night and with that and tonight's sighting, assuming they get it, they have insufficient points to plot a meaningful trajectory. I'm sure he'll understand that, realistically, it's impossible to extrapolate its flightpath accurately from so few datapoints. In fact, it could take as many as ten or even a dozen sightings to generate a really trustworthy projection..." then, slightly furtively, Dan added, "Oh! And by the way... In my opinion, there's nothing to be gained by mentioning to him our little... er... *variance.* It'd just confuse matters. And anyway, it should be rectified by tomorrow evening... And whoever finds their readings are out can simply re-run their data to compensate for the error..."

—•—

As Martha burst through the front door, she shouted Nicky. When there was no immediate response, she bawled "Nicky!" again, as she slammed the door behind her. The twins came hurtling out of the kitchen shoulder-to-shoulder, looking alarmed. Without waiting for them to ask her what was wrong, Martha barked at her son, "Get some things together... clothes... toothbrush... whatever you need. We're going to find Billy. I want to leave in fifteen minutes, twenty tops..." When he failed to respond instantaneously, Martha commanded, "Don't stand there gawping! Jump to it!". Nicky started to say, "I was only wondering..." but Martha snapped, "Don't wonder! Get a move on!" Turning to her daughter, she barked, "Claudette, come and help me make some stuff for the journey... God knows where he is but he's way ahead of us. We could be on the road for ages..."

Martha busied herself making sandwiches and drinks whilst Claudette gathered as many snacks as she could find in the cupboards and packed them all in a cool bag. All the while, Claudette had been asking about Billy, trying not to sound over-anxious. Finally, she asked the question that had been burning in her mind, "Why do you think Billy's run away, Mom?" Martha was tired of all the pointless speculation so she responded with a brusque, "I don't know". Sensing her mother's defensiveness but mistaking it for worry and her general preoccupation with the situation, Claudette continued with the packing quietly until she could no longer contain herself and cautiously broached the subject again. "What's Billy running away from?" Martha exploded, "Not you too! How the hell should I know?" Claudette was completely taken aback by the violence of her mother's response and stared at her in disbelief. After challenging the girl's frightened gaze, Martha bawled, "What is it, Claudette? Do you think he's run away because of me? Is that it? Is it?" Martha had advanced towards her daughter becoming louder and more belligerent with each question. As she bellowed the final "Is it?" straight into Claudette's face, it crumpled and the tears sprang from her frightened eyes. Claudette whispered a tiny, "No" then covered her face and sobbed into her hands, too hurt to speak but the tears leaked between her fingers and trickled down her arms. Martha stood back for a moment then, appalled and ashamed at her own cruelty, threw her arms around the girl and hugged her tightly. "I'm sorry darling. I'm so sorry. I didn't mean to upset you. It's just that I can't think straight. I'm so afraid for Billy." Claudette's sobbing abated a little and she managed to rasp, "So am I, Mom… So am I…" then, after a few moments, Claudette confided, "I don't know why but I'm afraid for us all." Martha rocked her daughter gently until she stopped crying. Claudette said, "I don't want to be alone, Mom. Can I come with you? If you're right, Billy's not going to show up here so there's no point waiting home for him."

Martha said, "Well… what happens if I'm wrong and he comes back and there's no one here? What then? I was hoping you'd at least wait for your father… When do we expect him home?"

"I don't know. When I spoke to Dad earlier, he said he didn't know… He sounded very tired… I think something's going on up there… He's being very cagey about everything… What he's doing… Why he went to the White House… He wouldn't tell me anything…"

Martha sent her daughter off to put some things in a bag. She was undecided about taking Claudette too and leaving the house empty, in case Billy should re-appear but she thought it better to be prepared anyway and she wanted a few minutes on her own to calm down and clear her head. Martha had already dialled Jack's mobile number when Margaret knocked; she put her head round the door and with a cheery, "Yoohoo! Anybody home? Can I come in?" entered without waiting to be invited. Martha gestured to her friend to come in and sit down, as she said, "Hi Jack, it's me…" Margaret sat opposite Martha, listening to the one-sided conversation as she briefly related the events of the last couple of days to her husband. Eventually, she said, "Claudette wants to come with me. She seems very upset and of course, I haven't helped by bawling her out like that but I don't want to leave the house empty in case Billy comes home…" Without giving a second thought to the fact that Martha was on the phone, Margaret blurted out, "You go dear. Take Claudette. I'll man the fort while you're away…"

Martha mouthed, "Are you sure? Won't Phil mind?"

Margaret waved her hand dismissively to indicate that she'd square things at home and said, "Don't you worry! You get off and find Billy."

—•—

Jack sat slumped on his sofa, his cellphone pressed to his ear. "I know Martha... I know. I miss you too... And I'm as worried about Billy as you are... but at least we know that, as of Saturday, he was alright..."

Martha cut in, "No thanks to you..."

Jack persevered, "But I really can't down tools and leave just like that..."

"Why not?" Martha demanded.

"Well... firstly, I'm in the middle of a really important sighting. Vital..."

"But you said there's cloud cover for the next few nights. So why can't you come out and help look for Billy until the sky clears again, then go back if you really must... What's so important that you've got to sit there twiddling your thumbs, waiting for the sky to clear when you could be out searching for your son? I don't understand!"

"You mean you *won't* understand, Martha."

"*Maybe that's because you're not telling me anything, Jack...*" Martha shrieked in frustration, "Or at least, anything that reasonably justifies your absence... Or not to my mind anyway..." then after a brief pause, Martha asked suspiciously, "What aren't you telling me, Jack?"

Jack said quietly, "I've told you all I can. I can't tell you any more... on the President's orders..."

"Oh! Very convenient!" Martha exploded.

Before she could say any more, Jack cut her off. "And if you'd just listen to me... Secondly, I have to go out to Mauna Kea tonight. I'm off to the airport in a few minutes to catch the redeye to Hawaii..." Martha was about to jump in with, 'With your blowsy little research assistant, I suppose...' when Jack said, "Keck I's in the middle of a major refurb and they're having trouble with Keck II... We're supposed to be working on this sighting together... They want me out there to help fix it... We can't afford to have both 'scopes out of action or we're right up the creek..."

The line went quiet for a moment before Martha said in a steely voice, "I hope you're not lying to me, Jack. It would be unforgivable at any time but at a time like this..." Martha trailed off into silence.

Shocked and somewhat bewildered, Jack responded, "Why would I lie to you, Martha?"

There was a strained silence between them as each struggled with their own thoughts. In a more even tone, Martha continued, "I've never had cause to distrust you before, Jack. You've never given me any... yet..." After a pause, she finished flatly, "I suppose I have to trust you now..." There was very little more that either of them could say. When they'd finished the call Martha sat quietly, her heart racing from sheer panic. As she calmed down, she mulled over what had been said. On reflection, she was extremely relieved she hadn't blurted out a direct accusation that would have told Jack she'd suspected him of being disloyal; if there was one thing that Martha would have staked her life on, it was Jack's fidelity.

Jack sat feeling unhappier than he ever remembered being in all their years together. He didn't understand where Martha had been coming from but he wasn't sure that her attitude was solely driven by her concern for Billy or what she might have concluded was his lack of concern. He was sitting, head down, long legs bent and slightly apart, arms outstretched with his hands on his knees when Dan walked in. "Come on, Jack! I've managed to delay the flight but Portland ATC say there's a storm coming in... They can only delay take-off so long... If you're not there in time, they'll be forced to leave without you, so you'd better look lively. I'll help you with your bags. Let me carry your toolbox out to the car for you..." Jack slung his laptop over his shoulder and picked up his briefcase in one hand and his flightbag in the other. As he was about to leave his office, he stopped and turned to Dan. With a quizzical look on his face, he said, "Unless I'm very much mistaken, Martha thinks I'm not joining in the hunt for Billy because I'm too busy having an affair..." Without hesitation, Dan shot out, "Don't be ridiculous! Now move it!" and with that, he marched ahead of Jack to the parking lot. As he waved his colleague off, Dan made a mental note to give Martha a call, strictly on the q.t. of course, to give her a heads-up. They were all under enough pressure as it was, none more so than Jack and Martha. He couldn't afford to let a stupid misunderstanding worsen an already difficult situation.

—•—

(Tuesday 3 August 2010, about 9.00am Pacific time)

Francis Doolittle said apologetically, "I'm real sorry, Mrs Culver. It seems Billy's dropped off our radar completely. Momentarily, I hope... The last sighting was in Salt Lake City... that was Sunday afternoon. We know he took the same bus as Mrs Col'houn out of Portland, so it's fair to assume that's how he got to Saltie, although we can't check with the driver on the leg from Boise, Idaho. She's not available. She's on compassionate leave... Whether or not Billy arrived in Cheyenne, we have no idea. Nobody's seen him since Saltie. All we can say with any certainty is that he didn't take the first bus of the day to Cheyenne, which is the one Mrs Col'houn's most likely to have taken..."

More to herself than anyone else in particular, Martha said, "So what do we do next?" Trying to be helpful, the Security Supervisor said, "Well, you could wait here Ma'am. We may get news that'd save you shooting off in the wrong direction entirely... Or you could drive to Saltie, to see if you could pick up his scent again there..." Martha sat deep in thought, then said, "I'd like to meet that woman... Mrs Col'houn... and her grandson. If Billy did travel to Salt Lake City with them, they may have some idea where he was going from there... How do I get in touch with her?"

The Security Supervisor said, "Oh Lord knows, Mrs Culver... If she is staying with her sister, I have no idea what her sister's name is, so I wouldn't have a clue as to how you'd find her property..."

"No... but Fred Chapel might be able to help. He knows where Mrs Col'houn lives. Maybe one of her neighbours knows where she's gone or how she can be contacted."

Francis Doolittle tucked the phone into his neck. As he was dialling, he said to Martha, "Fred lives over the river, on the outskirts of Minnehaha... If we can get hold of him, he might be able to... Hello, Fred... Yes, it's Francis here... Sorry to disturb you again on your day off but Mrs Culver's here about Billy. We haven't been able to track him down... She'd like to meet with Mrs Col'houn. She thinks she might be able to give her some clue as to Billy's whereabouts..." Francis Doolittle continued speaking for a couple more minutes then put the phone down and turned to Martha. "Fred's going to meet you and show you how to find the Col'houn place..." He motioned to Mrs Culver to join him by the wallmap and showed her how to get to the rendezvous point. "You take I-5 north over the river..." he said, tracing the route with his finger, "Get off here and head west on Fourth Plain Boulevard. Just before it turns into New Lower River Road, Fred will meet you at the intersection with Fruit Valley Road. You can't miss him. He drives a black sedan." Martha laughed as the Security Supervisor handed her a slip of paper and, with the faintest hint of sarcasm, she finished off his sentence for him, "But here's his cell number, in case I can't even find the Columbia River..." and then jokingly, with a twinkle in her eye said, "I suppose you think I'm a typical woman." It was Francis Doolittle's turn to laugh, as he said, "Far from it, Mrs Culver... but now I suppose you think I'm a typical man."

Martha thanked him for his help and the three of them left the Security Supervisor's office. Francis Doolittle stood at his office window. As he watched, Martha linked arms with her two children and he noticed a little skip in her step. He thought, 'Some lucky man's extremely fortunate to have a family like that... and such a lovely woman in his life. I hope he appreciates them...' then, 'Funny! You'd have thought he'd be leading the posse. I wonder what's so important that he's not here with her?' He watched until they disappeared down the steps to the parking garage then returned to his desk and sifted through the pile of paperwork that had accumulated since yesterday. Try as he might to concentrate on his work, he couldn't dispel the image of Martha Culver from his mind.

For some inexplicable reason, as they were walking to the car, Martha felt positive she would see Billy again and, for the first time in four days, she felt her heart lift a little.

—•—

Jack leaned listlessly against the cabin wall, looking out of the window. Down below, the sea sparkled and gleamed in the Alenuihaha Channel as the fifteen-seat island hopper jumped the strait between Maui and Hawaii. He'd had no sleep on the first leg to San Fransisco because he'd been turning over in his mind the telephone conversation with Martha. 'Does she really think I've been unfaithful? Surely not! Okay, there've been lots of opportunities whilst I've been away at conferences, as she well knows... And occasionally I've flirted with friends and neighbours at parties but that was only ever a bit of fun... and she knows that too because she's always been present... and she's never seemed to mind...' When he was in social situations with Martha, Jack enjoyed flirting. Martha didn't mind; in fact, in an odd sort of way, she was rather flattered. She'd never been jealous or felt threatened in any way and had always ribbed him about it afterwards but to the best of her knowledge that was as far as it had ever gone, although she had noticed that some of the other women took it far more seriously than Jack did. When he was without Martha, Jack made one simple rule which he always observed: never to openly encourage other women. He had always drawn the line there and had never crossed it, not because he didn't find other women attractive but partly because he couldn't bear the thought of deceiving Martha and abusing her trust even if she never found out and of hurting her and risking their happiness if she did. And partly because Jack already had a mistress, one he'd had since before he met Martha; she had followed them wherever they'd gone and Martha had come to terms with the fact that Jack had two all-consuming loves in his life. Currently, his other love resided in a large, white, hemi-spherical house on a mountain top about an hour-and-a-half's drive from their home. Martha had always known about her and had come to accept that Jack's work was the second love of his life; she'd always been confident in the knowledge that if he wasn't at home he'd be there with her. Consequently, Jack had never pursued another bird, even when it had shaken its tailfeathers at him and, until now, Martha had never though he might.

Jack's uncertainty over quite what Martha had been driving at on the phone clouded his thoughts. Whatever it was, it had depressed him. He'd been feeling very tired after waiting nearly two hours for his connection, so he'd

111

tried to put it out of his mind on the second leg to Honolulu but he hadn't slept nearly so well as he usually did on long-haul flights. Now, as the little plane skirted Mauna Kea on its descent into Hilo, Jack looked down on the twin domes of the W. M. Keck Observatory and the little gaggle of buildings squatting beside them, shining in the brilliant midday sun. At this point, Jack was normally filled with eager anticipation at the prospect of working with two of the Titans of the astronomical world but today he only felt disgruntlement, tinged with anxiety and resentfulness. Not, he reflected, a very conducive frame of mind to be in for tackling a potentially difficult fault-finding exercise. With a sigh, Jack stared into the distance and noticed the looming bulk of the mighty Mauna Loa volcano in the distance and, a little further away on its south-eastern flank, a plume of smoke rising from the summit of its younger, more active sibling, Kilauea.

Jim Murray strode up to Jack as he came into the baggage reclaim area. He extended his arm and shook Jack's hand vigorously. "Good to see you, Jack. I wish it could have been under less trying circumstances. I've had your bags expressed through. They're waiting to be collected so we can get going straightaway." On the way to the Observatory, Jim Murray appraised Jack of the problem with Keck II and the work they'd done so far to check calibration. To Jack's mind, it seemed as though the problem was instability in the positioning system, resulting in poor repeatability. That would surely affect the basic truth of the absolute coordinates they were working to. But what was its root cause? Jim Murray interrupted Jack's thought process. "It's Sod's Law, of course… Most of the work we've been doing recently has been comparative measurements using instruments mounted on Keck II. They're so super-sensitive they're accurate to a few tens of microarc-seconds. We've been looking for planetary systems similar to Earth that could harbour life. The main 'scope's only been used for fairly coarse aiming until we find the star cluster we're interested in, then the instrument's taken over… And we've been looking in a totally different quadrant of the sky from S241." Jim Murray broke off as he swung into his parking space. The two men climbed out and retrieved Jack's computer and toolbox from the back seat. As they walked into the main entrance, Jim Murray continued, "We've been plagued with problems lately. It seems as though the whole of the volcano system around here's woken up, with magma sloshing around and leaking out of every orifice. Even Mauna Kea's been grumbling after being dormant for the last four millennia. We've been suffering measurable tremors as often as two or three times a day… odd times even more frequently… although it hasn't happened for the last few days… But when it does… Oh brother! It plays merry hell with our most delicate instruments…" With almost uncanny timing, as though the giant that lived in the mountain had taken offence when it overheard the flea on its back complaining about its ill temper and bad manners, Jack felt the concrete floor under his feet give a barely perceptible shudder. Jim Murray said, "There it goes again… Not much of a disturbance as far as you and I are concerned but an absolute bugger when you're trying to measure to a fraction of a gnat's whisker…"

Jack sat in Jim Murray's office and stretched out his long legs. He was deep in thought. He sipped his coffee, then asked, "Have you had any tremors whilst you've been doing the calibration?"

"No, we've checked back and we've recorded nothing… or at least nothing significant… even down below minus four on the Richter scale… We have a fantastic new seismometer. I'll show you it, before you go…" Jim Murray added enthusiastically. Jack grunted his appreciation but didn't let himself be side-tracked; he wanted to bottom the problem then get the very next flight out of here.

"Has the Observatory shifted?" Jack asked, then added, "Most critically, of course, has it tilted?"

"Well… There are permanently-installed electronic inclinometers built into the foundations. They've registered a tiny degree of tilt over the last few months as the mountain's swelled but it's fairly negligible. Marginally less than two micro-radians. Certainly nowhere near enough to account for a discrepancy of this magnitude…"

"And what ground monitoring systems do you have on the mountain?"

"Laser distance measuring… Of course, they're restricted to line-of-sight surveying… and GPS sensors scattered all over the mountain. They're all linked by a telemetry system back to our own computer… And NASA's InSAR satellites provide us with topographical scans of the mountain on request… It's all done in conjunction with the US Geological Survey who help us interpret the data… All the evidence is telling us that the mountain's swelling which suggests there's some sort of volcanic activity going on down there…" said Jim Murray, pointing towards the floor, "…but hitherto we've always been able to adjust the calibration to compensate for those minute changes… Now it seems we can't…" Jack sat looking slightly bemused for a moment, then surmised, "It looks as though you've exhausted the external influences… I'm with you, Jim. It must be down to the 'scope itself, so let's get to work."

"OW!" Jack bellowed. He snatched his hand away and shook it violently, then tucked it under his other arm and squeezed it tightly. Alarmed, Jim Murray registered the pained expression on Jack's face. He leaned over and with a look of concern asked, "What is it, Jack? What's wrong?"

Jack said irritably, "Oh nothing... The wrench slipped off the bolt... I've just clouted my hand, that's all..." then added, "Nothing to worry about... It's so numb, I hardly felt a thing" pulling down the cuff of his glove and examining the gouge in the back of his right hand. The skin was broken and deeply indented between the metacarpals of the second and third fingers and a spot of blood was beginning to ooze up on the surface. A faint violet hue was already starting to develop under the skin and it hurt like hell. Jim Murray took Jack's wrist and examined the damage. "Come on. We need to get that seen to... And you need a break, Jack. Working in this thin air and freezing conditions is exhausting. You've been at it for more than twelve hours solid. It's past one in the morning..." When he sensed Jack's reluctance to stop work, Jim re-iterated more firmly, "You need a break! In fact, we should get you down to the crew room so you can get some shut-eye. You look exhausted..." Jack exhaled slowly, letting out a long sigh and said, "I guess you're right, Jim... We've already missed tonight's sighting, so I don't suppose there's much to be lost by breaking off for a while but I don't want to sleep. I'll just have a strong coffee and a bite to eat, then let's get back to it. I want this baby up and running again by tomorrow night. We can't afford to miss another sighting."

"Right-o Jack. I'll just ask Olo to remove that cover whilst we have a brew, then I'll organise some food for us... Oh! And by the way... I think you'll find that tomorrow is actually today..." finished Jim Murray.

The two astronomers sat going over their investigations so far. Assisted by Jim Murray and his best technician, Olo Peleakala, Jack had gone over the telescope meticulously, methodically working his way through the electrical and control systems as well as checking the mechanics. They had found nothing up to press and there was very little left to do. Jack was starting to worry that they may have overlooked something and have to start all over again. Feeling warmer and refreshed, Jack stretched and said in a more cheerful voice, "Right then! We won't find the problem sitting on our heinies in here. Are you ready to resume our hunt for the needle in the haystack?" Whether he was or not, Jim Murray sprang up and the two men donned their warm clothing and headed back out into the dome.

"Olo! Give me some more light in here... Thanks..." Jack gasped with the exertion of holding his own body weight steady as he peered awkwardly into the confined space. "There you are, Jim... I'll bet my boots that's what's caused it..." said Jack triumphantly, gently waggling the reader-head of the encoder that determined the angular position of the massive telescope's azimuthal axis. The movement was barely perceptible but it was there all the same.

Olo Peleakala leaned over Jack's shoulder and said, "I don't believe it! I checked that out yesterday... If I checked it once, I checked it a dozen times. How could I have missed it? More to the point... how could it have worked loose?" Jack said, "Well, it's easy to miss. The movement's tiny... and let's face it, it's pretty dingy under here... As for why, I haven't a clue... Let's have a look..." Jack gingerly backed off the two retaining screws holding the delicate sensor in place and tut-tutted under his breath. "There's no thread-lock on these screws. Whoever put this thing together didn't bother putting any adhesive on them to prevent them from working loose. They were barely finger-tight when I tried them... Obviously, you don't want to over-tighten them or it could crack the sensor... On the other hand, once they're set, you don't want them to move... Ever! Maybe the tremors have caused them to work loose now... Maybe they were never properly tightened up in the first place... We'll never know but I can tell you that you've been flying on a wing and a prayer. This was a failure waiting to happen..." There was a palpable sense of relief at having found something tangible. To minimise the disappointment if it proved not to be the case, Jack cautioned the two onlookers that this might not be the cause of the problem. However, this time, he secretly felt they'd struck paydirt. Whilst Jim Murray went off to warn the Control Room Manager that they would hopefully be starting a new calibration routine very soon, Jack carefully took Olo through a step-by-step procedure for correctly mounting and aligning the sensor, despite both of them being very weary. Even now, they were acutely aware that they didn't want this sort of thing to happen again.

"Well Jack, I don't want to celebrate prematurely but it looks like we've cracked it, thanks to you. We've been running the calibration procedure now for six hours and the readings we're getting are highly repeatable... Of course, we still have another forty-odd hours before the statistical analysis is finished but I really think we've bottomed it this time. We couldn't get this far two days ago. Now we've got to make sure the 'scope is precisely aligned. You're welcome to stay to help us out, if you want..." Jack shook his head and politely declined Jim Murray's invitation. "You're more than capable of carrying the baton from here on in, Jim..."

"Well, if not Jack, I've made enquiries about flights out... There's one in a couple of hour's time, at eleven-ten... I've provisionally reserved a seat for you... You could just make that one, if we hurry... If you want, I'll confirm it now..."

—•—

115

Martha said, "Yes, that's Billy's handwriting. Definitely!" She stared at the note for a while, then said, "It's remarkable!" Katherine Colquhoun waited a few moments for Martha to tell her what was so remarkable but when no explanation was forthcoming, she asked, "What is, dear?"

"Oh, not the fact that Billy can write. He writes a lot. Usually notes to himself... you know, little reminders or workings out... but they're usually in a kind of shorthand, one of his own devising but one that we can occasionally decipher. We call them his 'Billy-do'... But this one's unusual in that it's in sentences... short I know but to-the-point... *and* because he's *communicating* something to you... *something unsolicited*... something he feels sufficiently strongly about for him to write it down in the first place... But what?" After pondering a little longer, Martha continued, "It's strange... It reads like a command but it's not a command. It's not really an instruction, either... I've *never* known Billy to issue an order of any kind... Ever! I think it's more of an observation... a warning, if you like... his thoughts spilling out on paper because he finds it easier than putting them into words but something Billy wanted to get across to you all the same... *That's* what's remarkable." Martha sat silently, looking perplexed until Katherine Colquhoun ventured, "Perhaps it has some bearing on why Billy's run away. You say you think he's headed east. Maybe he thinks we should all head east... But why?" then, "If so, where do you think this fixation could've come from?"

Martha said, "I have no idea, Mrs Col'houn..."

Katherine Colquhoun interjected, saying "Please! Call me Katie. It sits far more comfortably..."

"Sorry... Katie... I really don't know but it's the second thing that suggests to me he's headed east himself... possibly, as I suspect, to his grandparents... but if that is where he's going, it's two thousand miles from where he was last seen. That's an awful lot of country for Billy to cross alone... and it presents an awful lot of opportunities for something... um... unpleasant... to happen to him" Martha gulped and concluded with a slight shudder.

Martha asked, "Before we go, may I have a word with George to see if he can throw any more light on Billy's whereabouts?" Katie Colquhoun ushered George in and went out again leaving him alone with Martha and the twins. At first the boy was reticent to talk about Billy or anything else but Martha gently coaxed him until he began to talk. Once he had overcome his initial shyness, George reverted to his normal, verbose self and Martha sat listening as he related a blow-by-blow account of their journey. Martha asked George a few questions. Nothing he said gave her any indication that he was aware of Billy's intentions. As the clock in the hall struck seven, Katie Colquhoun came in and clapped her hands together. "Dinner in five minutes!" she announced. Martha glanced at her watch and exclaimed, "Oh my! We've been here over two hours now... I'm so sorry to have kept you for so long... We really must be going... We've imposed on your hospitality long enough and we still have to find somewhere to stay tonight..."

Katie Colquhoun said, "Don't be silly, dear. I've spoken to our Jessie and she says you're welcome to eat with us, then you can bed down in one of the bunkhouses tonight. It's made up ready but the party that booked it has cancelled at the last minute..." Martha was about to protest but Katie Colquhoun cut her short, saying, "I won't hear of you travelling on this evening, Martha. You look dead-beat. You're all-in. It won't help find Billy if you drive off the road and into a gully... now will it?" Martha found the old lady's persuasiveness irresistible and gave in without a struggle, secretly relieved not to have to go on any further tonight. Martha said, "Of course, you'll let me pay for it..." but Katherine Colquhoun replied smartly, "Oh no you won't! It's already paid for..." then added testily, "Bloody cheeky New Yorkers... Only demanded a full refund and expected it too! Argued like hell, they did. And why? Because their whining brats changed their minds and wanted to go to Disneyland instead. Our Jessie told 'em where to get off. Damn straight she did!" then chuntered, more to herself, "Dreadful, brash people. I can't stick 'em at any price. They're so rude and arrogant and self-important... and they have absolutely no appreciation of the value of anything... America would be an altogether nicer place if they dropped a bloody great bomb on the city and wiped it off the face of the Earth. Still, even I wouldn't wish that on seventy million innocent rats..." then, after a moment's reflection, she concluded, "Oops! There I go again... 'Going off on one', as my sister would put it. I'm sorry, my dear, I really shouldn't be so judgemental. After all, there but for the grace of God go any of us, me included." Martha decided to maintain a diplomatic silence about where she hailed from.

With Frederick Chapel acting as guide, Martha had found the Colquhoun property. She had explained to the housekeeper who she was and why she was there and, with the bus driver's help, had managed to convince the skeptical woman that her story was real. The wary housekeeper had tried phoning her employer but had been told that both Mrs Colquhoun and her sister were out riding on the range; they'd taken a picnic and weren't expected back until the evening. After a fair bit of persuasion, the housekeeper had reluctantly given Martha the address and telephone number of Katie Colquhoun's sister's ranch which was on the edge of the plains, between Horse Creek and Iron Mountain, in the foothills of the Laramie Mountains. Martha had almost regretted – nearly but not quite – not having contacted Sergeant McKenna whose authority would have opened this particularly obstinate door with ease, whereas she'd had to prize it open bit-by-bit using a combination of obsequiousness and guile applied with lots of patience. She had reflected that she'd lost at least an hour that could easily have been saved but she had been reluctant to involve the police, especially one who'd already been under the Sheriff's malign influence. Before seven o'clock the following morning Martha had been standing outside the Security Supervisor's office in the bus station at Salt Lake City, waiting for him to arrive, having driven through the night. Besides replaying the CCTV footage which confirmed that Billy had indeed been in the bus station on Sunday afternoon, the Security Supervisor had been of no further assistance.

Before dinner, whilst the twins moved their few things into the bunkhouse, Martha called the security men at Portland and Salt Lake City but neither had any news of Billy. After dinner, Katie Colquhoun took Martha gently by the arm and said quietly, "Let's take a turn round the ranch before you hit the hay. It'll help you unwind..." Martha went without protest. As they walked, the older woman talked steadily about the ranch which was where she'd grown up, telling Martha that it had belonged to her parents who'd had over twenty thousand head of cattle at one time. "Of course, when Daddy died it all became too much for Mother to handle, so she sold off a lot of the land. When Jessie's husband died, she came to live here, to look after Mother in her last few remaining years. When Mother died, it left us both very comfortably off... Jessie lets out the bunkhouses to families who want a holiday on horseback. She has a couple of Shoshone guides who take them up into the hills for a few days... There's some stunning scenery hereabouts... Helps those cityfolks to re-connect with their roots, I say..." By this time, they were approaching the stables and Katie Colquhoun steered Martha towards the first of the loose boxes. "There's something I'd like you to see..." As they looked over the door, Katie Colquhoun called out "Tilly... Come here girl" in a low voice and a pretty little palomino pony, pale golden in color with a flowing white mane and tail, looked over its shoulder at them. As it saw the two women, it blew out its nostrils softly and came over to be stroked. "This is George's pony. I bought her for him in the hope that she would help bring him out of himself. She's very placid but he's still a bit timid so he doesn't ride her very much. When I was a girl, I practically lived on horseback... and I never shied away from anything... and if I fell off, I got right back up in the saddle again... I wouldn't be beaten by any fence... and I certainly wouldn't be beaten by our Jessie..." Then, after a few moments reflection, she continued with a tinge of sadness in her voice, "I wish he would... I'm sure it'd help shift the focus of his mind off whatever's troubling him... so much so that he's like an ill-sitting hen. He's even had to go to a special school because he was getting on so badly at his local school. He's getting on much better but he's still not fulfilling his potential... Thank goodness I've got the money to be able to pay for it because his parents haven't. Their business has been in the doldrums lately..." Katherine Colquhoun sighed and stood quietly as the pony nuzzled at her deep cleavage. It seemed to Martha as though the old woman had become so engrossed in her own thoughts that she'd forgotten Martha was there. She was about to move off when Martha said, "Billy attends a special school... Even then, he only goes two days a week. I send him so he gets the company of other children his own age. His teachers say there's no point sending him more often because they can't tell whether any of what they're trying to teach him is going in. It's not as though he's stupid or incapable of learning. It's... it's almost as though he's so completely preoccupied with his own thoughts there's no capacity left for interacting with the outside world..."

The two women stood outside the stable door talking about their respective boys, each revealing to the other frustrations they'd kept bottled up for too long. When they'd done, both felt a lot lighter in spirit. When they'd finished, Katie said, "Come and see my special boy..." and led Martha to the last loosebox. As they approached, she called out, "Ozzie! Ozzie!" Immediately the horse heard her calling it whinnied loudly then stretched its head over the door and tossed it vigorously up and down in greeting. It was clearly pleased to see the old woman who reached in her pocket and pulled out a carrot. As the horse munched on it contentedly, Katherine Colquhoun unbolted the door and led him out. She circled him round the yard a couple of times on his lead rope, then rubbed her hand across his flank. "Ah Martha. Don't you just love it? The smell of a horse's coat... I do... He's the most powerful thing I've had between my thighs since I lost the man in my life." Martha smiled to herself at the woman's candid disclosure which sparked a pang of yearning for her husband as she admired the beautiful, well muscled Appaloosa with the most striking markings she'd ever seen on a horse. "He's a fine animal, don't you think, Martha? I love riding him... My late husband bought him for me as a yearling shortly before he passed away... I called the horse Ozzie after him. His name was Ozark... Ozark P Col'houn... God knows what the 'P' stood for... if it ever stood for anything... Ozzie certainly didn't know... His father was a bit of a character... First generation Irish settler made good... Tough as nails... Called his son after the place where they thought he'd been conceived on their way out west... Gave him the 'P' because he said a man should always have a middle initial..." then, imitating her father-in-law's booming Irish brogue, "It makes him sound important..." Reverting to her own voice, she finished off, "Fancy choosing 'P'! I ask you..." breaking into a gale of unrestrained laughter. Martha joined in with a discrete little giggle. When she'd recovered, Katie Colquhoun put the horse back into his loosebox and bolted the door. She stood stroking the horse's nose and cupping his muzzle whilst Ozzie gently nodded; which of them found the intimacy of the contact more pleasurable Martha couldn't tell. Katherine Colquhoun became more serious and said, "Truth be told, he's what brings me out here so often and keeps me here so long. I love riding him… But something's been bothering me… like a burr under my saddle, you might say… since meeting Billy… I can't put my finger on it… I was thinking I might take George up to Yellowstone, to see Old Faithful but I don't feel so easy about it now. I don't know why… I can't get Billy's note out of my mind… So I've decided to cut short our stay and take George back home a couple of weeks early… His parents live on Lookout Mountain in Tennesee… overlooking Chattanooga… I spoke to my daughter last night and she said I'm welcome to stay with 'em 'til the end of the holidays…" Katherine Colquhoun looked directly at Martha. For the first time, she said with a hint of self-doubt in her voice, "You don't think I'm being a silly and superstitious old fool, do you, Martha?"

Martha looked straight into the old woman's soft, blue eyes for a long moment, then said, "No Katie, I don't… Although, like you, I don't know why?" Katherine Colquhoun perked up again and, patting Martha briskly on the arm said, "Thank goodness for that. I thought I might be getting a bit sentimental in my old age…" The two women strolled slowly back towards the bunkhouse arm-in-arm. When they arrived at the porch, Martha said, "Thank you Katie… and please thank Jessie for me… I won't ever forget your kindness… to us and to Billy… I hope we can repay it one day…" The two women embraced and kissed each other on the cheek. Katie Colquhoun said, "God go with you, dear… and give Billy a big hug from me when you find him…" and with that, she turned and walked back to the ranchhouse.

At five-thirty the following morning, Martha swung the car round to face the rising sun as quietly as she could and rolled it down the drive and past the ranchhouse without gunning the engine. Katherine Colquhoun stood in her bedroom window, basking in the warm glow of the early morning sun and watched the car as it emerged from the last dip then disappeared over the last rise, before dropping down to the road half-a-mile away.

—•—

Jack got out of the car and stood for a moment looking up at the house. It took on a faintly eerie glow in the light from the quarter-moon which filtered down through the thin clouds making the dappled shadows creep across the front and roof of the house. Jack took the few steps leading up to the front door one-at-a-time; lifting his legs to reach each tread seemed an effort. He felt dog-tired – even his bones ached. He turned the key in the lock and pushed open the door. The house was in darkness. He fumbled around until he found the lightswitch and turned on the lights in the entrance hall, then went to turn off the intruder alarm.

Before he'd left Portland International Airport, Jack had called Dan Ackland to tell him that he was going home for the night; he hadn't seen the place for a week now or slept in a proper bed – any bed, let alone his own – for the same length of time. He felt dirty, caked with the grime of travelling and his mouth tasted foul. He was looking forward to a shower and cleaning his teeth, then climbing in between cool, crisp sheets. Dan hadn't raised any objection; in fact, he'd positively encouraged Jack to go home and get a good night's rest, then come in refreshed the following day when he was good and ready. Tonight's sky had denied them a decent view of S241 but tomorrow did hold out a slender promise that the seeing might be better.

Jack sat slumped in the armchair, sipping his favorite bourbon. He stared blankly at the television with half a mind on CNN's late-night update. The headline news was all about the on-going conflict in the Middle East, about a massive car bomb in Israel that had killed thirty-four people and injured another seventy and about the latest US casualties in Iraq. There was a quirky article about a mass suicide amongst a Japanese doomsday cult with two hundred and forty-two members dead from cyanide poisoning but nothing more noteworthy. Towards the end of the broadcast, immediately before the sports feature, the anchorman announced that the Government was advising people nationwide to prepare shelters in their homes and workplaces as a precaution in the event of terrorist attacks or other emergencies but it was so low-key that it made little impact on Jack and he suspected it would be equally ineffectual on many other people. There was no mention of S241. Primarily, Jack was preoccupied in musing about Billy, wondering where he might be and what he might be doing. For some inexplicable reason, he wasn't worried about Billy's safety; above all else, Jack felt absolutely certain that his son would be okay. He tipped the tumbler up and held it to his lips for a few seconds whilst the last few dregs combined into a single, golden-brown droplet that trickled down the inside of the glass and into his mouth. He put it down carefully on the coaster, raised himself slowly out of the chair and went upstairs.

Jack was used to arriving home at all hours of the night, so he was accustomed to coming into a silent house and tip-toeing upstairs, trying to make as little noise as possible. Tonight, however, he found the stillness of the house oppressive. The thought of being alone in it dismayed him more than he could have imagined. Although he rarely checked on the twins anymore these days, he always looked in on Billy before curling up beside Martha.

Occasionally, if Jack returned well before sun-up, Billy would still be awake, his bedcovers neatly turned back suggesting that he'd been put to bed and had then got out again once Martha had retired herself. The French doors would be open in all weathers so long as the sky was clear and Billy would be there in his pyjamas and dressing gown, peering into the eyepiece of his mighty telescope, totally absorbed in what he was doing. Often, Jack would join Billy and the two of them would sit together looking at the stars until dawn's light put an end to their seeing. Usually, if the sky was overcast, Billy would be fast asleep and Jack would stand over him looking down on his son's passive face for minutes on end. When he'd done, Jack would softly shut Billy's bedroom door then go as quietly as he could into their own room. Invariably, he visited their beautiful en-suite bathroom first, which was tiled all in white, with a sumptuous cream-colored carpet and fitted out with an extremely expensive, white, Italian suite that they'd chosen on a trip to Europe to mark their twentieth wedding anniversary before slipping down the passage that lead into the master bedroom. Jack always looked forward to the moment when he slipped quietly into bed beside Martha who normally slept curled up on her side. Dependent upon how deeply asleep she was, Martha would either snuggle up to Jack's body and tuck herself into it as he wrapped his body around hers and put his hand on her belly, to gently ease her bottom towards his groin or she would wake up and they would make love. Either way, Jack usually ended up getting a good night's sleep.

As he reached the landing, Jack instinctively turned to Billy's room. He entered and stood looking around the shelves then went and sat on the bed. He studied the room and said to himself, 'Always such a tidy little boy... A place for everything and everything in its place...' then 'Where are you Billy? And why did you go?' He continued musing for a while and was about to get up to go to bed when he noticed that the telescope had been moved. Thinking it very strange because Billy had always been absolutely adamant that his 'scope should never be moved, Jack got up and sauntered down to the other end of the room. Without thinking, he unlocked the French doors and swung them open, letting in the sweet scent of the August night, then removed the dustcap. Casually he stared through the eyepiece but the image was dark and indistinct. Thinking that the correcting lens may be dirty, Jack went round to clean it. To his surprise, he discovered that the reason he could see nothing was because there was a post-it note stuck to it. He peeled it off carefully, avoiding touching the lens. To his even greater surprise, he read in Billy's hand-writing, 'billy go nannan'; Nannan had been Billy's name for his grandmother – Jack's mother – ever since he'd first learned to speak.

Jack sat on Billy's bed staring at the note. Although the blunt little missive simply confirmed what Martha thought, it rang in his head like a peel of bells. He sat clutching it between finger and thumb and tapped it thoughtfully on the thumbnail of his other hand. So Martha's intuition had been proved right after all but it still didn't throw any light on the question of 'Why?'. Jack continued staring at the note, willing it to reveal more than the obvious message it contained. Suddenly, Jack looked up at Billy's telescope. Why had he stuck the note there where it was almost guaranteed that no one would find it, with the possible exception of himself? Jack went up to the 'scope again and looked around it for other possible clues but there were none. He was beginning to believe that it had been a fanciful notion on his part. He took one last look before giving up. Out of curiosity, he switched on the computer that sat on the table nearby which automatically controlled the positioning of the telescope and displayed its actual coordinates. As he waited for it to boot up, Jack sat puzzling over the fragmentary pieces of evidence, trying to find meaningful links between the paltry handful of tenuous clues he had as to why Billy had run away but it was like trying to discern exactly what was going on in a dense fog from seeing only slight changes in its texture and hearing a few muffled cries. The computer gave a little beep and the monitor jumped into life, indicating it was ready and waking Jack from his reverie. The telescope's software was already running and the axis positions appeared boldly on the screen. Jack stared at them; they were familiar but his tired mind couldn't quite fathom out where he recognised them from. Eventually, out of frustration, Jack took out his cellphone and called his assistant. "Hi David, it's Jack..." Before David Johnson could exchange any pleasantries, Jack continued, "I need you to punch these coordinates into the computer and tell me exactly whereabouts in the sky they are... What would we be looking at?" Interrogating the log file, Jack added, "The last sighting was on... wait a minute... on July twenty-ninth, at twenty-three-fifty-seven hours precisely... That was when? Last Wednesday... no... last Thursday night..." Jack read them out and the phone went quiet whilst David Johnson concentrated on entering the data into the Observatory's computer. He read them back to Jack, to make sure they were correct. Jack confirmed, "Yes, that's right..." After what seemed an interminable wait, David came back on the line and said, "Well, give or take a few seconds of arc in both alt and az, they were the coordinates of last Thursday's sighting of 241..." David's revelation swept through Jack's mind like a sudden blast of wind and it blew away the fog in an instant. Absolutely dumbfounded, Jack sat there with the phone pressed to his ear. He was staring into the computer screen but his eyes were focussed on infinity. After a few seconds delay, David's voice rang in his head, "Jack, is everything alright? Are you still there, Jack? Jack!" Eventually, Jack replied, "Yes... Yes, I'm still here David..." With a distinct note of concern, David asked "Are you alright, Jack?" Sounding very vague and far away as though he'd just awoken from a dream, Jack said, "Yes, I'm okay... Look... I'll see you tomorrow David..." Before David could quiz him any more, Jack had rung off but he continued to stare into the computer screen.

"Martha, is that you?"

"Jack! Where the hell are you? Don't you know what time it is?" Martha rolled over to look at the bedside clock, its red digits glowing in the dark. "It's nearly one o'clock in the morning!" Martha sounded extremely crotchety; she had only just managed to drop off to sleep when her cellphone trilled in her ear. "What are you calling me for now? Just to tell me you couldn't give a damn where Billy is... or the rest of us for that matter..." she spat out viciously.

"No, Martha, of course not... I thought I'd let you know where Billy's gone... I found a note in his room..."

Martha abruptly interrupted. "Rubbish!" she snorted contemptuously; she was in a foul mood. "I scoured his room before I left. So did the Sheriff. There was no note..."

In an even tone, Jack cut in firmly, "I found it in his telescope, stuck to the lens... You wouldn't even have realised it was there, unless you'd removed the dustcap and peered down inside. I only found it by accident..." He read the note to Martha. It seemed to placate her a little, until she snapped, "So what are you going to do now, Jack? How about your fatherly duty... by getting off your arse and going out to look for him... Or going to the other end, to meet him..." Jack couldn't help but notice the sarcastic sneer in Martha's hard voice. This wasn't the woman he'd known for nearly twenty-seven years; she'd never been hostile towards him before, even when they'd had the occasional spat, certainly never to this degree. Before Jack could say any more, Martha demanded, "And just when are you planning to join in the search for Billy?"

With as much patience as he could muster, Jack said, "As soon as I've finished what I'm doing here which should be very soon... God willing!"

Martha exploded, "And what's so important you can't let someone else do it? It's your son we're talking about, for Christ's sake, not some itinerant... I can't believe you sometimes, you selfish bastard!" With that the phone went dead. Jack tried calling back but got Martha's answerphone. He sat on Billy's bed, smarting from the brutal finality of Martha's parting shot. His head hung down. His eyes started to tingle and he felt a lump rising in his throat which made him catch his breath but then his demeanour hardened and in a cold, unemotional voice, Jack said bitterly, "Fuck you, lady!" and went to their bathroom.

Jack stood on the bathmat, towelling his hair dry. He felt so much better, having brushed his teeth and gargled with a refreshingly-sharp mouthwash, then soaked under the shower. As he'd washed himself down under the hot jets, he kept replaying a mental recording of his conversation with Martha. He couldn't get the bitter invective of her last attack out of his mind and, as he played it over and over, it reinforced his resentment. It hadn't abated, even when he'd turned the shower down to cold and a thousand stinging needles had pierced his shoulders and back. He had stood there, brooding over Martha's treatment of him, until he'd begun to feel chilly then he'd stood there some more, trying to put a lid on the anarchy fomenting in his heart. Suddenly, he'd shouted "Bitch!" The explosion had alleviated some of the pent-up hurt and anger but the sudden expulsion of all that emotional energy had left his heart a few degrees colder. Jack had turned off the shower and stepped out onto the bathmat, pulling one of the luxuriously soft, white towels down off the towelrail and briskly rubbed it, yoke-fashion, across his broad, muscular shoulders.

As he was tousling his hair dry using both hands, Jack looked up and saw Margaret standing in the doorway. She was wearing Martha's white silk robe which she'd wrapped modestly around herself. Her left hand held one side of it across her front whilst her right hand held the other side closed. She stood, feet together with her head slightly to one side and her dark hair tumbling over one shoulder, looking at Jack. Jack's head had snapped up with the shock of seeing her there; until now, he'd assumed he was alone in the house. He abruptly halted what he was doing and stood frozen until he realised how coolly Margaret was regarding him. He quickly recovered from the initial shock and stared back at Margaret, meeting her steady gaze. As he relaxed, he lowered his arms then draped his towel around his neck and held the ends of it, his fists loosely clenched against his chest. The two of them stood like that without saying a word, the only contact between them being through their eyes, until Margaret slowly lowered her arms down to her sides and let the front of the robe fall open revealing her large, pendulous breasts, their smooth, rose pink nipples peeping coyly around the edges of the lapels, the gentle curve of her belly with a small, gold stud in her navel and the generous mound at the top of her thighs adorned with the narrow, dark stripe of her neatly trimmed pubic hair.

Chapter 6

(Wednesday 4 August 2010, late evening Eastern time)

"Reza, please, be reasonable. I told you when we arranged this vacation that I could be called away on urgent business. You can't say I didn't warn you... And Haroun and Seeti are some of our oldest friends in America. They're happy for you and the children to stay here while I'm away... and Mama, of course... They'll look after you 'til I get back... "

Reza wasn't going to be beaten without a fight. "Yes, Manni but why can't you delegate whatever it is you have to do? There's Mrs Bilhal... and that over-paid manager. Let him earn his corn for a change. You carry him. In the name of all that's holy, you carry them all. You deserve a break... And we haven't seen you for two months. God knows! Your mother hasn't seen you for nearly ten years... She won't always be with us, you know..." she chided then, more softly, "Don't we deserve to have you with us? Surely it's not asking too much, is it, my Bedouin prince?" she finished coyly.

Mansour Al Rashid said dictatorially, "I have to go, Reza. That's final! End of discussion!" but he disliked speaking to his wife so dismissively.

Reza Al Rashid leaned against the pillow hugging her long, slender legs to her chest, her smooth olive skin contrasting with the crisp, white bed linen. Her graceful neck dipped forward and her head rested on her knees, her dark, silky, flowing hair falling round her face, hiding it from her husband's gaze. She knew it would be no use getting cross but it didn't stop her from feeling utterly dejected. Gently, he cajoled her out of her sulk. "Look... all being well, my business should be concluded in a few days and I should be able to get back to spend some time with you... I miss you so when we're apart... You are my sun and moon, the soft desert wind that blows through the palace of my heart... Your love lights up my life. Its radiance shines on me and warms me to the very essence of my being..." He knelt in front of her speaking heartfelt words of devotion, tenderly kissing the top of her head and breathing in the delicate scent of her lustrous hair between each proclamation of his undying love for her. And he meant it sincerely; Mansour Al Rashid worshipped his beautiful wife above all other earthly creatures. In time, she turned her face up to him, her deep, dark eyes looking directly into his. She put a hand on the back of his neck and eased his head down until their lips met. Their kiss was delicate, as soft as the touch of a butterfly's wings and it lingered until Reza heard her husband's breathing quicken almost imperceptibly. She eased herself up, slipping her feet beneath her shapely bottom and knelt facing him. They remained like that, looking wondrously into each other's eyes, until he slowly reached out and lightly cupped one of her small, firm breasts in his powerful hand. He tenderly lifted it and kissed all

126

round the dark brown areola, his lips softly gliding over her flawless skin, then flicked his tongue lightly over the beautiful, conical nipple and gently sucked on it until it swelled into a turgid mound. He then transferred his attention to her other breast but continued caressing the first between finger and thumb so that it remained pert and aroused. All the while Reza stroked his chest, gently tweaking his nipples until they were likewise erect. As she sensed her husband's desire for her reaching its first peak, she leaned forward until their bodies touched and felt his great, thick erection firmly pressed into her belly. Their lips came together and this time their kiss was hotter and more passionate, exploring each other's mouths with probing tongues until she yearned to have him inside her.

They lay recovering from their exertions. He eased himself out of her, still erect but spent. She rolled onto her side and curled into a ball and he tucked himself behind her and wrapped his body protectively around hers, putting his arm over her and pulling her to him. He breathed in her body's delicate natural odour, heightened by the heat of their passion, mingled with the subtle, lingering aroma of her perfumed bath oil.

Their lovemaking had built steadily to a crescendo which culminated in a wracking orgasm that exploded deep in her loins, releasing a flood of powerful, confused emotions that left her feeling drained and completely overwhelmed. The tears streamed silently down her cheek and onto the pillow.

Mansour leaned over to kiss his wife. He gently turned her head and was surprised to find that she was crying. The tears welled up in the corners of her eyes. He was about to ask her what was wrong but she reached out and hugged him around his neck, pulling him down so that his face was next to hers. She clung to him tightly. It was impossible to ask her anything in this position, so he waited until her grip relaxed a little. "Reza, my darling, what's wrong?" When there was no reply, he said, "I don't understand. I thought you were happy... *we were happy*... I know you're disappointed that I have to leave you but... *in sa' Allah*... it'll only be for a few days, my princess... my flower of the desert... then I'll come and carry you off on my Arabian stallion, back to my tent where we will make love again and again until the Earth and Moon have passed away and the Sun and stars shine no more..." He realised his coaxing was having very little effect in lifting her out of her depression, so he asked more urgently, "Reza, what's wrong?"

"I... I don't know, Manni... Since I got back, when we've made love you've been very quiet... very intense... almost as though you thought it would be our last time together..."

Mansour Al Rashid held his beloved wife close and whispered, "Hush, Reza, mother of my children. I love you... I will *always* love you. Never doubt that..." Reza Al Rashid didn't; she had never been more sure of

127

anything than her husband's love for her but his earnest assurances did nothing to dispel the dull feeling of dread that had come to dwell in the deepest recesses of her heart. He slipped an arm under his wife's pillow, supporting her head and tucked himself behind her again. He put his other arm under hers and gently stroked and toyed with the soft flesh of her belly and breasts. Within a few minutes he had fallen asleep. She lay awake, listening to his shallow breathing and to the sounds of the night that came in through the open windows, until the cool night air gently nipped at her bare extremeties. Without disturbing him, she reached down and pulled the sheet over them both and, within minutes, fell into a fitful and uneasy sleep.

As the Sun's first rays pierced the darkness, Mansour Al Rashid unwound himself from around his sleeping wife and rolled over as gently as he could, trying not to disturb her, then swung his feet out of bed and stood up without a sound. He dressed and, before leaving the bedroom, leaned over and kissed his wife on the temple. He tiptoed out. On his way along the landing he called in on his two children, little girls of six and nine. Sharnia, the younger of the two, was lying on her back with both arms above the sheet and her hands on the pillow beside her head, fists clenched, looking like a little cherub. He bent down and kissed her lightly on the forehead, on each closed eyelid, then on the end of her button nose and, finally, on her open lips. He faintly caught the sweet scent of her breath. He pulled up the sheet slightly until it was under her chin and gently stroked her cheek, then went and stood over Shazea who lay on her side. Her dark hair tumbled over her shoulder and lay thickly scattered on the pillow and counterpane. As he was about to lean forward to kiss her she turned her head, opened her eyes and looked sleepily up at him. She yawned and started to ask him where he was going but he gently put his finger to her lips and softly shushed her. He sat on the edge of the bed stroking her hair until she fell asleep again.

Down at the boathouse, Haroun Hazami was finishing the preparations for putting out to sea. As Mansour Al Rashid appeared, he barked the final instructions to his younger brother, Zubin, then greeted his guest. "Good morning, my friend. She's all ready to go. The modifications have been completed and quicker than we've ever managed in rehearsals... She's been re-fuelled, the fresh water tanks are full and we've re-stocked the larder and drinks cabinet. The tide's running with you, so you should make good time for your pick-up in Hampton..." Mansour Al Rashid straddled the small gap and stepped onto the deck. The two men embraced and his host said quietly, "Allah go with you, brother. May He watch over you and guide your hand in everything you do." The two brothers hopped down on to the dock. One untied the lines holding the boat whilst the other opened the boathouse doors.

A thin veil of mist hung over the water as Mansour Al Rashid started the engines, then slipped the moorings and headed out into the channel.

—•—

(Thursday 5 August 2010, late evening Eastern time)

"Mr Davies! Good evening, Sir. Agent D'Angelo speaking, SAC Norfolk field office... Yes, Sir. We've just received reports from our watchers on Cape Henry and on Fisherman's Island on the Eastern Shore Peninsula as well as those overlooking the four navigation channels of the Chesapeake Bay Bridge. There's been lots of yachts sailing in and out, all day, as you'd expect at this time of year but only three cruisers going out of the Bay into the Ocean, none of which fits your description... Yes, Sir. There was 'Blythe Spirit' out of Portsmouth, owned by a holiday rental company... We've contacted the owners and they confirm she's currently being rented out to a family... the Morrisons... from Trenton, New Jersey. We're checking them out now... Then there was the 'Pride of Maryland', registered to one Luis Ruiz DaCosta, which is normally berthed at the Susquehanna Boat Club marina up in Havre de Grace... We've been unable to contact anyone there. The club secretary's vacationing somewhere down in the Keys. We haven't been able to contact him yet... and we're still trying to get hold of the Commodore. He's out in the Bay on his yacht... Anyway, both boats turned south towards Cape Hatteras and the Outer Banks of North Carolina... And finally there was the 'Maine Lassie', down from Kennebunkport... a real classy joint... She's headed north. Looks like they're homeward bound. We're still waiting for the report from our Boston field office about her owners... But no sighting of the 'Nesmat al-Rabiya'... No... No, Sir. I'm sorry... Yes, of course we'll keep our eyes skinned for her... Yes, I'm e-mailing my report to you now with photos of the three craft... I'll let you know immediately we have any news..." Alan Davies put his phone down. His head sank into his hands and he clutched his temples. What the hell was he going to tell the President?

His computer gave a little beep telling him he had mail. Alan Davies opened it and saw that it was the report from Special Agent D'Angelo in Virginia. He read the brief report then opened the first attachment. It showed a handsome, pale blue and white cabin cruiser with two young girls wearing bright orange life vests over yellow swimsuits leaning over the bow rail, looking down at the bow wave and a tall, slim woman with long, fair hair, presumably their mother, standing behind them anxiously holding onto their waist straps. He could just make out the name 'Blythe Spirit' on the hull beneath where the trio were unwittingly posing, oblivious to the fact that they had walk-on parts in the biggest security operation ever mounted in US history. Alan Davies quickly glanced at the photograph of Nesmat al-Rabiya. It was immediately obvious this was not it. He opened the second attachment and was immediately surprised. The 'Pride of Maryland' was nowhere near as pretty as he'd expected her to be. With a name like that he'd expected a real beauty queen with eye-catching proportions and sleek lines. Instead, the fire engine red superstructure looked cumbersome and ungainly and the bright green awning over the bridge was garish and unattractive. The whole thing looked discordant and clashed with his idea of what maritime elegance should be. And how unsightly those ugly, orange plastic floats looked, which some sailors hung along the sides of their boat to act as buffers so they could barge clumsily into the landing stage without damaging the hull rather than approaching it carefully and avoiding a collision in the first place. He looked a little closer and examined the busty peroxide blonde lying topless on the foredeck, then at the well tanned man on the bridge sporting a large, Pancho Villa mustache and wearing a loud beach shirt, a peaked Captain's cap and mirrored sunglasses. He said to himself, 'I bet those are silicone jobs. If they're not ersatz, I'm a Chinaman... Flashy Spic! There's a drug dealer if ever I saw one... Still, your luck's in today. We're trawling for bigger fish. I'll toss you back and save you for another day but your card's well and truly marked. I won't forget you in a hurry, Luis Ruiz DaCosta...' then promptly forgot him as he opened the third attachment. Alan Davies let out a long, low whistle. 'Now there's a floating gin palace worthy of a prince...'

—•—

(Friday 6 August 2010, about 08.10 Eastern time)

"You've done what, Mr Davies?" roared the President.

"We've lost Al Rashid, Sir..." and then added hastily, "Only temporarily, I assure you but I'm afraid to say he's given us the slip..."

"How in God's name did you manage to lose a forty foot cabin cruiser in open water? And, more importantly, what are you doing to find it again?"

"Well, Sir, it wasn't exactly open water... On Wednesday morning, they called in at Cape Charles on the Eastern Shore, to refuel, then headed across the sound towards Poquoson. We had a flotilla of boats shadowing them at a discrete distance, keeping visual and radar contact with them at all times. However, it became more difficult when they got close to land, what with all those other boats... Then a squall blew up. It'd been threatening all day. It only lasted about half an hour but by the time it'd blown itself out we'd lost contact. First both tracking devices went down then the satellite beacon. It may have been the lightning or they may have found the devices and tossed them overboard under cover of the storm. We don't know... Because of the

130

choppy water, we lost visual contact from sea level and the cloud obscured the view from the satellite overhead. Talk about 'luck of the Devil'. We had no idea where they were going, of course, so we assumed it was into the marina for safe haven..."

The President cut in, "But it wasn't..."

"No Sir..."

"There you go again, Mr Davies... Assuming too much... I warned you about that, didn't I?"

"Yes Sir... Anyway..." Alan Davies continued manfully, "...we had a dozen agents there as a reception committee but they never showed. There are lots of little inlets and side channels down the York River... and lots of private boathouses. They could easily have slipped into any one of those... We've called up helicopter and satellite surveillance... I've also instructed the local agents to search every pier pontoon and jetty, every inch of riverbank and every tributary for ten miles either side of Poquoson. We're doing everything we can but so far we've found nothing..."

"Well, Mr Davies, it doesn't look as though your best is anywhere near good enough, does it? So I suggest you try harder... Much harder!"

When Alan Davies and the other members of the NSC had left, the President turned to his adviser and said angrily, "I don't believe it, George! It looks like those bastards could slip the net after all... then 'Poof'! My presidency's finished... Just like that!" He shrugged his shoulders and threw up his hands, spreading his fingers wide, like a magician tossing the contents of his empty hands into the air in an act of sleight during a conjuring trick. The President sat glowering, clearly fulminating about the situation.

George Horowitz reflected on how much more difficult and agitated he was becoming with each day that passed, which had sharpened his temper but blunted his judgement. 'Still...' he thought, '...since we learned about the possibility of this latest terrorist threat... and Yellowstone... and S241... there's been no firm news one way or the other on any of them... Events are on the move. We all sense the end-game's fast approaching, whichever way the dice fall but until they do, we're in limbo waiting to see what happens... Now his physician's found a lump in his waterworks... Is it malignant? Is it benign? God knows! It's enough to test any man's mettle...' then, with an air of resignation, 'Well, we should know soon enough but in the meantime, it's enough to drive the sanest person completely mad...'

—•—

The sing-song voice floated up from the cabin. "Luis... Oh Luis, honey... Momma wants some more of your big, brown Latino cock... And get me another Bacardi and Coke... More ice this time, lover... and more Bacardi..."

After a moment's hesitation, a rather distracted reply came back, "In a momenteeto, my leetle chihuahua... I am just... er... leesning to de weather reeport on de raydeeo... Dere's a storm beelding and eet's headed towards de Caribbean... I wanna make sure eet ees'n coming our way..."

"Well hurry on down here, you sexy Mexxy cur or Momma'll hafta whup your ass like the naughty little puppy you are..." When Luis DaCosta still hadn't reappeared after a couple more minutes, the whining voice came again, a little less playful this time, a little more grating and impatient, "Come on Luis. Hurry up! I'm gett'n awful dry... at both ends..."

Mansour Al Rashid looked up from the radio. He said to himself, 'God! How I despise that vile bitch... Filthy, depraved American whore!' but his thoughts were interrupted by the brief message in an obscure Farsi dialect. "The wrath of Allah is upon the Infidels..." He looked at his watch then checked the GPS. Having satisfied himself there was still at least another hour before he needed to set off for the rendezvous, he calmly poured another couple of drinks and went down to the cabin.

As he took the last step down into the cabin, the boat rolled slightly with the gentle swell. He swayed with the motion but the ice clinked against the glasses. The woman raised her head and looked up, her little, piggy eyes staring up at him from her fat face, then sat up a little unsteadily and swung her legs over the edge of the couch. "Come on big boy... Come to Momma..." She reached out for one of the tall glasses and greedily emptied it, tiny rivulets spilling over the rim at the corners of her mouth, running down her chin and dripping onto her naked bosom. Her breasts sagged onto her paunchy belly which rested on her stout thighs and hid her unkempt, mousey pubic triangle from view. The taut rolls of fat on her midriff glowed livid red from too much sun. Mansour Al Rashid stood naked in front of the woman as she drank, looking down on the top of her head with its lifeless, brittle, straw yellow, permed hair which showed dark at the roots, trying not to give the woman any indication of his loathing for her. When she'd drained the first glass, he let her take the second from him without protest and she finished that one too. Looking up into his stern face she said, with a hint of a sneer in her slurred voice, "Don't think I don't know what you're trying to do, you wicked Mexicano. You're trying to get me drunk so you can take advantage of me, aren't you? Well it might work with your other women but not with me. Oh no! I'm wise to your little game..." and she broke into a raucous cackle of coarse laughter.

Suddenly, the woman pitched forward. The tall, swarthy man thought she was going to be sick and was about to jump back but she reached around his hips and, clasping his muscular buttocks with both hands, pulled him towards her. His long, thick penis hung in a great curving arc in front of her face. She took it in her mouth. As she worked her tongue over it, she felt the powerful muscles in his backside begin to tense. As it thickened and grew she gradually extended the action of her tongue, rolling her mouth round his swollen organ until it almost touched the back of her throat. When he was fully erect, the woman removed it from her mouth and, holding it upright, stroked the flat of her tongue up the length of his rigid shaft. She did this repeatedly, each time leaving a thin film of saliva on the shaft and over the engorged dome. She could sense his urgency increasing, the tension in his loins mounting. She dropped one hand from around his hips and probed her own vagina, making her juices flow. He savagely grabbed a fistful of dry, damaged hair at the back of her head and forced her mouth down further over his aching shaft which pressed against her tonsils, nearly making her heave. She fought back the urge to retch, knowing she would soon be handsomely rewarded for her brief moment of discomfort. She continued working hard on them both until eventually he relaxed his grip and, moaning with anticipation, ran his fingers through her hair. She knew he was ready to enter her.

With her mouth enveloping the end of his penis, the woman glanced up to see Mansour Al Rashid looking down on her upturned face. His eyes blazed with disgust and detestation which she mistakenly took for lust. He grabbed her roughly under both arms and hauled her up off the seat then spun her round and, putting one hand behind her neck, bent her over. Lurching forward under his weight, she found herself kneeling on the cushion of the well-padded couch, her forearms resting on the seatback. Her shins stung where she'd grazed them on the edge of the couch. She was about to protest that he didn't need to be so rough when she felt his powerful hands on her generous hips, his thumbs digging hard into her plump, well-upholstered buttocks, savagely spreading them apart. Her pouting labia gaped wide open. He guided his stiff penis between her lips then, when he'd found the opening, thrust it brutally into her. Unlike previous occasions when he'd started gently and savoured the moment, lingering to get the full sensation, then taken long slow strokes, gradually working up to a frenzied climax that could take thirty or forty minutes to achieve, this time he drove hard into her so that his loins slapped loudly against her bottom then he drew back and hammered into her again and again. At first, she enjoyed the aggressive intercourse, pushing herself back to meet his powerful thrusts so that the bruising blows excited her and made her beg for more. "Go on... Fuck me! HARD you big bastard! HARDER!

HARDER! HARDER!" The rythmic grinding went on until sweat poured off them both, running over his chest and belly and down his sturdy thighs and a little puddle collected in the dip in her back. He'd been gasping but now he'd found his second wind the new release of energy fuelled his vigor. The intense throbbing in his penis had subsided and with it his urgent desire to ejaculate as his shaft hardened and swelled further. She had been gulping in air, fanning the flames of her orgasm, the tremors spreading through her womb and into her pelvis. She had become so aroused that she momentarily suspended breathing and the hypoxia brought on by the interruption of oxygen to her brain only served to heighten the wild sensation. She felt as though the top of her head would burst. "Gag me! Gag me! Go on... get the rope and gag me... I wanna come som'ore... GAG ME!" He reached over for the soft, white silk halter they used for auto-erotic stimulation and looped it round her neck then pulled gently on the ends. He picked up the pace again and brought her to the point of orgasm once more. As she groaned, he felt her begin to quiver with excitement and pulled on the rope until it tightened round her neck, taking up whatever slack there had been. The thrill as he hammered into her from behind drove him on and she responded by urging him on harder and faster. "Go on... Fuck me! Fuck me! FUCK ME!" As she reached climax again, he started to apply pressure by pulling the reins tighter. He could feel the tension of the prolonged orgasm spread throughout the whole of her body, making it stiffen and shudder. He continued pounding into her, his large, powerful hands gripping the rope and his muscular arms pulling it ever tighter.

She'd often felt heady before and had even heard those tell-tale popping sounds in her ears but she'd never known the hallucinations or the starburst-filled blackness that she was now experiencing. From somewhere far off she heard a tiny voice in her head urgently whispering, 'Be afraid!' but it was too late. Her face had swollen and become puce and the veins in her neck and over her temples stood out like knotted cords. She clawed at the ligature but it cut too deeply into the soft flesh around her throat for her to get her fingers behind it. In an instant, she was overwhelmed with panic and swung her arms round wildly, trying to lash out at the monster on her back but in her weakened state she couldn't keep it up for long and, irrespective of that, it made absolutely no impression on Mansour Al Rashid; he continued hammering into her whilst he drew the rope ever tighter. As terror suffused her last conscious thoughts a stream of hot, acrid urine gushed out and ran down her legs, soaking into the cushion and spilling over into a pool on the floor; and still he continued unabated. As the last pulse of life slipped away, her body slumped forward from the waist and as a result of the sudden pressure it put on her bowels, she evacuated a jet of liquid faeces that spattered Mansour Al Rashid's belly but he took no notice of it. He was on the verge of exploding and kept pounding away, intoxicated by the exquisitely painful stinging sensations shooting through his inflamed penis, working himself up to the moment of frenzy. As he felt the explosive rush of fluid up his penis, the mighty blood vessels in his neck distended, his head went back and he bellowed like an injured bull. "Aaaaarrrrgghh… Aaaarrrgghh… Aaarrgh… Argh… Argh… Argh…" as he pumped his semen into the woman's vagina. The violence of his orgasm caused him such exquisite agony that for some minutes after he felt as though his guts had been ripped out. For her, it was too late to register any sensation; the life had already left her body. He stood behind her as the last few milky droplets oozed out of him, light-headed, exhausted, weak, shaky, leaning on her rump unable to move, the orgasm having robbed him of all his strength and coordination. His mouth gaped cavernously and his chest pumped up and down at a furious rate, sucking in huge quantities of air to replenish his oxygen-starved system, the sweat pouring off him, his leg muscles quivering with the exertion, until at last his flaccid penis slipped out of her and he staggered sideways and collapsed in a heap on the floor. He lay like that for some minutes, recovering, until he became properly aware of the noisome stench of the excrement that spattered his lower abdomen. Feeling no revulsion for her now but likewise feeling no pity either, he slowly rolled over and stood up, then eased her body from its kneeling position so that it lay recumbent. He examined the dead woman's tortured face, frozen in a ghastly rictus, the bulging eyes staring up at him accusingly and noticed that the whites of her eyes were shot with red where dozens of tiny blood vessels had ruptured under the awful pressure.

Mansour Al Rashid checked his watch. There was still plenty of time. He lifted the body under its flabby arms and hauled it off the couch, the heels landing with a dull thud on the floor, then dragged it through the cabin and up the stairs, laying it out unceremoniously on the afterdeck. He returned to the cabin and hinged up the lid of the locker under the couch on which he'd killed her and took out a fifty pound weight. He unwound the rope from around her neck and used it to bind the ankles of the corpse tightly together, then tied the other end of the rope securely round the handle of the half-hundredweight. With a little difficulty he lifted the dead weight of the woman's corpulent body over the stern and dropped it onto the transom, then reached for the iron weight and heaved it into the ocean. The rope went taut as it dragged her legs then her torso off the platform. As it slid into the water, it caused very little disturbance save for a few ripples. Mansour Al Rashid watched as it slipped into the murky depths, the hair streaming out behind in the turbulent wake and the arms flailing as though they were frantically waving goodbye. She had served her purpose.

Mansour Al Rashid dived off the side of the boat and swam out a little way, then idly trod water whilst he washed himself clean of the mess before swimming back to the boat and climbing up the stern ladder. He took one last backward glance to make sure he'd left no obvious signs that might give some clue as to the sinister deed that had taken place on the surface or what lurked down below in the darkness and noticed that a small shoal of fish had already gathered to enjoy the unexpected feast. He briskly dried himself and got dressed then went to the bow and weighed anchor. Back on the bridge, he pressed the starter button and heard the muffled roar as the big marine diesel engines leapt into life. He briefly consulted the GPS, set the compass then gradually opened the throttles and headed out to sea.

—•—

(Sunday 8 August 2010, early evening Eastern time / 27 Sha'baan 1431AH)

Alan Davies sat at his desk, clutching his head in his hands. Agent D'Angelo had just reported that, for the fourth day in a row, there'd been no sighting of 'Nesmat al-Rabiya'.

'Slippery bastard! Where is he? We've scoured every inch of coast from Cape Henry to Deltaville and both banks of the York and James rivers and every island, inlet and tributary in between and still nothing…' He seethed with indignation. He'd wasted the thick end of half a day attending a pointless meeting with the President to tell him… What? He couldn't give the President the reassurance he was looking for but he could have told him that over the phone had the Head of Homeland Security not insisted that he, Alan Davies, Head of the FBI's Counter-Terrorism Unit, attend to account personally for their failure to maintain contact with the suspected terrorists, purely so that it took some of the heat off her: Mrs Niara Marshall, Head of the Department of Homeland Security and career politician. Surely his time was better spent here, organising the search for the terrorists, than there at the White House shoring up the President's insecurity? And it was bad enough being carpeted by him but being taken to task by that jumped-up bitch was almost more than he could stomach. As he began to calm down, he remonstrated with himself, 'Maybe the President was right… How could we lose a forty foot cabin cruiser in open water? He must think we're a bunch of dummies… So where the hell can he have gotten to?' He continued turning over the same question in his mind, agonising over how Mansour Al Rashid could have disappeared so completely. 'Was the President right? Are we chasing the wrong man? Jesus Christ! Now I'm starting to doubt my own judgement… I've never been so spectacularly wrong before…' He opened up his e-mail account and scanned Agent D'Angelo's latest report. It was brief, to the point and totally devoid of anything that might bring him any comfort. He opened the attached images and briefly admired the graceful lines of the 'Queen of the South', an elegant

136

boat out of Newport News. 'Christ, they must be well breached to afford a beauty like that...' he thought to himself, a little enviously. 'I'd rather be sailing on her, oblivious to all this shit than stuck here drowning in it... For that matter, I'd rather be pretty much anywhere else than here...' then, after a moment's reflection, 'And if that bastard does evade us and gets through, my wish may be granted...' He continued browsing the attachments, showing cruisers coming into the Bay and going out into the Ocean. His attention was arrested momentarily when he pulled up an image of the 'Pride of Maryland' and he said to himself, 'There's the ugly old tub again, making her way home. I'll bet they've had a wonderful time fishing and screwing and Lord knows what... Speaking of ugly old tubs, where's Miss Silicone Tits?' then unjustly, 'Probably down below snorting a line of coke, at a guess... And there's old Pancho at the helm... I still haven't forgotten you...' He continued staring at the boat for a while. There was something unusual about it, something that puzzled him but he couldn't cotton on to what it was. He gently massaged the lids of his weary eyes and took another look. Eventually, he gave up and moved on and finished looking through the remainder of the photographs but none of them offered the faintest glimmer of hope. He sat gnawing at the problem or, more accurately, it gnawed at him. Suddenly, he said to himself, 'I wonder if it's been under our noses all the time and we haven't seen it? Could he have changed its silhouette? But how long might that take? Could it be in a boatyard even now undergoing a refit? No, probably not... Not if he intends to rendezvous with a ship this side of Ramadan, assuming that's what he's actually doing... No, if that's what he's done, he must have had it all in place... And if so, he must have had somewhere private to do it... and probably someone to help him... someone other than his wife...' His head started whirling with all the possibilities. 'Steady as she goes, Davies. Focus! Maybe the answer's here but you haven't seen it yet...' Alan Davies went back to Agent D'Angelo's first report and re-read it thoroughly then studied the photographs again. He progressed through Friday's and Saturday's reports. There was Mrs Morrison, from Trenton, New Jersey, looking far more relaxed as her daughters sat playing quietly in the well of the afterdeck. Maybe the novelty of being at sea had worn off and they'd got fed up with being cooped up in such a restrictive space so they'd stopped running around on the upper deck scaring the living daylights out of their mother. Or maybe they'd had a touch of seasickness from the ocean's swell which had taken some of the wind out of their sails. Whichever it was, Mom now looked as though she was really enjoying her vacation. He opened Sunday's report and continued reading. They were still waiting for the report on Luis Ruiz DaCosta; the Commodore of the boatclub was expected back this evening and an agent was waiting to interview him on his return. At that instant, the phone rang and Alan Davies picked up the handset distractedly and grunted into it "Davies".

Agent D'Angelo's deep, gruff voice boomed out, "Sir, just to let you know the Commodore of the Susquehanna Boat Club has returned and our man will be talking to him about DaCosta shortly. I'll report back to you as soon as we have something... But I wanted to let you know that most of our enquiries about DaCosta are leading us up blind alleys... We've been to his house... Nothing! It's fairly squalid. In fact, it looks more like a squat. The neighbours can't tell us anything because they see virtually nothing of him. He's seldom there. We've been on to the IRS and other Federal and state authorities... There's no record of him... It looks very suspicious to me. I think we need to put this guy under fairly close scrutiny... He could be a terrorist... a drug dealer... an arms smuggler... you name it... but whatever he does for his money, he's not paying his taxes on it so I'll lay you odds he's up to no good..."

Alan Davies snapped back, "Focus on DaCosta. We need to know all about him... We have no other viable leads so let's put all our weight behind this one. Okay?"

"Yes Sir"

"And see whether we can tie DaCosta to Al Rashid."

"Yes Sir"

This was a faint chink of light at the end of a long, dark tunnel. It was the first he'd seen and instinct told him he should go towards it. Alan Davies copied the photograph of the 'Pride of Maryland' from Thursday's report and pasted it alongside today's image and compared the two. The obvious differences struck him immediately. In the first, the 'Pride of Maryland' was headed east out into the Atlantic with the late afternoon sun coming from above and behind; in the second it was headed west under the Chesapeake Bay Bridge with the early morning sun coming in from the rear at a fairly low angle. In the first there was a blonde floozy toasting her buns on the upper deck; in the second, there wasn't. 'She's probably down below, totally out of it...' he thought to himself, not realising – taken literally – how close he'd come to the truth. 'There's Pancho, sporting sunglasses and that ridiculous peaked cap... and in this one he's not...' He continued contrasting the two images, building up a mental list of all the differences. 'Strange!' He looked again at the two images to make sure he'd got them the correct way round and then peered more closely. 'Surely that can't be right... She's riding lower in the water on the way home than she was on the way out... Can't be! It must be a trick of the eye... She must have used, I'd guess... what... six... maybe eight hundred pounds of fuel and water... and she's riding what... six inches lower in the water...' He checked that the images were of the same side of the boat and they were. In the first image, the orange floats along the side of the craft were a few inches above the water, whereas in the second image the very ends of one or two of the floats just dragged in the water. He did a quick guesstimate of the total plan area of the boat at the waterline and worked out the additional volume of water it displaced. 'Allowing for the loss in weight of fuel and so on, it must be a good three-and-a-quarter... maybe three-and-a-half tons heavier... It can't be! How in God's name can it have gained so much weight... It can't be drugs... The DEA would surely have known about a shipment of that size and we'd already have been informed of it long before now... And surely it couldn't be a bomb... *our bomb*... the one we've been waiting for... If it was, at three-and-a-half tons it'd be massive!' he thought incredulously. 'And it'd probably go through the bottom of the boat...' Then he remembered about the reinforcement of Nesmat al-Rabiya's hull and the need for heavily shielding such a bomb to avoid detection. A cold, sinking feeling began to settle in the pit of his stomach and his mouth and throat went dry. He peered anxiously again at the superstructure of the boat. He magnified the image and continued enlarging it until it started losing definition, then backed it off slightly until the image became crisp again and studied it carefully. His mind was racing madly ahead, one thought tripping over another. 'What's that faint white line? Is it a crack? No... It's too straight, too regular... Yes, that's it... a joint... a joint between two bright red fibreglass mouldings... No wonder we couldn't find the 'Nesmat al-Rabiya'... They've disguised it!' He framed the face of Luis Ruiz DaCosta on his monitor screen and blew it up as large as it would go whilst still appearing recognisably human. Looking more closely at the blurry lifesize image of the three-quarter view, he held up Mansour Al Rashid's photograph alongside and turned it away from him slightly, trying to imagine it seen from the same angle. There were definitely some striking similarities. He digitally removed the mustache and hair and gave Luis DaCosta Mansour Al Rashid's bald crown and temples and a grade one cut around the back and sides of his head and the likeness became even more alarming. The awful realisation of what that implied hit him like a thunderbolt. Thinking of the bomb, he said in a low voice, "Oh my God! It must be here..."

Alan Davies looked at his watch then checked the time of today's sighting. 'Christ, he has nearly ten hours start on us...' He reached down and pulled an atlas out of his drawer and opened it on the pages for Virginia and West Virginia. 'Assuming a maximum cruising speed of, say, twenty knots, that could put him anywhere... *literally anywhere*... in the Chesapeake Bay region... or up the James... the York... the Rappahannock... the Potomac... or Patuxent rivers... or even the Susquehanna come to that... At a push, he could even be in DC by now... bang in the heart of the nation.' He picked up the phone and called the Special Agents in charge of the FBI's Virginia, Maryland and Washington offices, getting all of them on a conference call. He briefly related to them his suspicions about Mansour Al Rashid and 'Nesmat al-Rabiya' and told them to mobilise all available agents in the search for their alter egos. He then called Niara Marshall, Head of Homeland Security, who confirmed that she would mobilise all the other agencies then inform the President but he warned her to be cautious in what she told him at this stage; there was a remote possibility that this whole thing could turn out to be a bizarre coincidence and an unfortunate set of assumptions on his part. He didn't want to lose any more face with the President than he had already.

Immediately he put his phone down, it rang again. Feeling good now that he had a real target to lock on to, he picked it up and answered it with renewed vigor. "Davies here!" he announced confidently.

Without preamble, Agent D'Angelo said, "We've had some interesting news from the agent who was waiting at the Susquehanna Boat Club to interview the Commodore... He's done that, by the way. I'll come back to that in a minute... When you suggested there might be a connection between Al Rashid and DaCosta, Agent Costello contacted the Annapolis Boat Club and got them to fax him a copy of Nesmat al-Rabiya's log, which he compared with Pride of Maryland's log. More often than not, when 'Nesmat al-Rabiya' was logged out of Annapolis, 'Pride of Maryland' was logged in at Susquehanna and vice versa... Occasionally, they were both logged out together... But here's the rub... They were *never* logged in at both places at the same time..." Alberio D'Angelo finished triumphantly, leaving the obvious conclusion to be drawn by his superior, then couldn't resist adding, "Of course, they wouldn't be, not if they're one and the same craft!"

Alan Davies thought for a moment, then said, "Not exactly proof positive. It could be a coincidence... but somehow I don't think so." He sat pondering the probability of it being a coincidence but all his instincts told him otherwise. He suddenly realised he was wasting time indulging in pointless speculation, so he asked, "What did the Commodore at Susquehanna say?"

"Well, he wasn't very complimentary about DaCosta. When Agent Costello showed him the photographs, he confirmed they were of DaCosta and his boat but he didn't recognise the woman. His impression of DaCosta was of a fairly theatrical, larger-than-life character. He said he always wore those sunglasses and cap. The one time he removed it, briefly, was when he doffed his cap... to the Commodore's wife, of all people. Apparently, she thought he was wearing a wig... He described DaCosta as loud, flashy, oily, a sleazy womaniser... Apparently, he only comes to the Club occasionally and when he does, he's usually accompanied by a different woman... Generally fairly tarty sorts, from what I gathered... He was fairly sniffy about DaCosta... Said they only took him on to boost the Club's income when it was down on numbers but now it had recovered, they wouldn't be renewing his membership... One of his comments did make me think, however... He said there are a couple of fluent Spanish speakers in the Club. One's Mexican, the other's actually Spanish by birth. Apparently, they've both commented to the Commodore that DaCosta's Spanish is very crude… by that I mean basic… One even described it as 'pig Spanish'… Apparently, when one of them asked DaCosta whereabouts in Mexico he came from, he told them he was from a tiny, remote village in the mountains… no name, he was very evasive… then quickly changed the subject. Clearly not keen to discuss his background or be questioned about it by others… All that would be consistent with somebody speaking Spanish as a third or even a fourth language as the cover for a false identity…"

Alan Davies interrupted, "If DaCosta is actually Al Rashid, he's done a pretty good job of maintaining his primary cover as a naturalized American citizen… He's only recently come to our attention after eight years. Who knows how long he was lying dormant and how long he's been active so, in that respect, he's had a lot to contend with. It must be difficult for him to take on yet another identity and be that person convincingly. He must feel positively schizophrenic at times…" Alan Davies suddenly stopped himself, realising that he was starting to sympathise with his enemy and changed the subject abruptly. His innate ability to empathise with his quarry was one of his great strengths – to think himself into his adversary's mind and see the situation from his point of view – which was why he was so good at what he did and why so often his instinct was correct. It was another thing entirely to sympathise with them; that could lead to errors of judgement which, in extreme circumstances, could prove to be a fatal flaw in any agent's armour. "Anyway, less of that…" Alan Davies continued, "There's another angle we need to pursue…"

Agent D'Angelo stopped him short, "Sir! If I may, there's another thing you may be interested in… Agent Costello also consulted the visitors' book and guess who appeared at the Susquehanna a couple of months ago… Al Rashid and his wife, no less, in 'Nesmat al-Rabiya'… The Commodore doesn't remember anything special about the boat but he does remember them both and her in particular… She must have been very memorable because, apparently, he went into raptures over the wife… Said she was stunningly attractive… as handsome as a thoroughbred, I think was the expression Costello used… He said the husband was also very good looking, cultivated and urbane and very attentive to his wife. A complete contrast to DaCosta, in fact… Of course, 'Pride of Maryland' was logged out at the time… But if Al Rashid and DaCosta are in fact one and the same man, his cover must be good because the Commodore never linked the two…"

Alan Davies said, "Probably testing his cover which obviously worked… but he probably also used the wife as a foil to distract attention away from himself… Very clever. He's clearly no fool…" This brought Alan Davies

141

back to the final matter he wanted to discuss. "Okay... We know Al Rashid's family were with him when he left Cape Charles. Nobody saw them transfer to another boat so the chances are he dropped them off somewhere or possibly left them in the care of friends or, more likely, fellow conspirators... We need to find them, the wife in particular... I suspect she has no knowledge of any of this... I couldn't imagine her going along with this for one minute if she knew about the woman on his boat... She might be able to lead us to him... I want you to saturate the ground with agents looking for them, the waterfront in particular..." squinting at the map, "...starting with the stretch from Virginia Beach to Gloucester Point and up the York and James rivers. Broaden the search if you fail to find them in that area. I can only guess that Al Rashid's left them with fellow conspirators who are also close friends... because that's what I'd do if I was him... So I can't imagine they'll appear much in public. Their instructions will be to keep a low profile... On the other hand if the wife isn't in on it, I can't imagine she'll want to stay cooped up for long. After all, they're on vacation... And it may be awkward for the people she's staying with to insist that she doesn't go out... If she feels like a prisoner, she might become difficult..." Alan Davies went quiet for a moment. Agent D'Angelo knew that his boss was trying to convince himself that his hunches were correct because there was so much more riding on this than his career. After a while Alan Davies concluded, "Considering the evidence we've got so far, my guess is she'll be with friends somewhere on or near the water, somewhere she feels at home, in a fairly pleasant and relaxed environment... possibly somewhere Al Rashid could work on the boat unseen... Draft in help from other offices if you need to but find them!"

"Yes Sir!"

"Is there anything else, D'Angelo?"

"No, Sir... Well, possibly one other thing. Do you think it's worth pursuing the blonde on his boat?"

Alan Davies responded wearily, "I doubt it. My guess is she's at the bottom of the ocean. He'll have got rid of her before he rendezvoused with the ship. He wouldn't want her witnessing that... We don't have any decent photographs of her... no description... no means of identificiation... She'll just be one of his dizzy bimboes... faceless... anonymous... Wallpaper to draw peoples' eyes away from him so they don't look at him too closely... Even if she told anyone where she was going and who with, she's unlikely to be missed for a while... No, I think you can write her off. Pursuing her at this stage would probably be a waste of time, unless you trip over evidence of her that leads us to him whilst you're about your business... which is stopping Al Rashid... Dead! Is that understood?"

"Yes, Sir!"

—•—

142

Agent Alfredo Costello used his shirt cuff to wipe the small pane of glass in the window high up in the boathouse wall, then stood on tiptoe and stretched to his full height to peek through the patch he'd just cleaned. The glass inside was dusty and festooned with cobwebs, so his view wasn't much improved even though he'd just created another piece of laundry for his new wife. He'd already tried the main double doors that gave vehicle access at the end of the boathouse as well as the side door, both of which were locked. In the gloom, he could just make out the upper deck of a cruiser. It was too dark to make out its color but as he strained his eyes, he could just discern the name on the bow: 'Pride of Maryland'. Even though there had been no sign of life, he instinctively dropped down then unholstered his pistol and retreated a few paces so that the line of shrubs was at his back. As he took out his satellite cellphone and dialled his Supervisor at the Baltimore office, he surveyed the boathouse. It was relatively large for such a small property in such a remote location, built a couple of years previously by a wealthy boating enthusiast whose dreams of becoming a specialist boat restorer when he retired had promptly foundered when his furniture manufacturing business failed.

"Marston here! Is that you, Al?"

"Yes Sir"

"What have you got to report?"

"I've found the Maryland…"

"Good work. Whereabouts are you?"

"I'm down on the Delmarva Peninsula, near a tiny hamlet called Kentmore Park, in Kent County, Maryland… One of the members of the Susquehanna said he'd seen DaCosta's boat at the mouth of the Sassafras River on two or three occasions, so I thought I'd drive down and look around before I knocked off… Most of the effort's being concentrated on the other side of the Chesapeake, so I thought I'd check out this side… Thinking about it, it's the perfect place for Al Rashid to use for a quick identity change between Annapolis and Havre de Grace… And it's within an hour's drive of his home… Agent Temperanillo came down as well. He should also be off duty, too… He's been on forty-eight straight. Bob took the north bank and I took the south so we could cover the ground more quickly…"

Their Supervisor chipped in, "I saw he was hooked into the call. I thought he'd be with you… Are you there, Bob?"

Special Agent Roberto Temperanillo replied, "Yes, Chief. I'm on my way down there right now."

Agent Costello resumed, "Anyway, it's in a boatshed in a fairly remote spot. The inlet's called Turners Creek. He couldn't have chosen a quieter spot for his clandestine goings-on but in this case it's probably worked to our advantage… You know how everyone knows everyone else's business in these small communities…" As he talked, his Supervisor uploaded the coordinates of Al Costello's location from the GPS navigator built into his cellphone then alerted the forensics team which was airborne within five minutes. "I was directed here by one of the residents who'd heard that a stranger had leased the property about a year ago. He didn't know his name but he said he'd seen him once or twice in passing and described him as looking a bit like a gaucho… You know, large drooping mustache, dark swarthy skin and so on. I showed him DaCosta's photo. He thought it might be him. He couldn't be sure… But the same person also said he saw 'Gaucho' headed out of here this morning, about seven o'clock, driving a white truck. On the back was a large wooden crate. Assuming it is our man, the bomb's probably on the final leg of its journey and it's got a good three hours start on us…"

Al Costello listened in to one half of the conversation as his Supervisor briefed the Special Agent in charge of the Baltimore field office. When he'd finished, the Supervisor said, "Al… You still there?"

"Yes"

"Forensics will be with you in about eighteen minutes… twenty tops… But if you're right, every minute counts. We've put out an APB for the white truck and you'll need to get a detailed description from the yokel who saw it when you've finished there. The SAC wants you to gain entry to the boathouse and have a quick look around to see if you can give us an early heads-up as to what we should be looking for. Can you do that?"

"Yes… but what about Forensics? Won't they want a clean scene?"

"Al, we don't have much time. Use your judgement. If you think there's any danger or if you think you'll contaminate the scene too badly, don't enter… But any time you buy us now would be invaluable…" A little hesitantly, Alfredo Costello agreed to try. He heard the voice of his colleague, Bob Temperanillo, cut in through his earpiece, "Be careful, Al."

Al Costello retrieved his tools from the trunk of his car and used the bolt cropper to cut the padlock off the side door, then dropped it in an evidence bag. He opened the door cautiously, standing away from the aperture with his back to the wall, pistol at the ready and shone his torch inside. He briefly glanced around and described what he saw to his colleagues in a running commentary. "The boat's here… She's been properly tied up, suggesting they weren't in a great hurry… It's definitely the 'Pride of Maryland'. It matches the photos… The hatch cover on the forward deck's been removed altogether… There's a small electric hoist on an overhead runway which starts over the dock and finishes over the vehicle bay. The hoist itself and its control pendant are parked above the hardstanding, which suggests it was used to unload something from the boat and onto a vehicle… There are tire tracks in the dust that go out under the main doors. How old I can't say but half-a-dozen at least... and a few footprints... The winch has a capacity of... wait, I can't see the markings properly... er... five tons..." then, after a brief pause, "I'm going in..." Stepping gingerly through the door, Al Costello continued, "There doesn't appear to be anybody here... Jesus! What's that?"

Agent Temperanillo's concerned voice came in through Al Costello's earpiece, "Al! You alright? What is it?" As the most senior agent in the Baltimore field office, Roberto Temperanillo had taken Al Costello, the youngest recruit, under his wing. The hard-boiled, time-served agent had willingly taken on the task of mentoring his inexperienced partner, trying to cram twenty-four years of hard-won fieldcraft into him in as many months.

"Just a rat... It must've come out of the cabin. It jumped over the side and into the water. It gave me one helluva start. Frightened the bejesus out of me, it did..."

Bob Temperanillo quietly advised, "Al, keep your eyes peeled. Any concerns, get out of there and wait for the Lab boys." He'd taken quite a shine to the eager, raw young man fresh out of Quantico.

Agent Costello advanced cautiously hugging the wall, his shoulder rubbing along it, the sleeve of his white shirt collecting more dirt and grime which made his wife's job of getting it clean that little bit harder. He peered in through the cabin windows but couldn't see a thing, it being far too dark inside the cabin to reveal anything. As he came to the stern, he crouched and swung round so that his pistol and torch pointed into the well of the afterdeck and made a cursory inspection, then briefly trained them on the bridge. There was nobody here; the boat was deserted. His Supervisor and colleague both remained silent, straining their ears to listen for anything from the man on the ground, not wanting to make a sound for fear that the slightest noise in his earpiece might distract Agent Costello at a crucial instant that could spell the difference between life and death. After a few moments, Al Costello's hushed voice came into their headsets, "I don't see anybody. Do you want me to go down into the cabin, Chief?"

The Supervisor's voice came back, "Use your judgement Al... Only if you think it's safe..." and Agent Temperanillo added, "If you do Al, watch for booby traps... Trip wires... antennea... tremblers... light beams... pressure pads... heat or movement detectors... If you want to wait, I should be there in fifteen..."

Not wanting the veteran to steal his thunder, Agent Costello said determinedly, "I'm going in..." He approached the boat and examined the seat that ran around the inside of the afterdeck. That looked okay. He extended one leg very slowly over the side, mantis-like and lowered it down gently until his foot rested on the cushion. The beam of his torch systematically swept around the open access hatch, the bright disc illuminating the stairwell and glinting off the chromed handles. His heart pounded in his chest. Hardly daring to breathe, he could hear the blood rushing through his arteries. He checked it was clear then climbed down onto the afterdeck. So far, so good. He crouched and shone his torch into the cabin, examining the interior. He could make out very little from up here, so he scanned the stairs thoroughly looking for any signs of danger. Nothing. He counted four steps down to the cabin floor. He switched off his torch then took a small canister out of his pocket and sprayed delicate puffs of an aerosol sensitive to infra-red light which glowed to illuminate the beams of optical sensors; they detected intruders who broke the beam and could be used as a trigger. Again nothing. Through his earpiece, Agent Roberto Temperanillo faintly heard the subdued hiss of the aerosol can and realised that his protégé was heeding all his careful warnings. Agent Costello leaned further into the hatch and sprayed the aerosol into the cabin, watching the ethereal cloud for tell-tale signs as it gradually filled the dark void. Still nothing. He put the canister back in his pocket then switched on his torch again and took out an ultrasonic sensor to listen for the signature given off by movement detectors but, again, nothing. With one last sweep, he carefully stepped down onto the well worn, non-slip tread of the top step and scanned the way ahead. He saw nothing that alerted him to any danger which only heightened his unease. He straddled the next step down and gradually lowered his weight onto the step below it. He repeated his scan of the cabin, then straddled the bottom step and descended to the floor of the cabin and said into his stalk mike, "I'm in…"

As he stood peering into the gloom, the Supervisor's voice came in over Agent Costello's earpiece. "Al, I'm just patching Marvin Spangler through. Marv's head of the Forensics team that's on its way out to you. He wants a word…" Alfredo Costello froze.

"Agent Costello. Agent Spangler here. We'll be there in three minutes… I don't want you on that boat… I don't want you contaminating any evidence that might be there, so re-trace your steps and get out now. That's an order!"

Alfredo Costello said, "Yes Sir. That's acknowledged…" He was secretly relieved that he'd been commanded to get off the boat. As he turned to go, he relaxed and breathed a heartfelt sigh of relief. Without thinking, he mounted the bottom step. As his weight came down on the wafer-thin, pressure sensitive pad that was bonded between the step and its non-slip tread, his body was instantly pierced by hundreds of jagged, lethal splinters of wood and glass-reinforced plastic, then a wall of searingly hot gas, expanding at many times the speed of sound, hit the young man and engulfed him. Alfredo Costello never had a chance to register what had happened. The explosion shattered the boat's superstructure, lifting it off the hull and blowing the debris through the roof of the boatshed, scattering it on the shore and into the creek for a radius of sixty yards around. As the pressure wave crushed the fuel tanks and ruptured them, the hot gas vaporized some of the remaining fuel which detonated, sending out a huge fireball that rose over the shell of the boatshed and spread to scorch the shrubs alongside it. The rest of the fuel leaked into the bottom of the hull where it fed the inferno that devoured every last vestige of combustible material, including Special Agent Alfredo Costello's tattered corpse.

As the helicopter cleared the last spit of land and swooped across Turners Creek, Special Agent Marvin Spangler saw the thick plume of oily black smoke rising over the creek from the burning hull of the 'Pride of Maryland' which was blazing fiercely. It banked steeply to come in upwind of the column which was gradually drifting northwards over the Sassafras in the gentle summer breeze and he was treated to a bird's eye view of the carnage. It hovered briefly whilst the forensic team examined the scene from their unique vantage point, looking about for any signs of Agent Costello but there was nothing useful to be gleaned from their eyrie, so the pilot descended and landed his machine well outside the debris field. As they climbed down from the helicopter, the first of the residents arrived, closely followed by Agent Temperanillo whose car bucked and wallowed as it sped over the rough track. It skidded to a halt alongside a brand-new SUV, kicking up small clouds of dust from the dry ground as the wheels locked momentarily. The grizzled old agent immediately hauled himself out of his car and, nodding grimly in the direction of Agent Spangler, busied himself ushering the morbid sightseers back from the gruesome spectacle then set about erecting a cordon beyond the furthest extremities of the debris. As he worked, he noticed small flakes of ash floating down from the smoke plume, amongst them the charred remnants of Agent Costello's grubby white shirt.

—•—

"I want a total news blackout for at least forty-eight hours. That'll put us into Ramadan… I don't want the terrorists to know we've found the 'Maryland', specially if it had no automatic warning system telling them their booby trap's been sprung… The bastards!" Alan Davies sat in front of his video-conferencing monitor with half a dozen channels open to the Special Agents in charge of local regional offices.

Just then, Marvin Spangler's voice came in over an audio channel, "Sir. Agent Spangler heading up the Forensics team down at the 'Maryland'…"

"Go ahead, Mr Spangler."

"Sir, we've picked up traces of radiation amongst the debris… Just the one isolated group of readings so far but sufficiently above the background level to convince me there was something radioactive aboard the boat… We're collecting a sample now. The chopper's taking it straight back to the Lab for analysis. I've told them to report to you as soon as it's identified..."

"Thank you, Mr Spangler..."

"Oh... Sir... One more thing... We've found what we think are Agent Costello's remains. It's difficult to say for sure because they were reduced to clinker in the bottom of the hull... or what's left of it. Most of it was consumed by the fire... It's only just cooled down enough for us to climb into it and it's on the verge of sinking... We're about to remove them now?"

"Very good, Mr Spangler. Who's going to inform Agent Costello's next of kin?"

"His partner, Sir, Agent Temperanillo. He's volunteered to tell Costello's wife... She's a teacher. First and second grade... She's taken them out on a field trip today and won't be back until this afternoon... Bob's going to... that is Agent Temperanillo's going to wait until she's back home. He doesn't want to tell her in front of her kids. It'll only frighten them if she becomes hysterical..."

"Kind thought, Mr Spangler. Please give Bob Temperanillo my best regards and tell him I'm real sorry to hear about his partner, will you?"

"Yes Sir"

Alan Davies turned back to the video console. Niara Marshall came on, tersely demanding to know the latest. She had just come out of a very difficult meeting with the President and was still smarting from his stinging comments about Homeland Security's amateurishness in letting Al Rashid get this far; there had been no reasoning with him about the sophistication and inventiveness of the terrorist's deception.

Alan Davies started, "We've called in every agent from every local office to join in the hunt... We've covered every route off the Delmarva, in particular Highway 301 north and south... We've got lookouts on I-95 and Route 40, in case they try coming down to DC via Baltimore... and on Route 50-301 in case they take the Bay Bridge via Annapolis... We've also covered the ferries. We've even covered the Chesapeake Bay Bridge-Tunnel, in case they choose to take a roundabout way via Virginia to try to throw us off the scent... We've nailed down every route into the Capital... We're even keeping tabs on routes north, in case the real target is Phili or New York... We've got reception committees at his offices in Washington and Wilmington and at his home in Newark... We're spread as thinly as we possibly can be whilst remaining effective. All I can do now is draft in more agents from further afield... Do I have your permission to do that, Mrs Marshall?"

Before she could answer, the Baltimore SAC's line became active. Alan Davies excused himself and mistakenly said, "Yes, Bernie, what's the news?"

"It's not Bernie, Sir. SAC Morillo's tied up. It's Tom Marston, Senior Supervisor. We've just had a radiation alert from one of the detectors on I-

148

695… the Baltimore Beltway… on the northern approach to the Patapsco River crossing. Fortunately, we're trying out a new, ultra-sensitive detector in the toll booths on the Outer Harbour Bridge… The video camera synched to the unit picked up a white truck carrying a big wooden box…"

Alan Davies exclaimed "Bingo!" For the first time, he felt that their luck was improving and the terrorists' was on the wane. He thought to himself, 'They can only have it their way for so long before the cards start falling in our favor…' He asked whether everyone else had heard the news and they confirmed that they had.

With more than a hint of panic in her voice, Niara Marshall said, "Stop them immediately before they get into the built-up area on the other side. If they detonate the bomb whilst they're on the bridge, it'll limit the damage."

Alan Davies hesitated. "Mrs Marshall, I think we'd do better to put a tail on it. If it is our man, he might lead us to the other members of the cell."

Thinking of the President's edict, Niara Marshall commanded, "Intercept it now, man! Don't wait! That's an order!"

Zubin Hazami checked his rear view mirror for a third successive time. He'd noticed the State Police cruiser pull off the ramp and into the traffic shortly after he'd left the toll booth. He accelerated up the gentle gradient towards the crown of the central span of the Francis Scott Key Bridge being very careful to stay under the speed limit. He didn't want to attract unwanted attention to himself. He subconsciously worried at the false mustache that he'd donned which made him look more like Luis Ruiz DaCosta. Being distracted by the view in his rear mirror, he didn't notice the FBI agents in the car alongside scrutinising him critically.

"Mr Davies, Agent Schiller here. We've just passed the suspect now… We've had a good look at him. We both think there's a strong resemblance to DaCosta… sufficient to justify apprehending him… and we've called for an interception team to meet us at the other end of the bridge… What do you want us to do?"

There was a brief silence until Alan Davies said, "How far before you're off the bridge?"

"We're not quite half-way yet, Sir… I'd say about another two minutes before we're clear off the other end. The traffic's a bit slow today."

"Well hold off but be prepared to intercept the suspect, Agent Schiller… And expect a violent response."

"Yes Sir"

Niara Marshall's voice came in, almost a strangled shriek, "I told you to intercept DaCosta, Mr Davies. Do it now!"

Alan Davies was about to respond to her when Agent Spangler came on the line again.

"Sir, Agent Spangler here at the Maryland. We've been going over the ground again. It's pretty hard and the tire tracks in the dust were pretty much obliterated by the blast but, from what evidence is left, I'd say there'd been *two different trucks* on the loading dock, not one as we originally thought... and possibly an automobile as well... Also, Agent Temperanillo's been unable to find the guy Costello spoke to earlier today but he interviewed a woman who says she saw *two trucks* coming into the village this morning whilst she was pegging out her washing... One white, the other a dark color... that's the best she can give us for the second truck... The white one came in first about six... the second, slightly larger one about five minutes later. The reason it caught her eye... she said she had to do a double-take because they both looked like they were being driven by the same man, which really threw her. When we showed her DaCosta's photograph, she said that both truck drivers bore a strong resemblance to his image... Unfortunately, she didn't see either truck leaving..."

Alan Davies thought quickly. "Mrs Marshall, I recommend we hold off pulling in DaCosta now. It could result in an uncontrolled firefight. I'd rather corner him somewhere we can take him out cleanly if that's what it comes down to... And it sounds as though there could be two bombs... If so, I'm sure both drivers are in regular contact with each other... If we pull in one driver, the other will probably know immediately... And I suspect the other bomb presents by far the bigger potential hazard... It's highly likely this one's a decoy... an early warning system, if you like... just to see if we're watching... Because my guess is this one's actually not as well shielded as the other one... Even then, it seems that this driver's doing his level best to avoid all the permanently sited detectors on the Interstates and major arterial routes into the cities... But if we're going to find one, gut instinct tells me they want us to find this one, so it distracts our attention away from the real threat... And if there is another one, it could be *anywhere*... We've got to keep tabs on this one whilst we find the other, so we can neutralise them both simultaneously. Do you agree?"

Reluctantly, Niara Marshall agreed.

As the State Police cruiser reached the south end of the bridge, it peeled off and took the ramp to Quarantine Road and Foremans Corner. As Zubin Hazami watched it go, he relaxed then called his older brother using a stolen cellphone. In the same obscure Farsi dialect Mansour Al Rashid had used, he reported that everything was going to plan. Haroun Hazami took the call on another stolen cellphone. "You're two minutes late!"

"Don't worry brother. For a while back there I thought I had company which is why I couldn't call sooner but it was a false alarm. Everything's alright now..." The line was open for fractionally longer than eight seconds.

The call would have been difficult to trace and the mobiles difficult to locate if the Federal Bureau of Investigation had known the numbers of the phones being used and more difficult still to interpret. As it was, it was impossible to trace the call back to the Hazami brothers.

"Mr Davies. Agent Willetts in Washington... We're at Al Rashid's office block on Connecticut. I've spoken to the Assistant Building Services Manager... a Polack called Willy Warzinski... a glorified janitor really, not very bright... This guy's been sick for the last few days. He's only come back on duty this morning... It seems he's quite pally with Al Rashid. He says Al Rashid treats him to the odd bottle of vodka every now and then, in return for favors done, no questions asked. Nothing serious, small things like special office cleaning jobs, helping him move heavy items of furniture in and out, etcetera... Little bribes to keep him sweet, so he doesn't put the jobs through the books, in which case he'd have to charge them to Al Rashid's company. And, of course, Warzinski doesn't tell anyone about their cozy little arrangement but we squeezed it out of him without too much persuasion... My guess is there's no harm in this guy, he simply likes his liquor... Apparently, Al Rashid mentioned to him a few weeks ago that he might be getting a safe and asked Warzinski if he'd take it up to his office for him in the freight elevator, strictly on the QT, of course. He told Warzinski there was a case of vodka in it for him. It seems Al Rashid's very cleverly been buttering this guy up for months. He's got him trussed up like a Thanksgiving turkey. If we hadn't been monitoring all calls in and out of the building and already knew most of it, I doubt Warzinski would have volunteered this information freely but when we questioned him about it and he realised his little game was up, the only thing he was worried about was that we didn't tell his boss about it... Anyway, it seems the safe should have been here first thing this morning, at six o'clock, before anyone was about but Al Rashid left a message on Warzinski's cellphone whilst he was on his way in to work to tell him delivery had been delayed and he'd call him later when he knew for certain when delivery would be... The reason we questioned Warzinski in the first place was because, about twenty minutes ago, Al Rashid called him on his cellphone to say the safe would be delivered later this morning. We picked up the call on the scanner but, unfortunately, we didn't have time to trace Al Rashid's location. Neither did the cellphone company. Warzinski told him the freight elevator was undergoing a routine safety check which started at nine o'clock and wouldn't be finished until one. Warzinski wanted to defer delivery 'til six tomorrow morning... I think he was bothered about his boss finding out... but Al Rashid was insistent it should be today... So, instead of the safe standing on the dock unattended for a couple of hours, Al Rashid's arranged for it to be delivered at two o'clock this afternoon... Apparently, its total weight is just

151

under two-point-five tons... Warzinski kicked off at that because it exceeds the weight limit for entry into the building's heavy objects register but Al Rashid just upped the ante and promised him two cases of vodka, which did the trick... It's the age-old story... Once you're in the mire, there's almost no limit to the depth you'll sink to... Anyway, there's a hoist over the dock, so they can get it off the truck easily... According to Al Rashid, it needs a pallet truck for moving it about which the delivery man from the freight company's bringing with him. He also told Warzinski that he'd be coming in personally to supervise positioning of the safe himself... Al Rashid made strenuous efforts to point out that the safe comes on its own plinth which also forms the base of the packing case, so all they need to do when it's in position is take the sides off the case. He assured Warzinski that the plinth was designed to spread the weight of the safe so it doesn't exceed the building's floor loading limits... It sounds well thought out. Al Rashid's clearly done his homework and covered every angle..."

Alan Davies instructed the field agent, "Well, it doesn't sound as though he suspects he's under surveillance, so he's made a serious miscalculation there... But don't under-estimate him. He's not stupid... Anyway, keep Warzinski under lockdown until this thing's over... Check out his boss and make sure he's okay. If you have no other option, take his boss into your confidence but maintain a very low profile in the building. We don't know whether any of Al Rashid's office staff are involved in this. I don't want him phoning in and being given the heads-up by one of them... And whatever happens, don't let Warzinski warn Al Rashid, even inadvertantly, that we're on to him..."

"What happens if Al Rashid calls Warzinksi before coming in at two o'clock... making one last recce to ensure the coast's clear? If Warzinski doesn't take the call, it may spook Al Rashid... If he takes the call but he sounds nervous, it may spook him..."

"Coach Warzinski in case Al Rashid does call him. There's a good reason why Warzinski should sound nervous. After all, he's doing wrong. He knows it and so does Al Rashid. Maybe you could tell Warzinski that if Al Rashid calls him he's to say that his boss will be taking a late lunch from half-one to half-two, which gives them just enough time to get the safe in place before his boss returns, then Al Rashid won't be so surprised if Warzinski has a hint of urgency in his voice... But he mustn't sound panicky... If that's the story you decide to spin, make sure it's a good one... And make sure his boss doesn't appear unexpectedly and blow the whole thing... Can you do that?"

"Yes, Sir"

"Well done, Willetts. Good work. Let me know immediately, if there are any developments."

"Thank you, Sir. I will."

Alan Davies sat turning over some pressing questions in his mind. 'Why the urgency? Why must it be delivered today? Why couldn't it wait until tomorrow? Is it to do with getting the bomb planted before Ramadan? Or am I fixated with Ramadan? Is it blinding me to some other possibility? And how big is the bomb? Assuming your average office safe weighs what… three-quarters… a ton even… is the difference really all bomb? My God! If it is, it's a big one! We've definitely got to stop it before it gets into the City…' Just then, his train of thought was derailed by Niara Marshall. He asked her, "Did you hear that?"

"Sorry, Mr Davies, my assistant came in and distracted me. I didn't catch it all… Please explain?"

"Al Rashid's expecting delivery of a safe at his office this afternoon. My guess is it contains the bomb… What better means of disguising and shielding it than a safe. It looks as though Al Rashid's convinced the janitor to take it up in its packing case, which means there's less likelihood he'll expect to see inside… And it looks as though the janitor's in his pocket anyway… We've got all the agencies on alert. What we've got to do now is try to second-guess these guys and work out what route they'll take to bring the bomb into the city."

"You do that, Mr Davies. In the meantime, I'll inform the President of the latest developments."

—•—

Mansour Al Rashid had waited until both trucks were safely loaded and on their way before going below to connect the electrical trigger circuits that would detonate the explosive charges hidden under the cabin floor and behind the bulkheads. He made one final tour of the boat to check he'd left behind nothing incriminating and had collected everything he needed for the next stage – the final stage – of their operation, then he'd gone to the bridge and removed the ignition key, pressed the starter button and held it for a count of thirty seconds on his watch then added five seconds more for good measure. Instead of the two big marine diesel engines roaring into life as he pressed the button, when he released it, a red light-emitting diode in the cover of a small, diecast aluminium box secreted beneath the instrument console lit up. The box contained an intelligent controller that monitored the triple-redundancy circuits which would detonate the demolition charges in the event that any one of the three parallel circuits was tampered with, irrespective of whether or not one of the triggers had been activated. The LED flashed for sixty seconds, giving Mansour Al Rashid ample time to get off the boat and into his car and to be more than a hundred yards away before it came on permanently. At the very same instant, a careful observer who had been very close to the open lid

153

of the console and who had been listening intently may have been able to hear the barely audible click that accompanied the steady illumination of the miniature beacon, as a tiny switch closed, arming the four cunningly concealed trigger circuits, any one of which could detonate the charges. All it needed now was for some unwitting person to come along and activate one of the triggers and… BOOM! Of course, if the hapless observer had been on the bridge when the electronic timer reached the minute mark, he or she would have been blown through the roof of the boatshed along with everything else because one of the triggers was cleverly concealed under the closure of the instrument console lid, making it virtually impossible to discover and extremely difficult to disarm.

Both of the Hazami brothers had turned north. The younger brother, Zubin, followed Route 301 until it intersected Route 40, Pulaski Highway, which he then took in the direction of Baltimore. The older brother, Haroun, had set off fifteen minutes later but, instead of proceeding to Route 301, he'd turned north at Galena and crossed the Sassafras from Georgetown to Fredericktown on State Road 213, then continued at a leisurely pace up to Elkton and stayed on it. As he drove, his initial tension eased and he'd become more relaxed. At Fair Hill, he'd turned west onto 273, eventually meeting Route 1 west of Rising Sun. He'd had the window down and had leaned his elbow on the ledge, enjoying the gentle Maryland countryside and the warm summer breeze wafting round his neck. He had plenty of time to get to Washington – he knew because he'd driven this route a dozen times before – and he wanted to savour the intoxicating pleasure of doing God's work. He followed the Conowingo Road as it crossed the Susquehanna River. As he approached the small town of Kalmia, his cellphone rang. He conscientiously pulled over and answered it. He exchanged a few brief bursts of Farsi with Mansour Al Rashid who told him that delivery had to be delayed by a couple of hours. Even that hadn't phased Haroun Hazami. They had a contingency plan for almost every conceivable eventuality so, just before reaching the communities of Marywood and Bel Air, he left Route 1 and took 23 to Jarrettsville; a small detour through towns with good, old-fashioned English names such as Hereford, Hampstead and Westminster would add sufficient time to the journey to get him to his destination for two o'clock. When he'd found himself on a lonely stretch of road with no other traffic in front or behind and no homesteads within view, he'd pulled over and removed the false whiskers that made him look like Luis DaCosta and donned a baseball cap and mirrored sunglasses that changed his appearance yet again, then hopped down and unpeeled the magnetic labels attached to the doors of the driver's cab which had told the world that his truck was registered to Marathon Trucking, Inc. He even found time to stop and pray.

At Locust Grove, Mansour Al Rashid had taken State Road 213 towards Chestertown where he'd crossed the Chester River, then continued through Church Hill and Centreville, picking up Route 301 just east of Queenstown. As he drove across the William Preston Lane Junior Memorial Toll Bridge in his second-hand Cadillac Deville purchased three months earlier for cash by one Ranaldo Alvarez Valasquez – another of his numerous aliases – and registered in Nebraska, half a continent away from his home and soon-to-be scene of his greatest triumph, he was oblivious to the spectacular view of Chesapeake Bay, blinded to it by his hatred of his mortal enemy. Although he turned over and over in his mind the fact that he was on a sacred mission, Mansour Al Rashid could not suppress the buzz he felt at actually beginning the final scene in the last act of a play whose script had been written nineteen years earlier at the end of the Gulf War when his revered father had been killed by Iraqi Imperial Guards whilst leading a popular uprising against Saddam Hussein's evil and cruel regime – an abortive and ultimately hopeless uprising – which had been encouraged by the USA but which it had then failed to support. Consequently, the insurgents and their families had been left isolated to suffer a terrible fate at the hands of the tyrannical dictator and his brutal henchmen. Mansour Al Rashid had mentally rehearsed his role in this living tragedy every day since. The sense of betrayal still smouldered in his heart and drove him on to attack the people he blamed for the loss of his father and his subsequent harassment and persecution which had ended up with him fleeing for his own life – ironically, the very people who'd taken him in when there were few safe places for him to run to.

Haroun Hazami drove steadily south though Olney on State Highway 97 until it met Highway 185 at the Gate of Heaven Cemetry where he turned off onto Connecticut Avenue and continued toward the Capital, staying one or two miles per hour below the speed limit. He checked his watch; it was one-twenty-nine in the afternoon of Monday August 9, in the year 2010 after the birth of the prophet Jesus, according to the calendar introduced in 1582 by Pope Gregory XIII or, for Muslims, 28 Sha'baan in the year 1431 after the Hijra which was when the prophet Muhammad ibn Abd Allah (peace and blessings be upon Him) departed Mecca the Blessed for Medina the Radiant to establish the first Islamic community there and two days before the glorious month of Ramadan. And here he was, the son of a dispossessed peasant farmer whose humble plot of land in Palestine had been forcibly taken over by the Israeli state to provide housing for Jewish settlers, transporting the retribution of the One God, which would rain down on the Infidels in their lair and drive them out, hurting them as they were hurting Islam and its followers. He quivered with anticipation as he took out his cellphone and called Mansour Al Rashid to make the final check that everything was on schedule before their rendezvous. Within the hour, his part in this glorious undertaking should be at an end.

Five miles north of the Capital Beltway, Mansour Al Rashid sat in the parking lot of a fast food restaurant off Turkey Branch Parkway overlooking State Highway 185. He ended the call from Haroun Hazami after seven-point-two seconds then briefly spoke to Mrs Bilhal on the office phone to let her know that he would be in shortly to see to his new safe. Other than being surprised to hear from him, his secretary sounded completely normal. She asked whether her boss was enjoying his vacation, then confirmed that "No…" she had neither seen nor heard any unusual activity. "Why? Are we expecting some?"

"Oh… no reason… It's just that I passed the office earlier and I could've sworn the cops had set up another of those mobile speed checks, that's all."

"Well I've seen nothing, Mr Rashid. Still, I didn't go out at lunch today. Mother's not feeling too well and she said she was going to rest, so she told me not to bother coming to see her… Said she might be better tomorrow…"

As Mansour Al Rashid rang off, Alan Davies said, "Damn! Was that a coded message telling Al Rashid she's not sure the coast's clear?"

Agent Willetts responded promptly, "I don't think so, Sir. We've followed Mrs Bilhal every day for the last two weeks and each lunchtime she's gone to see her mother. We intercepted a call from her mother earlier telling Mrs Bilhal not to come today. We know the old lady suffers from severe rheumatoid arthitis and has good days and bad days but we followed it up with her doctor, just in case… Her doctor told us she'd come in this morning for a gold injection which is used to treat sudden flare-ups and that she'd been advised to rest afterwards, so it seems genuine enough."

Alan Davies grunted his thanks but he was obviously getting agitated. "Where the hell are they?" he muttered under his breath, referring to Al Rashid and the second truck. He had personally been directing the hunt for the terrorists since Mansour Al Rashid and his family had left home early the previous Monday morning, during which time he'd had very little sleep. The constant anxiety was beginning to tell on him. And at the same time as trying to keep on top of this nightmarish situation and orchestrate the combined efforts of the entire anti-terrorist network, he'd been endlessly pestered by that arse-kissing bitch from Homeland Security instead of being allowed to get on with his job; of course, it wasn't his arse she'd been kissing. In fact, he had the uncomfortable feeling that his arse was probably being toasted even now in his absence. He simply hadn't felt the burn yet. Still, there was plenty of time for that, especially if the terrorists were successful and managed to detonate a dirty bomb in the District.

Alan Davies sat half-listening to the background talk, trying to block it out as he agonised over what the terrorists might do. What would he do in their shoes? He tried running various scenarios, uncertain even now that there wasn't some twist in their intricate plot. 'What had the President said?' he thought in a brief flashback 'This is all too pat... It feels like we're being set up...' but before he could wrestle with it any more, Agent Schiller came on the line and said, "Mr Davies, Sir... 'White Van Man's just taken a quick call on his cellphone and it looks as though he's about to move off again. He's within ten miles of Southern Avenue. Our marksmen are in position. What do you want us to do?" Agent Schiller had been sitting three cars away from where Zubin Hazami had been parked up killing time, in a rest area off Central Avenue, State Highway 214, east of the Capital Beltway, waiting for the instruction from his older brother to violate the heart of the Infidels. Alan Davies sat staring into the middle distance until Agent Schiller's quizzical voice interrupted his thoughts, "Sir... What should we do?"

Alan Davies made a snap decision. "Let him go... we haven't located the other truck yet... but don't lose him. Keep him in your sights..."

When Mansour Al Rashid saw the truck driven by Haroun Hazami go by, heading south towards the Capital on 185, he started his engine and drove out of the parking lot and smoothly joined the traffic, falling in unobtrusively about three hundred yards behind it. As the truck passed under the Beltway, he noticed the workmen's lorry parked on the hard shoulder behind the line of cones segregating the work zone from the traffic and the sign preceding it warning about the work zone ahead. He also registered the curious absence of workmen working around it. So intent was he on watching the lorry for any sign of activity that he failed to see the camera discretely mounted on the barrier of the central reservation, pointed at the oncoming vehicles.

Special Agent Frank Madison and his partner, Special Agent Evinrude Bolger, were sitting in their car on Spring Valley Road which joined I-495 eastbound to 185 southbound, watching the video monitor. Even before the image optimisation software had cleaned up the small amount of residual flare caused by the reflection of sunlight off the windshield that the polarising filter had failed to remove and the facial recognition software had stripped Mansour Al Rashid of his sunglasses then alerted them to the fact that this image was a good match with a better than ninety-six percent correlation with other known images of the wanted man, instinct had already told Agent Madison that this was the man they were looking for. As the on-board computer was making connections with umpteen other computers, automatically performing tasks such as checking the vehicle's registration details at the same time as alerting other watchers in the vicinity to this potential hostile sighting, Evinrude

Bolger was busy negotiating the traffic whilst Frank Madison called Alan Davies.

"Madison! I see him. Get closer! We need verification that it is Al Rashid... The computer's telling us the vehicle's registered to one Ranaldo Alvarez Valasquez, of Hebron, Nebraska. It could be another of Al Rashid's aliases. We know he prefers Hispanic IDs... Where is he now?"

"About a quarter-mile behind us..."

"Does it look like he's shadowing a truck? Are there any behind him? Or in front?"

"There are lots of trucks, Sir..."

"Give us names, Madison. Come on man, feed us the information!" Alan Davies barked urgently. As Agent Madison began reeling off the names on the trucks in his view, Agent Bolger gently slowed down, allowing the metallic blue DeVille to catch up gradually.

"Phoenix Trucking out of Casa Grande, Arizona... 'Get-up-and-Go' Freight and Haulage, from Oshkosh, Nebraska..."

Alan Davies interjected, "What's that like? Does it have a large wooden crate on the back?"

"No Sir. Just a few pieces of farm machinery..."

"No! Next!"

"Gaithersburg Collect and Deliver... It's a small, closed box van..."

"Next!"

"Er... Texas Road Runners, of Corpus Christi..."

As Agent Madison read out the names of the trucking companies and their telephone numbers along with the vehicles' make and registration number, other agents were frantically calling the companies named and speaking to their shipping managers to verify that the deliveries were legitimate.

"Doreen's Transport... No, I can see Doreen and she's definitely not our man... Tell City Products, Inc. out of Indiana. Looks like some sort of industrial equipment... Inchalla Express Deliverance, of Paradise, Maryland. A consigment of large cardboard cartons. No indication as to what's in 'em... Toledo Shipping..."

Alan Davies interrupted, "Wait a minute! What was that last one?"

"Toledo..."

"No! The one before..."

"Er..."

Alan Davies overheard Agent Madison telling his partner to catch up with the truck that had just overtaken them. As they pulled alongside it, Frank Madison read out, "Inchalla Express Deliverance, Sir..."

"How spelt?"

"India-November-Charlie-Hotel-Alpha-Lima-Lima-Alpha..."

Frank Madison heard Alan Davies muttering to himself, "Inch-alla... Inchalla..." then, as the realisation dawned on him, "Inshallah... *In sa' Allah...*" he blurted out. "It's Arabic for 'If Allah wills it...' It translates literally as 'God willing...' That must be them!"

As Agent Madison gave a detailed description of the truck, Alan Davies sat perplexed. The thought crossed his mind, 'Why advertise themselves so blatantly?' but in the next he concluded that the terrorists were either supremely confident that they wouldn't come under surveillance, in which case it wouldn't matter what was emblazoned on the side of their truck or they were becoming far too cocky or fatalistic for their own good. The thought was rapidly swamped by more pressing matters as he quickly gathered his wits. He checked the large-screen display showing a detailed map of the area indicating the location of the agents' car.

"Bolger, I have you just south of Jones Bridge Road. Confirm!"

"Affirmative Sir"

"Madison, have you ID'ed Al Rashid yet?"

"Negative... We're steadily dropping back, we haven't reached him yet... Just a minute..."

"For Christ's sake, hurry man! We haven't got a minute." Alan Davies snapped back brusquely. As he waited for Agent Madison's feedback, he issued orders to the interception squads to establish roadblocks at Chevy Chase Circle on Western Avenue and on Central Avenue and East Capitol Street where they crossed Southern Avenue and to search every vehicle crossing the perimeter roads before letting it into the District.

Agent Madison came back on. "Yes Sir. I'm fairly sure it's Al Rashid... Damn! I think he made us... Yes he has. He's speeding up... It looks like he's on his cellphone... Rudy, catch up wth him!"

As Mansour Al Rashid drew alongside the agents' car, he saw Agent Madison turn and look past the driver, scrutinising him carefully. He knew instinctively this was no casual glance. Something about them told him these were federal agents and they weren't simply carrying out a routine check; the driver was too rigid, looking ahead too intently, trying too hard to ignore the vehicle at his side. He accelerated aggressively, unleashing all the power that the four-point-six litre V8 NHP engine could deliver, going thirty yards ahead in a few seconds, to see if the car continued at the same pace. In his rear view mirror, Mansour Al Rashid saw the passenger mouthing something at the driver and gesticulating violently in his direction and, after a brief lag, it sped after him which immediately confirmed his suspicion. If his cover was blown, then it was highly likely the whole conspiracy had been compromised and there would probably be a SWAT team waiting to take them out long before they could plant the bomb in its intended site. He knew it would be impossible

159

to outrun the agents and anyway there would be nowhere to run to. His suspicions had already been aroused when the automatic speech dialler on the 'Pride of Maryland' had failed to send out its fourth, brief hourly message which should have been transmitted at ten-fifty-five that morning at the instigation of the intelligent controller, confirming that all was well. The fact that the subsequent two reports had also failed to come in had convinced him that someone had boarded the boat and inadvertently set off the demolition charges. And that someone would most likely have been either a federal agent or a state trooper. He'd been told that, if this happened, he wasn't to tell his fellow conspirators, so they remained unaware of the possible threat until it became a certainty; their mission mustn't fail simply because someone had panicked unnecessarily as the result of an equipment malfunction.

Mansour Al Rashid was under strict instruction not to activate the bombs prematurely, unless he was absolutely certain that they had been discovered and were in imminent danger of being captured or killed; either way, the success of the mission had to be in jeopardy. He had been told that, once he'd done so, they would have five minutes before the bombs went off. About half-a-mile ahead, where the 410 crossed the 185, he saw two sets of blue flashing lights pulling out into the road stopping the traffic and moments later a helicopter appeared over the carriageway. He reached for his cellphone which was mounted in its hands-free cradle on the dashboard and sent the text message – a five-digit code number – that he'd keyed in earlier in anticipation of this eventuality, which appeared simultaneously on the phones carried by the Hazami brothers and which instantaneously armed both bombs. Now, both bombs would detonate within five minutes, unless they received a pre-determined code to disable the trigger circuits, a code known only to Mansour Al Rashid and that had to come from his cellphone and no other. Mansour Al Rashid had memorised the code that would disarm the bombs but he was bound by his promise to God not to reveal it, on pain of being excluded from Paradise for eternity. What Mansour Al Rashid did not know was that, as an extra precaution against him disarming the bombs in a moment of Earthly weakness, the bomb designers had been told not to enable this function; once the bombs had been activated there was no way they could be de-activated by the terrorists.

Almost simultaneously, Alan Davies received messages from Agents Madison and Schiller telling him that both trucks had sped up and were weaving wildly through the traffic, heading for the Capital.

As he turned south onto 185 and saw the sign telling him he was now on Connecticut Avenue, Haroun Hazami experienced an enormous surge of exhilaration, a feeling of power and fulfilment that welled up inside him. It

160

came from knowing that he was in the service of his God who, he felt, was watching over their mission. Other than making and taking calls that kept him in contact with his fellow Jihadi, he constantly recited verses from the Holy Qur'an that he knew off by heart. The journey so far had afforded Haroun Hazami an excellent opportunity to reflect on his faith and he had not found himself wanting. Even now, the feeling of anticipation as he settled to the final round of his ultimate test of faith hadn't ruffled his sense of ease, right up until the instant he saw the squad cars with their blue flashing lights pull across the intersection at 410 and the policemen jump out to spread their X-Nets across the road in front of the traffic. He saw red brake lights illuminating in the distance and smoke rising from numerous tires as they squealed to a halt. At that instant, the text message came into his cellphone. A wave of nausea swept over him and his stomach churned with fear as he read it and realised that this was now a suicide mission; if they were discovered, his instruction was to deliver the painful blow as near to the heart of the Infidels as he possibly could – one that would make them reel – with no regard for his own life. He pressed the accelerator down hard, feeling the truck's automatic transmission shift down a gear and propel it forwards suddenly. As he saw the traffic backing up, he veered sharply across the inside lane and onto the hard shoulder, the truck rolling violently before righting itself, shedding some of the cardboard boxes, which revealed the top of a large wooden crate. As he approached the intersection at speed, a Harley-Davidson motorcycle pulled out of the queue, so that the unwary rider could look down the line of standing vehicles to see what was causing the hold-up. Haroun Hazami had no time to take evasive action. The truck struck it in the rear with a sickening crunch, ramming the bike into the back of the car in front and hurling the rider's broken body over the car roof. An irate passenger in a car six vehicles from the front of the queue, already late for an important business meeting in Bethesda, also suffered a similar fate when he impatiently opened the door and stepped out onto the hard shoulder to see what had caused the sudden stoppage, his body being instantly catapulted back inside the car by the terrorist's truck whilst the door slammed back against the front wing of the car and was left hanging at a crazy angle from one bent hinge. As the front wheels of the truck ran over the X-Net, the spikes on its leading edge embedded themselves in the tires, wrapping it around the wheels and front axle, which brought the truck rapidly to a halt less than fifty yards beyond the intersection. The sudden deceleration threw Haroun Hazami forward so that his sternum struck the hub of the steering wheel with enough force to wind him and his head hit the windshield, dazing him. Before he had recovered sufficiently to register what was happening, two burly SWAT officers dressed in body armour and wearing helmets had dragged him from the cab and pinned him spread-eagle, face-down on the tarmac, with their submachine guns stuck in the back of his neck.

Zubin Hazami was more alert to the possibility of being under surveillance than was his older brother. As he sat in the rest area off State Highway 214 west of Church Road, he stared curiously at the other vehicles. He was becoming more and more positive that he'd already seen that couple sitting in their silver Pontiac once before today, as he'd left I-695 on the outskirts of Baltimore and taken I-97 south then continued south on Crain Highway. Surely, they'd been driving a silver or gray car. He could have sworn on the Holy Qur'an that they'd overtaken him shortly before Pigeon House Corner then pulled into a fast food diner. Now here they were, three cars away, talking earnestly to each other, only occasionally glancing around. But how could that be? When he had received the message about the two-hour delay, he'd ignored the 214 to Washington and continued south on 301 until he'd reached Highway 4, then he'd taken two leaves of the four-leaf clover intersection and headed back on the northbound carriageway until he'd reached the Marlboro Pike where he'd turned off and sat in the rest area of a filling station to kill some time. He'd been vigilant at all times, scrutinising vehicles in front and behind him, even checking vehicles on the opposite carriageway. At no time had he suspected he was under surveillance... until now. He had resumed his journey northward on 301 and turned off onto 214, Central Avenue, towards the heart of Washington DC. As he'd negotiated one loop of the junction, he had checked in his rear view mirror for the thousandth time. He felt confident that he didn't have a tail. Even then, in his eagerness to fulfil his destiny, either he had driven too quickly or he'd failed to allow sufficient time at the last stop because here he was resting up again. He continued racking his brain, tormented by the nagging uncertainty, until the attractive, auburn-haired woman in the driving seat turned bodily towards her passenger and leaned forwards, lips pursed, to kiss him. Zubin Hazami decided that maybe he was being paranoid after all. As he reached out to answer his cellphone, Special Agent Louisa Mandelli put her hands behind Erwin Schiller's neck and pursed her lips, then gently eased his face towards hers and whispered, "He's taking a call on his cellphone..."

As he was approaching Randolph Village west of the Capital Beltway, Zubin Hazami glanced in his rear view mirror. What he saw made his stomach lurch and he stared hard. Unless he was very much mistaken that was the same silver Pontiac he'd seen in the rest area. It was now following at a discrete distance, separated from him by a bunch of vehicles but hugging the white line menacingly. He eased his foot down on the accelerator, gradually increasing speed. He kept glancing back; the silver car was pulling out to overtake the intervening vehicles, which made him feel more uneasy still until a truck and trailer combination pulled out to block their path. He breathed a sigh of relief and concentrated on the road ahead and getting his precious cargo safely to its destination. Less than two hundred yards from the intersection with Hill Road, Zubin Hazami's cellphone chirped, alerting him to the fact that a text message had just come in. He hardly needed to read it, knowing that at this stage of the mission it could only mean one thing. He snatched the phone out of the key tray and opened the message. The enormous rush of hatred he felt for the Infidels on reading it caused a sudden flux of bile. Ignoring the burning sensation in his throat, he put his foot down hard. Moments later, he saw the blue flashing lights of police cars that appeared to spring out of nowhere and began to congregate at the intersection. It was then that he noticed the yellow school bus pulling across in front of him into the left-hand lane, indicating its intention to turn into Shady Glen Road.

The second-grade children had been on an outing and were now going back to school. They had been singing "The wheels on the bus go round and round, all day long…" since they'd climbed on board for the return journey. The driver hadn't realised how many verses of this irksome, repetitive song a perverse imagination could conjure up and the tedious, discordant jangle of their childish voices had begun to irritate him. He was looking forward to dropping them off at school then getting back to the depot for a break. He was approaching the intersection a little faster than he normally would but not fast enough to be cited for bad driving. He glanced in his mirrors, then indicated and pulled across the traffic; that white truck was far enough back not to be a problem. He glanced in his rear view mirror again and was momentarily distracted by the white truck as it swerved wildly to pass him on his right-hand side; it must have been going much faster than he'd realised. As he looked forwards again, the police cars that had suddenly appeared at the intersection took him by surprise and he stepped heavily on the brake pedal, causing the nose of the bus to dive down violently and thirty-five children to squeal loudly in fright. As Zubin Hazami approached the bus, he reached for the heavily silenced submachine gun that lay on the bench seat beside him and pointed the muzzle of it forwards and downwards through the open window. As he drew level with the rear of the bus, he let off a long burst that strafed the entire length of its side, bursting both rear tires then the front tire in quick succession. As the rear tires blew out, the bus lurched clumsily to the right as the driver was trying to steer it into the left turn; as the front tire blew out, the ragged tread rolled off the wheel rim and the crippled bus tipped over onto its side and slid across the junction. The policemen and FBI agents who had been close by dived for cover when they heard the muffled hum of the automatic weapon and the metallic thuds as the bullets variously penetrated or ricocheted off the bodywork, interspersed by the loud reports of the tires bursting. The fender of Zubin Hazami's truck struck the front wing of the police cruiser that had stopped part-way across the junction and spun it sideways. He was clear of the intersection before anyone could unholster their weapon. The loud, staccato crash of the terrorist's truck striking the police car was immediately followed by an even louder bang as the bus rolled over, rounded off by the shrill screech as it slid the few yards to a halt on its side, all accompanied by a cacophony of screams from the terrified children inside. Whilst Agent Schiller radioed ahead to let the SWAT teams know that the suspect had broken through the cordon, Agent Mandelli aimed her car straight for the gap between the overturned bus and the wrecked police car.

When he saw the truck swerve onto the hard shoulder, Mansour Al Rashid realised that the road up ahead was completely blocked by standing traffic. He reacted quickly, diving through the gap between two cars as it rapidly closed and followed Haroun Hazami's truck. The driver of the car behind was so startled when the Cadillac DeVille suddenly cut across his path that he pulled his car hard right and skidded to a halt with the nose partially on the hard shoulder and bellowed "ASSHOLE!" through the open window, to vent his anger. He hadn't expected the lunatic to stop but neither had he expected the loud squeal of tires beside his door or the irate honking that followed it. He looked round, blazing with anger and yelled at the car alongside, "YOU TOO, ASSHOLE!" until he saw the powerfully built passenger aggressively thrusting a badge towards him and yelling back, "Federal Agents! Get out of the way!" The unfortunate driver was now boxed in by the car behind him which had also skidded to a halt inches from his rear fender, so when he failed to respond instantaneously, the burly FBI man leaned out of the window with his arm at full stretch, brandishing the badge more menacingly and bawled "GET OUT THE WAY!" After a few moments of chaos, the line of vehicles parted sufficiently to let the agents' car through and it sped off after the suspect's DeVille, kicking up gravel off the hard shoulder.

Mansour Al Rashid drove full bore into the dust cloud sucked up in the wake of Haroun Hazami's truck. As he approached the intersection, he saw the truck nosedive as it shuddered to a halt, hobbled by the stopping nets but he also saw that it had neatly cleared the junction of the traps in his path. He braked heavily into the corner and slewed the DeVille hard right, tires shrieking, fighting to straighten it up as he swung on to 410, then accelerated hard towards Bethesda. He heard three sharp reports as 5.56mm bullets shattered the rear window, one punching through the headrest and whistling past his right ear then exiting through the windshield to drop somewhere in the carefully manicured grounds of the Columbia Country Club, before the queue of oncoming cars standing in the opposite lane obscured the shooter's line of fire. As Mansour Al Rashid sped past the end of Meadow Lane, he looked in his rear view mirror and saw the agents' car, headlights full on, gaining on him rapidly; it must be capable of phenomenal acceleration to reduce the gap between them so quickly. He urged the DeVille on, seventy, eighty, ninety miles per hour, the tires protesting as he took the sweeping left-hand bend beyond Maple Avenue but the agents' car continued to grow larger in his mirrors. Mansour Al Rashid saw the burly agent in the passenger seat – the one whose scrutiny had first alerted him to their impending capture – cocking his machine pistol, the look of hatred on his face as he yelled at his partner to overtake the fugitive telling him that this man would have no qualms about using it. He knew they would soon be able to draw alongside him and, once they did, it would all be over in a hail of bullets. He pressed the control button fully to send his window down automatically, then reached for the canister lying on the passenger seat and, transferring it into his left-hand, thrust it out through the window and held it out at arm's length as far behind the driver's door as he could reach. He pressed the trigger to release the contents and watched in his rear view mirror as the trail of colorless vapor billowed out behind in the slipstream of his car and enveloped the following vehicle.

Agent Bulger remained tight-lipped, grimly determined not to lose control of the powerful pursuit vehicle. Agent Madison reported that the suspect had broken through the roadblock on 185 and was now headed west towards Bethesda on 410. He unfastened his seatbelt then reached over into the back and picked up the Heckler & Koch MP5/10 submachine gun and rested the stock on the seat between his thighs. He inserted the magazine, slid back the bolt and took off the safety catch. As the terrorist's car sped down the straight, oblivious to all other road users, Frank Madison saw Mansour Al Rashid's arm poke out through the car window. Not realising at first what the fleeing suspect was pointing in their direction, he said to his partner, "Looks like the bastard wants a firefight! Well, we'll give him one…" at which instant he recognised the canister from various photographs he'd seen of a previous atrocity. He exclaimed, "Christ, Rudy! Drop back! Shut the windows!" but it was too late. The agents' car cut through the cloud, the thick oily droplets fogging the windshield and swirling turbulently in through the open window, sticking to their skins and getting in their eyes. Almost at once, Evinrude Bolger's view of the road ahead became misty, as his eyes started watering and his nose began to run, then the view darkened as his pupil's constricted to pinpoints. He wiped his eyes with the back of his sleeve, which only made matters worse. Within a few seconds, his shirt was damp with sweat as he began perspiring profusely. He felt as though someone was gradually tightening his chest in a vice and he started to wheeze. Spittle ran copiously down his chin and dripped onto his shirt front. He could hear the rapid dubba-

dubba-dubba drumming in his ears as his heart began to race. As the wave of nausea swept over him, he knew it was impossible to continue driving, so he pressed hard on the brake pedal, relying on the vehicle's ABS to keep it in a straight line without skidding until it stopped. He heard his partner swear as he was thrown forwards against the dashboard, striking his forehead a resounding crack on the windshield. His throat was irritated and burning. He started hacking, a barking, rasping cough that racked his whole upper body but which brought no relief to his breathlessness. As it got worse, he vomitted violently, uncontrollably, over the steering wheel then, as it continued, he felt his bladder and bowels empty themselves into his underpants, rapidly soaking through to wet the seat. His limbs began to jerk spasmodically and the muscles in his face started twitching involuntarily and in less than a minute the shaking had become violent and continuous. As the Sarin permeated the furthest reaches of his central nervous system, Evinrude Bolger's eyes rolled back in his head until nothing but the whites showed and he slipped into unconsciousness. Within two minutes of inhaling the first few molecules of the lethal toxin, he was dead.

Mansour Al Rashid saw the agents' car dive down at the front as the driver braked hard and came to a swift halt. He continued to hold the trigger until the vapor trail ceased, then dropped the canister in the road. As he glanced in his rear view mirror, to check whether there were any other pursuers, he saw it bounce once before it disappeared out of his sight.

Zubin Hazami's thoughts raced frantically. He knew that if there was an interception team on this intersection, there would be one at the junction of every road into the Capital. The Infidels must have uncovered their plot and would be on full alert. His plan to use the school bus to block the road, preventing his pursuers from continuing the chase, had failed but it would surely guarantee that he would now be subject to the unrestrained wrath of the Infidels that awaited him. There was no means of fulfilling his mission or evading capture. And anyway, he was totally exposed on this highway and he could see that the silver Pontiac was still chasing him, closing the distance between them fast. He felt cheated of his moment of glory. On the one occasion he had been called upon to do something for his God – something pure, something unselfish, something that Allah would see as a selfless deed motivated only by this humble believer's desire to act in His service, something that would guarantee him immortality and eternity in Paradise – he had failed. For a brief instant, the thought of giving himself up crossed his mind and he lifted his foot off the accelerator and allowed the truck to cruise a short distance. He was momentarily overcome with indecision but before he could move his foot to cover the brake pedal he heard Satan enticing him to take the easy path in this life but one that would only lead to disgrace and to

166

him being spurned by God in the next. A black cloud of anger descended over his mind and he put his foot back down on the accelerator until it was pressed hard against the floor. His eyes sharpened to a pinpoint focus on the police roadblock at the intersection with Addison Road, as though he was seeing it at the other end of a long, dark tunnel, so much so that he failed to see the Boeing Apache AH-64D Longbow attack helicopter that rose above the junction and hung there, black and sinister, like the Angel of Death. He also failed to notice the silver car falling rapidly behind.

As the Apache settled to hover fifty feet above Highway 214, fifty yards west of Addison Road, the Co-pilot / Gunner said, "Target acquired, four hundred and fifty yards." He kept the truck in the crosshairs of the eyepiece of the integrated sighting system built into his helmet. The Pilot, who had been liaising with the FBI agent on the ground in charge of the interception team, had been given confirmation that their pursuit vehicle was now at least two hundred yards behind the truck although, from his vantage point, he already knew that and that they had been cleared to neutralise the terrorist threat. He spoke tersely into his microphone to the Co-pilot. "Hit it!" He heard the short, muffled buzz, lasting just under three-quarters of a second and felt the sudden jolt as the M230 chain gun mounted beneath the fuselage let off seven, thirty millimeter shells. All the shells either hit the truck directly or punched large pieces out of the pavement just ahead of it that flew up and struck the front and underside of it at supersonic speed. Miraculously, none of the shells hit Zubin Hazami although he was seriously injured by flying debris and shrapnel but the truck was crippled. It continued to roll on under its own momentum but it had been slowed down drastically by the impact of the shells and the damage they'd done. The Pilot ordered, "Hit it again!" and the chain gun delivered another five shells. This time the stricken vehicle veered left and came to a halt on the central reservation, thick black smoke pouring from its engine compartment. Slowly, the driver's door swung open and Zubin Hazami slipped to the ground, leaning against the truck for support. His left arm hung limply, blood running down it and dripping onto the grass. In his right hand he held a submachine gun fitted with a silencer although, due to the blood loss, he was rapidly becoming too weak to lift it. He was just over a mile from Washington DC and eight miles from the heart of the Infidels. Zubin Hazami was overwhelmed by a crushing sense of defeat. He tried to scream out in frustration and despair but the wind bubbled out of his punctured lung and the scream came out as no more than a hoarse wheeze. He had failed Allah, Islam, his people, his family and himself. As the tears streamed down his face, he heard a brusque command, "FBI agent! Drop your weapon!" He looked up and saw the attractive brunette indistinctly, her blurry face swimming in front of him and he was overcome with anger and self-reproach. He swung his weapon up but before he could level it in the woman's direction, Special

Agent Louisa Mandelli had discharged her semi-automatic pistol three times in quick succession, the first two shots shattering Zubin Hazami's sternum and knocking him back against the truck and the third delivering a hammer blow that smashed his nose as the nine millimeter bullet entered his skull and sprayed a mixture of blood, bone and gray matter inside the cab as it exited. The terrorist's lifeless body slumped down heavily and sat propped against the truck's front wheel; nevertheless, Special Agent Erwin Schiller kicked the submachine gun beyond the reach of his dead hand.

Chapter 7: Descent into Madness

(Tuesday 10 August 2010 / 29 Sha'baan 1431 - the day before Ramadan; about 6.30am Pacific time / 9.30am Eastern time)

"Jack! Jay Melosh here…"

Jack Culver leaned against the edge of his desk and said, "Yes, Jay, we've been waiting for your call. What have you got to tell us?"

Dr Jay Melosh, Professor of Theoretical Geophysics in the Lunar and Planetary Laboratory at the University of Arizona, in Tucson, and a leading authority on the effects of planetary impacts, continued. "I just finished running the analysis. I've e-mailed you the results. You should have 'em anytime now…" and then added more quietly, "…and they're frightening." After a brief pause he continued with a slightly tremulous note in his voice, "I don't want to question your findings, Jack… I guess you've been over 'em a thousand times already… but are you *absolutely sure* about the impact of S241? I mean, statistically speaking, Earth should only suffer an event of this scale every four billion years or so. I can hardly believe it's going to happen now, in our lifetime…" Jay Melosh finished desperately.

His old friend said patiently, "Jay, we've gone over our measurements time and again. It's going to hit Earth… and we now have confirmation from Keck II. Their projections of where it'll come down differ slightly from ours by a few hundred miles and theirs aren't so tightly grouped but they haven't been observing it as long as we have… It's a pity the sky didn't clear sooner or we might have known sooner but we had a couple of false readings caused by atmospheric distortion that threw us for a while… Anyway, we're now as certain as we can be that it's on a collision course… Christ knows, Jay, the level of certainty's high enough for JPL to be informing the President as we speak. He'll want a meeting, of course… immediately… and we'll need you there to tell him just how bad this thing's gonna be…"

"I… I don't know, Jack… What about my family? I can't abandon them at a time like this? For God's sake, Jack…"

"Jay, I know… There's nothing you can say because there are no words to express how any of us feel… But we've got to give the President every chance of organising some sort of rescue effort so we can salvage something from this… although God knows what he or anybody else can do…" Jack tailed off and the line went quiet as the two men struggled to come to terms with the likely magnitude of the catastrophe and the turmoil of their own thoughts.

Eventually, Jay Melosh said quietly, "Of course, Jack. I'll be there. Tell me what you want me to do…"

"Have everything ready to put on a succinct presentation. Give 'em all the facts then our job's done. We can get the hell out of there and try to do what we can to ensure the safety of our own families… because when S241 comes down, it'll be everyone for themselves…" After a brief pause, Jack continued, "Anyway, JPL will send the jet for us. We'll land at Tucson and pick you up on our way to Washington but you'll have to be ready at short notice."

"When do we go?"

"Probably today. Every second counts. We'll let you know when…"

"Okay. I'll be ready."

"We'll see you later… Oh! And don't forget, Jay… Keep a lid on it. The President doesn't want word of this leaking out without his say-so…"

"Don't worry, Jack. I haven't forgotten. I'll see you later…" With that the line went dead.

Jack sat for a long moment listening to the tone then put the handset down wearily.

—•—

Paul Kaufmann stood outside the restroom door and tapped on it gently. "Mr President… Are you in there?"

A raised voice from inside came back testily, "Who d'you think's in the President's john… Mickey Mouse? Of course I'm in here. Christ, can't I even take a leak in peace? What do you want?"

"Mr Harland of JPL's on the phone. He wants to talk to you right away, Sir. He says it's urgent. Apparently, he's already called twice but everyone he's authorised to talk to was tied up in briefings both times. He's very insistent…"

"Well, Christ man, you're not helpless. Can't you take a message? You're authorised…" then, more impatiently, "Jesus! I should've been in make-up five minutes ago and I'm supposed to be addressing the nation in half-an-hour… We've got to try to put a lid on this terrorist scare once and for all… Tell him I'll call him back later when we've finished the televised broadcast. Now I don't want any more interruptions. Is that understood?"

Paul Kaufmann sighed and said, "Very good, Sir." As he turned to leave, he faintly heard through the door a mumbled voice muttering, "My fellow Americans…"

At thirteen-fifty-seven hours on Monday, August ninth, two thousand-and-ten, two dirty bombs had exploded within seconds of each other just outside the limits of Washington DC. The bombs had been the work of Islamic fundamentalist terrorists and had been destined to be detonated in the Capital but their evil plot had been foiled by the FBI working in conjunction with the nation's other security services. One bomb, detonated just beyond the eastern perimeter had been relatively crude in its design. As best the forensics team could determine from its remains, it had comprised of a central core of high explosives surrounded by hundreds of small bomblets, each containing a potent mixture of a highly flammable, sticky, jelly-like substance similar to napalm that had been blended with about quarter-of-a-pound of finely powdered radioactive isotopes having half-lives ranging from a few tens to a few hundreds of years – primarily intermediate- and high-level waste from spent nuclear reactor fuel and industrial and medical equipment – which had been generously mixed with magnesium powder, to help dissipate any heat generated by the decaying isotopes. The crate containing the bomb had been lined with lead sheet which absorbed most of the ionizing radiation emitted by the noxious concoction. When the timer in the trigger circuit controlling the detonation had counted three hundred million microseconds, initiated by the call from Mansour Al Rashid's mobile telephone, the central core had exploded, shattering the wooden crate and dispersing its malign seeds over an area about two miles in diameter. Each bomblet had had its own small charge and detonator, designed to explode on impact with the ground or any other solid object or, failing that, within a minute of being blasted out of the mother pod. A couple of the bomblets had detonated prematurely as a result of the initial propulsive blast, showering the immediate vicinity around the truck with burning jelly that had stuck to everything it touched and half-a-dozen had failed to detonate and had been isolated, to be defused later by the bomb disposal squad once they had a better idea of how they functioned. And five hundred and seventy-eight bomblets had struck people's houses or smashed their windows and ended up inside their homes or landed in their gardens or in schools, shopping malls, gas stations, churches, community centers, hotels, motels and restaurants and myriad other places where people went about their daily lives, damaging or destroying them and completely swamping local emergency services with a tidal wave of minor disasters. But it wasn't the injuries, some fatal, or the visible damage that was most insidious; far more harmful was the radioactive fallout that spread over the area, carried by the heat of the fires started by the incendiary devices, which contaminated the very earth people dwelt on, the water they drank and the air they breathed, making the area highly poisonous and totally uninhabitable. It was this that did the real, long-term harm and spread the fear most palpably. The intended destination of this bomb was never known so the prospective victims remained ignorant of their possible fate but that didn't stop everyone who lived or worked in the Capital from heaving a collective sigh of relief that they hadn't been one of the unfortunate souls on the receiving end of such a vicious attack.

The other bomb, detonated beyond the north-western perimeter less than two miles north of Chevy Chase Circle had been more sophisticated. Like the first, it had contained multiple bomblets but fewer – forty-eight in number – each containing half-a-pound of powdered plutonium-238 and 239 in the same flammable paste, packed around a small blast charge to ignite and spread the jelly. The bomblets were discharged from tubes similar to mortar launch tubes which were housed inside a heavy-duty steel cabinet that had been cunningly designed to look like an ordinary office safe. When the five minutes had expired, cleverly concealed charges blew the front door and two adjacent sides off the safe, shattering the wooden packing case and scattering the cardboard boxes that had been hiding it from view, leaving the inside momentarily exposed. However, within a second, all forty-eight bomblets were blasted out simultaneously, the direction that each took being determined by the direction in which its launch tube was pointed. The safe had been loaded onto the truck with its door facing towards the rear. Consequently, when it exploded, the bomblets had been blown out to land in a sector spanning about one hundred and twenty degrees, at distances varying from half-a-mile to two-and-a-half miles. When the individual bomblets exploded, an area in a broad sweep from Glenwood and Alta Vista in the west to Woodside and Montgomery Hills in the east and everything inside that swathe was contaminated with plutonium. On examining Mansour Al Rashid's office, the forensic scientists found masking tape stuck to the carpet which his secretary, Mrs Bilhal, said marked the position of the new safe. When they subsequently superimposed a plot of the sites in which the bomblets had landed on a map of the Capital, with ground zero centered on the building in which Mansour Al Rashid's office was located and the safe was positioned in its intended orientation, the FBI investigators found that all forty-eight bomblets had been designated specific targets ranging from the Pentagon in the extreme south-west across the Potomac River to Union Station and the Capitol in the east and a comprehensive selection of Government buildings in between, not least of which was the J Edgar Hoover Building, headquarters of the Federal Bureau of Investigation. The White House had been singled out for special treatment with three of the bomblets targetted to land in its immediate vicinity. Unfortunately, these had landed in the grounds of the Columbia Country Club, helping to ensure that no one would ever play a round of golf there again. Fortunately, not one of the bomblets from either bomb had exploded within the District of Columbia.

Mansour Al Rashid's Cadillac DeVille had been found parked near the junction of Montgomery Lane and Wisconsin Avenue, close to the Bethesda Metro station. CCTV tapes confirmed that he had last been seen disappearing into the Red Line station carrying a holdall which was later found abandoned in one of the toilet cubicles in the Men's restrooms where, it was assumed, he had changed his appearance. In subsequent examination of video footage of the platforms, FBI investigators thought they could identify at least three potential candidates boarding trains, two of whom headed towards Metro

Center and the third towards the end of the line at Shady Grove. As well as killing the two FBI agents in the pursuit vehicle, the Sarin released by the fleeing terrorist had either killed or incapacitated dozens of other drivers on the East-West Highway. It had then drifted northwards on the gentle breeze, afflicting people as far afield as West Chevy Chase Heights and Rosedale Park with its ghastly effects. Fortunately, this same breeze had carried any radioactive fallout from the dirty bombs northwards as well, away from the Capital although it was still far too close for the comfort of the city's inhabitants, most of whom had understandably fled in panic. As of yesterday evening, Mansour Al Rashid now ranked Number One on the FBI's list of most wanted terrorists.

—•—

Alan Davies sat at his desk pondering the significance of the latest findings from 'Pride of Maryland'. He felt exhausted. Again, he'd worked all night poring over the multitude of evidence that had flooded in from every quarter. He had returned from the White House where he'd been since six-thirty that morning, briefing the President on the terrorist attacks. He had been there yesterday evening, summoned to his presence not to be thanked for his central role in stopping the terrorists before they reached the Capital but to be harangued at length for letting them get so close to the seat of power then failing to apprehend the principal protagonist. Throughout the dressing down, Niara Marshall had sat, looking a little chastened but otherwise very smug only one place removed from the President's right hand; clearly, she had told him about her insistence on neutralising the first terrorist on the Outer Harbour Bridge of the Baltimore Beltway as soon as he'd been identified without explaining the logistical reason why he, Alan Davies, time-served and battle-hardened veteran, had advocated doing otherwise. He could understand that the President's confidence had been shaken by the fact that the terrorists had come so close to fulfilling their ambitious scheme and by his realisation of the crippling effects it would have had on the nation's governance, as well as the implications it would've had for his presidency had they done so. He was also acutely aware of the nationwide outrage and panic that had ensued when the news broke that terrorists had successfully deployed radioactive dirty bombs and Sarin nerve agent in the vicinity of Washington DC. There had been a feeding frenzy without let-up by the news networks, with virtually continuous and repetitious coverage and instant updates every time another victim had succumbed to one or other of the lethal weapons. Yes, it also had to be acknowledged that there was a huge upwelling of anger, some of which was unreasonably aimed at the Government for failing to deter these latest atrocities by not dealing more harshly with previous ones. But how far could the President – any President – go? What Alan Davies couldn't understand was the President's apparent ingratitude which he felt was reserved specially for him. He had tried unsuccessfully to put the smarting criticism out of mind immediately he'd been dismissed from the meeting but, even now, fifteen hours later, it still rankled.

He had only called in at his office on his way back from the White House to collect the present for his wife that his PA had bought for him – he hoped it would be as good as an apology for having spent most of the last two weeks away from home – which he'd forgotten to take with him in his haste to get to the White House in time for this morning's briefing. As he'd reached for the beautifully wrapped gift, he'd noticed the little envelope symbol winking on his computer screen telling him he had mail. He was very tired and even more disillusioned. He picked up the gift and started to walk away but dint of habit and dedication to duty made him go back and open his mailbox. The first message was from Special Agent Marvin Spangler, reporting that one of the divers at the scene had found a small but very heavy, lead-lined, steel flask, still shiny and new-looking, in the mud at the bottom of the dock directly beneath where 'Pride of Maryland' had been tied up; the remains of the hull had already been removed. The logical assumption was that it had been dropped overboard – either accidentally or on purpose – as opposed to being blown out of the boat by the explosion. On taking it to the laboratory for analysis, it had been found to contain traces of strontium-90 and caesium-137 – both highly radioactive by-products of the fission process carried on in nuclear reactors – the same radioactive substances that had been found amongst the debris of the Maryland and two of the many toxic substances in the dirty bomb discovered at the Patapsco River Crossing. He sat wondering, 'Why would a terrorist go to the trouble of carrying a sample of something radioactive... something that could easily be detected by an investigator with a Geiger counter... in a container to shield it from detection, then empty out its contents so it could be readily found... sooner or later? Obviously the container was to protect the person carrying it... I can't believe they spilled it accidentally but why empty it out on purpose? Why? It doesn't make sense...' He mentally shifted his perspective, so he saw the thing from various viewpoints but he struggled to make sense of this new twist in the plot. Suddenly the thought crossed his mind, 'The assumption so far has been that the material found in the debris of the Maryland had leaked out of one of the bombs accidentally. Maybe they wanted it to be found to alert us to the fact that they really did have a dirty bomb in case we hadn't taken the threat seriously... But why? Surely that would just make us look harder. After all, we've foiled their plans... We won this particular battle, they lost... But why do anything that might increase the likelihood of discovery even slightest?'

Then a chilling thought struck him, 'Or have they lost? Was this only their opening gambit?' Before he could question further what motive the terrorists might have had for wanting their plot to be uncovered, his PA knocked and stuck her head round the door. She seemed in an upbeat mood.

"Excuse me, Mr Davies. Your wife rang whilst you were out. I told her I'd let you know... Oh! And just to remind you... The President will be speaking to the nation in five minutes... I hope you get a mention for your role in this triumph, Sir. You deserve it, you really do."

He thanked his PA for her faith in him. He reached for the remote control with one hand and switched on the television then muted the sound, waiting until the President appeared whilst he dialled his home phone number with the other. As he waited for his wife to answer, he opened the second e-mail and began scanning it but his mind was elsewhere, distracted by dark thoughts that raced pell-mell through the shadowy recesses of his mind.

His concern and alarm over the high numbers of casualties amongst his agents and members of the public had killed any euphoria or even relief that Alan Davies might have felt at this outcome. But there were aspects of this that puzzled and concerned him, aspects that had nagged at his subconscious but which now surfaced again with this particular issue. He thought, 'Why? Why have they advertised their presence so blatantly... Why put the one bomb in a simple wooden box? They took the trouble to fabricate one safe... Why not make two? It would've made the other bomb virtually undetectable, especially as it was emitting much higher energy radiation... I can understand why they had two different designs of bomb... They could only get their hands on a relatively small amount of plutonium... it's so tightly controlled... so they wanted to use it to maximum effect... That's why they plumped for filling the other bomb with nuclear waste... and in truth it's probably far more harmful in the short term than plutonium, although plutonium is probably far more emotive. It has much greater propaganda value... And why 'Inchalla Express Deliverance'? When you think about it, it's so obvious. It's a dead giveaway... And why purposely contaminate the site of the Maryland with radioactive material after the event? Was it to focus our attention and drive home the fact that this is a real radiological threat... once we'd found it, of course... Is that what this is all about? Grabbing our attention...' His wife's voice interrupted his thoughts momentarily. "Estelle! Hello darling. I'm sorry! I know I said I'd be home by nine-thirty but I was at the White House longer than anticipated, then I got held up at the office... Yes, I'll be leaving soon. I'll watch the President's address then come straight home... How's Mother?" Alan Davies and his wife passed another minute making small talk but she could tell by his monosyllabic answers to her questions that he was preoccupied, so she gently brought the call to a close by telling him that her invalid mother, who lived in a granny flat attached to their house, was calling for her assistance even though she knew for a fact that her mother was dozing in her wheelchair.

Yesterday afternoon, before he'd gone the White House, Alan Davies had circulated an e-mail to all FBI Field Offices, which read:

To: all ADICs / SACs

Status: TOP PRIORITY – MOST URGENT: REQUEST FOR IMMEDIATE ACTION

Background: At approx 1400EST today Muslim terrorists linked to al-Qaeda (all naturalised American citizens of Middle Eastern origin) detonated two dirty bombs just outside Washington DC limits. Both bombs contained radioactive materials. One was housed in a specially constructed steel cabinet, effectively shielding any radiation, made to look like a normal office safe (overall dimensions approx 76"H x 48"W x 36"D – see fotos attached, no manufacturer's mark or other distinguishing features). It is thought that the bombs were assembled in Yemen and brought to USA by ship, then transferred to a cruiser (probably outside 12-mile limit) owned by one of the terrorists (Mansour Al Rashid a.k.a. Luis Ruiz DaCosta and Ranaldo Alvarez Valasquez – see fotos). The bombs were landed at a private dock and transported by road to Washington separately by two other terrorists in the cell (brothers Haroun and Zubin Hazami – see fotos). Al Rashid had leased an office on the top floor of a high-rise in DC within striking distance of the White House and many Federal buildings which we think were the intended targets of the bomb in the safe. Al Rashid had also bribed one of the building services staff to do small jobs for him that were not put through the service company's books and so were not charged to Al Rashid's company. This was the route by which the safe was going to be taken to Al Rashid's office without it being drawn to the attention of the building's management. We think that, had the plot been successful, the bomb would have been detonated high above the Capital, which would have contaminated Washington with plutonium seriously disrupting Government. I am concerned that other bombs as yet undiscovered may have been planted covertly in other US cities, possibly disguised to look like office safes or similar.

Action: Make enquiries of the management company of every privately-owned commercial property, starting with high-rise office blocks leasing space to third parties, about safes or other large cabinets brought in by tenants. This will necessitate management companies making a complete search of the building (every office, room, etc.). In particular, we need to be informed immediately about safes that have been brought in covertly (i.e. without authorisation and without being entered in the building's heavy items register, if it has one). Management companies should use their pass keys to enter any unmanned offices (occupied, or not) and must immediately report to the local FBI Field Office any refusal by occupants to allow access. Management companies must also provide a list of all safes brought into the building with their knowledge and / or permission within the last three (3) months. These may be searched for terrorist weapons by a Federal Agent at the discretion of each ADIC / SAC.

Coverage (Priority 1): All major cities having an FBI field office

Coverage (Priority 2): All other towns and cities having (i) an FBI Satellite Office, or (ii) a strategic military installation and / or nuclear power plant located within a 20-mile radius

Term: To be actioned immediately and continued until complete

Supplementary information: ADIC Washington Metropolitan Field Office is tasked with compiling a list of all safes sold in USA in the last three (3) months by safe manufacturers, importers, distributors and retailers, which will be circulated to all Field Offices by 1000EST tomorrow, Tuesday August 10. Lists provided by management companies of safes installed are to be cross-checked against our master list. Any installations that are considered suspicious for any reason will be investigated by Federal Agents.

Legality: There is a blanket warrant no.78650101/B currently in place, issued under the Prevention of Terrorism Act, Special Regulations (2010) that allows Federal Agents access (with forced entry, if necessary) to any privately-owned property without the owner's or occupant's consent if there is any suspicion, however slight, that elements hostile to the USA are or might be at work therein.

Note on Legality: Representatives of management companies do not have the right *per se* to demand to examine the contents of a safe, even if its owner has given their permission for that representative to establish that it exists. We only need to know from them that the safe exists. We will deal with any further enquiries as to its contents thereafter.

Alan Davies briefly read the e-mail from the Assistant Director in charge of the Washington Metropolitan Field Office, which had arrived at 0953EST, four minutes after Agent Spangler's e-mail. It contained a surprisingly comprehensive list of most safes sold within the last three months in the USA, with very few dealers claiming to need more time to put together the information. He was about to open the attached list when his attention was caught by sudden flashes from the television screen on the far wall. He looked up as the President appeared on stage hand-in-hand with the First Lady. Without exception the audience, comprising almost exclusively of hard-bitten journalists and reporters, stood and applauded the leader of the most powerful nation on Earth; it hadn't gone unnoticed that throughout the impending threat, the President and his family had resolutely remained in the White

House despite pressure from the Secret Sevice special agent in charge of the Presidential Protection Detail responsible for their security who had insisted they withdraw to the relative safety of Air Force One. He watched as the President modestly acknowledged the plaudits, then raised both hands and motioned for the audience to sit down before accompanying his wife to her seat. He held her hand considerately as she descended genteely, knees together, on to the chair. As she tucked her straight skirt tightly under her shapely thighs, Alan Davies thought how smart and elegantly understated she looked in her expensive, lightweight, gray silk, two-piece suit. When the hubbub had died down, the President stepped up to the podium. As he silently mouthed the opening words of his speech, "My fellow Americans...", Alan Davies reached for the remote control to restore the sound and noticed how haggard and sunken the man's eyes looked which no amount of make-up could disguise.

—•—

Dan Ackland sat forward in his sumptuous, leather upholstered chair and said impatiently, "There's no wonder JPL can't get through to anybody at the White House. They're all tied up in this three-ring media circus... How in Heaven's name do they think they'll pass this one off as a victory? And if they do, it'll be interesting to see what they make of it when the news breaks about S241..."

In a rather more placatory tone, Jack Culver said, "Well, Dan, you can understand it. People are scared and angry. I guess the President's just trying to calm their fears about something that's nearer to home and far more tangible for most people than S241. After all, it'd hardly inspire confidence in him if he ignored these atrocities. He's got to try and reassure people that he can... that we all can deal with these big, difficult, painful issues successfully. I think, on balance, he's doing the right thing... in fact, *the only thing* he could do under the circumstances." He leaned against the edge of Dan Ackland's desk, his long legs stretched out in front of him, with his back to his boss and long-time friend and continued watching television intently.

Dan Ackland grunted then grudgingly acknowledged, "I suppose you're right, Jack... And anyway, Wayne Harland's pre-empted the White House by sending the jet for us to avoid any more delays. It should be here within the hour..." Realising that Jack was only half-listening to him, Dan Ackland shut up and concentrated on the televised message.

In his opening statement, the President had given a highly precised but basically accurate account of events culminating in the explosion of the two dirty bombs and the release of Sarin nerve gas and their gruesome aftermath. There was little point going over them in detail. It would simply have been to reiterate what had already been played out over and over again on most television news channels. He continued, "We have overwhelming evidence that the terrorists intended to perpetrate these wicked crimes in the Capital itself, which may have resulted in many more casualties and may also have had a seriously damaging effect on the process of Government if temporarily. I am pleased to say that the brave men and women of our security services foiled the terrorists' evil plans and that no harm was done inside the Capital although, sadly, not without the loss or injury of a number of our valiant defenders. However, my deepest sympathy lies with those unfortunate victims in the state of Maryland and their families who bore the brunt of this terrible attack and have suffered its horrific consequences..." Here he paused briefly before continuing, "The military term for these dirty bombs is 'Area Denial Weapons'. It would seem that the terrorists were determined to deny us the use and enjoyment of our great capital city, an endeavour in which they failed totally. To those people who lost their homes, I assure you that once a full assessment has been made of the situation, we will set about clearing and decontaminating the affected areas and rebuilding your communities. And if that's not possible we'll help everyone to become re-established elsewhere..." The President paused to take a sip of water, then continued, "Coming to the terrorists themselves, we have one in custody, one is dead and a third is on the run. No effort will be spared to apprehend this man and when we do, he will be brought to justice... American justice!" he said emphatically. At this, there were murmurs of approval from the audience. After pausing to allow the ripple of accord to die down, he took a fresh grip on the lectern and visibly braced himself before continuing with greater gravitas. "In the broader sense, I am currently re-appraising the whole of the terrorist situation and how we deal with it but until that process is complete, I give you my solemn pledge that we will continue to be vigilant on all fronts in the protection of our interests at home and abroad and rigorous in eradicating terrorism wherever we find it..." The President continued in a similar vein for another five minutes, talking in measured and reasonable tones about the ongoing problem and the Government's response to it. When he had finished, he concluded with, "Thank you, Ladies and Gentlemen. And now I'd like to invite questions from the floor..." at which fifty-odd hands shot up in unison.

Jack Culver turned to Dan Ackland and commented, "Not bad. No insincere, meaningless rhetoric. No wild promises. Just a common sense, down-to-earth approach. Let's hope he has chance to carry it through..."

The President nodded in the direction of a woman in the middle of the third row and said, "Yes, Miss Silver..."

The woman stood and announced herself. "Monica Silver of the Washington Post, Sir. I'd like to ask what you meant by 're-appraising the terrorist situation and how we deal with it'... How will future policy be different and what guarantee is there that a change of direction will be any more effective?"

The President cleared his throat and appeared to falter momentarily but only because he was trying to shape his answer. He started cautiously. "As you'll no doubt appreciate, I can't say too much about our deliberations at this stage because as of today they're not complete but what I can say is this... We have to try and live with everyone on this planet... yes, even those who bear us malice and would do us harm... We have to understand why they feel as they do and what has shaped their malign view of us so we can try to re-educate them or at least try to change their perception of us... After all, we're not the tyrants they clearly take us for..."

Before he could continue, another journalist stood up uninvited and without announcing himself, asked forcefully, "So is what you're saying, Mr President, that America will step back from its role of trying to bring democracy to other countries, particularly in the Middle East and Third World?"

The President turned his gaze on the man and responded, "Thank you. Albeit it was univited, I'll respond to your question directly because it helps to complete my answer to the first question..." Before he could elucidate another, blunter voice came from somewhere in the audience, from someone who remained seated, "Or is what you're talking about appeasement? Caving in to the terrorists? In other words 'America running scared'..." and another dissenting voice joined in angrily, demanding to know "And if that is the case, how do we deliver this so-called 'American justice' you talk about so glibly... Just what is it anyway? And how do the ninety thousand innocent Americans who've already died at the hands of Muslim terrorists obtain any sort of justice?"

Like a rumble of thunder, the wave of dissension rolled through the audience. The President waited until it had abated, staring into the sea of faces in front of him, then held them with a steely eye as he said, "Before you criticise this approach or dismiss it out of hand, stop a moment and ask yourself what the alternatives are..." He waited momentarily for them to respond to the challenge he'd laid down then, when it had calmed again, continued, "We can't simply go on as we are... allowing the situation to spiral out of control... and the costs, human and otherwise, to escalate... to get us where? I'll tell you. Precisely nowhere! We're no better off now as a nation for having lost ninety thousand innocent souls than we were before the killings started in earnest with the World Trade Center on September eleven, two-thousand-and-one... But also, we're not under attack because the terrorists don't like the way we comb our hair or knot our ties or... or the fact that we put maple syrup on our waffles. There are some people... *many people*... worldwide... that have a deep-seated dislike and distrust of America... a hatred even... with what they believe to be just cause... Yes, I personally believe in and uphold democracy and I think it's the only fair system of government for all peoples, so we'll continue trying to persuade nations to move in that direction but we must also accept that, once democracy is in place, other nations have a right to their own sovereignty without our interference. The difficulty we face today is how we achieve that... That's what the on-going debate is about and I would respectfully ask that you accept that position..."

The audience sat quietly, chewing over the President's pithy comments. In a jocular tone, he said, "It looks as though I've stunned you into silence... If there are no further questions, I must get on... We have detailed recovery plans to formulate..."

Before the President could take his leave, a hand in the front row went up. He nodded in the direction of the hand and the reporter stood up and said, "Bob Green of the New York Times, Mr President. May I ask what implications your last statement has for Iraq? It has a crude form of democracy... imperfect I know and not working very smoothly... but it seems to me that it only exists at all because of the presence of US forces there... What happens if we withdraw?"

The President looked straight at the man for a few moments, then admitted candidly, "To be frank, I don't know how we resolve the situation in Iraq, Mr Green... or indeed for that matter, in the whole of the Middle East. But that, of course, is what the current debate is all about. All I know is that it has to be resolved... And that means including the views of all parties, however distasteful we might find them..."

The mood was strangely subdued.

Dan Ackland said to his colleague, "Uncharacteristically honest for a politician. Not at all what I'd have expected..."

A small, well-tanned hand went up and the President again nodded. The speaker stood up and said, "Anwar Al-Fawr of the Arab Free Press, Mr President. May I ask, what of Saudi Arabia?"

Sensing that this was a loaded question, the President tried giving himself time for thought by expanding on the answer slowly. "In what respect, Mr Al-Fawr?"

"In respect of the withdrawal of all American infidels, military and civilian, from the Kingdom, Sir."

"Well, as you know, the United States has a legitimate presence there at the direct invitation of the King and the ruling Al-Saud family..."

The questioner interrupted, "But not at the invitation of Allah or many of the people who follow Him. With all due respect, Sir, to them, you are unbelievers and consequently unwelcome in that place... And so I would ask you again... What of Saudi Arabia?"

The President tried again. "We are there at the invitation of our friends, the Saudi royal family, who are also custodians of the holiest cities of Islam and keepers of the Muslim faith. If they were to withdraw their invitation and ask us to leave, we would obviously have to accede to their wishes, as we have done in the past but in the meantime…"

The little man cut in determinedly, "There are six thousand princes in the Saudi royal family… devout Muslims maybe but a tiny minority in a nation of twenty-five million Muslims and a worldwide community of one-and-a-quarter billion Muslims, many of whom consider America's presence there offensive and a desecration of Islam's holiest places. We all know that you are only interested in the Middle East because it sits on top of half the World's oil reserves and the Saudi royal family want you there to underpin their hold on power which is the source of their wealth… Effectively, your presence in the Kingdom is to maintain the material interests of six thousand individuals… and ultimately, of course, your own material interests… with no consideration for the feelings of the other one-and-a-quarter billion Muslims…"

The President asked confrontationally, "So you claim to speak for all one-and-a-quarter billion Muslims…" but before he could finish, the dogged little man said in a level voice, "With all due respect, I do not claim to speak for anyone, Sir. I am merely asking the question so I will ask it one last time. What of Saudi Arabia?"

The President stood stony-faced for a long moment, looking directly at his inquisitor. All eyes in the room had swung from the swarthy, dapper little man in the immaculate gray suit and were now fixed on the President. After what seemed like an age, he said flatly, "I cannot answer that question."

—•—

As Alan Davies watched the President, he thought, 'So that's the route he's chosen… To pursue the diplomatic option… And he's neatly circumvented the Department of Defense by declaring himself publicly… Very clever… and very brave… Of course, it'll not go down well with the hawks at the Pentagon. Let's hope it doesn't backfire on him… Still, I don't think I'll be here to worry about which direction they take. My instinct tells me my days in post are numbered… It'll be down to some other poor sod to take on the thankless task of trying to keep the nation safe… Even the Director seems to be distancing himself from me. He must have sensed which way the wind's blowing…' He rubbed his sore eyes and decided he would go home as soon as the President had finished his address without waiting for the question and answer session. After all, it would be staged like all Q&A sessions in his experience. He was about to switch the set off when the President chose his first questioner. Alan Davies thought, 'Monica Silver, the hottest hack in Washington and sharp as a razor. I hope he knows what he's doing because she takes no prisoners. He might end up wishing he'd chosen someone else because her line of questioning could easily lead him into a minefield…' He continued watching for a few moments longer, interested in the question and how the President would reply to it. 'I bet that one was off-script. Naughty naughty, Monica…' he said to himself, silently admonishing her. 'Still, he did raise the subject, so it's fair game. She has every right to pursue it…'

The telephone rang and he picked it up, keeping half his attention on the screen.

"A.D.I.C. Neery here, New York Field Office…"

Alan Davies said expansively, "Hello Rubin. Long time, no see. How are you, old friend?" but Rubin Neery was clearly in no mood to exchange pleasantries.

"Alan, we've got one helluva firefight going on here in a high rise downtown in the business quarter… The building services manager became suspicious when he tried to get access to an office leased to a company trading as Al Yamamah Exotic Materials Inc… The manager thought they were dealing in porn and sex aids and so on but it turns out to be precious metals… You know, silver, gold… They're bound to need a safe for storage purposes… At first, they wouldn't answer the door so he thought there was nobody in and tried his pass key. That's when he found out the door was locked from inside. He called us and we sent out a team to investigate… At first, they tried contacting the occupants by phone but no reply. Eventually they tried forcing an entry which lead to two of my agents being shot. One's dead, the other's badly hurt but we can't get him out. They're dug in tighter than a tick on a hound and they've got some real heavy artillery in there. I've sanctioned a complete evacuation of the building and full containment…" When more than ten seconds had elapsed with no reply, Rubin Neery said querulously, "Alan… are you there?"

"Yes…"

"Did you hear what I just said?"

Alan Davies had been listening intently to the Assistant Director in charge of the New York Field Office but he had also been watching the unnerving exchange between the President and the diminutive Arab reporter on the television. He felt a cold clamminess begin to creep over him, as all the scattered pieces of the jigsaw dropped into place to reveal a terrifying picture. "Yes…"

Rubin Neery had the presence of mind to realise that his superior was preoccupied with something important so he waited quietly. Suddenly, Alan Davies shot out, "Rubin, forget containing the scene. Evacuate the building… No! Evacuate the whole area for ten blocks in each direction…"

Rubin Neery blurted out, "Why Alan? Do you think they have another…" but before he could finish, Alan Davies commanded, "No! Evacuate the entire city… On my orders!"

Rubin Neery gasped, "Have you gone mad? You can't be serious…" but Alan Davies cut him dead. "Do it, Rubin!"

Rubin Neery's tremulous voice came back, "I can't do that, Alan. I don't have the authority… or the grounds…"

Alan Davies cut in, "No, but I do! I'm going to speak to the Mayor and tell him to start the evacuation immediately. Then I'll speak to the Director. We should be able to get presidential sanction for it straightaway…"

"Jesus, Alan! Think hard, man. If you're wrong, they'll fire you. At least get the Director's say-so. Let him take the bullet for it if anyone has to…"

"I suspect my time here's finished anyway, Rubin. Whatever happens, I'd rather go out with a bang… Trust me, old friend, I know what I'm doing. Evacuate the city. Don't hesitate. Do it. Now!" and with that, he slammed the handset down. As he frantically scanned his electronic telephone directory looking for the number of the direct line to the Mayor of New York City, Alan Davies bawled out at the top of his voice, "Mary! Mary!"

His PA burst in, a look of alarm on her face. "What is it?" she gasped urgently.

"Get me the Director. Now! It's a matter of vital importance. He's at the White House."

His PA left the room even quicker than she'd entered it, as Alan Davies hit the speed-dial button. The telephone at the other end of the line seemed to ring interminably before a distant voice said, "Good morning, the Mayor's office… How may I help you?"

—•—

Martha knelt in front of the toilet, clinging to the seat, her head over the bowl. As she retched for the third time, she heard Claudette outside the bathroom door urgently asking, "Mom… Mom… Are you alright? Do you want me to get a doctor? Is there anything I can do?" It was the third morning in a row she'd felt queasy but it was the first time she'd actually been sick. Martha tore off a strip of toilet paper. She wiped her chin and flushed the toilet, then rinsed her mouth out. "No… No, it's alright, thanks darling. I've got a gippy tummy. It must've been something I ate. I'll be alright, once I've rested up."

Martha sat on the bed, leaning against the raised pillow. They were in a hotel in Portage, Indiana. Claudette brought her a glass of water and she took a few sips. "Thank you, darling. I'm feeling a lot better now…" She thought to herself, 'God, I hope this isn't what I think it is. Especially not now, at a time like this…'

After they had taken their leave of Katherine Colquhoun, the Security Supervisor at the bus station in Cheyenne had shown them video footage that gave a few brief glimpses of Billy in the terminal in the early hours of Monday morning, August second, three days previously. This was further confirmation that Billy was headed east but Martha was concerned that he was so far ahead of them. She had been frustrated by the slow progress they'd made since leaving Cheyenne. Martha had looked at the map and, like Jack, concluded that if Billy was making his way to Jack's parents, he would go by the most direct route, if possible. The obvious route was to take I-80 as far as Cleveland.

They'd had a puncture just outside North Platte, Nebraska which delayed them a couple of hours. Then, as they'd approached Lincoln, the fuel pump had packed up. The car had to be towed to a main dealer for urgent repairs but as the dealer didn't have a replacement in stock, it necessitated an overnight stop. The car had been delivered back to them at mid-day, as promised but not before Martha's patience had worn thin. She'd lost her temper with Nicky. Why? For being on the phone to his girlfriend at home when the car had been returned, delaying their departure by a few minutes. The twins had noticed that their mother was becoming increasingly irascible, particularly in the mornings but they had put it down to her anxiety over Billy. When they saw the CCTV tapes at the bus station in Omaha, they had caught sight of a woman with two boys in tow, the younger one of whom bore such a strong resemblance to Billy in looks and mannerisms that Nicky was convinced it was him. The boy hung back behind his mother, as a consequence of which they only caught infrequent and fleeting glimpses of him. Martha and Claudette were unsure whether it was Billy. When the Security Supervisor discovered that the woman had bought a return ticket to Kansas City for three passengers, Martha was even more doubtful it was Billy. Why would the woman buy a ticket for a stranger only to bring them back to the same place they'd started from? But Nicky had argued that as it was their only lead, however flimsy, they should at least follow it; if it lead them up a blind alley, he argued, they could always retrace their steps.

As it so happened, the woman had organised to take her sons to visit Westport and Independence, to visit the heads of the California, Oregon and Santa Fe trails, the Arabia Steamboat Museum and Kansas City Museum, to help with the older boy's studies of pioneering and the opening up of the west as part of his school history project. She had planned to reward them for their diligence with a visit to the Worlds of Fun theme park and its sister attraction, the Oceans of Fun water park. Had the woman's arrangements gone to plan,

Martha would never have run her to ground. But the boys had had a secret agenda and had only gone along with their mother's plans on a pretext. As soon as they'd arrived in KC, the boys had badgered their mother to take them to see their father who now lived near Wichita with his new wife and whom they hadn't seen for three months. Hurt by their duplicity, she had reluctantly spoken to her ex-husband after much wrangling then put the boys on a bus to Wichita.

When Martha watched the CCTV footage in the KC bus station, she saw the family. The mother looked decidedly fractious as she snapped at the younger boy and motioned for him to join her at the ticket counter, where Martha got a clear view of him for the first time and saw it wasn't Billy. She had known in her heart that it was unlikely to be her son but when it was confirmed, the disappointment combined with the fact that they'd lost another day and made a three hundred and eighty mile detour for no good reason hit her like a slap in the face. As the three of them returned to the car, she could barely contain her hurt and anger. So when they were rear-ended as they joined I-35 north to Des Moines, Martha had exploded and screamed at Nicky for his stupidity in dragging them all this way on a wild goose chase which set an uncomfortable tone for the next leg of the journey. What rankled with Martha was the fact that, had she not been persuaded by Nicky, the accident – albeit relatively minor – wouldn't have happened but what rankled even more was the fact that, if she'd obeyed her instinct, they would never have deviated from their eastward path in the first place.

There was no record of Billy having been in the bus station in Des Moines, so they had done the only thing that made sense to Martha which was to continue eastward. At the bus station in Davenport, the security tapes from early the previous Tuesday morning showed Billy walking determinedly across the terminal to the departure area. As of today, he was at least six days ahead of them. There was no wonder Billy hadn't been apprehended so far; the runaway child alert put out by Francis Doolittle at Portland must have arrived after the Security Supervisor had gone off duty Monday evening and by the time he saw it Tuesday morning, Billy had already gone. When the Security Supervisor studied the tapes, the best he could tell Martha was that, from the stands in that part of the terminal, Billy was headed east, possibly to Chicago. Martha told him that they knew Billy was headed east to Jack's parents in up-state New York.

The Security Supervisor said, "Well, he seems to be single-minded in his quest. Your boy must have been travelling virtually non-stop to keep up such a gruelling schedule." The man thought about Billy's progress for a few moments, then said, "If you know where he's going, why stop at every town along the way? It takes time and you're falling further behind. Why not go straight to the other end and meet him there?" then added, "Assuming he makes it, of course."

Martha said, "I did consider that but as there's a reception committee at the other end, I thought he'd be better served if we came along behind to pick him up if he can't get a ride..." then added, a little incredulously, "I'd never have guessed he'd pass through here so soon after leaving Cheyenne if I hadn't seen it with my own eyes."

The Security Supervisor said, "Well, Ma'am, that should say something about the efficiency of our transit service..." Then, with a slightly troubled look, added, "It doesn't explain why he hasn't arrived yet. He should've been there some days ago if he'd continued making such good progress."

It was Martha's turn to look troubled as she said quietly, "That's what worries me... and that's why we're visiting every stop along the way to make sure something hasn't happened to him..."

Martha was convinced Billy would continue east on I-80 using buses, unless anything happened to prevent him from doing so and she said so. The Security Supervisor agreed. Still smarting from his mother's harsh words, Nicky cautiously suggested they should at least investigate the possibility that he'd gone via Chicago. The Security Supervisor chipped in usefully that many of the long-distance services went via Chicago but Martha didn't want to deviate from the path she was certain Billy had taken. It was probably the reassurance of having seen Billy on video as recently as six days ago and her certainty that he was determined to see his quest through that had calmed Martha sufficiently so that she answered Nicky coolly, "You go and see if Billy's been there if you like but I'm continuing straight east..." Looking at the map on the Security Supervisor's office wall, she said, "You take the bus to Chicago and see what you can find. Claudette and I will continue east and meet you tomorrow in... er... Gary, Indiana... Can you manage that?"

"Yes."

"Well, make sure you're there by mid-day at the latest. We'll check into a motel somewhere thereabouts... It'll probably mean you leaving Chicago by..." Here she checked the bus timetable and pointed to an entry "...here, using this service... by ten-twenty a.m. It gets into Gary at eleven-thirty, which should give us plenty of time to check out then pick you up from the bus station..."

As Nicky dashed back to the car to get his overnight bag, the Security Supervisor said, "I must warn you, Mrs Culver... Most security systems operate using a suite of seven tapes, one for each day of the week, which are rotated on a cyclic basis... I know ours does... If your son gets a week ahead of you, they'll be taping over the previous week's footage before you have chance to see it. You can't afford to fall any further behind..."

187

Martha thanked the man for his assistance and the two of them went to see Nicky off. Secretly, mother and son were relieved to be out of each other's company for a while because the acrimony of their arguments had left both feeling a little hurt. Both felt that the separation, albeit brief, would give them time to lick their respective wounds.

Martha looked at the bedside clock and back at her watch. "That's odd... I forgot to put my watch forward. It's still on Central time but we're in Indiana... I thought Hoosiers were on Eastern time..."

Claudette said, "Yes Mom, they are. But here in this corner of Indiana, I think they're on Central..." Martha continued to play with her watch and fidget about on the bed. Her daughter thought, 'Mmm... She's getting itchy... She clearly wants to be off after Billy... I bet she regrets letting Nicky go off to Chicago yesterday, especially as there was no sign of Billy...' but Claudette was surprised when, a few moments later, her mother said, "I hope he's okay... Nicky, I mean... You know how uncomfortable these big cities make me feel nowadays..." Then, a couple of minutes later, "I do hope Nicky's alright..."

A message appeared on their television screen as it did on the television in every room, sent from the reception desk, informing all guests that the President would be making a televised broadcast to the nation in five minutes and on which channels it would be shown. Claudette switched the television to channel thirty-two and sat beside her mother.

Nudging her daughter and pointing to the screen, Martha said excitedly, "Robert Green! As I live and breathe. Would you credit it? We were at high school together, Claudette. He was a year below me. He had a crush on me like you wouldn't believe. He actually asked me to go out with him... At the time, I was one of the cheer-leaders for the school's football team and I was going out with the quarter-back... I didn't fancy him anyway... he was such a weed... but when I told him I couldn't go out with him, he was heartbroken. In fact, he was so upset, he rode his bicycle straight off the levee and into the Hudson River. God! It was so funny! Well, it would've been if he hadn't nearly drowned... A couple of longshoremen had to fish him out... At the time, I thought he was completely mad but in hindsight it was a very romantic gesture... Crazy but romantic..." Martha concluded, then added a little wistfully, "Odd... I haven't thought about that for years but I remember it like it was yesterday... That's what unrequited love does to you. I wonder if he ever thinks about it now?"

Claudette said distractedly, "Probably not. Not if he's moving in such elevated circles..." but her focus was on the small, brown man who was

188

progressively backing the President further and further into a corner like a terrier cornering a rat before going in for the kill.

—•—

In response to the finality of the President's answer in the negative to his question, Anwar Al-Fawr said respectfully, "In which case, Sir, would you kindly oblige me by asking your technicians to turn the monitor to channel twenty-eight... or thirty-two, or thirty-six, or even thirty-eight for that matter..." For a moment, the President looked perplexed then nodded to the broadcasting studio manager. The monitors to left and right of the stage flickered momentarily, then stabilised. The picture was divided down the center, showing the President on one half looking quizzically around the studio. In the distance, raised voices shouted instructions and doors slammed as the Secret Service agents, sensing something was wrong, tried to take command of the situation. On the other half of the screen was a picture of a city seen from a great distance through a telephoto lens. As the President stared, trying to make out which city it was, one of the reporters from the west coast said, "Isn't that downtown LA? Yes! There's the Griffith Observatory in the foreground and I'm pretty sure that tall building in the background's the US Bank Tower..." Another voice concurred and with that a ripple of recognition spread through the audience. As they watched, the image of the city slowly diminished, so that the Observatory receded into the far distance until it was almost too small to distinguish. The picture now showed a panoramic view of most of the Los Angeles metropolitan area; it would have shown it set against a beautiful backdrop of Santa Catalina Island and the deep blue Pacific Ocean had the view not been obscured by the thin veil of smog that hung over the city. As they watched transfixed, a swarthy man with a full, dark beard walked into shot and stood in sharp focus in front of the camera, blocking out most of the city. The President's stomach lurched as he recognised the man from the FBI's surveillance photographs.

Mohammad Faisal Qureshi waited a moment, then said, "Good morning, Mr President. I would like to thank you for calling all these good people together in the first place and then for humoring Mr Al-Fawr's request... Oh! And before I go on... Before you detain him indefinitely without trial at your Guantanamo Bay facility, Mr Al-Fawr is completely innocent of any complicity in this... He is simply following instructions given to him by his editor in asking you the question. Mr Al-Fawr knows nothing of what is to come... Anyway, to get down to business. You have the undivided attention of most of the population of the United States of America..." then, in a more menacing tone, "Now, thanks to you, so do I..."

—•—

189

As he'd waited for the Mayor of New York City to come to the phone, Alan Davies had switched to channel twenty-eight then zapped the other three channels mentioned by the diminutive reporter from the Arab Free Press and had seen the same image on all four. He hadn't recognised the city but he overheard the impromptu comments from the studio audience which informed him of the location. Immediately the terrorist leader appeared, a chill ran down his spine and a feeling of dread settled in the pit of his stomach. As he watched intently, a brusque voice came in his ear, "We have a Code Red alert, you say! On whose authority? This hasn't come from the Department of Homeland Security so what's the problem?"

Without preamble, Alan Davies said, "I have good reason to believe that terrorists have taken over an office in a high rise downtown and they have some sort of weapon of mass destruction which they're going to set off any time now. My advice is to evacuate the city immediately. Don't hesitate! I'm waiting for my Director to speak to the President to get his sanction but if you'll take my advice, you'll start evacuating the city now…"

The voice at the other end was tinged with disbelief when the Mayor said, "It's no small thing you're asking, Mr Davies. I can't do that without direct instructions from the DHS… What evidence do you have?"

Struggling to contain his anger and frustration, Alan Davies briefly recounted his conversation with Rubin Neery whilst trying to listen to the television. In the end, he barked into the phone, "For Christ's sake! If you don't believe me when I tell you something's very wrong, just look at the television…" then added hastily, "But whatever you do, don't hang up!"

Mohammad Qureshi continued, "I am spokesman for the Islamic jihadi group 'Metraqat Allah'… That is 'The Hammer of God' to you. It was us who put on this little show for the specific purpose of attracting your attention. My brave brothers worked hard to ensure that you uncovered our little plot. We couldn't believe how many clues we had to give your security services before they realised the threat was real… in particular your FBI who were very slow on the uptake, very clumsy and leaden-footed… and how many more clues we had to give them before they were able to track us down. We couldn't have been more helpful and obliging. Even then, when they were handed to you on a plate, your FBI let one of our most accomplished freedom fighters slip through their fingers. And even now, they still can't see what is beneath their noses… We knew that if we managed things so that you intercepted our heroic freedom fighters before they could detonate their bombs in your capital city, you wouldn't be able to resist the temptation to boast about it to your public. And you couldn't have played into our hands better if you had read the script, Mr President… So now it is our turn to hold center stage and your turn to listen… You know that according to the Islamic religion you are infidels…

190

unbelievers... and the presence of American infidels in the Kingdom of Saudi Arabia defiles our holiest places. It is the most profound insult to Allah and a grievous offense against Islam. This does not need to be explained to you because you are well aware of the bitter hatred, the deep resentment and the ill feeling that it causes... However, you arrogantly assume the right to maintain your presence, even though you know you are unwelcome and your presence is unwanted by millions of Muslims... Again, today, you have reiterated that you will not vacate willingly, so now we are here to persuade you to leave, however unwilling you may be to do so. And whilst our main concern... *our only concern...* is to uphold and protect the purity and sanctity of the Holy Kingdom by cleansing it of all infidels, we would also remind you that you are usurpers throughout the Islamic world... in Iraq, in Afghanistan... through your puppets the Israelis, in Palestine... and elsewhere... and your presence is not wanted in those places either... I must warn you that whilst you remain there, America will know no peace..."

The Mayor of New York City heard Alan Davies' detached voice at the other end of the line as he snarled impatiently at his television set, "Come on, you bastard! Cut to the chase."

Without hesitation, the terrorist continued, "As far as we are concerned, your refusal to respond to our polite requests... or our threats... or even gentle coercion... means that we must resort to using violence to force you to go. Consequently, unless you acquiesce to our wholly reasonable demands and announce your decision publicly on television, we will destroy one American city every hour until you agree to a complete and unconditional withdrawal... Nothing less will do." Looking at his wristwatch, he said, "The time in Washington is now ten-twenty-eight... You have until eleven-thirty to announce to the world that the USA is pulling all its military and civilian personnel out of Saudi Arabia and twenty-four hours thereafter to begin your withdrawal. Failing that, we will destroy one American city after another until you do... And so you take us seriously and understand that we mean what we say, we will leave you with this as a demonstration of our power and our determination to carry out God's will... We will unleash the wrath of Allah on Los Angeles and its eighteen million inhabitants..." As a parting shot, the bearded man said, "We expect to hear from you in one hour's time..."

Mohammad Faisal Qureshi stepped aside out of the camera's field of view, briefly revealing once again the view of greater Los Angeles, until someone out of shot closed the rear door of the van in which the camera was mounted. The window through which the camera now pointed was heavily tinted by a highly reflective material that attenuated the bright view of the distant city, so that only an occasional glint of sunlight off some shiny architectural feature reminded countless millions of viewers that the camera was still gazing wide-eyed at the city. As the second finger of the clock on the studio wall reached top dead center, telling the President that the time on the Eastern seaboard was exactly ten-thirty, the faint image of the distant city instantaneously became filled with a brilliant white light that completely obliterated everything. On the other half-screen, the view of the President standing mouth agape and eyes wide open, staring in dumb-struck disbelief, reflected perfectly the expressions on the faces of many of the hundred-and-eighty-million viewers. A few people noticed the First Lady, still sitting behind the President, who buried her face in her hands to hide her eyes from the horror then began to shake violently and sob inconsolably once she had recovered from the initial shock, which broadly mirrored the reaction of the rest.

A few seconds after the initial flare, the image danced around wildly as the van was violently buffeted twice, first by the shockwave then a few seconds later by the powerful winds from the thermonuclear explosion. As he watched the huge fireball spreading over where the city had once stood, Alan Davies heard a hoarse whisper in his ear imploring, "Dear God! Sweet Jesus, have mercy on their souls…"

Without the slightest trace of emotion, Alan Davies said bluntly, "What more evidence do you need?"

The Mayor of New York City recovered sufficiently to ask, "And you think that's what we could be facing?"

"I think you're next… within the hour… unless the President agrees to their demands."

Three weeks previously, representatives of Metraqat Allah had secretly transported an ex-Soviet nuclear warhead having a nominal yield equivalent to one-point-eight million tons of trinitrotoluene, into the Los Angeles offices of Al Samari Rare Metals, Inc. which was a legitimate front for Muslim sympathisers linked to the terrorist organisation. The warhead had been hidden inside a specially constructed, reinforced steel cabinet made to look like an office safe. The box around the warhead had been lined with specially shaped blocks made from a tungsten-rich alloy that reflected the initial blizzard of neutrons emitted in the first few millionths of a second by the chain reaction back into the core, which ensured that a greater proportion of the fissionable material was converted into energy before the core was blown apart than would otherwise have been the case, effectively increasing the yield of the weapon to about two-point-four megatons. There were also dozens of sachets of powdered cobalt inside the cabinet which in the nuclear maelstrom produced the highly radioactive species, cobalt-60. Al Samari's offices had been on the twelfth floor of a modest, old-fashioned tower block, about a hundred and fifty feet above street level. The blast excavated a crater about fourteen hundred feet in diameter and over two hundred feet deep where the office block had once stood. It blasted highly radioactive debris out in all directions to a distance of about a mile all around. The shockwave and subsequent wind levelled everything out to a distance of two miles. Beyond that, the occasional skeletons of steel reinforced structures remained partially standing, twisted and distorted into grotesque forms, up to a distance of four miles, at which point most of the steel frames remained largely intact but without walls, windows, or occupants. Not one single family residence remained standing within four miles of ground zero and most out to a radius of eight miles had either collapsed or were so badly damaged they were beyond repair. The fireball, which rose steadily to a height of two miles, burned so fiercely that the thermal radiation ignited everything combustible for a radius of six miles; even if it hadn't been directly exposed to the intense glare, the ensuing firestorm that was fanned by the powerful up-draft created by the mushroom cloud engulfed everything within the malign view of its withering eye. But the most long-lasting damage was done by the fallout, made highly radioactive by the bomb's close proximity to the ground and by the cobalt it had been salted with. The dirty, gray-brown cloud churned and roiled, drawing up enormous quantities of irradiated dust from the ground, lofting it as high as the upper atmosphere where the winds carried it vast distances. The cobalt-60, which has a half-life of five years and decays by the emission of gamma rays – the most penetrating and harmful form of radiation – ensured that its poisonous effects would be felt wherever it landed for at least fifty years before humans could safely enter the area again. And who in living memory would want to resettle an area that had once been so thoroughly contaminated with something so toxic it had even killed the cockroaches? The loss of life was impossible to determine, safe to say that all four-and-a-quarter million inhabitants of the city of Los Angeles perished, most within seconds as a direct result of being vaporized, crushed by the initial shockwave, impaled by flying debris, or blinded by the light – more brilliant than a thousand Suns – then burnt to a crisp by the searing heat. The firestorm and the intense radiation, both of which made it impossible for rescuers to approach within ten miles of ground zero, also guaranteed that the few souls who miraculously survived the bomb's immediate effects would have succumbed to one or the other long before they could get out of the worst affected zone. Of the remaining fourteen million people in the metropolitan area, as well as millions more downwind of the city who were liberally sprinkled with the fallout over the next few hours and days, more than six million people died within a week from burns, blast injuries, or exposure to lethal doses of radiation. Millions more suffered the agony of a long, painful, drawn-out death with no relief from the ghastly symptoms of radiation sickness; every hospital for hundreds of miles around was completely overwhelmed by the scale of the disaster and the emergency and rescue services were totally unable to cope. Within twenty-four hours, the military had thrown a cordon round the 'hot zone' preventing

193

anyone from entering it for the sake of their own health. Eventually, the exodus of fatally contaminated people leaving the zone dwindled to a trickle then stopped altogether, condemning those still inside the cordon who were too ill and didn't have the strength to reach the makeshift border to a lonely and miserable death.

—•—

Without realising what she was doing, Claudette had reached out and taken her mother's hand. Now, as the screen whited out, Martha clasped it with such force that the girl would have cried out in pain had she not been so stunned by the terrifying image. Mother and daughter stared at the screen until the fireball had cooled and gained sufficient definition to be instantly recognisable when Martha put her other hand to her mouth and gasped, "Oh my God! Nicky! Oh God, I hope he's okay..." After a few moments, Martha let go of her daughter's hand and scrabbled amongst the clothes scattered on the bed, looking for her cellphone. Claudette sat trembling with fear, tears streaming down her face. When eventually she found it, Martha frantically dialled her son's cellphone number but there was no service available and it failed to make the connection. She swore and tried again, still without success. She tried the hotel phone but that also failed to make a connection. Claudette rocked backwards and forwards, wailing in a small, plaintive, frightened voice, "What do we do, Mommy? What do we do?" and then, "What about Billy, Mommy? Is he alright? What about Daddy?"

In a panic, Martha snapped, "How should I know, Claudette?" and then screamed hysterically, "How the hell could I know?" When she saw the effect that her response had had on her daughter, Martha calmed immediately and knelt beside the terrified girl and put her arms around her, hugging her tightly. She said, "Oh God, I'm sorry Claudette. I'm just so frightened for Nicky... for Billy... for Dad... for us all... But what happens to Nicky if Chicago's next? I should never have let him go off on his own like that..." The girl buried her face in her mother's neck and sobbed while Martha silently berated herself for her own stupidity.

—•—

Since the first mention of the possibility that terrorists were planning to explode a dirty bomb in the Capital, the Secret Service had been ready to whisk the President and his family away to safety at a moment's notice. At all times, Marine One had sat on the helipad, manned by the duty crew with at least one relief crew on stand-by. As the President left the stage, he motioned to Paul Kaufmann and George Horowitz, who were anxiously waiting for him just beyond the stage, to join him. He took them both by the arm and drew them to him. "George. Get down to the Situation Room. Tell them I'll be along in a minute. We've got less than an hour to hash out a response to this threat."

George Horowitz snapped out, "Yes Sir" and turned on his heel and went.

The President then turned to his assistant. "Paul, I want you to get my wife and kids out of here. Get the chopper to take them to Andrews. They can wait for me there if they like but I want them ready to take off at the first sign of danger."

Before the President could finish giving his instructions, the Secret Service agent in charge interrupted him. "Excuse me, Sir. I've had word that the VP's missing. We can't contact him. Air Force Two's stuck on the ground at LAX. It looks like the electromagnetic pulse from the bomb knocked out the air traffic control system and two planes have collided on the runway, so it's chaos down there. It's impossible for anyone to take off. I insist you leave now for Air Force One. The next city the terrorists destroy could be this one and you mustn't be here if that happens."

The President glowered at the Secret Service man and said, "You can insist all you like but I'm not leaving. There's no time to get to another studio before the next broadcast's due... Now, I have a meeting downstairs with the NSC. They're all present... In the meantime, I want you to get my family out of here."

The Secret Service agent could see that the President wouldn't be budged, so he said, "Very good, Sir but I insist that you hold your meeting in the Emergency Ops Center. At least that way, if the next bomb goes off here, there's a good chance you'll survive. But you'll have to be prepared to go at a moment's notice if we perceive a real and present danger."

"Understood!" The President snapped back tersely. "Alright! Tell everyone to decamp to the Ops Center. I'll be there in a minute" then he turned to his aide. "Right, Paul. Now for the difficult bit..." The President approached his wife who was still very shaken but had recovered sufficiently to be comforting one of the White House press secretaries. When he told her that he wanted her to take the children and go to Andrews Air Force Base, she adamantly refused which was the reaction he'd anticipated.

"I'm not leaving without you! If it's safe enough for you to stay, it's safe enough for all of us..." but the President cut her dead abruptly, "I'm going down to the bunker..."

"We'll come with you..."

"You can't. The NSC's meeting down there. It'll be full. There'll be no room for you ." As he saw the desparate look in his wife's eyes, his tone softened and he continued, "I need you away from here. I can't function

195

properly unless I know you're safe, darling... You and the children... So please go for their sakes and for mine..."

The tears welled up in her eyes and she nodded, barely perceptibly and murmured, "I'll take them... for their sakes and for yours. But you be careful and come back to me safe when this thing's over... Promise?"

He whispered, "Promise" but it was one he secretly felt unsure of being able to keep. He hugged his wife tightly and they exchanged a kiss then, with a final parting squeeze of her hands, the President strode off in the direction of the East Wing.

—•—

The members of the National Security Council had been watching the President's televised broadcast in the Situation Room, located in the basement of the West Wing, until the Secret Service agent had come and asked them to move to the Presidential Emergency Operations Center, a heavily-reinforced, blast-resistant bunker buried deep beneath the East Wing of the White House. Without them realising it, the President followed them as they streamed down the short passage leading to PEOC. He noticed that they had divided into their familiar little cliques, each talking animatedly amongst themselves, with the exception of General Landsbergh and the party from the Department of Defense who stayed obdurately silent. As each of them took a seat, the President walked in and announced his presence, "Be seated, ladies and gentlemen" then, without preamble, "I presume you're all aware of the terrorist's demands and the fate that's befallen Los Angeles as a foretaste of what'll happen to other American cities if we don't meet them..." at which there were nods from every quarter. "We have very little time to formulate a response before their deadline for destroying another American city expires... And, at this stage, we have to assume the threat is real. Does anyone have anything to add?"

The Director of the FBI spoke up. "Sir, I've just been informed about a stand-off in a high rise in the middle of New York. The occupants are probably Arab terrorists. At least, the business operating out of those premises has an Arabic-sounding name. They're heavily armed and extremely hostile. Alan Davies believes they have another bomb in there and they're there to protect it and prevent us from disarming it, in the event of it being discovered. If so, it'll probably be the next one to be detonated and they're probably willing to go up with it... If that's the case, they'll be prepared to fight to the death to stop us from getting anywhere near it... Of course, it could be a bluff to try and force our hand..."

The President interrupted, "We can't take that risk..." He turned to Niara Marshall. "Give instructions to evacuate the city."

196

The Director said, "Alan Davies has already told the Mayor to evacuate the city. When he saw what happened to Los Angeles, Alan said he actioned it immediately without waiting for further instructions…"

Niara Marshall added, "I've had reports of people flooding out of every city, thinking it might be next… Every city's gridlocked. People aren't going anywhere. The roads can't take such heavy traffic… And accidents, panic and roadrage are making problems worse. It's causing havoc. The situation's approaching anarchy."

The President thought for a moment, then said, "There are two issues to address… First! Can we assess how serious the threat of another attack is? After all, we thought it was impossible for terrorists to get hold of one nuclear bomb… Was this the only one? Their ace in the hole. They've played it. Now they have to rely on bluff. Or did they get more? And if so, how many more? How can we find out? Pronto!"

General Landsbergh volunteered, "This was a big bomb. D.o.D analysts estimate at least two megatons… Assuming it was a standard military warhead, which it probably was… and assuming it wasn't from the stockpile of one of our NATO allies, which is unlikely… it was probably of Russian origin… To the best of our knowledge, none of the nuclear wannabes have anything of that size, although Pakistan and Iran both have nuclear weapons programs and are predominantly Muslim nations. One or other may have developed something secretly we don't know about and supplied it to the terrorists but I doubt it. They're much more likely to keep it for use against their neighbours… And of course, the Russians have a large number of surplus warheads, a decommissioning program that's in total disarray, lax security, underpaid guards, a ruthless Mafia and corruption is rife, so there's no shortage of possibilities from that quarter. For my money, I'd start by asking the Russians if they're missing any materiel although whether they'd know… and whether they'd tell us if they did… is another matter… And that's assuming this isn't a Russian conspiracy to drive us out of the Gulf…"

The President swung round. "George, get me the President of the Russian Federation on the phone. Now!" Whilst he waited for the call to come through, the President said, "Second! And far more important… How do we respond if we find out these lunatics have more of these weapons or if we can't be certain they don't?"

The audience remained silent, nobody wanting to commit themself first, some having no idea how to respond. Some looked about to see whether their neighbours showed any signs of stepping up to the plate, others remained impassive and expressionless. General Landsbergh was the only one whose face showed any emotion – it was fixed in a stony scowl. The President scanned the faces around the table, which remained motionless without a flicker. Suddenly, the room seemed very small and claustrophobic to most of its occupants, many of whom wished they could be anywhere else but here under these circumstances. Eventually, General Landsbergh turned and looked directly at the President.

"Yes, General?"

Slowly and deliberately, the General said, "The widely held view among the Chiefs of Staff is that, should America come under nuclear attack, we retaliate immediately with overwhelming force…" Here he paused to allow his words to sink in, before continuing, "This situation is somewhat different from the normally envisaged scenario in that the enemy is not a nation state and therefore is not well defined or readily identifiable but it is an enemy that has declared itself all the same. We are at war with Islam! And irrespective of whether all Muslims support this action… or indeed all Muslim nations for that matter… the fact remains that this is a clear declaration of war and one we must respond to. Therefore, as Chairman of the Joint Chiefs of Staff of the United States Armed Forces, I recommend we go to Defcon One immediately then…"

Pre-empting his proposed response, the President said forcefully, "Go to Defcon One by all means but I will not… I repeat not… sanction a retaliatory strike on…" but before he could finish, George Horowitz interrupted and said, "Sir! I have the Russian President on the line…"

As the President rejoined the meeting, the voices round the table hushed. "I've had a very enlightening conversation with the Russian premier. He was watching the broadcast and saw it all…" With heavy emphasis, he continued, "He *claims* to have received an *unsubstantiated* report within the last twenty-four hours that *some nuclear materiel* has gone missing from one of their military bases. He doesn't know what or how much but when he heard the reports about dirty bombs and now Los Angeles, he put two and two together and figured out that the missing materiel must have found its way here in the hands of Muslim terrorists. He's going to put pressure on local authorities to find out exactly what's gone missing but until they get back to us, we're none the wiser. We're still playing a game of high-stakes poker with an opponent who might just be holding all the aces. So… What do we do, ladies and gentlemen? Time's running out…" This time, every member of the National Security Council had advice to give, with the exception of the Department of Defense.

—•—

The President stood at the podium and nervously cleared his throat. He stared at the camera waiting for the red light to come on telling him he was on air.

As he'd made his way hurriedly to the Press Center, Paul Kaufmann had fallen in step with him. "Sir, we've received messages of support from the Prime Minister of Great Britain, from the office of the Israeli Prime Minister, from Canada, Mexico, Australia, New Zealand..." Paul Kaufmann reeled off a list of countries that had offered their support. We've had messages of sympathy from others including the Germans, Japanese, Russians... The French have asked us to... er... do nothing hasty we might not be able to undo..."

"And the Saudis?"

"Nothing, Sir... as of yet... Or from any other Arab country for that matter... In fact, no Muslim country... yet..."

He glanced at the clock, the minute hand hovering round the five o'clock mark. Just as he muttered "For God's sake, hurry up!" under his breath, the lamp came on and he saw his image jump into life on the monitor screens. He started hesitantly. "I am now... er... speaking to the terrorists of Metraqat Allah..." After a short pause, he continued a little more positively. "Before I expand on what the United States is prepared to do to meet your demands, I will say this... Today, by your barbaric and unprovoked attack on the innocent and defenseless citizens of Los Angeles, you have driven a wedge so deeply between the two great religions of mankind... Islam and Christianity... that the rift may never be healed. Furthermore, as the world's greatest democratic superpower... no, the world's *only* democratic superpower... America has a duty to try to bring peace, stability and democracy to lands that are ruled by dictators... whether they be political or religious and benign or tyrannical... and we will not be bullied, bribed or blackmailed by you into reneging on our obligations. Coming now to your demands... For the time being, as a first gesture, we will pull back all non-Muslim US citizens currently stationed in the Kingdom of Saudi Arabia to coastal ports or military air bases from which they can depart the country and that are situated as far away from the holy cities of Mecca and Medina as is reasonably possible, preparatory to discussing with the ruling Al-Saud family whether they wish us to withdraw from the Kingdom altogether. Ultimately, we will act in accordance with their wishes... US citizens of the Muslim faith who are there for legitimate religious purposes not associated with military or commercial activities we will leave to their own judgement as to whether they leave the country or not... Finally, coming to you, the evil perpetrators of these heinous crimes... America will hunt you and all terrorists down relentlessly with the intention of bringing you to justice..." The President suddenly became aware of George Horowitz gesticulating wildly from the side of the stage. He turned away from the camera. "Yes?" he asked abruptly, putting his hand over the microphone.

Looking pale and drawn, his senior adviser hurried over to him and said quietly, "Sir. Reports are coming in... It's as we feared... New York... Another bomb's gone off... It's wiped out the entire city..."

The President raised his hand and the studio director gave immediate instruction to stop broadcasting.

—•—

As he entered the Presidential Emergency Operations Center, all heads turned towards the door and the President felt the eyes of everyone in the room boring into him, tacitly accusing him of failure to prevent this latest attack. He took his place at the table silently and sat for a few moments before saying, "We now know the terrorists managed to acquire at least two nuclear weapons. It's reasonable to assume, therefore, that they have more. How many more we don't know but we can't wait to find out the hard way. If we want to avoid the destruction of other American cities and further loss of life, I see no option but to comply with their demands and announce our immediate withdrawal from Saudi Arabia and the Middle East. At least that way, America will be safe..."

Without waiting for the President to finish, General Landsbergh stood up and with a steely edge to his voice said, "Safe my ass, you defeatist son-of-a-bitch..."

The President bellowed, "Sit down! Or I'll have you removed..." but before he could finish, the General, determined to be heard, continued, "You can't! And let me tell you... If we pull out of the Middle East now, nowhere in the region... *in fact, nowhere in the World*... will be safe from these lunatics. America will retreat into itself like a whipped dog hiding in its kennel and die of shame. We'll become isolated... marginalised... a laughing stock. No one will ever take us seriously again... Then who'll police the World and keep it safe? And whilst you've been trying to flannel your way out of trouble, we've received reports about a massive outbreak of fighting in Israel between Jews and Palestinians... and popular uprisings in Saudi Arabia, Jordan, Egypt and other pro-Western Arab nations, all sparked off by these acts of terrorism... The situation's already gone super-critical, it's on the brink of meltdown. We're the only ones who can stop it and here's you talking about throwing in the towel before the fight's hardly begun... Did you really believe what you said about America being a superpower... a champion of democracy... or was that just political bullshit? What's the point of spending trillions of dollars to become a superpower and arming ourselves to create and defend that reputation if at the first sign of difficulty we cave in? I say, 'Take action!' Hit the bastards hard right where it hurts... In the Ka'aba... That'll provoke the most militant and dangerous ones to rise up and we can deal with 'em en-masse and it'll subdue the more timorous and less committed ones and we shouldn't hear another peep out of 'em. And if we do, we can pick 'em off at our leisure. The Pentagon already has a prioritised list of targets starting with Mecca and Medina that we can take out in an instant. Our Commanders are ready, the coordinates are locked into the missiles and the warheads are armed. All you need do is give the order, we turn the keys and push the buttons and the birds are in flight…"

Thrusting a forefinger hard against his own chest, the President said flatly, "Yes… and I notice it's me who has to give the order… That it's me who'll go down in history alongside mass murderers like Adolf Hitler, Josef Stalin and Pol Pot… Where's the legitimacy for such an act of genocide?"

Not expecting any response to his rhetorical question, the President was taken aback when, for the first time, his Counsel, a small, owlish man with round spectacles, spoke up in a dry, matter-of-fact voice. "Well… er… actually, Mr President, if I may proffer a view… There is no unequivocal legal definition of when nuclear weapons may be used… but on July eighth, nineteen-ninety-six, the World Court… formerly the United Nations International Court of Justice… issued a non-binding advisory opinion requested by the UN General Assembly which stated that…" and here he picked up a sheet of paper and read from it. "…'The use or threat of nuclear weapons generally would be contrary to international law, except possibly for self-defense, if a state's very survival were at stake…' From a purely hypothetical standpoint, it would be impossible to say categorically that our very survival was at stake until so many cities had been destroyed and so many people killed that the USA was no longer able to function as a viable entity… However, no reasonable person would expect any nation to wait until it had reached that dire extreme before defending itself… Therefore, it is my considered opinion that a retaliatory strike against a known or identifiable aggressor… purely for the purposes of self-defense, of course, as a response to the attacks we've already suffered and as a deterrent against further attacks… would be well within the purview of the Court's opinion and a fair interpretation of it… In short, in law, we can hit back if we choose to do so… Of course, the only identifiable aggressor here is Islam, which gravitates around the cities of Mecca and Medina… which represent its most tangible physical assets and the focus for all its activities, good and bad…"

The President sat quietly with his head bowed, elbows on the desk, clutching his temples. After a moment, he looked up and said, "Do we really think retaliatory strikes on Mecca and Medina would deter further attacks if the terrorists do have more bombs? Surely, they'd be so enraged it'd guarantee they used them…"

With cold logic, the bespectacled lawyer said, "Surely, unless we acquiesce to their demands unconditionally, which means that terrorism wins through the use of blackmail and coercion… and which we should have done *before* New York was destroyed, if we were going to do it at all… then they're going to use them anyway… And I think we must also bear in mind that capitulation now would open the floodgates for every nutcase with a grievance and a stick of dynamite…"

The President reflected for a moment, then said, "So, we might be able to retaliate legally but can we do it morally? And can we do it without precipitating a blood bath in the Middle East? God knows… And if the Russians or the Chinese choose to get involved is it likely to spark off a world war? What shape would it leave the world in?"

Before the President could expand on his concerns, General Landsbergh cut in, "And what about your duty to the American people… the people who elected you and put their faith in you… the people you swore to protect? Was all the rhetoric you spouted before polling day about defending the interests of the United States more bullshit? And what do you say to the people if we don't respond? As for Russia and China, I somehow can't see them wanting to get embroiled in this at the risk of antagonising us further… and we'll warn them off getting involved through diplomatic channels when we decide to take action. Of course, once this situation's resolved, we'll have to take up with the Russians the matter of the damage to our cities caused by their warheads… I should think that'd be involvement enough for them."

The President asked desperately, "How would it look to the world if we destroy these religious centers full of innocent worshippers at prayer, instead of military targets? How do I… how do any of us live with that on our conscience?"

The General responded forcefully, "That's exactly what the terrorists are relying on… That we'll be sitting here mired in indecision, wringing our hands in despair, agonising over the morality of taking action… They're counting on us being too soft… too constrained by rules and etiquette and a sense of fair play… too concerned about how it'd look to all those armchair critics who haven't had to suffer the direct consequences of having nuclear bombs detonated in their backyards… to respond at all… that we have no stomach for a real fight… Let's face it, there are no rules here… there can be no rules to govern this scenario because it's one nobody's ever experienced before and one that could hardly have been envisaged. We have to call it as we see it and I see no option but to respond to the use of absolute force with absolute force… unless, of course, you want to see America sidelined and consigned to the scrapheap of history with all the other failed empires…"

The President asked, "Are there no other… er… more appropriate targets that would have an equally damaging effect on the terrorist psyche?"

The General came back promptly, "None that I can think of. We can hardly launch an unprovoked attack on a nation state. Which would we choose? None have declared war against us... No! Islam is behind these attacks. It's the source of all the malice, venom, hatred and hostility that's directed at us and that's fuelled these attacks. We have no option but to excise the heart of Islam..."

The President said, "But for Christ's sake... that'll simply provoke nation states throughout the Muslim world to rise up against us... Then what?"

The General replied coldly, "We're ready for them."

—•—

As the clock approached twelve-ten Eastern Standard Time, George Horowitz reached out and gently laid his hand on the President's forearm. "Mr President... Sir... May I remind you that time is running out. We have twenty minutes before the next broadcast... With all due respect, Sir, may we know what decision you've come to?" The President had been sitting absolutely motionless, silently staring into the middle distance for the past five minutes. A deathly hush had descended over the room, with no one moving a muscle, everyone trying to second-guess which course of action the President would opt for and dreading his eventual choice, whatever it was. George Horowitz stared into his face for a long moment and for the first time saw with alarming clarity just how deeply etched the lines around his eyes and mouth had become and how gaunt and sallow he looked. But what concerned him most as he examined him at close quarters was the blank, expressionless stare of those tired, sunken eyes. He squeezed the President's arm a little more firmly. "Sir... We need to know what decision..."

Before he could finish, the President, sounding very vague and far away, said softly, "I'm sorry George... I can't tell you because I don't know... I... I... I just don't know what to do..." and his voice drifted off into oblivion.

After what seemed like an eternity to everyone around the table, the silence was broken by the barely perpectible creak of someone rising from their chair. Whilst most eyes remained fixed on the President, George Horowitz looked up to see General Landsbergh marching purposefully down the room. He stopped a few yards short of the President and in a powerful, authoritative voice said, "Mr President! By the power vested in me as Chairman of the Joint Chiefs of Staff of the United States Armed Forces... and finding the nation at war and without a competent Commander-in-Chief... I am relieving you of that duty forthwith and assuming it myself..."

George Horowitz immediately leapt up and roared at the General, "You can't do that... It's mutiny... Insurrection..."

General Landsbergh turned his icy gaze on George Horowitz and said, "I think you'll find I can, Mr Horowitz and I am. The President's title may have been fine in peacetime but we are now at war and, with all due respect for his position, he is a career politican with no experience of combat let alone commanding military operations under hostile conditions..." George Horowitz was about to protest but the General silenced him summarily by continuing, "Furthermore, he is unfit and incapable... We've all seen his indecisiveness. We have the perfect example of it here and now... His self-delusion about his power to talk problems away... His serious health problem and his stubborn refusal to get treatment for it which in itself shows poor judgement but which is also clouding his judgement on all other matters... and his heavy drinking... Mr Horowitz, we cannot leave the fate of America in the hands of a lush..."

George Horowitz responded sharply, "That's grossly unfair..." but the President pulled him back down to his seat and said, "No, George... No it isn't... I need help because I can't cope with this situation... General Landsbergh's right. I'm completely out of my depth here... I will not oppose him taking over as C-in-C. He does it with my full approval."

The General said, "Thank you, Mr President. As of now, I am imposing martial law... These changes in no way restrict your role as Head of State or as Chief Executive, Sir..."

At that moment, Paul Kaufmann hurried in and said breathlessly, "Sir, the Russian premier's on the line."

The President said, "General, I think you should take this call..."

In less than two minutes, the General returned. "He says they're missing three warheads... So where's the third?"

With the phone to his ear, the Director of the FBI said, "I'm on to Alan Davies... He says that, so far, there have been no further reports from possible locations, so God knows where the third one might be. It could be anywhere..." He continued sitting with the phone pressed to his ear, listening to the silence at the other end. Suddenly, he exclaimed, "What! How do you know?"

Alan Davies said, "I don't know it for a fact but it all fits... Qureshi went out of his way to humiliate us... the FBI, that is... for our incompetent detection skills... I thought he was trying to undermine public confidence in us... But he also said something else that's been bothering me... Something about us not being able to see what's right under our noses... Don't you see? The first two bombs went off in cities having main metropolitan field offices under the control of an Assistant Director... There are only three..."

The penny dropped and the Director of the FBI finished Alan Davies' sentence for him. "And the third one's here in Washington..."

Without waiting for further explanation, General Landsbergh said, "Mr President. I respectfully suggest you leave for Air Force One immediately. You may not realise it but with the exception of the Vice President who is currently missing, most of the people in the presidential line of succession are either here in this room or within the environs of Washington..."

George Horowitz and Paul Kaufmann had propelled the President up the steps of the waiting Boeing seven-four-seven which was standing at the end of the runway. It had already run up its four General Electric CF6 turbofan engines in anticipation of his imminent arrival. Immediately the President and his party were on board the door had been closed and locked and the ground crew rolled the steps away. With a thunderous roar from its engines as the pilot opened the throttles, the mighty aircraft accelerated at a rate that kept its occupants firmly pinned in their seats. Marine One, the Lockheed Martin US101 helicopter that had whisked the President from the lawn in front of the White House to Andrews Air Force Base, rapidly receded into the distance.

The First Lady had been there to greet her husband as he entered the plane and had ushered him to a seat. He flopped down wearily into it and sat crumpled, looking like a man utterly defeated as she fastened the belt round his waist then took his hand in hers. Without speaking, he stared down the length of the cabin at the clock on the bulkhead. As it came to twelve-thirty, he turned and looked out of the porthole at the once-bustling metropolis, now eerily deserted except for a few stray dogs roaming loose in the streets and the odd wino slumped on a park bench enjoying the unusual tranquility and the warm summer sunshine. As Air Force One passed eleven thousand feet, the city suddenly disappeared from view as the sky was instantaneously filled with a brilliant light from horizon to horizon. The President saw the shockwave that radiated out as an ever-expanding dome, spreading out in every direction from its epicenter at an alarming rate but as it reached them, now more than twenty miles from ground zero and struck the three-hundred-and-seventy ton airliner, it had become sufficiently dissipated that the jolt barely disturbed its equilibrium. He continued staring at it until he could no longer bear the sight. When at last he turned his head away from the awful spectacle, the pupils of his exhausted eyes constricted to tiny black pinholes as a result of the intense glare, the First Lady saw that his sunken cheeks were streaked with tears.

Chapter 8

(Monday 16 August 2010)

Six days later, during which time the hatch that for the last sixty-five years had remained firmly battened down on Hell had been lifted to reveal to the world the madness that was festering down below, Jack Culver, Dan Ackland and Jay Melosh sat on board Air Force One, stationed temporarily at a United States Air Force base somewhere in the mid-West, waiting for the President to appear.

Since taking off from Andrews Air Force Base, his whereabouts had been kept secret for fear of terrorist reprisals. The pilot of the Learjet that had brought them had only been informed of their final destination once they were airborne. Two Secret Service agents, both capable fliers themselves, had flown with them, with strict orders to take over the aircraft and if necessary, immobilise the pilot if he deviated from their instructions by the smallest degree. Even then, they had been accompanied by two fully armed and combat-ready USAF F-16 Fighting Falcons all the way until they touched down and taxied to the opposite end of the runway farthest from the President's plane; had the passengers known that the Air Force pilots had orders to shoot down the Learjet if it strayed from its approved flightpath, they might have been even less enthusiastic to be on board than they were already. Wayne Harland should have been with them but after frantically trying in vain for three days and nights to contact the roving equivalent of the Oval Office, he had collapsed and died of a massive heart attack brought on by the sleeplessness, stress and anxiety. Discounting the two hundred and forty-two members of the Japanese doomsday cult who had committed mass suicide for reasons unfathomable to anyone outside the group, Wayne Harland had the singular if somewhat dubious distinction of being the first victim of asteroid 2010 AS241; it would be impossible to discern who would be the last.

—•—

After Wayne Harland's sad demise, Dan Ackland had taken it upon himself to contact the President. He had tried steadily, firstly calling the White House numbers they'd been given at their last meeting but to no avail, then going through the operator, the emergency services and all the branches of the Armed Forces in vain. All air travel was suspended indefinitely and road travel into and between cities and other main centers of population was prohibited under martial law with the exception of critical supplies which even then could only be moved with a special permit, in an effort to prevent the free movement of terrorists. Effectively, the country was in stasis. Telephone traffic was severely curtailed with the National Security Agency eavesdropping on all private calls, listening for further evidence of terrorist activity despite superficial damage, such as cracked windows and low-level contamination with radioactive fallout, to its headquarters at Fort Meade, Maryland, about twenty miles north-east of the heart of Washington DC. All available lines were virtually continuously jammed by callers frantically trying to ascertain the whereabouts of friends and relatives and whether they were safe which made the process extremely slow. Eventually, figuring that if anyone knew how to make contact with the President it would be the United States Secret Service who were entrusted with his care and protection, he was about to try calling the local Secret Service bureau in Portland when they came calling on him. Two burly and intimidating special agents carrying barely-concealed pistols in shoulder holsters and displaying their most business-like, no-nonsense attitudes, barged uninvited into Dan Ackland's office and demanded to know why he had been trying to contact the President of the United States during a time of national emergency. Dan Ackland revealed to the agents as much as he could within the guidelines laid down by the President, without telling them explicitly about S241. At first they were skeptical but when he showed them the business cards he'd been given during their visit to the White House and explained that he'd been trying, with no success, to contact the President's staff via their direct lines to submit an urgent report that he was expecting, their attitude softened slightly and they said they would contact the President who would then make contact with him if he still deemed it necessary. What they didn't tell him – which was not publicly known at the time because of the news black-out imposed under martial law – was that there was no one at the White House to take his calls because it no longer existed; the only evidence that it had once occupied the site which now remained was the head of the passageway leading down to the hardened Presidential Emergency Operations Center where it surfaced through the scorched and shocked earth.

Sensing that he had failed to impress upon them the urgency of the matter, Dan Ackland had tried insisting that they make the call immediately from his phone, assuring them that the President would want to hear from him straight away but the agents weren't about to let a member of the public dictate the President's agenda. What they did not know, however, was that the President was in no fit state to take the call anyway, having just had an operation to remove a malignant growth from his prostate gland. What no one other than the President, his physicians, his wife and his senior advisers knew, was that the malign seeds of the cancer had already spread to his lungs, lymph glands and ribs before the primary cause had become a serious enough problem to cause him any real discomfort. It was now highly unlikely that either radiation treatment or chemotherapy would halt the relentless advance of these aggressive secondary tumours.

Within a couple of hours of leaving Dan Ackland's office, one of the Secret Service agents had called him back. This time, the agent spoke in a slightly more respectful tone, saying that he had spoken to Paul Kaufmann, the President's Principal Aide, who had confirmed that the President would call him and that he was to stay near his desk. Later that evening, whilst Dan Ackland and Jack Culver were going over the projections of S241's flightpath for the thousandth time, the phone rang. Dan Ackland picked up the handset and said curtly, "Ackland!"

The voice at the other end said, "Mr Ackland, Paul Kaufmann of the President's staff here. I understand you've been trying to get hold of the President. You have something to report, I presume. He apologises for not getting back to you sooner but he's been tied up... If you'd wait a moment, please, I'll put him on."

The President sat hunched over a small globe, staring at north Africa. Paul Kaufmann said, "I have Mr Ackland on line one, Sir."

The President looked up and said quietly, "Thank you Paul" and picked up his handset. "Hello, Mr Ackland. I gather we've been giving you the runaround. I apologise for not getting back to you sooner but you'll understand why that wasn't possible. Now... I guess you have some news for me, Mr Ackland... Is it good? Or bad?"

"It's not good, Sir... It's bad... In fact, it's very bad. Our latest sightings show that S241 is on a collision course with Earth... and our findings have been corroborated by the Keck Observatory."

Hardly daring to ask the question directly, the President asked, "So... the impact site... How far out are we from your original prediction of August first?"

Dan Ackland went quiet for a moment. The President heard papers being shuffled, as the astronomer turned back to the chart generated from the sighting of July thirty-first. "Well... er... actually, Sir... remarkably close... The latest projections confirm that the actual impact site is only about eight- or nine-hundred miles east and a little north of our original impact site..."

Before he could continue, the President interrupted him and Dan Ackland thought the President's voice seemed slightly lighter. "So by my reckoning S241 should be coming down... er... just north of Riyadh... in the heart of Saudi Arabia... if I'm not mistaken."

There was a long pause before Dan Ackland replied, "Well... actually, Sir... I'm afraid you are mistaken..."

Paul Kaufmann, who was sitting opposite the President, saw the look of apprehension appear in his eyes. When Dan Ackland told the President where

S241 would actually hit the Earth, Paul Kaufmann saw the color drain from his face which turned a pale shade of gray. The President stuttered, "But... but... how? I cross-checked the impact site from your original chart on my globe... I measured its position from the Greenwich Meridian, which put the original impact site somewhere in northern Egypt..."

Dan Ackland said, "If you assumed the bold line on the chart is the Greenwich Meridian then possibly... but it isn't... It's actually the International Date Line. In fact, if you look closely up near the North Pole, where the line is broken, it actually says 'IDL' in capitals, although admittedly the letters are tiny at this scale..."

The President's own words rang in his ears and he felt as though he'd been kicked in the guts. Eventually, he said quietly, "We need a meeting, Mr Ackland. I would respectfully ask you to come here straight away..."

Dan Ackland started to ask, "Where's 'here', Mr President... And how do we get there? There's a ban on all flights... Our plane's been grounded and the pilot's been kicking his heels for a week now, waiting to fly us to Washington for this meeting."

Before the President could respond the Secret Service agent, who'd been listening in on another phone, interrupted and said, "Excuse me, Mr President... Mr Ackland, you don't need to know where 'here' is... We'll get Secret Service agents from your local bureau to make all the necessary arrangements for you to rendezvous with the President but we may need the use of your plane... The JPL pilot is ex-Air Force. We've already run a security check on him and he's been cleared... Will there just be yourself, Mr Culver and Mr Harland?"

Dan Ackland replied, "No, Sir. Wayne Harland's dead. He died a couple of days ago of a heart attack but we hope to bring with us a Professor Jay Melosh. He's the expert on planetary impacts who can predict how much damage S241 will do..."

Dan Ackland passed the phone to Jack Culver who gave the Secret Service agent his friend's personal details.

The President cut in, "Mr Culver, is there anyone else you think needs to be present at this meeting to give us the fullest possible picture of forthcoming events? Bear in mind we don't have long to respond to the threat..."

Jack Culver thought a moment, then said, "In terms of possible effects, it may help to have a competent geologist... one who's familiar with geological conditions on the North American Continent... maybe even worldwide... but I'm afraid I can't be of much use there because I don't know of anyone..."

The President said, "I do, Mr Culver. I'll contact him and arrange for him to be here. In the meantime if I put you in touch with him, can you give him all the details?"

"Yes, I'll do that, Sir."

"Thank you, Mr Culver."

—•—

Paul Kaufmann ushered in a tall, slightly stooped, rather shambling, gray haired man. "Gentlemen, please let me introduce Graham Tandy of the US Geological Survey. Mr Tandy is currently Scientist-in-Charge at the Yellowstone Volcano Observatory… Mr Culver, you're already acquainted with… His colleague, Dan Ackland, who's Director of the Observatory… and Dr Jay Melosh, who's Professor of Planetary Sciences at the University of Arizona…" The four men shook hands over the table then sat and looked at each other for a long moment. In a rather somber tone, it was Graham Tandy who broke the ice by voicing everyone's thoughts. "Well, Gentlemen, we're living in extraordinary times. I wonder if we'll all live long enough to look back on them?" Before anyone could respond, the door in the far bulkhead opened. George Horowitz entered and announced, "Gentlemen, the President of the United States."

The four men rose smartly as the President, immaculately dressed in a dark suit, white shirt and pale blue silk tie, shuffled unsteadily in. The three men who'd met him two weeks previously were shocked by the extent of the change in the man. His hair was visibly grayer than it had been and his face was gaunt, the cheeks pale and sallow. But it was his eyes which had burned so brightly when they'd last met, even in the face of adversity, now dull and empty in dark, sunken sockets which told them that this was a broken man.

As the President approached the table, he said, "Please be seated." When Paul Kaufmann had finished the introductions, the President said slowly and deliberately, "So, Gentlemen, I know the news isn't good… How bad is it?"

The four visitors looked at each other momentarily, until Dan Ackland said, "Mr President, as I told you on the phone, we're now as certain as we can be that asteroid S241 is on a collision course with Earth. Our latest projections show it coming down in the Pacific Ocean approximately seven hundred and fifty miles west and a little south of San Diego or within a two hundred and fifty mile radius of that point. Time of impact will be around one-forty-seven a.m. Pacific time on the morning of Saturday, August twenty-first. That's less than five days from now. Keck's observations concur pretty much with our own to within a few seconds and a few hundred miles…" Jack Culver, who'd been watching the President, thought that he appeared to physically shrink at this news. Dan Ackland continued in the same unemotional, deadpan tone. "Briefly, for your information, Mr President, the key statistics we gave to Professor Melosh about S241 for him to work out its impact effects were as follows… We estimate its mass to be thirty-two point three trillion tons… Impact velocity is one hundred and one thousand, six hundred and thirty-five miles per hour… and impact angle is eighty-five degrees relative to a plane tangential to Earth's surface. In other words, it's coming down near-vertical… Total impact energy is equivalent to seven-point-two *billion* megatons."

When the silence had persisted long enough for the President to safely assume Dan Ackland had completed his delivery, he said quietly, "Thank you, Mr Ackland…" then turned to the two newcomers and asked, "And how does that translate in terms of damage done?"

Jay Melosh turned to Graham Tandy and said, "I'll lead off, if that's okay with you…" to which Graham Tandy responded with a brief nod of his head.

Whilst Jay Melosh handed round sheaves of papers clipped together and turned his laptop computer to face the audience, he spoke steadily. "An impact of this magnitude is an extremely complex event, Mr President, so before I go on to give you my prediction of its effects, I'd just like to preface it with a couple of comments… Firstly, this simulation on my PC is fairly crude but it'll give you some idea of the scale of events. Obviously, we need a lot more processing power for a more realistic visualisation… And secondly, many of the calculations are empirically derived based on data from nuclear explosions, small-scale hyper-velocity experiments and the like… and on observations of cratering on the Earth, Moon and other terrestrial planets… and where no data is available, on theory… so I can't guarantee that all our predictions will be entirely accurate… but where they're not, we've probably erred on the side of caution and under-stated the effects…"

Jay Melosh proceeded to run the program demonstrating the impact of S241 visually but the fact that it appeared on a small screen, sitting on a desk in the air-conditioned comfort of a plushly carpeted and upholstered lounge tended to diminish its impact on the viewers' minds. Providing a commentary to the simulation, Professor Melosh said, "From naval charts, I estimate that the Ocean is between twelve- and sixteen-thousand feet deep at the impact site, although the precise depth makes little difference to the final figures… As you'll see from the graphic, S241 displaces the water down to the seabed creating a hole approximately two-hundred and fifty-two miles in diameter. The water has to go somewhere which, of course, results in massive waves that radiate out from the impact site… The impact itself will vaporize or melt the underlying rock, throwing out about sixty thousand cubic miles of debris and creating a transient crater in the Earth's crust about one-hundred and fifty miles in diameter by fifty-three miles deep… The impact will be equivalent to an earthquake at that point of magnitude eleven-point-two on the Richter scale… Far more powerful than any 'quake ever recorded on Earth… Once the sides of the transient crater have finished collapsing, the final crater will be about three-hundred and ten miles in diameter by over a mile deep… Hopefully, these bald figures should give you some sense of the magnitude of the event... One piece of good news... *possibly the only piece of good news I can give you today...* is that the Earth should suffer negligible loss of mass and there should be no noticeable effect on its rotation period, the tilt of its axis, or its orbit... In other words, the Earth isn't going to be smashed to smithereens or go careening off into oblivion, so it should continue as a stable platform for life... Of course, whether the post-impact environment continues to be hospitable for us is another matter..." The audience sat in absolute silence. Mistakenly thinking that his opening presentation hadn't properly grasped the President by his vitals, Professor Melosh continued with added vigor, "Now, turning to the printed hand-outs... Each sheet deals with a different impact effect, of which there are five major physical effects that will be widely felt beyond the impact zone. These are..." and here he started counting them off on the digits of one hand, "...thermal radiation generated by the near-instantaneous conversion of some of the asteroid's kinetic energy into heat and light... Seismic shaking similar to an earthquake... The ejection of debris from impactor and target... A huge shockwave followed by terrific winds... And of course, coming down in deep water also means that the impact will generate huge tsunamis, as well... I'll deal with each of these effects in order... Please bear two things in mind... Firstly, our model is useful for an area about six thousand miles radius centered on the point of impact. Beyond that distance, it becomes less reliable... Secondly, the results are based on S241 coming down seven-hundred and fifty miles west of San Diego... If it comes down at the most easterly extreme of its projected target area, which would be two-hundred and fifty miles closer to the west coast, the damage there would be substantially worse... although given the scale of the devastation, I'm not sure that matters a lot as you'll see..." He poured himself a glass of water and took a sip before continuing. "Anyway, coming to the first sheet..." Each sheet in the bundle contained a map showing the North American continent and Pacific Ocean as far west as the Hawaiian islands, on which had been superimposed concentric circles centered on the point of impact of S241, blocked in in colors varying from bright red in the inner ring to pale yellow at the extremities. "This chart shows the distribution of thermal radiation... The impact will create enormous temperatures and pressures that will melt or vaporize the entire asteroid along with some of the underlying crust. The resultant fireball will be many times larger than the impactor itself but, initially, it'll be hidden from view by a plasma of ionized air surrounding it that will absorb most of the heat. As the fireball expands, the air around it will cool. When it reaches a temperature of about three thousand Kelvin, it'll become transparent to radiation in the infra-red and white light part of the spectrum. About fourteen seconds after impact the fireball will suddenly be unveiled, like switching on a gigantic light that'll shine for at least a couple of hours, radiating heat that'll ignite everything combustible that's in line-of-

212

sight within a radius of sixteen or seventeen hundred miles... Just to give you some idea of the intensity, the chart shows that from San Diego and Los Angeles the fireball will be about a hundred times larger than the Sun and a thousand times brighter... In San Francisco, it'll be about seventy-five times larger than the Sun and six hundred times brighter... and in El Paso, Albuquerque, Santa Fe, Denver, Salt Lake City, Spokane and Seattle it'll be at least ten times bigger and twenty-five times brighter than the Sun... Thereafter, intensity will drop off rapidly until at seventeen-hundred and fifty miles it's about the same size and intensity as the Sun... and beyond that distance it's hidden below the horizon... Effectively, all of California, Arizona, Nevada, Oregon and Utah... most of New Mexico, Colorado, Wyoming, Idaho and Washington... possibly even west Texas... as well as Baja California, most of Sonora, Chihuahua and Durango in northern Mexico... will go up in flames... And the situation's made worse by the fact that it's the height of summer and everywhere's tinder dry. The only places that might be spared being torched by the direct glare are places in the shadow of intervening mountains but even they may be engulfed by the ensuing firestorm..." Looking at the chart, the President asked, "And beyond that the rest of the country's safe?" Professor Melosh replied guardedly, "From the radiation... yes... but not necessarily from the other effects..."

The President sat silently brooding over the chart, his eye drawn magnetically to the unshaded area beyond eighteen hundred miles. Eventually he said, "Please proceed, Dr Melosh but you can dispense with the detailed explanations. I have to trust that you know what you're talking about. Just give me the facts."

Jay Melosh said, "Very good, Mr President. Coming to the second chart, this shows seismic effects. Within four or five minutes of the impact, you'll see from the map that the west coast from San Diego to San Francisco suffers magnitude-six tremors which equate to values of six or seven on the Mercalli Intensity Scale. In other words, the ground will shake violently making it difficult to stand. Weak masonry will fail, plaster will come off walls, some chimneys will collapse and there may be damage to things such as concrete drainage channels... The shockwave will continue to propagate outwards, giving a similar ground effect out to about two thousand miles when it starts to attenuate. Beyond that, the shaking becomes progressively less severe causing only modest damage and being less frightening for people..."

The President asked, "So, if we move the population out of the Pacific time zone and get them east of Texas, Oklahoma, Kansas, Nebraska and the Dakotas... effectively into the Central time zone or even further east... there's a good chance they won't feel either of these effects?"

"No, Sir, they might not... But with all due respect, we also need to consider the other effects..."

213

"Well, please go on, Dr Melosh."

"Next we come to the ejecta... that is material thrown out by the impact... and it has two distinctly unpleasant effects... Firstly, you'll see from the chart that the model predicts the depth of the debris at various distances from the epicenter and its average size... It assumes that, at a given distance it'll be uniform but in reality it could comprise anything from fine dust to bombs of molten rock the size of a house... But in general, the further out from the epicenter, the less likely you are to find huge projectiles raining down on you..." Referring to the chart Dr Melosh said, "You'll see that San Diego and LA will be buried beneath a blanket of debris sixty feet thick, the bulk of which will be dumped on them about six minutes after the impact... The depth gets less the further away from the impact site you are but it'll still be five feet thick at the edge of the thermal radiation zone seventeen hundred miles away, three feet thick at two thousand miles and a foot thick at three thousand miles... Bearing in mind that the ejecta is essentially rock which could be travelling at a velocity of five or six thousand miles per hour, anyone in the open would be killed instantly by it. The only way to survive the blizzard would be to be underground, in some sort of shelter... And with a density of a hundred to a hundred-and-eighty pounds per cubic foot, dependent on how well it's compacted, most people within two thousand miles of ground zero will find themselves buried alive. I think it'd be well-nigh impossible to dig yourself out if there was any greater overburden of ejecta... That radius, of course, encompasses two-thirds of the continental United States..." This time, the President said nothing. "The second problem comes from ejecta blown clear out of Earth's atmosphere. This will rain back down over the next few hours and days. As it re-enters the atmosphere, the air will be shock-heated changing the chemistry of the atmosphere, in particular damaging the ozone layer... But the bigger problem by far will be at ground level where the super-heated air will spontaneously ignite wildfires. Given the magnitude of S241, the model shows these will break out all around the World..."

Feeling a little uncertain about the President's reception of his last missive, Jay Melosh turned to his next chart with some trepidation. "This chart deals with the air blast and the following winds which I've considered separately..." He looked up momentarily and saw the President was studying it, so he continued, "Firstly, the shockwave will expand out from the impact site as a hemispherical bubble but it's the shock front at ground level that concerns us. This causes a sudden increase in air pressure that can destroy buildings... A peak over-pressure of just one pound per square inch will shatter glass windows... Five p.s.i. will destroy most timber-framed buildings such as family homes... At seven p.s.i. most multi-storey, wall-bearing, brick and masonry buildings will collapse... At thirty p.s.i. virtually all man-made structures including steel-framed buildings and truss bridges will be severely

214

distorted to the point of collapse and at thirty-five p.s.i. girder bridges and motor vehicles will be completely destroyed... The human body can just about withstand a momentary over-pressure of thirty p.s.i. albeit at some risk of internal injury... Anyway, if you look at chart four-A, you'll see that at two thousand miles from ground zero, peak over-pressure is about thirty-three point five p.s.i., sufficient to level every man-made structure. Nothing is going to survive even partially intact within that area... What's really worrying is that virtually no habitable structures are going to remain standing within a three thousand mile radius of ground zero which includes most of the USA, Canada, Mexico and Central America. Windows will probably be broken as far afield as Chile, China and New Zealand..."

Jack Culver checked the map and noted that his parents' home was just over three thousand miles from the point of impact, where peak over-pressure would be equal to about one atmosphere above ambient. He thought, 'God only knows... Billy might have lead us as far away from the impact area as his imagination could take him but is it far enough? Will we be able to survive even here if that's the extent of the devastation?' His thoughts were jerked back to the proceedings as his old friend said, "Coming now to chart four-B... Irrespective of whether a structure survives the shock front, it still has to contend with the powerful winds that follow it. These probably present the greater danger to humans because of the risk of being hit by flying debris or being blown bodily into other objects. Even out at the eastern-most extremities of the United States, our calculations show that wind speed will be in excess of three hundred miles per hour, typically twice the speed of the most powerful category five hurricanes. That's enough to rip up every tree still standing. The model even predicts cat five winds in Japan and the Carribean... and hundred-and-thirty-mile-an-hour winds powerful enough to bring down three-quarters of the trees in China and the rainforests of South America..."

With a hint of desperation in his voice, the President asked quietly, "Is there absolutely no relief from these catastrophic effects, Dr Melosh?"

Jay Melosh thought for a moment then said, "Well... possibly some relief... The model assumes the target is a perfect sphere which, of course, Earth isn't... Between the impact site and the eastern half of the USA are the Rocky Mountains... and the Sierra Madres further south... all part of the American Cordillera that runs in a virtually unbroken chain down the western side of the North and South American continents which separates east from west... The Rockies top out at over fourteen thousand feet. No doubt they'll help break up the shock front and the following wind but they won't stop them altogether... and they'll probably stop some of the ejecta that's blasted out on a fairly low trajectory but most of it will simply clear the mountains... Of course, this also implies that everywhere west of the Rockies will simply receive an even greater battering... but, as I indicated earlier, I don't think that'll matter because west of the Rockies conditions will be so hostile that all life will be extinguished within a few minutes of the impact."

Like a drowning man clutching at any straw that presented itself, the President said, "So... getting people as far east of the Continental Divide as possible is likely to increase their chances of survival, would you say?"

Jay Melosh offered the qualified opinion, "Of surviving the initial impact... definitely!"

"But not necessarily its aftermath?"

"I couldn't speculate, Mr President. It's impossible to hazard a guess but I'll come to that shortly... Would you like me to continue?"

With a sigh of resignation, the President said, "Yes, please, Dr Melosh."

"Chart five shows the effect of the giant wave created as S241 comes down in the Ocean. It'll displace upwards of a hundred and fifty thousand cubic miles of water... which will act as a cushion and take a little of the energy out of the impact... Unfortunately, not a lot..."

George Horowitz cut in, "Wait a minute... Won't the water simply quench the fireball?"

Thrown by the interruption, Jay Melosh thought for a moment before replying, "Well... certainly not initially... Bearing in mind the impact will impart a huge impulse to the water ... that is a sudden massive momentum that'll cause it to flow outwards, away from the impact site... and it'll take a long time for it to flow back to fill the hole, by which time the thermal radiation will have ignited everything on land it's going to ignite... Not only that... When it does eventually flow back, it wouldn't quench the fireball very quickly... it's far too massive and has too much latent energy for that... Anyway, getting back to the immediate effects. The wave will hit the west coast with enormous force, travelling inland for hundreds of miles, unless its progress is impeded by mountain ranges... Bearing in mind the extent of the damage already done to the west coast by the other effects, I didn't think it was worthwhile computing its exact effects... Far more important are the effects on the Pacific islands and other nations around the Pacific rim... Any small, low-lying sandy atolls will simply be swept away, whereas high, rocky islands will be scoured clean. Suffice it to say that no one will survive... Countries across the Pacific, such as Japan, China, Taiwan, the Philippines, Indonesia, Papua New Guinea, Australia and New Zealand, which face the oncoming wave will be hit by tsunamis some hours after the impact in the middle of their night. Their only hope is to evacuate people to high ground as far inland as possible... The effect on the west coast of Canada, the north-west USA and Central America will be subtly different because here the wave will be running pretty much parallel to the coast, so they'll probably see a huge surge, like an extremely high tide then it's passed... although it'll probably inundate low-lying parts of Central America, such as Nicaragua and Panama, so much so that it'll spill over into the Atlantic... Alaska and the Aleutians will also be hit by the full force of the wave. However, the wash from it will slosh backwards and forwards around the World, affecting sea levels everywhere for days before it finally settles..."

The President suddenly snapped, "I'm not interested in the rest of the world! I'm concerned with America and what we can do to save our nation. We'll warn other nations, yes but then it's up to them what they do to save themselves. It's my duty... *no, it's our duty...*" indicating everyone around the table, "...to see that the United States survives so I'd ask you to focus on that one objective..."

Feeling a little awkward at the President's outburst, the scientists sat quietly. Not knowing quite where to look, they sat studying the charts. Eventually, Dan Ackland broke the uneasy silence by saying in an uncharacteristically gentle voice, "Excuse me, Mr President. I know it's not easy to comprehend the gravity of this situation when you're presented with the facts for the first time... whereas we've had a few days to take them in and consider the consequences... but you do realise that the United States isn't going to survive this disaster? Or at least not in its current form..."

The President slammed the table with his fist and shouted, "I won't have such defeatist talk! We're not done for until we're done for and I for one refuse to give up the fight before it's even begun. Do you understand, Mr Ackland? Do you?" But no one around the table felt his tirade was backed by any genuine conviction, with the President sounding like a man in his final hour railing against the dying of the light.

Dan Ackland sat quietly, his steady gaze meeting the President's glaring challenge until George Horowitz said diplomatically, "Dr Melosh... You said you'd be coming to the long term consequences... Would it be appropriate to consider these now?"

"Yes, it would."

George Horowitz turned to the President and said, "With your permission, Sir..."

After a brief pause, during which the President seemed to deflate completely, he said sourly, "Go ahead! You might as well drive the final nail in the coffin..."

"As I said earlier, this is a very complex event... Another effect of the impact that must be considered is the disruption to the ionosphere which is a layer in the upper atmosphere used for the transmission of radio waves... Effectively, this will make terrestrial broadcasting impossible for some time after the impact. How long I don't know but weeks, maybe months. It'll also knock out huge portions of the electrical power grid nationwide which will be destroyed by the ejecta and winds. That and the destruction of radio and TV stations, cable networks and the like will effectively make communication by

217

radio, television and telephone impossible... The only systems that might continue working are direct military and government comms links that were designed to survive a nuclear attack... So any information or instructions you want to give people will have to be given before the impact because afterward it'll be impossible..."

"What about transport... mobility? Will people still be able to get about?"

"I was coming to that, Mr Horowitz. There'll be any number of problems to contend with and they'll all be major... many will be insurmountable... Firstly, the ejecta, the air blast and the winds will level most of the infrastructure across the nation... Power generation and distribution... Fuel and food production and distribution... Industry... Road, rail and air transport... You name it, the initial impact and its immediate effects will destroy it. It'll also kill most agricultural livestock and crops. Secondly, the nation will be buried under a blanket of ejecta... *literally*... Even in New England and the maritime provinces of eastern Canada, the model shows it'll be at least six inches deep. This will make it extremely difficult to re-establish agriculture on any significant scale... Finally, the impact itself will put vast quantities of dust into the atmosphere and the ejecta will cause wildfires around the World that'll consume vast tracts of forest and scrub putting enormous quantities of soot into the atmosphere. The combined effect of dust and soot, which will reflect a significant proportion of the sunlight back into space, will be severe global cooling which may persist for years... it may even trigger another ice age... which will make it even harder... *no, virtually impossible*... to re-establish agriculture on any scale, especially in the Northern Hemisphere. Without agriculture, we can't sustain a viable population... And these effects won't just be local... *They will truly be global*... As I see it, life on Earth... at least all higher-order life, including mankind... is in grave danger of extinction. Quite frankly, it'll be a miracle if we survive..."

The President asked bitterly, "Are you saying it isn't worth doing anything because everything we do will come to naught?"

Showing more emotion than he had up until now, Jay Melosh said heatedly, "No, that's not what I'm saying. I don't know how bad things are going to be in a week, a month, a year from now. On the other hand, you don't want me coming here spouting meaningless platitudes, downplaying the risks. I'm trying to open your eyes to the worst possible scenario in the hope that, by some miracle, we don't have to confront it... If I thought it was totally hopeless, I wouldn't be here now. I'd be at home spending my last few days with the people I care about most..."

A flicker passed through the President's eyes. "Now that's what I wanted to hear, Dr Melosh. Fighting talk! Yes Sir! We might go down in the end but we'll go down fighting. So, do you have anything more to contribute?"

"Nothing concrete. The future's all speculation, so I don't see any point in going there. I suggest we focus on surviving the impact and its immediate aftermath. That's more than enough for mere mortals. Thereafter, we have to put our trust in God."

In a far more business-like tone, the President said, "Bravo! Well said, Dr Melosh. Thank you. Now, Mr Tandy, I presume you also have something to contribute…"

Graham Tandy nodded and said, "Yes, Sir, I have… but I'm afraid it's not good news."

"Well, Mr Tandy, good or bad, let's hear it."

Graham Tandy cleared his throat and said, "Unfortunately, I haven't had long to consider all the consequences of this impact but I have identified a number of possible knock-ons from it… Firstly and of greatest concern is the Yellowstone Volcano…" As an aside, Graham Tandy said, "I've already appraised these gentlemen of the situation at Yellowstone…" before continuing, "We estimate that the seismic shaking at Yellowstone will be about magnitude five-point-five on the Richter scale. My assistant and I did some quick calculations and there's a significant chance… about fifty-fifty… that the tremor will crack the cap over the magma chamber, triggering an eruption. It's also possible that the shockwave travelling through the Earth's interior could cause a sudden pressure pulse in the magma chamber that could blow its lid off… If Yellowstone were to erupt, the immediate effects of it would be more localised than the impact of S241 but it would still cause widespread devastation over an area a couple of thousand miles in diameter, making conditions in the mid-west even more hostile… But, worse than that, Yellowstone would contribute greatly to the pall of dust in the atmosphere, worsening and possibly extending any period of global cooling… and the huge amounts of sulfur dioxide and other constituents of acid rain it belched out would worsen the long-term damage to nature and agriculture…"

The President interruped, "Is there evidence from other impacts that gives us any clue as to what may happen here?"

Graham Tandy thought for a while, then said, "Well, there's a strong parallel here with the Chicxulub disaster sixty-five million years ago that wiped out the dinosaurs. At around the same time, there was a massive volcanic eruption in what is now India… called the Deccan Traps… which may have contributed to the mass extinction by making the environment even more unhealthy… If that was the case, then there may be an even greater probability of S241 triggering Yellowstone than we originally estimated… There's no hard evidence to tie the two events together. It may just have been coincidence… On the other hand, the Chicxulub asteroid which was smaller than S241, could well have triggered the eruption of the Deccan Traps. It's probably highly significant that, sixty-five million years ago, the landmass that became the Indian sub-continent was at about the antipodal point to Chicxulub... that is, at the point on the other side of the globe directly opposite the impact site, where the shockwaves that radiated out from it would have met and concentrated. Fortunately, Yellowstone is nowhere near the antipodal point of S241's impact site which is actually in the Indian Ocean off the coast of Madagascar... but, unfortunately, that too is a volcanic hot spot with Piton de la Fournaise on the island of Réunion, which is one of the World's most active volcanoes..." Graham Tandy noticed the President staring at him intently. "I'm sorry, Mr President but there's no easy answer where such complex matters are concerned..."

The President said calmly, "I understand, Mr Tandy. Please go on."

"Another major concern is the Cascadia fault which runs up the west coast from northern California to Canada. This is a little-known underwater fault in the subduction zone at the edge of the Pacific plate where it dives under the continental North American plate. It's similar in size to the Sumatran fault that caused the magnitude nine earthquake on December twenty-six, two-thousand-and-four, which resulted in the giant tsunamis in the Indian Ocean that killed two-hundred and thirty thousand people... Cascadia has ruptured catastrophically four times within the last two-and-a-half thousand years, at intervals as short as three hundred years or so, causing massive earthquakes on the west coast and giant tsunamis here and on the opposite side of the Pacific. It's not well known outside of the geological community simply because it's been quiet since before the time the area was settled by Europeans but the evidence of its existence is indisputable. Unfortunately, it last ruptured about three hundred years ago... in January, seventeen-hundred, to be precise... and there's no reason to think the pressure hasn't been building steadily ever since. By the time it reaches the fault zone, the magnitude of the tremor emanating from the impact will be about five-point-five. There's a good chance it'll cause the fault to rupture again, which would result in a major secondary seismic event and another huge tsunami..." After a brief pause, Graham Tandy said, "I know this offers us no comfort in the immediate term but the shockwave from S241 will probably release other, huge, pent-up stresses in the Earth's crust such as Cascadia, which would avoid such events happening at a time in the near future that would hit survivors of S241 just as they were trying to get back on their feet. The cruel dilemma this presents us with is that surviving the impact of S241 will be difficult enough in itself, without compounding the problems with other major events triggered by it..."

The President said briskly, "As Dr Melosh rightly pointed out, we might as well know the worst that could happen and be prepared to face it now in the hope that conditions for survivors are more benign. So, do you have anything to add, Mr Tandy?"

"Well Sir, only that S241 could also trigger the eruption of other volcanoes around the World, particularly those around the Pacific 'ring of fire'... Of greatest concern are the volcanoes running down the backbone of America, from Alaska, through Canada, the Cascades and California, into Mexico and Central America, most of which would erupt explosively, putting a lot of ash and fume into the atmosphere. S241 could trigger an eruption of any of these which would only make local conditions even worse..."

"But you can't say categorically whether two-forty-one will trigger any of these events?"

"No, Sir, not with absolute certainty..."

"Well, in that case, let's hope and pray it doesn't..."

The President sat quietly for a while then said, "I've heard mention of global cooling and 'volcanic winters'... even the threat of another ice age... Realistically, what's the likelihood of any of these occurring?"

Graham Tandy thought how best to approach the problem before saying, "Strictly speaking, we're in the middle of an ice age today... one that began forty million years ago... because we still have permanent ice sheets and glaciers in higher latitudes. For the last ten thousand years the ice has been retreating, making the weather milder. The relevance of that will become clearer in a minute... The dust and soot from S241 and the fires it starts will cause global cooling on a dramatic scale. The eruption of Yellowstone or any other volcano would increase the amount of dust... We know from the geological record that there was an intense cold spell after Chicxulub but the climate eventually recovered to become quite hot and balmy. To the best of our knowledge, it didn't result in an ice age but that was probably because it happened during a fairly temperate period in Earth's climate... With S241, we have two conflicting conditions. Firstly, the amount of dust and soot will probably be greater than Chicxulub which will cause profound cooling. That'll result in an extended winter and we may not see significant warming in the summer because the skies will still be overcast. Set against that, the fires started by S241 will put a lot of carbon dioxide into the atmosphere which is a powerful greenhouse gas. Along with the increased level of carbon dioxide already in the atmosphere from burning fossil fuels, it may be enough to kickstart the process of warming, once the dust settles... That could take years, of course... But the most worrying thing is that Earth is already in an inter-glacial period. The real problem is that scientists can't agree on whether a swing back towards glaciation is already overdue or whether we can expect this mild climate to continue for another ten or even twenty thousand years. However, what many scientists do agree on is that, if the climate gets so cold that snow which falls one winter fails to melt the following summer reflecting more of the Sun's energy back into space, the climate may find itself in a downward spiral from which it can't recover. The condition becomes self-accelerating... It may only take one or two seasons of intense cold to push the Earth into its next period of glaciation."

Sensing that Graham Tandy had finished, the President said, "So where does that leave us, gentlemen? We need to formulate some sort of strategic response to S241..."

They sat in silence until George Horowitz volunteered, "It seems to me that the first step is to evacuate everyone into the Eastern time zone. After all, if they stay west of the Rockies they're guaranteed to perish. If they stay in the Central time zone, their chances of survival improve but they're still at risk. The further east they go, the greater their chance of survival will be..." He looked around the table at the four scientists who stared back at him skeptically.

Eventually, the President said, "Well, gentlemen, what are you thinking?"

After a brief pause, Dan Ackland said, "With all due respect, Sir, I don't think you realise the logistical problem... or should I say the impossibility... of moving a third of the population of the United States a distance of two thousand miles or more in four days... It'll take at least twenty-four hours after making the announcement to clear the cities...There are very few major roads running east-west and the few there are will become completely snarled with congestion within hours of the announcement... The average American automobile has a range of about three-hundred and fifty miles on a full tank of gas and to get from the west coast to the Eastern time zone is eighteen hundred miles. That's at least five tanks of gas. There isn't nearly enough fuel in all the gas stations en route to support such an almighty exodus... Notwithstanding that, that's not nearly far enough away from ground zero to guarantee anyone's survival. The chances are, people would be left stranded somewhere on the road... Even if they did reach the mid-west, where are they going to shelter when S241 comes down? The likelihood is they'll be caught in the open with nothing more to hide in than their cars which will be destroyed or buried... And assuming they survive that, where are they going to live and what are they going to live on? The situation for locals will be hard enough without having to contend with a huge influx of refugees all competing for the same meagre resources... And before any of that could happen, all travel restrictions would have to be lifted..."

The President interrupted. "What are you saying, Mr Ackland?" he asked in disbelief. "That we do nothing and stand by while millions of people perish without lifting a finger to help them?"

"*Billions* of people are going to die, Mr President... If not within a few minutes or hours of S241 coming down, then within a few days or weeks... Not just here but around the World. That's the awful reality of it..."

Paul Kaufmann, who'd been studying the charts, spoke for the first time. The audience couldn't fail to register the note of desperation in his voice. "I see what Mr Ackland's saying. I can't see how an influx of refugees from the west would help people in the east... But couldn't we evacuate some of our people abroad... possibly to Europe... by sea or by air? At least that way some of our people would have a better chance of survival?"

George Horowitz said, "After the... er... condemnation of our recent actions by the French and Germans and other European nations, I can't see them welcoming our people with open arms... Can you?"

Dan Ackland interjected. "Forget the moral arguments, Mr Horowitz. It'll be more fundamental than that. I'd be surprised if Britain which is supposed to be our closest ally, would let any of our people in simply because Europe's already densely populated, nowhere more than Britain. Farming there's going to be hit just as hard as everywhere else. They won't be able to feed themselves let alone refugees... When S241 comes down it'll be a case of everyone for themselves... And on a purely practical note, Mr Kaufmann, nobody's going to want to be caught on a ship in the middle of the Atlantic with enormous waves whipped up by two-hundred-mile-an-hour winds... And using the whole of the American airliner fleet, you could maybe evacuate two million people by August twenty-first if you started now... How would you pick which two million were to be evacuated when you're leaving two-hundred-million to face certain death and the remainder to a very precarious future? And coming back to my first comment... Where would you evacuate them to?"

The President remained deep in thought for a long time before saying, "So, Mr Ackland... In reality, is what you're saying that we should do nothing? Make no announcement, formulate no plans because in the long run it won't make any difference..."

"No, Sir, that's not what I'm saying. Even if you'd announced it two weeks ago when we first brought the possibility of S241 hitting Earth to your attention, there would still have been nothing you could've done to change the outcome. You might have had time to evacuate at least part of the population... but to where... You could have forewarned people sooner but that would have done very little to help them survive the aftermath... Bear in mind that after S241 there'll be no government because there'll be no one to administer it. People will be too busy with the day-to-day demands of survival to have any loyalty to anyone but themselves and their close group... There'll be no organisation... no law and order... no communications... no emergency services... no medical facilities... no infrastructure to provide food, water, fuel, energy, health care, housing... You name it, it won't exist. What we're talking about for the survivors... not just here in the United States but worldwide... is a return to a primitive society where the biggest communities

223

will be organised around family groups or small enclaves of families in a locality... I suspect that if you'd warned folks sooner it would simply have led to rioting, looting and mayhem sooner... Think what happened in New Orleans in the aftermath of Hurricane Katrina... and that was only a localised disaster with help from outside the stricken area just a few hours or, at worst, a few days away. This time there'll be no outside help because everywhere will be stricken... It'd be anarchy on a massive scale as supermarket shelves empty and pumps at the gas stations run dry, with folks killing each other over a loaf of bread or a bottle of milk, not really grasping the reality of the situation... That when they've exhausted their own provisions, they'll have to make do with whatever they can scavenge for the foreseeable future... I see no way in which you could prepare people for what's to come after S241 because it'll be like nothing anybody's ever experienced before. At the end of the day, how you play it is your decision, Mr President but if you want my advice, I suggest you keep it as low-key as possible... Inform other governments, by all means, then announce it to the world simultaneously. Stress the need for people to take shelter in their own homes, warn them about the probability of power outages, advise them to get in a sensible stock of provisions... but don't try and embark on a complete evacuation of the west. Doing so will only provoke widespread panic and mass hysteria, leading to a complete breakdown of order which will result in anarchy and all the problems we highlighted a few moments ago."

"But Mr Ackland... I was elected to protect the people of the United States... To preserve people's lives and keep them safe... It would be a dereliction of my duty if I did what you're advocating..."

With a firm note in his voice, Dan Ackland said, "With all due respect, Mr President, my advice is to accept that you can't protect people from what's coming. You can't do anything to preserve life in the aftermath of what's about to happen. The chances are you won't survive it yourself. The forces lined up against us... *against humanity*... are so many orders of magnitude greater than any force man could exert, even if everyone on the planet pulled together in the same direction. That's not being defeatist, it's simply being realistic. What's more, people aren't going to survive because they deserve to. The devout... those who pray hardest... aren't going to be singled out for survival. Even the survivalists... those who've been preparing for the Apocalypse... won't necessarily survive. If there are any survivors, they're going to be chosen by fate, not by you or anybody else. When you consider how brutally harsh and difficult life will be afterwards, you can't even say it'll be the lucky ones who survive... And those who do survive will only do so because they adapt to the primitive conditions most successfully..."

The President looked at each of the scientists. "Is this the opinion of you all?"

In turn, starting with Jack Culver, the other three men concurred.

The President looked them hard in the eye. "And would you be saying differently if you were all back at home rather than here?"

After a tense pause, Graham Tandy said softly, "As you probably know from my security file, I'm a confirmed bachelor. I don't have anybody else to worry about. But speaking for myself, I am going home... well, home to Yellowstone that is... as soon as you've dispensed with my services. If I'm going to meet my Maker, I want to live out my last few days on Earth in God's own country surrounded by the beauty He bestowed on it... I'll be on Yellowstone Lake, fishing for those magnificent cutthroat trout He so generously stocked it with. I'll take my chances alongside my neighbours. So no, Mr President, I think I have a reasonably balanced view..."

The President held Graham Tandy's steady gaze until Jay Melosh volunteered, "Unlike Mr Tandy, I do have a family that I care about very deeply. When I've finished here I'm also going home. I must confess when I found out about S241 a week ago... *literally hours* before the attack on Los Angeles and the imposition of martial law which prevented all movement... I would've taken my family and gone east. Where to and to what fate I don't know because, by that time, I also knew the effects of S241... But I can't argue with Dan Ackland's assessment of the situation, however much I wish I could. On balance, I think our chances of survival in Tucson are now probably no worse than the chances of survival anywhere else we could reach in the time available. And if we aren't lucky enough to survive, the end should be mercifully swift... So no, Mr President, I'm not being biassed either."

The President said, "Thank you for being so candid. With the same view coming from opposite ends of the spectrum, I have to believe you're sincere... And I value your opinions, although whether I can agree with them unreservedly is another matter. I'd be obliged if you'd indulge me a little longer and give me some time alone to consult with my advisers. So if you'll excuse us for a while, my wife has some refreshments ready in our lounge..."

In unison, the four men stood up and one of the Secret Service agents lead them out through the door that the President had entered by an-hour-and-a-quarter earlier.

—•—

The four men sat sipping home-made lemonade, making small talk with the First Lady. After about half an hour, Paul Kaufmann appeared and asked Dan Ackland to join them. To break the silence that followed, Jack Culver turned to Graham Tandy and said, "I don't know why but the moment I saw you, I had you down as a fisherman. I'm a golfer myself when work permits but I haven't had much time for it lately."

225

Graham Tandy said, "Golf's not a game for a loner. I tried it once but I felt ridiculous slicing into the rough with no one to rib me about my mistakes... And I found it very lonely with everyone else going round in twos or fours... No, fly fishing is much more suitable for the solitary sportsman... And it allows you time to think. The pace is determined by the fish and the solitude of being out on the lake early in the morning when it's still and tranquil is absolutely glorious... whereas with golf you're so completely preoccupied with your own game... or your opponent's... that you can't enjoy nature. Or at least I couldn't..."

The President's wife asked gently, "Have you never been married, Mr Tandy?" to which he replied, "No Ma'am..." and then added rather shyly, "I was engaged once but my fiancée was killed in an accident shortly before we were due to be married. I guess I immersed myself in my work and never got out of the habit. Thereafter, I never met anyone I wanted to be with as much as Yvette although, if truth be told, I probably never encouraged it."

The President's wife said, "I'm really sorry to hear that, Mr Tandy. That's very sad... So much promise unfulfilled..."

Feeling that, in telling these strangers something he'd only told two or three other people in the last thirty-five years he had revealed too much, he hurriedly went on, "August is a fine time for fishing Yellowstone Lake... Of course, its weed beds are deeper than most freshwater lakes so there are lots of insects hatching... And the cutthroat trout is very amenable. It'll easily rise six feet to take your Callibaetis imitation..."

Not wanting to exacerbate his mild embarassment, the First Lady asked politely, "What are 'Callibaetis' Mr Tandy?"

"Mayflies, Ma'am... One of the staples of the trout's diet..."

The conversation lapsed into uneasy silence, leaving the three men with the impression that there was something that had so far gone unsaid. Eventually, the First Lady turned to Jack Culver and ended the pregnant pause. "My husband regards you very highly, Mr Culver. You made a powerful impression on him at your first meeting..."

A little taken aback by the unsolicited compliment, Jack Culver said, "Do you mind if I ask why, Ma'am?"

"He said you were very forthright... straightforward and plain spoken... and clearly an expert on top of your subject..."

Jack Culver cut in, "As we all are, Ma'am. I'm no more expert in my field than my colleagues are in theirs..."

"Perhaps not, Mr Culver but for some reason he took a particular shine to you. So now I'm asking you to speak plainly to me..." Jack Culver saw the steely look in the woman's eyes. "I know why you're here. My husband told me about S241... or enough for me to grasp the significance of forthcoming events. And I know it's the worst possible news or you wouldn't be here at

226

such short notice at a time like this... But... and I say this in the strictest confidence, you understand..." All three men nodded. "...my husband is consumed with guilt. Guilt at not taking action sooner when he first found out about S241. Guilt about being responsible for countless deaths that could have been avoided if he'd acted sooner which is eating away at his soul. Is he right to blame himself, Mr Culver?"

Jack thought deeply before saying, "If you want the plain truth, Ma'am, the reality of this situation is such that no human being... not even the President of the most powerful nation on Earth harnessing the combined effort of every individual on it... could alter the outcome of this event to any meaningful degree. To imagine you could would be to deceive yourself..." After a brief pause, Jack Culver continued, "I must confess I was surprised there'd been no public warning about S241 before now, or what to do in the event of an impact but, at our first meeting, it was only an outside possibility and there was no certainty about the location of the impact. It was all too nebulous to justify causing the widespread panic that would inevitably have followed... On the other hand, I did notice a steady increase in low-key safety announcements, which could equally well have applied to surviving a terrorist attack as to S241, so I assumed something was being done to prepare people for a forthcoming disaster without scaring the living daylights out of them. Perhaps a little too subtle but something at least..."

The First Lady interrupted, "Yes, that was all part of his strategy..."

"If there was any self-deception, it was possibly to think he could use the situation to his advantage against his enemies but even then it would have been a pyrrhic victory..." Jack Culver left the sentence hanging, watching for a response but when he saw none, continued, "...because when S241 comes down, it'll wipe out whole populations indiscriminately irrespective of color, creed, birth, or status... As for his guilt... If he's guilty of anything, the only thing he's guilty of is wishing harm to his enemies... But if he'd known the true nature of S241, I don't think he'd have wished it on his worst enemy..."

Chapter 9

Within an hour of the destruction of Washington the military, in conjunction with the National Guard and Reserve, had imposed martial law nationwide. Within two hours when no further cities had been destroyed, radio announcements began assuring people that there would be no more bombings and it was safe to return but it still took the remainder of the day to shepherd the majority of the frightened inhabitants back to their homes. Even then, many resolutely refused to re-enter the cities, taking refuge wherever they could find accommodation remote from any major conurbation. For many of the survivalists who'd been anticipating and planning for Armageddon, it wasn't only an opportunity to put their preparations to the test but it was the bugle call they'd been waiting for. Many retreated deep into forest or wilderness, determined to lead a self-sufficient life off the land, some of whom were ready to kill anyone they perceived even remotely posed a threat to them. Unfortunately, with the subsequent clampdown on travel, those that would have liked to return home found it difficult to do so. Once people had recovered from the initial shock, the annihilation of the three principal cities of the United States by terrorists using nuclear weapons had raised people's levels of fear, paranoia, hatred, anger and abhorrence in pretty much equal measures to hitherto unknown heights and the military response to the attacks had exacerbated some still further as much as it had quelled others. The fact that the President had been in evidence very little during this period and the Vice President not at all only served to heighten people's anxiety. It was against this background that the President now struggled with the prospect of breaking the news about S241.

The next problem the President had faced had been convincing the Joint Chiefs of Staff of the United States Armed Forces that the danger presented by S241 was real and imminent. With military control over all public announcements, news broadcasting and movement, it was necessary to get their cooperation before anything could be done but the most difficult obstacle to overcome had been grabbing their attention in the first place and holding it long enough to drive the message home when their focus was entirely on developments in the war abroad and security at home. In frustration, the President had called Dan Ackland into the conference call to provide an expert view in an effort to make the Generals understand that this event eclipsed anything they might be wrestling with at the moment. The call ended with General Landsbergh demanding that the President and his team meet with the other members of the JCS at a secure base near Washington before they would consider lifting any restrictions; General Landsbergh himself was still trapped underground in the Presidential Emergency Operations Center from where he was directing military operations. After the call, the President had asked Dan Ackland if he would become his special scientific adviser on all matters related to asteroid S241. Before agreeing to join his entourage, Dan Ackland asked cautiously, "What about my colleagues?"

The President responded, "What about them? I assume they'll all want to go home. I see no reason to detain them. We don't need them, do we? You've heard their forecasts about the damage. You've got their charts. Can't you speak for them?"

A little hesitantly, Dan Ackland said, "Yes, Mr President but…"

"But what, Mr Ackland? You don't have anyone to go back to yourself… or at least not according to your security file. So why the hesitancy?"

"It's not for myself, Sir. It's for Jack Culver. Jack would have left two weeks ago to join his family in up-state New York. He only stayed on at the Observatory at my request to help us through this period, until we were certain whether S241 was on a collision course or not. He should've been heading out the day martial law was imposed and he's been trapped there ever since. I can't leave Jack in limbo when his family's waiting for him to join them back east."

Sensing that an impasse had been reached, the President said, "I applaud your loyalty, Mr Ackland but aren't you being a little hypocritical? Aren't you doing precisely the opposite of what you advocated earlier? Surely, Mr Culver stayed knowing he might be sacrificing himself?"

Dan Ackland said quietly, "Had Jack Culver known he wouldn't make it, he'd still have stayed anyway out of a sense of duty. But I can't abandon him to God knows what fate when he only stayed at my behest."

The President held his gaze with a wither eye long enough for Dan Ackland to start to feel uncomfortable before he said quietly, "Perhaps now you appreciate how impotent I feel, Mr Ackland but two-hundred-million-times worse… Alright, we'll take him with us. We'll drop him off as close as we can to his destination, then it'll be up to him to make his own way home. That's the best I can offer, Mr Ackland. Take it or leave it."

"Thank you, Sir."

Within two minutes, Jack Culver was bidding farewell to his old friend, Jay Melosh; within five minutes, Air Force One was thundering down the runway beginning the last leg of the last journey it would ever make.

—•—

(Tuesday 17 August 2010)

As the Sun peeped over the distant horizon, piercing the twilight with the first golden rays of the day, Martha sat at the intersection tut-tutting impatiently, waiting to join the unbroken queue of traffic on I-80 headed east at no more than walking pace, interspersed with long and inexplicable periods with no movement at all. With the exception of the dull throb of a thousand engines turning over at little more than idling speed, the endless columns of vehicles which occupied both east- and west-bound carriageways and stretched as far as the eye could see in either direction, were eerily quiet. Radios played continuously but most of them were tuned to news channels and were talking in very muted tones. For the most part the occupants were subdued with adults in the front staring intently into the rising Sun and the children sitting quietly or slumped in the back seats asleep.

Just before seven o'clock the previous evening Martha had received a call on her cellphone from Jack, the first she'd had from him in a week. It was very hurried. He'd only just had time to tell her to turn on the television when he said urgently, "I have to go!" Martha had sat listening to the tone until the line automatically disconnected itself, leaving her feeling lonelier than she could ever remember feeling in all their marriage. They were still in the same room, in the same hotel in Portage, Indiana that they had been in when they saw the President's confrontation with the diminutive Arab reporter, trapped there by the travel embargo imposed under martial law. Claudette had raced in from the bathroom, her panties askew. "Is that Dad? Can I speak to him?" But when she saw the bleak look on her mother's face and her hands lying in her lap clutching the silent phone, she had burst into tears and retreated back into the bathroom. Sick of watching television, with its endless litany of unpleasant and depressing news about targets destroyed, uprisings put down and American losses, Martha had switched it off that morning. Now she switched it back on again. As it had done a week ago, the message on the screen announced that the President would be addressing the nation but this time at twenty-hundred hours Eastern time.

Martha had selected channel thirty-five and seen the President sitting behind a table in a makeshift studio, looking drawn and troubled. This time there was no audience and no air of jubilation. As the camera pulled back, it revealed General Corfield, the spokesman for the Joint Chiefs of Staff who by now had become a familiar figure in most households, sitting at the President's right hand. As the shot pulled back a little further, Martha was astonished to see Dan Ackland appear in view. While she watched, he turned to his left and said something to someone just out of camera shot.

The President had opened by saying, "My fellow Americans, I have some extremely grave news to give you, news that is being announced even now to all the peoples around the World by their national leaders... Recently, I learnt that for some time now astronomers have been watching a distant asteroid which they termed S241, that they thought might come close to Earth. They have been plotting its course through the heavens to determine whether it represented a threat to us... I have to tell you now that, as of this morning, I was told that S241 will strike the Earth in the early hours of Saturday morning, August twenty-first, just over four days from now. The best estimates show that it will come down somewhere in the Pacific Ocean, between Hawaii and the west coast of the United States. I am also told that there is nothing we can do to prevent this collision, so we will have to ride out its effects as best we can... Before I hand you over to my colleagues who will give you practical advice on what action you should take, I want to say this... The effects of this impact will be felt on a global scale. Nobody on the planet will be unaware of it or will go untouched by its effects and many people will perish, here and around the World. The scale of this event... *no, this disaster*... will be greater than any mankind has ever experienced, so no one's certain how serious it's going to be. The only way you can help ensure your own personal safety and the safety of your loved ones is to follow the advice that is to follow. So without further ado, I'm going to hand you over to my special scientific adviser on asteroid S241, the man who led the team that discovered it, Mr Dan Ackland..."

"Thank you, Mr President..." Dan Ackland spoke slowly and precisely. "I know many of you will be frightened by the prospect of asteroid S241 hitting the Earth and worried about the effects of the impact and you have every reason to be. However, if you follow the simple guidelines we are going to give you, you have the best chance of surviving the impact and its immediate effects... I will come to the longer term issues shortly... Firstly, you are advised to stay at home. If you have a basement or underground shelter, get in it at least two hours before the impact and remain in it for at least twenty-four hours after. Announcements will be made on radio and television telling you when you should take shelter... Secondly, take a stock of food and water into your shelter sufficient to last at least a week or longer if you have room to store it..." Dan Ackland continued talking steadily, his even tone giving terrified people some hope and reassurance that S241 would be survivable. "As and when you do emerge, be very careful. Examine the sky and the area around you for any signs of small projectiles, like pebbles, falling to Earth. If there are any, return to your shelter immediately and don't come out into the open for at least an hour after they've stopped falling... When you do finally emerge, the landscape may be very different from the one you left behind... The impact will eject a lot of debris in varying sizes from pebbles to large rocks. The nearer you are to the impact site, the bigger and deeper the debris will be... You may also find that trees, as well as buildings and other structures have been blown down or badly damaged by the powerful winds that will follow the impact, possibly even as far away as the eastern seaboard of the United States and that hot debris or ruptured gas mains or fuel tanks may have caused fires to break out, particularly if you live in cities or heavily wooded areas…"

Martha thought, 'All the time this was what Jack was being so secretive about. So he was telling the truth when he said he'd been sworn to silence by the President…' and she was suffused by guilt for having suspected him of being involved with another woman. 'Why didn't I trust him when he needed it most?' She berated herself, "How could I have been so stupid? Stupid! STUPID!" she shrieked angrily, which brought Claudette dashing in from the bathroom to see what the commotion was all about. Ignoring her question about what had made her cry out loud, Martha briefly told Claudette about S241, then mother and daughter sat hunched together on the bed watching the rest of the announcement. As General Corfield summarised the relaxation of travel restrictions, Claudette turned to her mother and asked quizzically, "Do you think this has anything to do with why Billy ran away?"

Being preoccupied by this latest bombshell, Martha replied distractedly, "Don't be ridiculous!"

Martha sat on the bed chewing her fingernails, something she only ever did if she was extremely anxious. Her mind raced back and forth between going back for Nicky or going on to find Billy. Eventually, she managed to get through to her mother-in-law on the telephone who told her that there had still been no sign of Billy. Conjuring up any number of terrible, nightmarish reasons why Billy still hadn't arrived at his destination and the terrible images that went with them, Martha made the snap decision to go on on the basis that, at seventeen, her elder son should be better able to look after himself than a boy of twelve with severe communication problems.

Suddenly, in exasperation, Martha exclaimed, "Christ Almighty! This is no good. We're never going to find Billy at this rate… And I can't get out of this bloody traffic queue. I'm totally blocked in… Why the hell didn't I take the back roads…" After a few moments, she viciously thumped the steering wheel and spat out with an equal degree of frustration, "Where the hell do these people think they're going? Surely they heard the advice, didn't they? 'Stay at home! Do NOT leave! Take shelter in your basement!' Why the hell didn't they do as they were told?"

Claudette said, "Calm down Mom. It's no use blowing your top. These people could be saying exactly the same thing about us. They have as much right to be here as we do. And they're probably as frightened as we are… Maybe more so. At least we have the assurance of knowing that Dad's been aware of S241 for a while now and if there had been anything to be really worried about, he'd have taken us away long before now, as soon as he found out about it. That's more than all these other people can say… We've still got a long way to go and you've got to keep your cool or we'll have an accident or something… Then where would we be?"

Smarting from the scolding – Martha knew Claudette was right, about remaining calm at least – the two sat in stony silence for the next hour, during which time they travelled just under four miles. Eventually, Martha said, "Get the map, Claudette. We're getting off at the next intersection. We're going to find a different route to South Bend, one that misses this tail-back." Claudette rummaged around in the back seat until she pulled a crumpled road atlas out from under a pile of clothes, then studied it for a while. "There's a junction in about… er…" checking the nearest mile marker, "…three miles. I suggest we get off there and take State Highway forty-nine south to U.S. Highway six, then go east on six until we reach U.S. thirty-one, then take thirty-one north to South Bend… and failing that, we'll go cross-country…" Mother and daughter gave each other an old-fashioned look and Martha said, "Well if that ain't the dangedest set of directions I ever heard, I don't know what is…" and for the first time in what seemed like a lifetime they laughed at the tongue-twister. After a little while, as they found themselves sitting in another interminable hold-up, Martha turned and put her arms round Claudette and hugged her, saying, "If I had to drive clear across the United States under such conditions… *no, under any conditions*… there's no one I'd rather have as my travelling companion than you, my darling daughter…" and gave her a kiss on the cheek. Claudette sat quietly as Martha continued, "I guess you might not have chosen me, especially the way I've been acting recently. I know I've been a real bitch at times and I'm sorry for it but I haven't been feeling myself lately. And what with that and worrying about Billy… and your Dad… and now Nicky… it's all been a bit much…" Martha tailed off, feeling a little embarrassed at admitting to such a lapse but Claudette put her hand gently on Martha's forearm and said, "It's alright Mom, I understand… And I still know you're the best friend I'll ever have…" at which it was Martha's turn to shed a few tears.

—•—

In exasperation, Jack savagely kicked the motorcycle with his heel of his shoe, unleashing the full fury of his boiling anger and it toppled over onto its side with a dull metallic crunch as he cursed it, "Harley heap of junk!" As soon as the engine had cut out and the warning light had come on he'd known intuitively that the alternator had failed; he'd had exactly the same problem with his own Harley-Davidson, twice, which is why he'd got rid of it and bought the awesome Suzuki Hayabusa GSX1300R instead and had never looked back. Now, his latest bike, a Limited Edition 2006 model, the second Hayabusa he'd owned, was sitting in his garage, three thousand miles away when he could desperately have done with it here. He had coasted to a stop at the roadside and he now sat on the verge turning over in his mind what to do next.

Air Force One had landed at Dover Air Force Base, in Delaware (on the basis that terrorists armed with man-portable, shoulder-launched surface-to-air missiles may be waiting in ambush somewhere in the vicinity of Andrews AFB, with the intention of trying to bring down the presidential jet as it came in to land – ironically, possibly using Stinger missiles originally supplied to the Mujahideen, in Afghanistan, by the CIA, for use against the occupying Soviet forces) from where the President had broadcast the chilling news about S241 to the nation. Jack had been party to the meeting with General Corfield and two other members of the JCS. When they had explained the consequences of S241 and the General had overcome his initial incredulity, he had gone as white as a sheet; Jack wondered whether it was white with fear at the prospect of what was to come or white with rage that it would spoil his war. However, once they had been convinced they'd moved very swiftly and decisively, contacting General Landsbergh and appraising him of the situation, then helping to formulate the President's plans ready for his forthcoming announcement. Being hard-boiled pragmatists with up-to-the-minute experience of managing a crisis, they had broadly agreed with the scientists about how much should be revealed to the public and how much should be kept hidden but they had insisted that the ban on public transport remain because of the threat that buses and planes in particular might be hijacked and used as weapons of mass destruction, although that phrase now seemed far less apt in light of both recent and forthcoming events.

After the broadcast, Jack had tried calling Martha a dozen times but he'd found that the networks were completely choked with terrified people desperately trying to contact their loved ones and it had been impossible to get through. Unbeknown to Jack, Martha had tried calling him and found herself equally frustrated. Immediately the broadcast was over, the President had whisked Dan Ackland and the members of the JCS off for a briefing and Jack had found himself at a loose end. The base commander had been present, watching the broadcast. Jack had buttonholed him afterwards to ask if he could suggest how Jack might obtain some transport, hoping it may elicit the use of one of the base vehicles but it hadn't. Not having eaten much all day, Jack had asked where he could get a hot meal and was directed to the mess. That was how he'd found himself standing in front of the notice board reading a personal advert offering a motorcycle for sale:

'1999 Harley-Davidson Softail Custom. 23,000 miles. Custom paint w/ghost flames. BUB pipes, SE-3 cams, Mikuni carb, new tires, backrest, extra seat, Harley flame pegs and grips, drag bars and much, much more. $13,500. One careful owner. Sale forced due to arrival of twins. I offered to fit genuine leather saddlebags but the wife said "NO!" A real sweet ride (the bike, that is). It will break my heart to see her go (ditto)'

Jack stood examining the photograph which showed a beaming Airman sitting astride the bike which was clearly his pride-and-joy. He'd tried the cellphone number a couple of times but failed to make contact, so he unpinned the advert and took it down and went off in search of someone who could point him in the direction of Senior Airman Vince Price.

As it so happened, S/A Price had been on duty that evening but Jack had discovered whereabouts on base he lived and that he should be home the following morning. Beginning to feel very isolated, Jack had gone in search of Dan Ackland and found him walking across the apron from Air Force One coming in search of him. In the dark, the armed guard had challenged Jack as he'd approached the cordon around the plane and Jack heard the quiet snick as the guard released the safety catch on his semi-automatic rifle. Although Jack had explained that he was with the President's party, the sentry had made him wait until Dan Ackland had reached the perimeter, rather than allowing Jack to enter it. As the two of them had walked away from the plane, Jack sensed that the basis of their long friendship had shifted very slightly but had shifted all the same. After a pause, Dan Ackland had said, "I've arranged for you to bivvy in one of the officers' quarters tonight, Jack. Thereafter, we'll have to see what tomorrow brings…" before continuing, a little more hesitantly, "Unfortunately, the President won't intercede on your behalf and requisition one of the military vehicles for you to use. He says it's up to you to make your own arrangements as far as transport is concerned."

Jack told Dan that he'd already approached the base commander who'd been unreceptive to any such suggestion, so he'd already taken steps in that direction himself. The two had stood uneasily for a few moments, until Jack had said, "What about you, Dan? What are you going to do?" then, before his friend could answer, said "Why don't you come with me? We could go up to my parents' together. They have a big basement… certainly big enough for one more… and I'm sure they'd be glad to see you again…"

Dan replied quietly, "The President's staying here, Jack. There's a bunker where everyone can sit out the impact. He says he's going to try to re-establish some form of government in the aftermath of S241… if there's anyone left to govern… and he's asked me to stay and help him. I said I would. I feel I owe that much to my country… He also says you're welcome to join us, if you want… Maybe you could join Martha and the family later… when the dust's settled, so to speak…"

Jack Culver thought for a moment, then said, "Dan, it was you who convinced him… *you certainly convinced me… you convinced us all…* of the futility of such a course of action. I agreed with you then and I'm still of the same opinion. So what's happened to change your mind?"

"Oh, I haven't changed my mind, Jack. If anything, the more I check the calculations, the more *I'm convinced*... It's just that I think it's human nature not to give up without a fight in the face of adversity. After all, if we have no hope, we have nothing..."

Jack cut in, "Yes, Dan. I agree. But have you actually taken a long, hard look at the man? Unless my eyes deceive me, he's not well. In fact, irrespective of 241, I'd go so far as to say he's not long for this world."

"You're right, Jack. The President has cancer. His doctors have given him a few months... maybe a year at most... and that's with treatments that may not be available after 241. He confided in me when he told me about his plans and asked me to be part of them..." Dan Ackland had continued, "He's worried that the only section of society with any real chance of survival is the military... Every base has hardened bunkers, control centers, underground storage facilities, armories, ammunition and explosives stores, blast-resistant aircraft hangars, places where people and material can survive the impact... And large parts of our armed forces are scattered around the World where they're also heavily protected... They have enormous stockpiles of food, fuel, medicine, arms... You name it, they have it in abundance... Of course, their might isn't sustainable in the long term without the industries that produce and support their weapons and most of those will be destroyed by 241. But in the short-to-medium term, they can take whatever they need by force from other survivors... And after the way we've prosecuted this war on terrorism, the President's convinced that the lunatics have taken over the asylum... And he was the one who handed them the keys. It's a nightmarish prospect. He doesn't necessarily think he'll be able to bring about a return to democracy because the infrastructure for it will have been completely smashed but he hopes to be able to wrest some control from the military and influence those actions he can't control, to bring a degree of moderation to them..."

"Very laudable, Dan but ultimately futile. The President's a spent force. He's already lost control of the military. After 241, the military may continue to have some power for a short while. And they won't share it or give it up lightly... And who's going to make them? But I predict it'll wane as soon as their provisions run out..."

"So should I take that as a 'No' then, Jack?"

"Yes, Dan."

Noting the finality in Jack's voice, his friend changed the subject, "And what about Billy? Has he turned up yet?"

"Not so far. Martha's seen him on camera at various bus depots across the States which confirms he was headed east but the most recent sightings were two weeks ago..." then, with the first hint of doubt that Dan had heard in

Jack's voice, "I don't know, Dan. I was so sure Billy'd turn up but now I'm beginning to wonder…"

As the men walked to their billet they discussed small, inconsequential things, feeling that all the big topics had been exhausted.

As he'd lain naked and sweating on his bed late that night, the air conditioning whirring away, his cellphone had rung. It had been Martha. "Jack! Thank God I've got through at last. I've been trying to call you since the announcement about this asteroid… I saw Dan on TV. I presume you're with him…" Jack had given Martha a brief account of his situation, then had asked abruptly, "What news of Billy?" Martha had told Jack that she'd spoken to his mother earlier that evening and no, Billy still hadn't turned up. She had also told him that, as far as she'd known, Nicky was still trapped in Chicago, in a transit center set up by the military specially for displaced persons but as she'd heard nothing from him for the last couple of days and his cellphone had been off, she couldn't be absolutely sure. After a brief pause, Martha explained that Nicky had only gone off to ease tensions because they'd fallen out and now she felt guilty for having been so short with him. Jack had been able to tell that Martha was crying although she'd tried to conceal it from him. Although there had still been a slight tremor in her voice that gave it away, Martha had calmed down again sufficiently to ask, "What about this asteroid, S241, Jack? Just how serious is it?"

Jack had asked, "Is Claudette there?" When Martha had told him that she was asleep, he'd said, "Good!" Martha had known it wasn't going to be good news when Jack had continued, "I don't want you telling her any of what I'm about to tell you. It'll only make her more frightened than she must be already…" and he had given Martha a highly condensed but no-holds-barred account of the consequences that could be expected to follow the impact of asteroid 2010 AS241, which were far more dire than any impression Martha had been left with based on Dan Ackland's comparatively soothing presentation. When Martha had asked, "Can we survive it?" in a voice no louder than a whisper, Jack had said, "If we'd been at home when it struck, almost certainly not. We'd probably have perished within hours if not minutes of the impact. Here, three thousand miles from ground zero there's a fair chance we can survive the impact, assuming we're in a decent shelter. As to whether we can survive the aftermath… God knows…"

Martha had remained silent for a few moments, before saying quietly, "Jack, I'm sorry… really sorry… for being so angry with you. I had no idea you were dealing with something like this…" but Jack had cut her dead, saying, "There's no time for that now. We've got to figure out what to do next."

Martha said, "I've decided I'm going to continue on to your parents'. I'll call in at every bus station along the way if I have to. I've got to try to find Billy before this event overtakes him. After all if he hasn't seen a TV, he may not even be aware it's coming..." but Jack had said, "Oh, I think you'll find he is. I think that's why Billy ran away in the first place... And I think he ran away knowing we'd come after him."

Martha had remained silent as the implications of what her husband had just said sank in, before she said, "What about you, Jack?"

"I'm trying to arrange some transport for myself but I won't know about it until tomorrow morning..."

"And what about Nicky?"

Martha had sat listening to the silence at the other end until Jack had said, "I don't know... I agree with your decision to press on. There's no point going back for him unless you know where he is and you've arranged to rendezvous... And don't forget, Nicky knows precisely where you're going... If his phone's fritzed or he's lost it and can't make contact with us, I hope he has the gumption to make his own way there. There's no point any of us going off half-cock on some wild goose chase looking for him. So unless we hear from him, we have to rely on him to get himself home. In the meantime, I'll try and make some enquiries at this end but I don't hold out much hope of tracking him down."

They had continued talking over plans for a little while longer until the conversation had begun to dry up and Martha said, "Anyway, Jack, I'd better let you get some sleep. You sound whacked..." and Jack had confirmed that he was. "I love you, Jack... And I'm sorry I..." there had been a brief pause before Martha concluded, "...doubted you... but it has been a bloody awful couple of weeks..."

"And I love you too, Martha. I always have... And you're right. It has been a bloody awful two weeks, the worst of our lives..." But Jack had left his darkest thought unspoken. 'And unless I'm seriously mistaken, things are going to get much, much worse before they get better.'

The following morning, Jack had woken early and gone straight to Dan's room but it had been empty. As he'd walked into the refectory intent on grabbing a quick bite of breakfast, he'd bumped into Dan Ackland coming out and had said, "Dan, I've been looking for you. I'd like to ask you a favor. I need help to locate Nicky. He was in Chicago, in a transit center set up by the military. He had his cellphone with him but we've been unable to raise him on it for the last couple of days. There might be a problem with it... I have no idea how to go about finding him... I was wondering if you could ask the President to pull a few strings to find out where he is now?"

Dan had said, "I doubt the President will be able to help. He's got his hands full already... But I'll see what I can do."

Jack had thanked him, taken a couple of muffins that he could eat on the move and a carton of orange juice to wash them down and had gone off in search of Airman Price's family quarters.

"I heard there was some dude from the President's posse looking for me. Well now you've found me... You're interested in the hog..."

Jack had said guardedly, "I might be if the price is right..."

Senior Airman Vince Price had taken Jack round to the back yard to look at the bike. "Ever ridden one of these afore?", to which Jack replied, "Yes... In fact, I've had three over the years..."

"Real beaut, ain't she?"

Not wanting to over-egg the pudding, Jack had said, "Well, you sure have prettied her up a bit but I'm not interested in her for her looks..."

As Jack examined the bike, Airman Price pointed out all the features that were blindingly obvious to Jack. Mrs Price had stuck her head out of the kitchen door and said, "About time he got rid of that ugly monstrosity. I've told him enough times already, mister... 'It's like a hole in the ground you keep pouring money into.' We can't afford to run that and twins..." at which point Airman Price had shushed her up and shooed her back into the house. As an afterthought, his wife had poked her head out again and added, "Oh, excuse me, Sir, I'm forgettin' my manners. Would you like a coffee? If you would, say so now because when one of 'em starts bawlin' it sets the other off and then all hell's let loose." Jack had declined the coffee and the woman went indoors, a little deflated.

He'd said, "Before I make you an offer, I'd like to take her for a test drive..."

The airman had said, "With all due respect, mister, I ain't open t'offers. The price is thirteen-an'a-half... but if you're willin' t'pay it, you can take her for a spin if you like. I'll just come along for the ride if you don't mind... No offence intended..."

As Jack had swung his leg over the seat, he'd said, "None taken" but when he'd checked the fuel tank and rocked the bike from side to side, he'd said, "She's nearly empty. That won't get me far..."

The airman had said, "How far d'you want to go on a test ride?"

Jack had said emphatically, "I'm not interested in the bike unless it comes with a full tank."

Airman Price had started to object. "Gasolene's like liquid gold at the moment. You can't get it for love nor money..."

Mrs Price must have been listening at the door and sensed an obstacle to a successful sale because she'd appeared again and scolded her husband, "If the man wants gas, give him gas! You've got a five-gallon can of it in the garage. If he'll take the damn thing, fill it up and be done with it!"

Jack had struck up the engine and revved it a few times, waiting for Airman Price to climb aboard. He closed the throttle and let the engine idle for a minute; he'd forgotten how lumpy and uncomfortable it had been sitting at traffic lights, waiting for them to change, as the exhaust pipes burped their crude "potato-potato-potato" signature tune. Jack had steered the lumbering, ungainly bike out of the yard and onto the road with some difficulty and pulled away; he'd also forgotten how sluggish and unresponsive it was compared to his latest ride. Jack had carefully negotiated the roads round the base until they'd got out onto DE-1. After winding the twistgrip back hard a few times then cruising for a couple of miles he'd satisfied himself that the engine was in reasonable condition. Not wanting to run out of fuel and get stranded a long walk from the base, Jack had turned round and gone back.

As the pair of them had dismounted, Mrs Price had been hanging out her washing. Jack had said, "I'll take it at the asking price but only with a full tank."

"The price with a full tank is fifteen gees, mister, take it or leave it."

Suddenly seeing the prospect of a sale slipping away, Mrs Price had swung round, alarmed and snapped, "Oh no you don't, Vincent Price! Fifteen hundred dollars for a tank of gas is grand larceny…" but Jack had upskittled her when he brought the hammer down on the sale and said, "Done!"

"Cash! Not cheque!"

"Agreed"

As Vincent Price went inside to get the papers for the bike, Jack counted out fifteen thousand dollars from the money belt round his waist and handed it to Mrs Price; it had been fortunate that Vincent Price hadn't known that Jack had been carrying thirty-five thousand dollars on him, which he had brought along in case of such eventualities.

As Jack roared away down the road, Vincent Price had snatched the money out of his wife's hand and exclaimed in amazement, "God damn it, Selena, he paid it. He actually paid it. He must've wanted it real bad. I wonder how much more he'd have paid if I'd upped the ante? And we still have a shed-load of accessories we can sell…" and he'd gone indoors waving a fistful of dollars and singing, "We're in the money, We're in the money, We've got a lot of what it takes to get along!"

Mrs Price had stood listening to the throaty roar getting fainter as it steadily receded into the distance and thought, 'Well, that's eased our money problems… for a while, at least… I'll have to make sure 'Lumphead' there doesn't go and waste it on some other useless knick-knack…' Then, after a moment's reflection, 'He didn't look like a flashy sort'a guy. I wonder why he was so willing to part with his cash so readily? He must have more money than sense… Enough to burn, no doubt. It certainly can't mean as much to him as it does to us? Still, he's one of the President's men. He can probably afford it…' And, as an afterthought, 'I wonder if he knows anything about that rock that's headed this way? I never thought to ask him…'

Jack had seen Dan Ackland from a distance, walking towards Air Force One. When he'd pulled up at his colleague's side, Dan Ackland had said, "After what you said about the last one, I never thought I'd see you on one of these again, Jack."

Jack had replied dryly, "Needs must when the Devil drives, Dan." Then, with a slightly troubled look, Dan Ackland had said, "I'm sorry, Jack. No news of Nicky, I'm afraid. I did ask and one of the President's Secret Service men made some enquiries… It would seem that, after the relaxation of travel restrictions that came with yesterday's announcement, the military disbanded the transit center and had sent everyone on their way by first light this morning. I know that doesn't help you much and Nicky still has the problem of getting home without the aid of public transport but there's not a lot more I can do."

Jack had thanked his friend and the two had stood looking at each other, until Dan Ackland said slowly, "Well, Jack, it looks like this is 'farewell'. We come to the parting of the ways and I doubt our paths will cross again…" Jack had nodded, indicating that he felt exactly the same sentiments. "Go carefully, Jack… and God's speed… I'll pray for you."

With a look of mild surprise, Jack had responded, "And I never thought I'd hear you say that again, Dan."

"As you said yourself, Jack, 'Needs must when the Devil's nippin' at your heels'. Anyway, take care, old friend and I hope your missing sheep return to the fold."

The two men had shaken hands, each holding the other's wrist tightly with the left hand. It had struck Dan again just how powerful Jack's forearms and hands were. After a long moment each had sensed the other's hand relax and the two men let go their grip. Jack had pulled in the clutch lever, dropped the box into first gear with a dull, mechanical clunk and, without another word, had ridden off. Dan had stood watching Jack's back until the bike had disappeared from sight then had continued to stand, listening to the powerful throb of its exhaust until it became an almost inaudible rumble and then was lost altogether in the muted cacophony of background noises. And he had continued to stand there for some time after, quietly conscious of the warm midday sunshine and the gentle breeze playing on his back, reflecting on everything that had brought them to this momentous juncture and wondering what fate had in store for them all and whether any of them would ever have the leisure to stand in the sun again.

As Jack had cruised steadily on I-495N, trying to keep the engine on that sweet spot where its effort seemed least strenuous in order to eke out his precious reserve of fuel, he'd kept a sharp eye on the other vehicles around him, looking for telltale signs that one might suddenly change lanes without warning and knock him off, but the driving had been far more orderly and courteous than any he could ever remember. Maybe they were all trying to conserve fuel or maybe they all understood the consequences of having an accident and being without transport, now more than ever. He had been able to see umpteen columns of thick, black smoke rising angrily into the sky directly ahead, perhaps twenty or more miles away but for the moment had been unable to place where they might be coming from. His first reaction had been one of surprise that so much heavy industry had still been operating in light of current events but, as he'd got closer, he'd become less convinced that his first assumption was correct. The traffic had gradually slowed and become denser until eventually it had stopped altogether. He'd looked down the lines of standing traffic, trying to make out what the hold-up was but hadn't been able to see anything. Off in the distance he'd been able to see the first sign telling him that he was coming up to the junction with I-95 to Philadelphia, so he'd checked that nothing was coming up behind him and carefully slipped into the gap between two lanes of vehicles. Threading his way gingerly he'd made wary progress, alert to the possibility that some over-anxious rubber-necker might suddenly open a door directly in his path, until he'd reached the head of the queue. A Delaware State Trooper had been holding back the traffic. Jack had pulled up alongside him and let the bike stand idling for a few moments. Hearing the noise of an engine running at his side, the Trooper had turned and said, "You might as well shut her down and save gas, mister. You ain't goin' nowhere in a hurry."

Jack had asked, "Why, Officer? What's the hold up?" and the Trooper had explained, "We're waitin' for a bunch of emergency and rescue vehicles out of Wilmin'ton to go through."

"Why? What's happened?"

"D'you see that smoke yonder? That's Philly burnin'… Last night, after they broke the news 'bout this meteor, the city went mad. Folk rushed out to the stores to get stocked up. When the goods ran out or prices went sky-high so's folks cun't afford 'em, people started riotin' in the streets… Lootin'… Smashin' up the malls, takin' 'way anythin' they could carry. Then it turned real ugly. The Army wuz called in to try an' restore order an' that's when the shootin' started. They said it wuz like Dodge City down there f'rawhile… Rioters set fire to cars an' buildin's, to create smokescreens an' keep the'mergency services busy. The result… Anarchy! The world's gone plumb loco… They're callin' in ev'ry 'vailable firefighter and fire truck from all over the state of Pennsylvania and beyond. Lord knows what they'll do if there's

242

another outbreak of madness akin to this one elsewhere and they're needed there as well?" And then, as they'd heard the first faint wailing of sirens away in the distance, the Trooper had observed flatly, "Dun't seem as though there's much brotherly love there right at this moment in time..." nodding toward the city eighteen miles distant.

After the convoy of fire tenders, pump ladders and ambulances had passed, their blue lights flashing furiously, Jack had asked, "Can we go now? Are you going to move those Stingers?" indicating the tire deflation strips that had been deployed across the road. The Trooper had told Jack to remain where he was. He'd gone over to his cruiser and reached in through the open window and spoken into the handset. He'd come back a few moment's later and said to Jack, "Not yet awhile, Sir" and the reason had soon become obvious as half-a-dozen trucks filled with Delaware National Guards came tearing past, heading for The City of Brotherly Love. He'd gone to his patrol car again and consulted the radio for a second time. This time when he'd come back, he'd said to Jack, "I can tell you that the military are stopping anyone from entering the city and they've closed I-95 through Philly. If you want Trenton, you're out of luck. You'll have to find a different route to New Jersey. All traffic's being diverted north on four-seven-six..."

Jack had said, "Suits me fine! I'm headed north toward Scranton and New York State..."

As the Trooper had pulled back the Stinger, Jack had fired up the engine and roared through the gap. With the empty road stretching out ahead, he'd had to rein himself in sharply and remind himself to go easy on the gas; he still had no idea how he was going to get the second tank of fuel he'd need to cover the four-hundred and ten miles to his parents' house.

"Fat lot of good that did", Jack said to himself as he sat looking at the overturned bike. He pulled the map out of his jacket pocket and studied it. He'd barely come a hundred and thirty miles. The sign up ahead told him that he should get off I-476 here if he wanted Allentown, which he didn't, but sitting at the roadside hoping some kindly Samaritan might take pity on him and offer him a lift wasn't going to get him home in a hurry either, so he heaved the six-hundred and eighty pound machine upright with some difficulty and pushed it the three-quarters of a mile to the off-ramp at exit fifty-six. As he arrived at the unmanned toll booth, sweat pouring from him, his shirt wringing wet and clinging to him, Jack noticed that the arm of the barrier had been snapped clean off. It still lay where it had landed. He pushed the bike along US highway twenty-two, all the while scanning the road ahead looking for somewhere he might find assistance. He passed a couple of closed gas stations with signs outside telling a disappointed clientele that they had sold out of everything – fuel, food, drink, cigarettes, even charcoal for traditional barbecues and bottled gas for the smokeless, modern variety. Everything! The shelves in the shops were as bare as if a plague of locusts had swept through them. He continued pushing the bike until he came across a small repair shop. The main door was open. He could see flashes of blue-white light bouncing off the walls and hear the telltale crackling that told him someone was arc welding inside. As it stopped, Jack knocked on the door and announced himself. A cheery voice came back, "Hi! I was just fixin' this here generator. I figured it might come in handy over the next coupl'a weeks. We're closed but 'never turn away trade', that's what I always say. So what can I do for you?" Jack strode up to the young man in grubby coveralls and explained his problem. "Well, you might just be in luck. There's a Harley dealer 'bout ten miles away, in Center Valley. They might be able to help... And if they have the part in stock but can't fit it right away, I could probably fit it for you..." the young mechanic finished helpfully.

"Oh, that's kind of you but I could fit it myself if I had the right tools..."

"Well then, let's call 'em. If they have it, I'll run you over there to pick it up."

But when the young man found the phone number and tried calling, there was no answer. "Probably closed..." he surmised, hanging up. "After all, who'd want to buy a bike now. You never know what you might need to conserve your cash for after... after what's comin'... because it sounds to me like it could do more than a peck'a damage..."

Before he'd realised what he was saying, Jack said, "Oh! Believe you me, the damage will be catastrophic. It's just a suspicion but I think your skill at fixing things will be far more useful than cash for paying a repair man."

As they went out of the workshop, the young mechanic let out a long, low whistle. "I've always fancied one of these but I could never afford it... or perhaps I should say, I could never justify the indulgence... especially with a family to support... But there's no sin in feasting the eyes..."

The two men stood by the bike which was leaning on its side-stand in front of the workshop door. The metal cover with its retaining screws lay on the concrete in the shadow of the bike. In an effort to be helpful, the young man pointed to the stator and said, "There's the problem. There's a short on one of the poles. The winding's burnt out..." but Jack had already seen it. "So what do we do now? Easy enough to fix if we had a replacement part but we haven't... I'm not sure what to suggest next..."

Jack said, " I need transport to get me back to Rochester. I don't care what it is, so long as it gets me there..."

The young man caught Jack eying his gleaming new recovery truck. "Oh no! I'm sorry, Sir. I need the truck for ma business. I couldn't possibly part with it... and I doubt you could afford it. Lord knows, I can barely afford it myself… And I couldn't sell it anyway. Leastways, not without the bank's say-so. I only own the wheel nuts. They own the rest…"

Jack was about to ask whether the young man could suggest anyone locally who had a vehicle for sale or hire when he said, "But there is my old truck. I got this one to replace it and I wuz gradually doin' it up with a view to sellin' it… I just have to fit a new water pump and the jobs a good'un but I haven't bin able to get round to doin' it lately…"

Jack said, "How long to get it ready?"

"Oh. Two, maybe three hours at most…"

"If we can fix it, how much do you want for it?"

"Well, I have no idea what it's worth. Not much. Fifteen hundred dollars. Two thousand max…"

Jack said, "I tell you what. If we can fix it and you can let me have enough fuel to get me home with some to spare, I'll let you have the bike…"

The young man looked at Jack askance. With a sense of *déjà vu*, Jack said, "What? Bad deal? But you said it was only worth a couple of gees…"

"No! No, it's not that. It's far too generous. I couldn't take advantage of you in your time of need. It'd be against my principles. Your bike must be worth all of ten thousand dollars. I couldn't possibly take it for my beat-up old truck and I certainly couldn't afford to make it right with you."

Jack had already noticed the small symbol of the fish on the tailgate of the new truck encompassing the Greek word *ikhthus* and the sticker with the legend '*W.W.J.C.D?*' in the back window. He said, "Rest assured, you wouldn't be taking advantage of me. In fact, you'd be doing me the biggest favor…"

—•—

The two-hundred-and-sixty mile drive from South Bend had taken Martha nearly nine hours, having been stopped numerous times at checkpoints manned by National Guardsmen wanting to know their destination and the purpose of their journey. Now that they were in the city there was a barricade at every major intersection, which slowed them down even more but at least the Ohio National Guard seemed to have deterred most of the looting and anarchy and the streets were relatively safe, even though the light was fading rapidly. As she turned off East Ninth Street onto Chester Avenue looking for the bus terminal, her eyes were dry and sore, her mouth tasted foul and she felt weary, sticky and dirty from travelling. She was quietly seething, having just paid eighteen-hundred-and-fifty dollars for eighteen-and-a-half gallons of fuel at a small gas station on the outskirts of Cleveland but, as the car had been running on the fumes at the time and she had already been to half-a-dozen gas stations that had sold out completely, she'd had no option but to pay the exorbitant price demanded by the owner. To add insult to injury, he'd insisted on taking her car key and credit card before dispensing the gasolene so that she couldn't drive away without paying, not that the thought had even entered her tired mind. Claudette had been unaware of the extortion, having laid her seat-back down flat and fallen fast asleep shortly after they'd passed through Huron. At first, Martha had been irked at the thought of having to navigate into the city herself, as well as doing the driving but she'd calmed when she reflected that her daughter was probably as tired as she was herself.

Once they'd managed to get off the interstate, Martha and Claudette had reached South Bend without too much trouble. They had found the local bus stop easily which was located at the regional airport. The approach road to the terminal was blocked by a barricade. As Martha had driven slowly towards it, two men wearing combat fatigues and carrying automatic rifles had come forward and flagged her down, motioning to her to stop. One of the Guardsmen had walked cautiously up to Martha's window and asked her what business they had there. When Martha had explained that she wanted to see the bus line's security supervisor and why, the Guardsman had told her that there was no one on duty at the terminal because all flights and bus services had been suspended under martial law by order of the Joint Chiefs of Staff. Trying to make light of it, Martha had turned to her daughter and said with forced cheerfulness, "Well, Billy's not likely to have gotten off the bus in this one horse town so let's not waste our time looking for him here".

As she'd swung the car round and headed back towards the entrance, Claudette had asked quietly, "Did you see those soldiers, Mom? The ones behind the barricade, I mean… pointing their guns at us… Do you think they'd have shot us?"

Martha said dismissively, "Oh I very much doubt it, darling… On the other hand, you know what they say… 'Give a redneck a gun and he thinks he's got to kill something, he just doesn't know why.' " But the thought had stayed with Martha for a while until she finally managed to put it out of her mind. Then she asked, "Where next?"

Claudette had been studying the map and the bus company's service schedule. She said, "Toledo, I guess… It's about a hundred and fifty miles by my reckoning…"

Martha had been surprised to find anyone at the bus terminal in Toledo but, as they'd entered, they had almost bumped into the security guard as he'd rounded a corner on his way back to his office. He had been very genial and had said, "Well, ladies, this is a nice surprise. I didn't expect to see anyone today, except possibly the odd looter. What can I do for you?"

Martha had said apologetically, "We're looking for my son, Billy. He's twelve... He ran away from home a couple of weeks ago. We know he came this way, probably on Tuesday, August third or Wednesday fourth... We're looking for any clues as to where he might be. I wondered if you'd seen him or if he'd been caught on security camera..." As they accompanied him back to his office, Martha had shown the gently-spoken man Billy's photograph and briefly explained the circumstances of his disappearance. He led them to a pinboard on the office wall on which there were about thirty similar photographs, mostly, with the exception of seven or eight boys, of teenage girls. Most were old and faded whilst a few were fairly new and glossy. The watchman had studied the pinboard for a moment then pointed to a shiny new picture in the bottom row – the one that had been circulated by Francis Doolittle in Portland – and said, "There's your boy, Ma'am... And no, we haven't seen him. If we had, we'd have apprehended him and reported it."

Martha had stood looking at the pictures for a while, then said, "So many lost children... Are they all runaways? Where do they go to? And why?"

The guard had said, "As far as I know, Ma'am, yes... Where they go, I have no idea. It's probably more a case of wanting to be anywhere other than where they are... As for why... Some just go for the adventure, others go off in a huff because of a fall-out at home... They're generally the ones we can help and they're usually back home within a very short time because home's really where they want to be... But most of the poor little wretches have either been kicked out or they're running away from something... From broken homes, abusive parents, violent step-dads... or moms... rape, incest, God knows what. You name it, most of 'em have probably suffered at least one..." He'd stopped abruptly, suddenly feeling very uncomfortable when he saw Martha staring at him and realised that she must be wondering what he was thinking about why her own son had run away. She had sensed his discomfort and knew the reason for it. Indicating the pictures on the board, he'd continued diplomatically, "At least these kids have parents who care enough to put out a missing person's bulletin which is more than you can say for some... Many parents are only too glad to see the back of 'em..."

To break the uneasy silence that had ensued, Martha had asked, "Do you ever help any of these children get home again?" and the guard had said, "Oh, occasionally Ma'am... But some of 'em don't want to go home. In fact, it's the last place they want to be... They think they're escaping... Unfortunately, what many of 'em don't realise is that the streets are often more dangerous than home because out there there's always some unholy bastard... if you'll pardon my language, Ma'am... waiting to prey on vulnerable and unsuspecting kids..."

Tapping the board at the gaps in the rows with her finger, she'd asked, "Were these the ones you helped return home?" indicating the pictures that had been taken down.

"Some of them, yes Ma'am…"

"But not all?"

"No Ma'am…" the guard had replied, reaching out to remove the drawing pins that held the picture of a handsome black youth, Spike Griffiths, to the board. "It seems that Spike Griffiths here wasn't lucky enough to make it home. His body was found in a dumpster in Pontiac a few days ago. In fact, I'd just received notification from the police Tuesday morning last week and I was about to take his picture down when we were told to evacuate the city… The police usually let us know the outcome of their investigations if we've helped them with their enquiries and in the case of this particular boy, I'd reported that he'd been through here a few days before… It's a pity that I'd only seen him on video after he'd gone or I might have been able to do more…" and the guard had finished with, "Very sad."

After a respectable pause for quiet reflection, Martha had asked whether it would be possible to view the video tapes for the days in question but the security guard had thought for a moment then said, "You say you think your boy came through here Tuesday the third, Ma'am… I'm sorry but the footage from that day was taped over on the tenth… I know because that was the day all hell broke loose. I set the video running myself first thing in the morning and what with all the panic when Los Angeles went up and then the rush to escape the city in case Toledo was next, I didn't turn it off… I just grabbed my family and we fled… It'll have wiped out any record of your boy coming through here if that's what he did… We weren't operating on the eleventh, of course, because of the travel restrictions but as I only live round the corner I came in anyway… and I'm fairly sure I ran the security tapes that day as well… A matter of habit, I'm afraid… I'm sorry, Ma'am."

Martha had thanked the man and assured him he had nothing to be sorry for. As they turned to leave, she'd stopped and asked him, "If you don't mind my asking… Why are you here? I mean, why aren't you at home with your family making preparations for… for what's coming? I presume all the other employees are…"

The man had looked at her and said, "The company doesn't want looters stealing its buses or its fuel or anything else for that matter. They want to be able to start up services again as soon as possible after… after what's comin'… They're planning on business as usual. It's all part of the recovery process. They want us t'be first back on the road with no holdups, as soon as the 'all clear' sounds. That way we can win market share from our competitors… As for me, I've put all my preparations in place. The good lady's at home bottling the best of the fruit from our trees and putting the finishing touches to our basement. We couldn't be better prepared for getting through it if we'd had a month's notice. And the company's offering double pay to security guards who work the week running up to… well, you know… It was too good to pass up." Martha had thanked him again. As they'd turned to leave, he'd said, "I hope you find your boy, Ma'am." Martha had called out, "Thank you", over her shoulder and thought to herself, 'And so do I… And I hope you live long enough to enjoy your wife's bottled fruit and spend your overtime pay'.

Mother and daughter had been very subdued as they'd walked back to their car. Martha had started the engine but before pulling away she'd let out a sigh of resignation and said quietly, "The trail's going cold, Claudette. God knows if we'll ever find Billy now."

Claudette had said nothing in reply but simply studied the map and said, "I think we should avoid the interstate and take the lakeshore road instead. It's likely to be quieter…"

They had set off in silence but as Martha had turned off South Summit Street onto Clayton Street and the approach to the Maumee River crossing, she had braced herself and said, "We'll give it one last go. If we don't find any trace of Billy at the next stop we'll have to give up the search and get on and hope he can find his own way to Nannan and Grandad's…" but she'd left unspoken her darkest thought, 'But I daren't even begin to think about why he hasn't arrived there already…' then, with a more positive note in her voice, Martha said, "Right Claudette! Next stop, Cleveland!"

The terminal itself was gloomy and deserted. A number of buses were parked up with their doors locked. The stillness and lack of activity seemed a little eerie, as though it spoke silently of things to come. On the far side of the concourse, Martha could see a dim light glowing in one of the offices and headed towards it, although there was no sign of movement from within. When she reached it, the label on the door read, 'Security Supervisor'. She knocked lightly and waited. After a few moments Martha knocked again, a little more firmly this time. When there was still no answer she gently pushed the door. It had shut to on the automatic closer but because someone had carelessly dropped an empty cigarette packet that had missed the wastebin, which had prevented the door from latching properly, it swung open under the modest pressure Martha applied to it and she went in. "Hello! Anybody home?" A cigarette burned low in the ashtray and the column of smoke lazily wound its way upwards until it dissipated itself in the thick layer of fug that hung just above head height, obscuring the bare fluorescent strip lights that were suspended from the ceiling on short chains. Another, half-empty packet of the same brand which lay on the desk and the large number of butts in the ashtray confirmed that someone had been here for some time and had only recently gone out. Not knowing quite what to do next, she hovered uncertainly in the doorway hoping someone would come.

After a while, Martha was overcome with curiosity and began to look around the office. The computer monitor was turned off but the black-and-white screen of the CCTV surveillance system glowed in the corner. Martha went over to it, hoping to catch sight of the security guard on his rounds as the door closed quietly behind her. She watched the views from each of the cameras for a couple of minutes but nobody appeared. She was about to leave when she noticed the pinboard on the wall, which had been hidden from her view by the filing cabinet when she'd been standing by the door. She went up to it and studied the array of photographs on the board, some of which she recognised from Toledo and elsewhere but Billy's wasn't amongst them. She thought it odd that Francis Doolittle would bother to forward it as far as Toledo but hadn't sent it to Cleveland. Martha stood for a few moments puzzling over why this might be but gave up. She slowly scanned the office, looking for any other information about runaways but there was none. Starting to get fed up waiting for the guard to return she idly browsed through the calendar, admiring the beautiful russet and gold colors of the autumnal scenes for September and October and the pristine snow scenes for the next two months, then her eyes lit on the framed picture of Jesus Christ, arms outstretched invitingly, with a beatific smile and glowing halo, that was hanging slightly askew behind the desk. There was a raffia cross pinned either side of it and another one above it but what caught Martha's eye was the corner of a photograph secured by a black plastic-capped drawing pin which peeped out from behind the picture. Martha looked over her shoulder, to reassure herself she was alone, then swung the holy picture further to the side and was shocked to see Spike Griffiths looking back at her. But what made her blood run cold was the fact that someone had adorned the youth with a halo, applied in thick, black fibre-tipped pen and a pair of angel's wings that had been drawn in above the shoulders. The letters 'R.I.P' had been added underneath. Martha swung the religious icon further aside to reveal photographs of other runaways, all boys, another one of which had also been given a halo and was being enjoined to rest peacefully in the hereafter. Just then, Martha heard the telltale electronic 'beep-beep-beep-beep-beep' as someone entered their access code into the lock. Martha straightened the picture as the electromagnetic catch snapped back and the office door swung open and in came the security supervisor carrying a cup of coffee. He halted so abruptly and his head snapped up so violently at the unexpected sight of Martha standing in his office that he spilled the entire steaming contents of the cup down his front. "JESUS CHRIST!" he exploded, dropping the cup and violently shaking his hand as the scalding liquid soaked into the grubby bandage that swathed his hand from knuckles to wrist, leaving only his thumb poking through, then tugged the front of his shirt away from his body to distance the hot coffee from his skin. "How did you get in?" the guard snarled, followed by, "What do you think you're doing here, lady? Don't you know this is private property?" He was livid and his face flushed red with anger and pain. He wasn't big; in fact, he was a small, pudgy, balding man but the hostility that burned in his eyes frightened Martha far more than his physical presence did.

Martha started, "I... I tried the door and it was open..." but he cut her dead, saying, "Don't gi' me that crap, lady! I shut it when I went out. Now what d'you want?"

Martha said quietly, "I'm looking for my son, Billy... He's twelve... He ran away from home and I thought he might've passed through here..."

In a slightly less threatening tone, the guard said, "Well, I ain't seen no 'Billy' passing through here, lady, so you'd better get off company property. Now! Let me escort you to the exit..." But before he could do so, Martha thrust Billy's photograph at the man, saying, "Please! Look at this and tell me if you recognise him." The guard reached out and took the picture, looked at it quickly and said, "Thousands of people come through here, lady. How do you expect me to remember one in a crowd?" then, "No, I don't!"

Martha said, "Please look at it again... Properly this time..." but the man was having none of it. He grabbed Martha's upper arm and started to propel her towards the door.

She responded rapidly, saying, "Take your hands off me! My husband's waiting in the car. If he sees you mauling me, he'll have something to say..." but the man sneered and said, "Oh yes, lady! So it's your car parked outside, is it? Well, it looked pretty empty to me when I passed it. So, has your husband got fed up and run off with another woman, then? Or what?" The fact that Martha's bluff had failed made the man somewhat cockier and he increased his grip on Martha's arm so much so that it hurt. Martha whirled round and grabbed his wrist, yanking his hand off her arm and spat out, "Get off me, you bastard!" And it was then that she noticed his wristwatch. Martha stared at it for a moment, then looked the man hard in the eye and said, "Where did you get that watch?" When he hesitated, Martha said again, more aggressively this time, "I said, 'Where did you get the watch?' "

For a moment he seemed lost for words, then stammered out, "I... er... I bought it..."

"Where?"

"I... I don't remember..."

"When?"

"Er... about a year ago..."

Martha looked him straight in the eyes with a cold, hard stare and said in a low hiss, "You lying bastard. It wasn't on sale a year ago..." then, as the enormity of the lie hit her, screamed in his face, "YOU LYING BASTARD!" Now it was the guard's turn to be alarmed. Martha pushed him back with such force that he stumbled and tripped, falling heavily on his back. She spun round and grabbed the icon, violently yanking it off the wall. There, pinned just below the hook on which the holy picture had been hanging, was Billy's photograph. Two red drawing pins had been stuck into the eyes and a pair of horns and a goatee beard had been drawn on it in red ink, with the words 'Rot in Hell' savagely scrawled across it. Martha reeled backwards, away from the ghastly apparition and collapsed into the chair. A wave of nausea welled up and nearly swamped her. As she gulped in air, trying to calm herself and clear her head, questions raced through her mind. 'What's that monster done with my little boy? Where's Billy now?' And most importantly, 'Is he still alive?' Martha recovered sufficiently to push herself up out of the chair but as she spun round to face the man he ran bodily into her and slammed her back against the desk. The impact winded Martha and the pain which shot up into the small of her back and down her legs, as the backs of her thighs struck the edge of the desk, made her feel sick. The man grabbed Martha savagely round the throat and squeezed hard, pushing his thumbs into her windpipe, trying to crush it but he couldn't apply much pressure with his injured hand. Martha clenched the muscles in her neck with all her might, trying to resist the awful pressure. She clawed at his face but her well bitten nails failed to penetrate the skin deeply. The man seemed to take perverse encouragement from the fact that Martha's frantic struggling was doing very little damage and he leaned forwards, his foul breath directly in Martha's face and taunted her with vile words, in a hoarse, rasping voice. "Yes, I've seen Billy, the little prick. I had him right here, in this office, over this very desk..." All the time his hands squeezing harder. "He begged for mercy... He begged me to stop... He offered me his watch, thinking I'd let him go but I took it anyway..." Continuing to squeeze Martha's throat. "He had such a tender little heinie, like two ripe peaches... and I fucked him up the ass... Hard! He was cryin' all the time..."

Martha was gagging, the air from her lungs forcing its way out through the tightly constricted airway, making a harsh bubbling sound as her vision started to go black and bright lights burst in front of her eyes. The thought of this evil, sadistic pervert sodomizing her terrified child filled Martha with rage. As though through a haze she saw the monster's leering face swimming directly in front of her own and in desperation she stopped trying to claw at it and grabbed his head with both hands, brutally gripping his ears and sinking her thumbs into his eyes. Too late, the man realised what was happening and violently threw his head back, trying to shake Martha off but not before one of his eyeballs burst sending a spray of aqueous humour into the air as Martha's thumb sunk deep into the socket, until his ear tore off and his head slipped out of her hands. The man screamed in agony as the sudden, seering pain suffused the whole of one side of his head and he put his bandaged hand up momentarily to cover the empty eye socket, relinquishing his grip on Martha's throat. As she gulped in lungfuls of air, there came the loud crashing of someone hammering violently on the window and Martha heard her daughter screaming "MOM! MOM! MOM!" and saw Claudette's terrified face looking into the office. As the man spun round to see what the noise was, Martha lunged past him and snatched up the holy picture from the desk where she'd dropped it and smashed it down over his head from behind, the glass shattering into a multitude of jagged shards. As his head burst through the canvas, Martha violently yanked the picture towards herself with all her might so that the bottom of the frame was under his chin, then dragged him backwards until she pirouetted round and flung him hard against the office wall. As his legs crumpled beneath him, the man slumped down until he was sitting on them. Winded by the exertion, Martha staggered over to him. Blood from his severed carotid artery pulsed out and onto the wall, wetting his clothes and running in rivulets onto the floor so that he ended up sitting in a red puddle. Martha gripped his lower jaw tightly and roughly pushed his head back into her other hand so that he was looking up into her face. Through gritted teeth, she said, "Where's my son?" As the breath whistled through the hole in his trachea where it had been punctured by a large splinter of glass, he stared into Martha's eyes and his face contorted into a ghastly grin. Martha asked again, "Where's Billy?". This time he whispered something that Martha couldn't quite catch because of the bubbles of blood and saliva that foamed out of his mouth, which muffled it and because of the noise of Claudette screaming hysterically and beating her fists on the office door. Putting her ear closer to his mouth so that she could better hear him, Martha asked again, more urgently this time, "Where's Billy?" and she heard the man feebly wheeze, "Fuck you, lady!" with his last breath, before his body went limp and the weight of his head sank down into her hands.

Martha stood over the dead man cradling his head in her hands until the grotesque realisation hit her that this monster was getting more tender human contact in his last dying moments than her son would ever have had and the thought repulsed her. As the bile rose in her throat, Martha became overwhelmed with rage and repeatedly smashed the dead man's head against the wall, screaming from the very depths of her despair until the skull became such a bloody mush of bone fragments that she could no longer keep a grip on it and it slipped from her hands. As the certainty that Billy was gone beyond her reach sank in, Martha hunched over the monster's corpse, her stomach heaving and was violently sick. Suddenly, Martha felt very heavy, almost infinitely heavy, as the cruel reality that she would never see her son again flooded her mind. Robbed of all their strength, her legs seemed too weak to bear her terrible weight and she dropped to her knees. Then the tears rolled down her face. Martha stayed like that for an eternity, her nose running and saliva dribbling from her open mouth, gulping in air until she eventually calmed down. The thought struck her that she had never gotten to know her son and now she never would.

Gradually, the tears ceased and she found herself staring down at Billy's wristwatch. The beating on the door had stopped and Martha could hear her daughter on the other side of it, sobbing. Martha slowly reached down and unfastened the strap and removed the watch from the man's wrist. She stood up and was about to go when her eyes fell upon Billy's photograph on the wall. She took it down and, after looking at it for a few seconds, she took the man's cigarette lighter and set fire to one corner of it. As the flames licked up around Billy's face Martha dropped the picture which fluttered down and landed on the floor. She stepped over the tiny funeral pyre and walked slowly to the door and opened it. Claudette was tucked up in a ball on the ground outside the door, still sobbing. Martha stooped down and took her daughter gently under the arms and coaxed the girl up. Claudette was trembling violently. She put her arms round her mother and buried her face deep in Martha's neck, as Martha hugged and shushed her distraught daughter until her crying subsided. Eventually, when she had calmed sufficiently, Claudette whispered, "I... I was so scared... I... I thought that man was trying to kill you... Why would he do that? Why?" Martha remained silent, not knowing how to break the news but when Claudette again asked her why, Martha said simply, "Because he was a very bad man... An evil man... He killed Billy... He hurt Billy then he killed him..."

Claudette pulled away from her mother slightly with a bewildered look on her face and stammered, "But... but... he can't have... Billy's alive..."

"*What?*"

"That's what I was coming to tell you... Whilst you were gone, your phone went off. It woke me up. It was Nannan calling to tell us Billy's alive and well." Martha's mouth dropped open and she looked at Claudette aghast. When Martha had recovered sufficiently to speak, she said, "But that man told me he did unspeakable things to Billy... Are you sure? Are you absolutely certain she said Billy's alive?"

"*Yes!*"

"Well, where is he?"

"He's up at the cabin. Big Grandad went up there today... that's where he wants to be when... when... you know... and he found Billy. He's been living up there for the last couple of weeks, getting things ready, getting food in and everything... Nannan's been trying to contact us all evening to let us know..."

Martha stood in stunned silence for a minute, tears of relief welling up in her eyes. She wiped them away with the backs of her hands, then let out a little laugh and exclaimed in astonishment, "I don't believe it! I'll never cease to be amazed by that boy..." then, a little more somberly, "But what was that all about?" indicating the scene in the office over her shoulder. "Why did that man tell me he'd done all those cruel, wicked things to Billy? Why did he let me think he'd harmed Billy... killed him even?"

Claudette said, "I... I don't know, Mom... I'm just glad he didn't..."

Martha stood for a moment deep in thought, then said, "Come along, Claudette. We've got to get cleaned up, then we must get off... His blood is on my hands... *Literally!*"

Claudette asked hesitantly, "Is... Is he dead?"

"Yes, darling, he's dead."

"Well, shouldn't we tell the police then?"

As if she'd been stung, Martha snapped back, "No Claudette! No, we shouldn't..." then taking her daughter firmly by the shoulders, she said emphatically, "We mustn't tell anyone! Not now! Not ever! Do you understand?" But Claudette said, "Surely, we have to inform someone, don't we? Isn't that the right thing to do? It'll be alright, won't it? It was self-defense... Wasn't it?"

Martha took a deep breath and said firmly, "Yes, Claudette, it was self-defense. He attacked me, to try to prevent me from finding out what he'd done to Billy... I had to defend myself... to fight for my life... But it is a killing, all the same. If we go to the police, they're bound to hold us for questioning while they investigate it. How long that'll take, God knows... And we've only got three days left to reach the cabin, so we have to get off now if we're going to stand any chance of getting there in time... Do you agree?"

Martha looked Claudette directly in the eye, a look that challenged her to disagree. After a brief pause, Claudette said a little uncertainly, "Yes, Mom, I agree..."

As Martha steered her daughter across the darkened concourse back towards the car, she thought, 'And anyway, in four days time, if half of what Jack tells me comes true, it'll all be academic because there'll be so many dead bodies here and everywhere else that nobody'll notice one more.'

—•—

As the pick-up started its ascent of the gradient, the third consecutive switchback in the gently folded landscape, Jack thought to himself, "It seems to be getting a bit sluggish. It certainly doesn't want to tackle this one like it did the last two..." He kept his foot pressed down hard on the accelerator but instead of the pick-up pulling smoothly up the incline, the engine started chugging and panting as the speed dropped to a crawl and it struggled to crest the brow. "Hell's teeth! What now?" Jack shot out. He checked the temperature gauge and this time the needle was well into the red zone. He thought, 'I wonder if the radiator needs topping up again? Maybe I still haven't got all the air out of the system yet.' As he reached the crown of the hill, Jack pulled over onto the grass verge and it was immediately apparent to him what was wrong; wisps of steam were escaping from under the hood and the front wheel arches. As he got out, he could hear it hissing out of the overheated engine. When he lifted the hood, a cloud of hot, sickly-sweet-smelling vapor billowed out and engulfed him and he could hear the sound of liquid bubbling aggressively.

After they had fitted the new water pump and tested it for leaks, the consciencious young mechanic had warned Jack that he might need to top up the radiator a couple of times, to fill up any airlocks in the cooling system. Consequently, he had hefted a large plastic container filled with water into the back of the pick-up alongside the four, five-gallon cans of gasolene which acted as Jack's reserve tanks. Jack had already stopped three times to top up the radiator; he'd only done fifty-five miles but he'd already used close on a quarter of the water he'd set out with. Now it was impossible to remove the filler cap because of the pressure of steam behind it. And anyway, now that the moon had set so low that it perched precariously on the horizon, it was too dark to see the filler cap; if he tried to top up the radiator, there was a good chance he'd pour half of his precious coolant reserve down the side of the engine block. So Jack climbed back behind the steering wheel of the truck then swung his legs up onto the bench seat and opened the pack-up that Emily LeBlanc had made up for him. As he sat savouring the succulent roast pork sandwich, made up with left-overs from their evening meal, his cellphone rang. "Hello… Hi, Mom! Is everything okay?"

Mabel Culver told her son that Billy had turned up. Astonished, Jack exclaimed, "What? He's been there all this time… Does Martha know?" His mother explained that she had told Claudette who'd told her that Martha wasn't there and that she must be off pursuing another line of enquiry but that she would go and let her mother know immediately, so she didn't waste any more precious time on what was now a pointless exercise.

When Jack had reflected on it for a while, he said, "It all fits, of course it does…" then, "Is Dad there? Let me speak to him."

Mabel called her husband who came to the phone. "Hi, Dad… What do you mean, 'Good news'. It's fantastic news! Listen, I've been thinking… I think the cabin will be a far safer place to be than your home. After all, it's pretty much sheltered from the west by that rocky outcrop… you know, the one that puts it in shadow as the Sun sets… which should help protect it from the worst of the impact blast… It's in a large clearing. I don't think there are any big trees near enough to fall on it and if there are, we can soon fell them… And there's the bear pit where we can all take shelter when the time comes…

What's more it's solidly built, it's warm in winter, it has clean, running water, wildlife galore some of which is bound to survive the impact and fruits of the forest all nearby, unlimited firewood on the doorstep... and a generator... until the fuel runs out, of course..." and then, as an afterthought, added, "And there'll probably be far fewer people up there competing for the meagre resources that are left."

When his father started, "I don't know, Jack... Your mother seems mighty set on staying here..." Jack cut him dead, saying "Dad! Don't you see? Billy must have come to the same conclusion. All this time, he's been leading us there... *to this one special place...* He's probably not made his whereabouts known to us before now because he thought we'd come and take him away..."

Jack's father butted in, "But how did Billy know we'd find him?"

"Oh, he could be fairly confident he'd be found in good time because he's heard Grandpa Sam saying often enough that when his time comes, he wants to end his days up at the cabin..." then, speaking very earnestly, Jack continued "Billy's not done this thing haphazardly. He's chosen this place purposely... *because he thinks we can survive there...* And thinking about it, so do I!"

Father and son continued talking for some time about the relative merits of weathering the coming storm in their holiday home in the Adirondack Mountains until, eventually, Jack's father agreed that, yes, it probably would offer them the greatest chance of survival. "I'll try and persuade your mother, although it'll break her heart to leave the old place."

"Dad..." Jack said sympathetically, "It would also break her heart to see it razed to the ground... If she lived long enough to see it, that is..."

Jack had wheeled the disabled Softail into the workshop and the obliging young man had locked the door. He'd said, "The picks-up's at the house. We'll go an' work on it up there..." Jack had expected them to jump into his new recovery truck but he was surprised when the young mechanic had lead him round to the rear of the workshop and up a grassy bank to a gate in the chain link fence that surrounded the property. "Our home backs onto the workshop. Very convenient for getting to work..." The pick-up had been standing forlornly on the drive outside the garage.

As the young man had swung the garage door up, Jack had called out over his shoulder, "Are you sure we can fix this thing in a couple of hours? I really would like to get off as soon as possible..." but the young man had reassured him it could be done. At the sound of the door opening, a tall, pretty young woman wearing a bright red, figure-hugging summer dress and flat sandals, her long, chestnut hair tied back in a pony tail, had appeared round the corner of the house. "Oh... My wife, Emily... I'm Matt, by the way... Matt LeBlanc..." Jack had shaken the woman's outstretched hand. "John... John

Culver… But please call me Jack. Everyone else does. It avoids any confusion with my father…"

Looking Jack squarely in the face, Emily LeBlanc had said softly, "Welcome to our home, Mr Culver". He had been struck forcibly by her gently spoken manner but he'd been completely captivated by her eyes which were the clearest, most intense blue he'd ever seen. After her husband had explained what they were doing she had gone back to the kitchen and Jack had noticed that, as she went, she brushed the wall of the house lightly with her fingertips.

Jack had been impressed by the orderliness of the garage but he hadn't been able to get the image of those piercing blue eyes out of his mind.

After a while Jack had said, almost unconsciously as the vocal expression of his secret thoughts, "Your wife has lovely eyes…" then when he'd realised he'd said it out loud, quickly added, "I hope you don't mind my saying so…"

Matthew LeBlanc had said, quite genuinely, "Well thank you, Jack. I'll tell her. She'll be flattered…" then, "I saw you watchin' her as she went back to the house…" Jack had wondered guardedly what was coming next but the young man had continued, "She pretty much has to feel her way round everywhere these days, even places she knows well. Emily has a degenerative form of retinopathy, somethin' she inherited from her mother. There's no treatment for it. Her mother was already blind when I met Emily…" This revelation had struck Jack deeply and he'd suddenly felt very sad. Perhaps it was the thought that those beautiful eyes would never behold the World and all its wonders again. After a moment's reflection, Jack had thought darkly, 'Considering what's coming perhaps it won't be such a great loss…' then immediately rebuked himself for his callousness.

The two men had worked steadily for a couple of hours. As they'd finished fitting the new water pump and Matthew LeBlanc had said, "Well, the moment of truth is upon us… Now we need to fill her up and see if she leaks…" his wife had come out and said, "Dinner's almost ready, you two. You will join us, Mr Culver. We'd be delighted to have you…"

Jack had felt it would be churlish to decline such a gracious invitation even if he'd wanted to, which he hadn't. He had felt curiously attracted to the woman, so much so that it would have been impossible for him to say, "No". So he'd said, "Yes. Thank you. I'm ravenous!" with such enthusiasm that Emily LeBlanc had let out a spontaneous little laugh.

Matthew LeBlanc had said, "You go and get cleaned up, Jack. Emmy'll show you the way. I'll be there as soon as I've topped her up."

Jack had willingly downed tools and followed the woman indoors. He'd freshened up in the spotless little cloakroom that led off the hall. When he'd emerged, Emily LeBlanc's melodious voice had called out, "Through here, Mr

Culver" and he'd gone into their sitting room. A little boy had been sitting on the carpet, legs apart, with a small wooden mallet in his hand hammering brightly-colored pegs into a block of wood. "This is Morgan. He's three… Say 'Hello' to Mr Culver, Morgan." The little boy had looked up momentarily and said, "Hello", before resuming his industrious endeavours with even greater seriousness.

"This is Miles…" and Miles had stepped forward and shaken hands. "Pleased to meet you, Sir."

"And this is Lara, after my Russian *babushka*." The little girl had held the hem of her dress daintily between fingers and thumbs and curtsied deeply. Jack had squatted down and gallantly held out his open hand, palm up. The little girl had shyly offered hers and Jack had taken it and kissed it lightly. As he'd looked into the little girl's delicate face he'd seen the same trusting, radiant blue eyes that her mother had been blessed with.

Emily LeBlanc had asked, "Do you have children, Mr Culver?" and Jack had told her, "Yes. Martha and I have the twins, Nicky and Claudette. They're seventeen. And Billy. He's twelve." The two of them had continued chatting about families for a few minutes, until Emily LeBlanc said, "About ten minutes until we eat, Mr Culver."

"Is there anything I can do?"

"Oh, no thanks. Everything's under control. I just have to serve up…"

"Would you like a hand to take things to table?"

"No. That's alright, I can manage. I'm sure the children would like to keep you company."

As Emily LeBlanc had left the room, her daughter had taken hold of Jack's hand and lead him to an easy chair. "Would you like to sit down, Sir?" Again, the invitation had been irresistible. As Jack sat down, the little girl asked, "Would you like me to dance for you?" and Jack had said, "Yes, please." The older boy had sat at the piano and started to play a romantic waltz whilst the little girl skipped round lightly on her toes, the skirt of her dress fanning out to form a cone as she pirouetted round. Jack had been enchanted by the delightful display, never having seen quite such an innocent and joyful spirit, even in his own daughter when she'd been Lara's age.

When Emily LeBlanc had come in and said, "Children, it's time to wash your hands. Dinner's nearly ready" the two children had been sitting either side of Jack in the generous armchair, taking it in turns to read passages from 'Black Beauty'. Miles had said, "May we finish this chapter, Mommy? There's only two paragraphs…"

"Okay darlings but then we must get to table. Mr Culver's very hungry and he still has a long way to go once we've eaten."

Emily LeBlanc had taken the toddler away to get him ready whilst Lara had finished reading then asked to be excused and had gone to wash her hands. As Miles had finished the final paragraph of the chapter, the little girl had come back and taken Jack's hand and accompanied him to the LeBlanc's dining room.

"Mommy says 'Would you like to sit here, Mr Culver?' "

Jack had sat admiring the spread laid out before him as the LeBlanc tribe assembled. There had been a stuffed loin of pork, its skin roasted until it had turned a deep tan color and hard as the Devil's forehead; so crisp, it had almost shattered under a firm bite. Jack's favorite! The vapors that had risen from it had made Jack's mouth water. There had been a large tureen of baby new potatoes still in their skins, each one shiny and glistening like a wet pebble, glazed with a sheen of melted butter and flecked with green shards of chopped parsley freshly picked from Emily LeBlanc's own carefully tended herb garden, another tureen of small, yellow and orange cubes, diced early pumpkin and squash that had been delicately steamed and a large bowl of mixed, green salad garnished with a light sprinkling of chopped walnuts and fresh cilantro leaves. And a jug of gravy, made with the meat juices, to which Emily LeBlanc had added pureed apricots and a splash of dry white wine, which had been reduced to make a rich, slightly tangy but subtly sweet sauce for pouring over the meat.

Matthew LeBlanc had been last to come in and sat at the head of the table. Jack had noticed how calm the children were when Emily LeBlanc said, "Children! Hands together…" and three little heads had bobbed down. He'd been taken completely by surprise when Emily LeBlanc said, "Jack, before we eat, would you like to say grace?" Jack had flushed momentarily until he'd suddenly remembered something they'd said before meals at his private school. He'd put his hands together and said, "For what we are about to receive, may The Good Lord make us truly thankful… Amen" and in unison, four hushed "Amens" had come from around the table. Emily LeBlanc had reached over to the high chair and was about to prompt Morgan when he'd said, "Amen".

As Matthew had expertly stroked the carving knife along the steel, he'd said, "Well, Jack, I filled her up. After dinner, we need to check for leaks and if there are none we'll see if we can get her started…" Using the back of the blade, he had tapped the crackling to break it up into manageable pieces which he'd arranged on the platter around the joint, then had carved thick slices of meat which curled away from the end of the joint like breaking waves, to reveal the solid core of stuffing that ran through it. He had put a generous portion onto the plate on top of the stack in front of him and asked, "Jack, would you like crackling?"

When Jack responded enthusiastically, "Yes, please! I love it!" his host had heaped the crispy skin from about quarter of the joint onto his plate, at which Jack had exclaimed, a touch dramatically, "My word!"

The two older children had helped themselves to vegetables then served their mother, whilst their father had put out a small portion for their young brother then cut his meat into tiny pieces and mashed up his vegetables.

Once everyone had been served, the table had descended into silence as they all tucked in. After he'd eaten his first fork-full of meat, Jack had declared, "That stuffing! It's delicious! I'm sure Martha would love the recipe. Do you mind if I ask how you made it?" Emily LeBlanc had said modestly, "Not at all... Soften a chopped onion and a little garlic in olive oil. Add ground pork and gently fry it, then add some pureed apricots and apricot juice... I reserve the rest for the sauce... Breadcrumbs to soak up the juice... A handful of toasted pine nuts... Herbs... seasoning... then a beaten egg and some *fromage frais* to bind it together... It helps keep the meat nice and moist while it's cooking..."

When she'd finished, her husband had said, "Go on, Jack, try some of Emmy's spicy peach chutney. It'll knock you out", pushing a small pot of the home-made condiment towards him.

Jack had watched fascinated as Emily LeBlanc had tentatively reached out and felt the rim of her plate with movements so subtle they'd been almost imperceptible, then had picked up her precisely positioned cutlery and, holding it delicately, had slid it in from the rim of the plate until she'd located her food. He'd noticed that her husband had thoughtfully given her all small, carefully selected, bite-sized pieces of meat that needed no further dissection. Slowly but surely she had cleared her plate as thoroughly as everyone else.

At one point, Emily LeBlanc had said, "Mr Culver, would you like a little more?" Still having lots of meat left, he'd said, "I'd like some more of those lovely vegetables, please. They have such a fresh, earthy taste... And the salad's so crisp..." and Matthew LeBlanc had said, "They're from our own garden. They were still in the ground this morning. We grow most of what we eat. Emmy has green fingers and the children love helpin' Mommy in the garden... don't you, children?" at which Miles and Lara had both responded with vigorous nods of the head. Matthew LeBlanc had concluded, "Simple fare, Jack, but the best."

Thinking of home, Jack had said, rather wistfully Emily thought, "What with one thing and another, it seems a long time since we all sat down to a meal together..." and she'd said, "My grandmother used to say, 'A family that eats together, stays together' and I agree with her. That's why I try to put a proper meal on the table every day..."

"It's a good job you're not looking for a lodger or I might not go home again..."

Emily LeBlanc had laughed and said, "Oh, we don't eat this well every day, Mr Culver. Usually only on high days and holidays..."

"So what's today's special occasion?"

261

"It's our tenth wedding anniversary…"

"Oh! If I'd known, I wouldn't have intruded…"

"Don't be silly, Mr Culver. We've enjoyed having you as our guest, haven't we Matthew?" Matthew had confirmed that, yes, he'd enjoyed Jack's company.

"Well, congratulations! If I'd known, I'd have brought you a present…"

"According to what Matthew tells me, you have… Perhaps not one I'd have chosen for myself, given the choice, but something he values all the same…"

As Jack had laid his knife and fork side-by-side on his plate, he'd declared, "Well, that was wonderful! Thank you. It's the best meal I've had in ages…" and Emily LeBlanc had added quietly, "I've done it today because we don't know when we'll next have an opportunity to sit down together like this…" For the first time, Jack had seen a cloud flit briefly across her sunny countenance. But as quickly as it had come on, she had dispelled the gloom, as she'd said, "Right children! Warm pecan pie and ice cream for pudding…" at which cheers of delight had come from all three children, "…by special request…" then, for Jack's benefit, "It's Daddy's favorite. Isn't it, Matthew?" Then, in a slightly teasing voice, "Do we have any takers?" Three little hands had shot up as Miles and Lara said, almost in unison, "Yes please, Mommy" and in an urgent bid not to be overlooked an eager little voice had piped up excitedly, "Me me me…"

When everyone had finished, the two older children asked their mother, "May we leave the table, Mommy?"

"Yes, darlings… And please take your little brother with you." The children had got down from table, Miles dutifully lifting his brother out of his high chair and carrying him to the sitting room to continue practicing his handicraft skills.

As Matthew LeBlanc had gone to the kitchen to make coffee, his wife had asked, "So what do you think of this asteroid… S241… Mr Culver?"

Reluctant to admit its looming presence into this idyllic scene, Jack had asked cautiously, " 'Think'… In what respect?"

"Of the threat it poses…" then, when Jack hesitated, Emily LeBlanc had said quizzically, "You do know what I'm referring to?"

Slowly, Jack had replied, "Yes… Unfortunately, I know exactly what you're referring to… to a greater extent than you could ever imagine…" Not knowing quite what inference to draw from this cryptic message, Emily LeBlanc had looked at Jack with an expression of frustrated curiosity, so he'd continued, "I was… in fact, technically, I still am… Director of Astronomy at the observatory that discovered S241. It was my assistant, David Johnson, who first identified it. My boss, Dan Ackland, is the President's spokesman and advisor on S241. As for thinking about it, I've barely thought about anything else since we first realised it would cross Earth's orbit... As to the threat it poses, that cannot be overstated..."

"The announcements, the safety measures, the guidelines given by your colleague about surviving it... They sound so reassuring, as though S241 is survivable and life would return to normal after the impact... Is that true?" Jack had sat silently, looking troubled until Emily LeBlanc had said, "Please, Mr Culver, tell me the truth. I suspected things may be worse than they were actually letting on to. Now, your reticence reinforces my misgivings..."

In an even tone, Jack had said carefully, "Here, at this distance from the impact site, you have a good chance of surviving the impact if you observe the instructions and take shelter underground. Even here, above ground and in the open, you'd probably be killed by one or other of its effects... But no, I'm sorry to say, life will never return to normal... or at least nothing that would vaguely resemble the normality you're used to. But the real challenge won't be surviving the impact but surviving in the wasteland it'll create..."

Emily LeBlanc had stood and said, "Would you please come with me, Mr Culver? I'd appreciate your view on something..." As she'd turned to leave the table, she'd stumbled over a chair that one of the children had carelessly forgotten to put back. She'd put her hands out, a look of mild alarm on her face; it was the first time she'd done anything that had openly demonstrated her condition to Jack. She had regained her equilibrium almost immediately and set off across the room towards the hall but Jack could see from her slightly tentative steps that her confidence had been shaken.

Emily had opened the door to the basement then switched on the light before descending the stairs. She said, "You probably realise I put the light on for your benefit, not mine, Mr Culver..." Jack stood looking round the walls which were completely lined from floor to ceiling with shelves stacked high with cans, jars, bottles and packets of edible provisions, a well-stocked medicine chest, candles, matches, firelighters, toilet paper, torches, batteries, bleach, detergent, disinfectant, soap, toothpaste, toothbrushes, clothes, boots, blankets... You name it, it was there.

"I started laying down this store of food for other eventualities... For when my sight failed altogether... I wasn't sure if I'd still be able to do things like bottling or preserving... Most of the other things we've been laying down against a rainy day, although I don't think we'd ever envisaged a drenching on quite this scale..." Everything was very tidy. "Do you think we can survive down here, Mr Culver? And how can we improve our chances of survival?"

"Well... The floor above's made of concrete slabs which should support the weight of the house if it collapses. Down here, you should survive the impact... These provisions should allow you to subsist for some time but eventually they'll run out. The only thing you'll have to fall back on then is your will to survive... and possibly other qualities you've never had to exercise before, such as ruthlessness, selfishness, guile... things that might run contrary to your principles but which might need to be exercised to stay alive... because those survivors who have nothing are going to look to those who do to provide them with what they need to stay alive... This lot won't go far if you start sharing it with others. And if others find out you have it, there'll be some who'd kill you and your family to get their hands on it..." Jack had seen the look of horror and disgust that suffused Emily LeBlanc's face and said, "I don't know how to prepare you for how bad things will be afterward, safe to say that people will probably be eating each other to stay alive. I know that must sound shocking to you but that's how drastic this situation's going to be..."

Emily LeBlanc had crossed her arms defensively across her chest and turned her back on Jack. "In a way, knowing is worse than not knowing... Part of me wishes I'd never asked you, Mr Culver..."

"Part of me wishes you'd never asked, too..."

Matthew LeBlanc had descended the first few steps until he'd been able to see Jack's back and, over the other side of the basement his wife with her back to their guest. "Coffee's brewed. I'm goin' to check on the truck. You join me when you're ready, Jack."

"Okay! I'll be right with you." As Matthew LeBlanc's footsteps had receded down the passage, Jack had been able to tell that Emily was crying silently. More than anything, he had wanted to go over and put his arms round her and assure her everything would be alright. But he hadn't. He hadn't been able to because he knew it wouldn't.

Sensing that Jack was in limbo, Emily LeBlanc had dried her eyes and said, "It's not your fault, Mr Culver. You're just the messenger. You can't help being the bearer of bad tidings. I did ask after all. I... I just don't want the children seeing me like this. They don't understand what's happening... what's about to happen... We were determined to shelter them from what's already happened and we're even more determined to shelter them from what's coming. Matthew and I have tried not to talk about it any more than we have to and we've tried to downplay it for their sakes. We were determined to survive this awful war without it harming them and we've taken the same attitude to S241. We've put our trust in God to see us through if he sees fit to do so. We've done everything we can to prepare ourselves. Now we have to throw ourselves on His mercy..."

When they'd started working on the truck, Matthew LeBlanc had put its battery on charge. Once he'd satisfied himself that the cooling system hadn't leaked whilst they'd been having dinner, he'd secured the battery terminals then called to Jack, "Start her up!" Jack had turned the ignition key three or four times and the engine had turned over but hadn't fired up. He was beginning to feel disheartened when it had coughed then backfired, filling the yard with a sooty cloud of black smoke and started throbbing a lumpy and uncomfortable rhythm.

As the two men had stood by the truck listening to the irregular beat of its iron heart, Matthew LeBlanc had said quietly, "I guess Emmy wuz talkin' to you 'bout this asteroid... S421..."

"S241..." Jack had corrected him before replying, "Yes... She's scared... for the children mainly... She was asking my views about survival..."

"Emmy thinks it's God's punishment on America for wagin' this evil war... and God's punishment on mankind for wagin' war on each other in His name..." After a moment's pause, Matthew LeBlanc had continued despondently, "I don't know what to think... Thinkin's not my thing. I prefer to be doin' any day... Emmy's the thinker, the one with the education. She studied English and Education up at the university. She also speaks Russian and French which she learnt at home when she wuz growin' up... But she's a homebird really. All she ever wanted to do wuz raise a family... We've chosen to school the kids at home because we're tryin' to instill our values in 'em, in the hope it'll make a difference... Emmy takes care of all that... But I'm startin' to think we're fightin' a losin' battle when you look at what a wicked place this world's becomin'..."

Within the hour, Jack had been ready to leave. He'd turned off the ignition and Matthew LeBlanc had removed the spark plugs and cleaned them. The engine had started first time and run far more smoothly. When the thermostatic valve had opened, the water level in the cooling system had dropped with a gulp but they'd topped it up again and there had been no further signs of loss so they'd topped up the oil and filled up the fuel tank. They'd reckoned that that should be enough to get Jack to Irondequoit with a good margin for error.

Matthew had told his wife their guest was leaving. Emily had come out carrying Morgan with Miles and Lara skipping along beside her. She'd handed Jack a brown paper bag saying, "A little something for the journey, Mr Culver. Sustenance for body and soul..." Jack had thanked her, then he'd picked up Miles and Lara in turn and given each of them a hug. He'd pinched Morgan gently on the cheek, then kissed Emily and shaken hands with Matthew. He'd swung himself up into the driver's seat and started the engine. The LeBlanc's had gathered by the driver's door to see Jack off and he'd wound down the window. Matthew had said, "God be with you, Jack" and Jack had replied, "And with you" and he'd driven off, waving through the open window. He'd looked briefly in the rear view mirror and seen the family group, huddled together, waving back. They had all been smiling, with the exception of Emily LeBlanc who had worn a slightly troubled look.

After a couple of miles Jack had pulled over, his curiosity piqued by Emily LeBlanc's parting comment. He'd opened the bag. Inside was a sandwich and some fruit, a bottle of water and a small book. He'd reached in and taken out a slightly dog-earred old copy of the Bible, the King James version, with a carefully folded sheet of paper roughly at the center of the volume between the pages separated by the red ribbon that served as a bookmark. He'd opened it and taken out the paper. It had been Emily LeBlanc's recipe for stuffed loin of pork, written out in her beautiful flowing hand with a short personal note to Martha accompanying it. Without reading it, he'd folded it back up then turned his attention to the Bible. When he'd looked more closely, he'd noticed that it had been open at Psalms, number twenty-three. Someone had made a tiny, unobtrusive mark alongside the fourth verse: 'Yea, though I walk through the valley of the shadow of death, I will fear no evil; for thou art with me; thy rod and thy staff they comfort me.'

"So what do you want me to do, Son?"

"Get Mom, Martha, Claudette… everyone… up to the cabin as soon as you can…"

"What about Nicky? Shouldn't we wait for him?"

"Is there any news of him? Has he been in touch yet?"

"No… At least, not for the last few days."

"Then no, I don't think so. I think you should get up to the cabin as soon as possible. If that's going to be our place of safety, I don't think you should jeopardise your chances of getting there by leaving it to the last minute before you go…"

"Won't Martha want to wait for Nicky?"

"I don't know. Probably yes and no… Yes, she'll be concerned about him, particularly as he doesn't know we're going to the cabin. But she'll also want to see Billy. Don't forget, she hasn't seen him for the best part of three weeks. Even if she's difficult, you must persuade her to go…"

"And what about you, Son? Where are you now? How are you getting there? And when should we expect you?"

"Don't worry about me, Dad?" Jack briefly explained his circumstances then told his father that he would come to their home on Lake Ontario and wait for Nicky, so that the others could get off to the cabin at the earliest possible opportunity. "I'm having a bit of trouble with my transport but I should be there some time tomorrow… Thursday at the latest. Whatever you do, don't wait for me. Get off as soon as you can. That goes for Martha and Claudette, too. And don't take 'No' for an answer from Martha. You know how stubborn she can be. If you've gone before I arrive, just leave me a key in the usual place. I'll let myself in. Hopefully, Nicky should arrive in plenty of time for us to get up to the cabin. We'll see you up there."

After finishing talking to his father, Jack ate what remained of the sandwich then folded his jacket and put it behind his head and within a couple of minutes had fallen asleep.

—•—

(Thursday 19 August 2010)

The cabin, which had been the Culver family retreat since the early nineteen-fifties when it had been built by Jack's grandfather, Samuel John Culver – affectionately known by his great grandchildren as 'Big Grandad', to differentiate him from Jack's father – on a piece of land that had been left to him by his grandfather, nestled in a natural amphitheatre formed by a roof-high rocky outcrop covered in coarse, tussocky grass, wild blueberry and deep moss, topped with gnarled old-growth spruce and fir, which enclosed it on three sides leaving its south-facing front aspect open to enjoy the best of the day's sun. Here and there, where the underlying rock showed through the cover, it was adorned with a soft gray-green lichen.

The road up to the cabin struck off State Highway seventy-three just outside of Lake Placid. It passed through a number of tiny, sparsely-populated hamlets before it turned into an unmade track which wound in a southerly direction through dark stands of tall, dense timber and beside crystal-clear, tumbling streams, climbing steadily as it approached the lower slopes of Mount Marcy. The further they climbed, the further they left behind the man-made forests with their serried ranks of arrow-straight pine trees and entered an altogether more natural landscape and one that was far more pleasing to the eye, of virgin woods made up of conifers mixed with aspen, birch, maple, witch-hazel and other deciduous trees, a landscape that had remained largely unspoilt by man since the retreat of the last glaciers approximately eleven thousand years previously.

As soon as Martha had cleaned the man's blood from her hands and face using the wet-wipes she always carried in the car for freshening up and for emergencies (although she'd never foreseen an emergency of quite this gravity) and had changed her blouse, she'd tried calling Jack's parents. Their phone had been engaged so whilst Martha had driven she'd set Claudette the task of charting their course out of the city, in the hope it would take her mind off the gruesome scene she'd witnessed. Trying to put it out of mind, Claudette had concentrated on giving her mother accurate directions.

Once they were clear of the city, Martha had been struck by the worrying thought that it was a long way to the cabin, much further than it was to Jack's parents' house on Lake Ontario. Claudette had studied the map a little longer and said, "About five-hundred-and-thirty-five miles by my reckoning if we avoid using I-90 and all the other major east-bound roads but only a few miles shorter if we use the interstate and risk all those hold-ups…"

Martha had done some quick mental arithmetic and said, "In which case, I think we're short of fuel by at least a hundred miles… maybe a-hundred-and-twenty… and the chances of getting some en route are very slim."

She'd tried again and had eventually got through. After Mabel had reassured her that Billy really was alright and that she'd also let Jack know the good news, Martha had spoken to Jack's father about her concerns. He had agreed with her that it was unlikely she would find any fuel now, having tried unsuccessfully himself to buy enough fuel locally to fill his wife's car. Once the shock of the evening's violent confrontation had worn off, Martha felt absolutely drained and she had guessed correctly that Claudette felt equally exhausted but she had been afraid that if they parked up overnight, they would be at risk from gangs intent on hijacking the car or stealing its fuel, so she had determined to press on to Jack's parents' without stopping; they had already passed hundreds of vehicles abandoned at the roadside, most of them having run out of fuel, leaving the hapless occupants stranded in the middle of nowhere. Jack's father had discussed the situation with Martha awhile, then told her that he would siphon the remaining fuel out of his wife's car and transfer it to Martha's. He'd estimated that there was five or six gallons left in the tank, enough Martha thought to get them to the cabin. It would seem that Jack had also persuaded his parents that, in light of forthcoming events, it would be better for them to go up to the cabin because before ringing off Jack's father had told Martha that when she was ready to leave, they would travel together in convoy.

Martha had told him that she wanted to leave as soon as her car had been fuelled but when they arrived at five-thirty the following morning Jack's mother had taken one look at Martha's and Claudette's ashen faces and dark, sunken eyes and had insisted that the two of them get some sleep before continuing. After putting up a token protest, Martha had agreed that they would take a nap whilst Jack's father was transferring the fuel to her car but that they should leave immediately it had been done. The two women had taken a quick shower and climbed into bed in the guest room. By the time Jack's father had finished the job an hour later, they were both so soundly asleep that Mabel had insisted they be left undisturbed. At about eleven-thirty, Claudette had been woken by her mother's fitful whimpering and had climbed sleepily out of her own bed and into her mother's. Claudette had gently rolled her mother onto her side then cuddled up to her and put an arm around her until Martha had calmed. The two had slept on, providing comfort for one another, until three-thirty that afternoon when Martha had suddenly awoken with a start. It had taken her a few moments to come round from her deep sleep but, once she'd checked the bedside clock and realised what time it was, she'd shaken Claudette vigorously then leapt out of bed and dressed hurriedly, all the while chivvying her daughter to do the same.

Martha's first reaction had been one of anger that they'd been allowed to sleep on well past the time she had said she wanted to be up and away but when she'd seen the gray, drawn faces of her mother- and father-in-law, she'd realised they were just as tired and just as worried by the dread prospect of forthcoming events as she was. Mabel had said quietly, "I'll go and make you some breakfast, dear" and Jack's father had said, "Jack's given us some idea of what's coming. He's given us instructions about preparing for it and we've packed as much as we can get into the truck. He says he wants you all to get some warm, hard-wearing clothes and boots suitable for cold, harsh conditions…"

Martha said hotly, "I know! That's what he told me to do but when have I had the opportunity? We've been travelling solidly for the last two weeks, chasing after Billy or cooped up in that bloody hotel in Indiana waiting for the curfew to be lifted. What with one thing and another we haven't had time for shopping. And since this latest scare, shops have sold out of *everything*… or been emptied by looters… and now they're all shut and locked. How the hell could I shop under those circumstances?"

Jack's father had seen that Martha was getting very agitated and had cut in gently, "Don't worry, Martha. I've arranged with some friends of ours who have an outdoors outlet in town to open up for us this evening… You know, hiking and camping gear and the like… They've got plenty left in stock… It seems most of the looters are far more interested in wide-screen TVs and DVD players and fancy sport shoes… We can go and pick up what you need later…"

Martha had tried impressing upon her father-in-law that they couldn't wait and needed to get off now but he'd said firmly, "Martha, you need to be prepared for the worst and from what Jack's told me this could just be the worst scenario you'd ever envisaged. If needs be, there's plenty of time to get up to the cabin tomorrow." Martha had kicked off at the idea that they should wait another day but her father-in-law had gently calmed her down again, saying, "You were damned lucky not to get waylaid last night, Martha. I've been watching the news. The interstates are largely blocked and traffic's pretty much at a standstill. Thousands of cars have either run out of gas or overheated and boiled dry or simply broken down, so that means we'll have to avoid them altogether. And there's been dozens of reports of people being held up at gunpoint and even killed on small, country roads, particularly at night. It's much safer to travel by day and to stick to the main roads where there's more likely to be regular checkpoints and National Guards on duty to deter outlaws. Don't forget, we've still got the best part of three hundred miles to go and there are a lot of desperate people out there prepared to do desperate things to survive. We don't want to fall victim to one of them…"

Martha had acquiesced, not wanting to fall out with him, knowing that her father-in-law only had their best interests at heart and was talking common sense. They had set off early the following morning with both vehicles loaded to the gunnels with food, clothing, medicine, tools and anything else they'd thought might be useful for survival in the wilderness but not before Martha had seen her father-in-law empty his gun cabinet and stow his hunting rifle and ammunition safely in his truck. She'd also noticed that he'd slipped a loaded revolver into his driver's door pocket, careful not to let his wife see what he'd done and he'd quietly mouthed to her, "Travel insurance", with a serious look on his face. Whilst Claudette had helped her grandmother prepare food for the journey, Martha and her father-in-law had pored over the map, planning the route in minute detail. He had sternly instructed her to make sure they stayed together and what to do in the event that they became separated.

As it happened, the journey had passed uneventfully, with the exception that Martha's car ran out of fuel shortly after they'd passed through Saranac Lake and her father-in-law had had to tow it the last few miles. Fortunately, the five-point-seven litre HEMI V8 engine of his Jeep Commander had more than enough grunt to pull them both up the two or three steep slopes on the track to the cabin and its intelligent four-wheel drive had sufficient bite to ensure it tackled them with ease.

As his truck crested the last rise where the track emerged out of the trees, he swung it round in front of the cabin so that Martha's car stopped directly in front of the open door. The porch was in deep shadow but there was Billy standing in the doorway. Mother and son remained frozen for a long moment, until Martha slowly got out of the car and went and stood at the edge of the stoop. The two regarded each other then Billy stepped forward and shyly said, "Hello Mom". As the tears rolled silently down her cheeks, Martha stood, unable to speak, or move, or barely even breathe. After what seemed like an eternity, she mounted the steps and took Billy in her arms and, pressing her face into his neck, wept steadily. Tentatively at first, Billy slowly raised his arms then put them round his mother and, for the first time in his life, Martha felt Billy hugging her in the way that she'd always longed for. Not wanting to intrude upon their reunion, Martha's father-in-law went quietly round to the back of the cabin, to find his father, whilst Mabel, concerned that the girl had been overcome by the emotion of the moment, went to the car to comfort Claudette who had suddenly broken down and was sobbing.

Eventually, when Claudette sensed that mother and son had bridged the abyss that had separated them for twelve long years, she too went up and put her arms around Billy and Martha hugged them both tightly.

After they had unloaded the cars and Mabel and Claudette had set about preparing the evening meal, Martha took Billy out onto the porch and sat with him. The two remained sitting slightly apart on the swing seat, with Billy staring at his hands which were clasped between his knees and Martha staring at the top of Billy's downcast head. They sat like that for some minutes. Not knowing quite how to open the conversation with her son, Martha said quietly, "I met George, Billy... And his grandmother... George asked me to say "Hi!" when I saw you... And his grandmother sends you her love. It seems you made quite an impression on her... On them both, in fact... She told me she was taking George back home to Chattanooga early on account of you..."

Without looking up, Billy said quietly, "To Lookout Mountain. One-thousand-three-hundred-and-twenty-five miles from Cheyenne, about forty miles more from their ranch..." then, after a long pause, "She must have found my note."

Martha sat making small talk about their journey. She occasionally asked him questions about his, to which Billy gave his customary monosyllabic responses. Eventually, the conversation dried up altogether and the two sat in uneasy silence until Martha reached into her pocket, saying, "Billy, I have something for you..." and pulled out his wristwatch. She laid it in the palm of her hand and, without a word, offered it to Billy who sat looking at it but did not reach out to take it.

After what seemed an excruciatingly long and painful pause during which Martha agonised over what her son must be feeling, Billy said very quietly, "He didn't hurt me, Mom..."

Martha gazed at her son, her eyes starting to fill up and said gently, "Are you sure, Billy? You can tell me, darling... He told me he did some horrible things to you. Are you sure he didn't hurt you?"

After a brief pause, Billy said, "Yes... He tried to hurt me but I hurt him instead..."

"How, Billy?"

"I bit him... hard... on his hand... I sank my teeth in and wouldn't let go..."

Martha suddenly let out a little laugh and threw her arms round Billy's neck, hugging him close to her. After a moment's reflection, she said, "Do you realise, Billy, you probably saved my life... and you probably saved Claudette's life, too?" to which Billy simply replied, "Yes".

As the bus had pulled into the Cleveland terminal late in the evening of Tuesday, August third, Edmond Xavier O'Shea, the Security Supervisor, had been sitting at the desk, a lighted cigarette smouldering in the ashtray at his elbow, idly watching the grainy images on the monochrome monitor of the CCTV surveillance system. He had panned the camera round slowly until its cold, expressionless eye fell upon the main door of the bus, then zoomed in so he could observe more closely the stream of weary passengers as they alighted. A woman leading three children off the bus caught his attention, not because this was unusual in itself but because the boy bringing up the rear of the party hung back from the main body a little and scanned the concourse furtively before stepping down onto the platform whilst the other two children followed her obediently. There was something familiar about the boy. He'd turned to look at the pinboard and saw the photograph, sent to him the previous evening by one of his colleagues in Portland, Oregon, which he had pinned up that very morning and the similarity was striking. When the boy peeled off and slunk unobtrusively away in the direction of the restrooms, Edmond Xavier O'Shea had known instinctively that here was more prey.

Edmond Xavier O'Shea had been born to Catholic parents. His mother had been an extremely devout woman who attended mass twice daily, every day of the week. His father had been less committed but had exculpated himself for his failure to make such regular devotions by looking after their only son whilst his wife was out at church. The fact that the couple had had a child at all was something of a miracle, as Mrs O'Shea regarded all carnal knowledge as sinful, especially after the miserable and traumatic time she'd had bringing young Edmond Xavier into the world, which had guaranteed that that was the extent of her husband's knowledge of her. To quench any smouldering desire on his part, she had insisted that Mr O'Shea accompany them to mass just as soon as Edmond Xavier was old enough to participate in the ritual. Quite when the tampering had started Mrs O'Shea couldn't be sure and when, at the age of twelve, she had first noticed the telltale stains on the boy's underwear her initial reaction had been one of abhorence at her son's self-abuse. But when she eventually discovered the truth of the matter, Mrs O'Shea had secretly taken the boy away and left her husband to go to the Devil. Thereafter, she had cleaved to the boy to such an extent that she had completely smothered him so that, forty-one years on, he still lived with his mother who was by now frail and bed-ridden and totally dependent on him for support and companionship, barring the occasional visit from the local parish priest. The fact that her son had failed to develop – no, had been prevented from developing to the extent that they had been almost forbidden – normal, healthy relationships with others meant that the only close physical contact he had ever experienced in his formative years had been the sexual attentions of his father, carried on furtively in darkened rooms against the boy's will and as the price he'd had to pay for being allowed the smallest privileges in an otherwise ascetic and disciplinarian household. But once they'd fled, his mother had taken away even the few harmless children's books he had enjoyed – his sole source of solace and his last refuge from the unpleasant reality of his sad and lonely existence – which had left him with only the Good Book to read. And now, for the privilege of being allowed to pass through his domain, he exacted a similar price from the lonely, often frightened boys who crossed his path as they fled from one demon or another, coerced by the threat that he would return them to face their own particular demon if they refused to pay it. And they usually paid it. With the exception of William John Culver, who had stood mute whilst Edmond O'Shea made his overtures in his darkened office, who had silently taken off his prized wristwatch and offered it in return for his safe passage, who had stood rigid whilst his tormenter had pulled down his trousers and underpants then unzipped his own flies, who had remained unbending when he had tried to force his stubby little erection between the boy's tightly clenched buttocks but who had then started to emit an unearthly wail, low at first, like the moan of an animal in pain but getting steadily louder until the Security Supervisor, terrified of the unwanted attention it might attract, had panicked and tried to silence the boy by placing his hand over his mouth. And it was then that Billy had sunk his teeth into the man's hand and clamped down on it with all his might.

Edmond Xavier O'Shea was desperate: desperate for love, for affection, for human contact physical and emotional but he had laboured for so long under such an overwhelming burden of guilt, of disgust at his own sinfulness and the weakness of his own flesh and of obligation to his mother, that it presented an insurmountable obstacle to him ever knowing happiness. Instead, he had had to suffice himself with the occasional gropings that passed for fulfilment in these brief, sordid encounters. Out of gratitude he had created a little shrine, to venerate all those whom he had anointed with his own sacred unction. Only a couple of weeks before he'd met his nemesis, he had pinned up the picture of Spike Griffiths and had added the halo out of respect when he'd received news about the youth's sad demise. But Edmond Xavier O'Shea had been no cold-blooded killer. When this small, mute boy had inflicted pain on him such as he had never felt before, even his agony and his inclination to cry out loud had been swamped by his fear of discovery and exposure. He had let go of Billy and pushed him away, pleading with him to unlock his jaws and promising to let him go unmolested. Billy had backed away from him, all the while watching the man out of the corner of his eye, until he was at arm's length when he released his bite and let go of the man's hand, then shuffled to the office door where he hurriedly pulled up his trousers and grabbed his rucksack and let himself out, leaving his watch on the desk.

Burning with detestation for this wicked creature that had spurned him and turned on him, his first instinct had been to destroy his image but then, in his warped mind, he saw the boy as the angel that had resisted God's will and as a consequence had fallen from grace and he damned him to go to Hell where he belonged. He had put up Billy's image to remind himself that he had survived his encounter with Satan. Unable to punish the boy or put him out of mind, Edmond O'Shea's impotent rage had festered until it had developed into a full-blown desire to... to... to... To what? What would he do to punish the boy if he ever met him again? And then, completely out of the blue, the boy's mother had presented herself in his office and it had taken the least provocation for him to realise how he could hurt the boy most. And who would ever find out, bearing in mind forthcoming events? As he had lain on his back, sprawled out on the floor of his own office, looking up at Martha's back, his shrine desecrated, a lifetime's pent-up pain, humiliation and isolation had erupted and fired his sudden and overwhelming desire to kill someone. Anyone. And who more fitting than the mother of the Beast. But what Edmond Xavier O'Shea had failed to reckon with was how fiercely a loving parent would fight to protect their child.

Spike Griffiths had been less fortunate. When he'd been twelve years of age, his mother had installed a new lover, the latest in a long line that had come and gone. This one put up with her moodiness, her foul temper, her binge drinking and her drug addiction not because he loved her but because of his easy access to her youngest child. Spike's brother who was six years older and whom Spike looked up to, had gone to live with his girlfriend in Detroit shortly before the new partner had become ensconced. His mother put up with the new man in her life because he made very few demands on her sexually and because he kept her supplied with the drink and drugs that kept her stoned which ensured that she failed to notice the demands he put upon her son. After two years of abuse, he had gone to his mother in desperation and told her everything. Desperate to ensure the continued flow of hard liquor and hard drugs, she had flown into a rage and dismissed the boy's story, accusing him of manufacturing the whole tissue of lies, telling him that he had never liked his new step-father and had never tried to make him feel welcome, as a consequence of which Spike Griffiths had phoned his older brother and told him of his miserable situation. His brother had told him to get out immediately and to stay with a friend until he could send a bus ticket, which is how Spike Griffiths found himself in the terminal in Buffalo, waiting to catch a bus to Detroit. Seeing the note that the boy had left for his mother before she had read it, her partner had screwed it up and thrown it in the trashcan. With the boy gone there was no point in continuing to fuel the bitch with expensive bourbon and crack and very little point in being there at all, so he had packed his few belongings in his battered holdall and left. And in a rare moment of lucidity that followed her enforced abstinence and sobriety, his mother noticed that Spike had disappeared. Rummaging through the empty liquor bottles in the trashcan, looking for any remaining dregs that might slow down her headlong plunge into withdrawal, she had found her son's note telling her that he was running away to live with his brother in Detroit. Vaguely recalling their conversation when the boy had expressed his profound unhappiness at the hands of his tormentor, his mother had been stabbed by a sudden pang of guilt and had gone to the police and filed a missing person's report and in doing so had signed her son's death warrant.

For three days, Edmond Xavier O'Shea had watched the arrival of every bus coming from Buffalo but Spike Griffiths hadn't been among the passengers. He had almost given up hope, thinking that the youth may have taken a different route to Detroit. Now, as the late bus pulled in and the passengers alighted, he focussed the CCTV camera on its door and, sure enough, there he was. He had cornered the boy in an area of the terminal he knew was not covered by the surveillance system and after letting him know that he had been reported missing, asked the youth to accompany him to his office. Not knowing that his tormentor had done a flit, the boy had pleaded with the Security Supervisor not to turn him over to the police who would arrange for him to be returned home. So in the darkness of his unlit office, the sad deviant had put his proposition to the frightened youth. Having been used countless times before, Spike Griffiths had decided that once more wouldn't make much difference if it let him continue on. And Edmond Xavier O'Shea knew that the youth wouldn't report him to the authorities if he was so desperate not to be returned home that he would agree to his proposition in the first place. But what neither of them had known was that Spike Griffiths would never make it to Detroit because waiting for him in the bus station in Toledo was a beast of an altogether different nature, a far more dangerous and cold-blooded predator and one with whom no deals could be struck. Billy had been fortunate: he'd been making such rapid progress that the beast had realised he was prey only after the boy had passed through his lair. The detectives from the Pontiac P.D. investigating the murder of Spike Griffiths would fail to make any connection with Edmond Xavier O'Shea whose dark secrets would go with him to the grave because, like everyone else on the planet, they were overtaken by a far greater turn of events.

—•—

By the time Jack arrived at his parents' house, as hot and fuming as the engine of the truck he was driving, the others had already been gone more than three hours. It limped up the long drive with steam hissing out from under the hood. This time it had only managed to cover six miles – fortunately, the last six miles – since he'd last filled up the radiator.

When he'd awoken, with the first light of dawn peeping over the horizon, it had felt surprisingly chilly, the penalty of a clear night. Jack had rubbed his upper arms vigorously to stimulate the circulation, trying to take the chill off his bones. Once he'd managed to restore some warmth Jack had sat munching on the fruit that Emily LeBlanc had packed for him, waiting for the light level to be sufficient to see by, then he'd topped up the radiator. He had been surprised by how much water it had taken to fill it up to the point where he'd decided to check again for any leaks when he'd sneezed, causing him to miss the filler spout and spill water over the engine. "Damn!" He had peered down into the gloomy recesses of the engine compartment but hadn't been able to see much. When he'd crouched down and looked underneath, he hadn't been able to see much either but had been able to make out droplets of water falling from various points on the engine. When he'd checked it again the container had been little more than quarter full. He'd said to himself, 'This can't be right… It must be more than an airlock. There must be a leak somewhere… But where?'

Jack had driven on steadily, keeping a watchful eye on the temperature gauge. Gradually, after about fifteen miles, it had started to creep up again. As the truck had struggled to reach the top of a modest rise, Jack had recognised all the symptoms of overheating so he'd let it coast down the other side, willing the cool morning air to suck as much waste heat out of the radiator as possible. From the top of the rise he'd seen the creek below him, off to the left of the road amongst the trees, so he'd rolled to a halt at the bottom of the hill, on the bridge that spanned the little tributary before it flowed into the creek.

He had scrambled down the steep side of the gorge in which the little stream ran, made slippery by the ground water that leached continuously out of the hillside, and filled the container. When he'd tried climbing back up with his heavy burden he'd slipped back until, on the third attempt, he'd struck his ankle a heavy blow on a sharp piece of rock. "Urrgh!" he'd gasped as a wave of nausea swept over him. Eventually, as the dull, sickening pain had begun to subside, he'd pulled up his trouser leg and gingerly rolled down the cuff of his blood-stained sock to reveal the ragged shreds of loose skin. When it had stopped keening quite so much, he had massaged his leg, trying to avoid the area of grazed flesh.

As he'd examined the embankment, trying to work out how he could get back up, he had heard a car approaching in the distance. It was a lonely stretch of road at the best of time made lonelier by the fact that it had been so early in the morning, which had made the chances of summoning assistance even more remote. So as it reached the bridge, Jack had called out, "HELP! HELP!" at the top of his voice but the car had continued on without stopping. He had managed to catch a quick flash of red and heard the growl of its exhaust as it had begun to pull up the opposite slope then it was gone. Jack had looked around for a way out. He had decided it would be too hazardous to go downstream under the bridge because, as it emerged on the other side, the stream disappeared over a lip where it fell into the creek twenty feet below. He had also considered wading across the stream and trying to climb the opposite bank but as that was as steep as this one, he had discounted that option, too. By a process of elimination, the only option left open to him had been to go upstream.

It had taken Jack the best part of an hour to get out of the ravine. It would have been physically trying under any circumstances but with a badly bruised ankle and carrying a heavy container of water, it had been extremely difficult and had severely taxed Jack's stamina. At one point, he'd nearly abandoned his burden but, having decided that the whole exercise would have been pointless if he returned without the water and that there was no way he'd be able to get home without it, he had persevered.

After he'd filled up the radiator, this time being careful not to spill a drop, which had taken about half the water in the container, he had put the filler cap back on then screwed the lid firmly on the container and put it down on the road in front of the pick-up. He'd then laid down on his back in front of the truck and, hanging from the fender, hauled himself underneath. Jack had watched for a couple of minutes, expecting to see dripping water that would give away the location of the leak but had seen none. 'That's odd...' he'd thought, 'I wonder if it only leaks when the pump's working and the system's under pressure. I guess I'd better start her up and see...' He'd pulled himself out from under the truck then heaved the water container back into the truck. As he'd delved in his pocket for the key, Jack had suddenly been struck by an arresting thought. There was something odd about the truck, something missing. 'Where were the fuel cans?' He'd spun round and looked over the tailgate. "WHERE'S THE FUEL CANS?" he'd exploded. 'For Christ's sake, Culver, you idiot!' he'd berated himself. 'How could you have been so stupid as to leave them in the open for anyone to take? It was tantamount to putting up a sign inviting people to steal them.'

Even with the reserve fuel it was touch-and-go whether he could make it all the way to the cabin; without it, he certainly couldn't; he may not even have enough fuel to get him to Irondequoit. Furious at his own stupidity and seething with anger that someone could have done this to him, a torrent of questions had flooded wildly through Jack's mind. 'Who could have taken it?

Which way had they gone? Where were they now? How could he get it back? *Could he get it back?* If not, could he replace it? How? Where?'

He had looked in both directions but seen nothing that might suggest which way the thieves had gone and, anyway, they could easily have an hour's head start. Jack had jumped into the truck and started the engine and thrashed it up the incline. His boiling, turbulent rage had quickly cooled and condensed into a cold, hard malice towards the bastards that had put him in this difficult situation and he'd thought, 'It's a bloody good job I locked the truck and took the key with me. I'd have been right up Shit Creek if they'd taken that too…'

As Jack had thundered over the next rise a panoramic vista had opened up before him, illuminated by the soft golden glow of the early morning sun coming in low from the right, as the landscape flattened and became gentler. He could see the road directly ahead as it came out of the last hollow and ran into the distance. Parked at the side of the road just beyond the point where it levelled out onto the plateau about a mile distant, Jack had noticed a red car. And trudging slowly up the slope towards it had been two very rotund figures, each one with both arms hanging straight down by their sides carrying two heavy objects – Jack's reserve fuel cans.

As the Beaufort twins had come to the end of I-476 north there had been a barrier across Exit 131 leading to I-80 north. A Pennsylvania State Police vehicle, with its battery of roof-mounted warning lights flashing lazily, had been sitting on the approach to the exit and there had been a State Trooper to wave motorists on, although at six o'clock in the morning it had been a fairly lonely vigil with just a handful of vehicles passing by. As they had approached the exit, Jedediah Beaufort had said to his twin brother, "Shee-it, Zeke! Looks like they closed the road. Pull over'n see what's goin' on" and Ezekiah Beaufort had responded, "Don't tell me what t'do all the goddam time, Deke. What d'ya think I wuz slowin' down fa? Dumb ass!"

The State Trooper had waved the car down. As it ground to a halt at his side, Ezekiah had wound down his window and the Trooper had said, "I-80 north's closed. There's bin a nasty accident up yonder just afore the Carbondale Road intersection. Road's completely blocked. You'll haf'ta take a diff'runt route." Which is how they had found themselves going north on Highway eleven about ten minutes behind Jack.

As they'd torn over the bridge, having taken full advantage of gravity to accelerate them to an alarming speed and had passed the stranded pick-up truck with its hood propped open, Zeke Beaufort had observed, "Lonely place t'break down. If we see the poor critter walkin', I'll stop'n giv'm a lift…" and his brother had said, "Just keep y'eyes firmly on the road ahead, ya mad fool! Y'know this old shit-box Dodge ain't no good at speeds 'bove thirty…" and the two had continued bickering until they'd been approaching the last brow

278

when the engine had juddered a couple of times, picked up momentarily as the last few dregs of fuel were sucked into the cylinders which had just been sufficent to propel the vehicle over the brow of the hill before it had cut out altogether.

As it had coasted under its own momentum, gradually losing speed, Jedediah Beaufort had let out an explosive report that had summed up their situation to a tee. "SHEEEE-IT!" The two had sat arguing about whose fault it was that they'd run out of fuel until Zeke had said, "This ain't goin' t'git uz home. You'll haf'ta go n'git help n'I'll stay n'look after the vee-hickle…"

"Why do I haf'ta go? It wuz you who ran out of gas, fool! You go n'I'll mind the car…"

Eventually, they had both agreed that as no one was going to drive it away and it was unlikely anyone would want to strip an eighty-four sedan for parts they would both go in search of fuel. After two more minutes of heated debate over who should go in which direction, they had both agreed they would walk back along the road towards the truck they'd passed and town, on the basis that they'd seen no signs of homesteads ahead. And they had barely been able to believe their good fortune when they'd looked over the tailgate and seen four fuel cans in the rear of the pick-up. They had looked around; they had even looked under the truck and over the parapet of the bridge into the ravine but they had seen no one who might have laid claim to the truck and its contents. So after checking that the doors were locked and having shaken the cans to check they were full and removed the lids to check it actually was gasolene they were taking, they had heaved the four cans out of the truck and set off back in the direction they'd come from.

With a touch of guilt Zeke had said, "Shun't we jus' take a couple? That should be more'n'enuff t'git uz home…" but Deke had salved both their consciences by observing, "Well, if it weren't us as burrered it, some other varmint wud'a dun… 'N wot d'folks expect, leavin' it about like that at a time of nashnul shortage?"

Before they'd reached the top of the first hill, Deke had wheezed, "I need a rest… Jus' stop awhile, will you, Zeke?"

Being the soul of concern for his brother's welfare, Zeke, who was slimmer by all of five pounds in two-hundred-and-eighty-five pounds, had said, "C'mon, tubby…", which had rather smacked of pot calling kettle black, "Keep goin'… Th'exercise'll do ya good" but fifty yards further on, Zeke had panted, "I agree… Let's rest awhile…"

Each brother had stood his cans side-by-side and had sat astride them. First one had taken off his spectacles and wiped his sweat-beaded forehead with the back of his arm, then polished the lenses with his shirt-tail, then the other had unconsciously copied his twin's actions exactly without either of them realising it. Zeke had taken a packet of cigarettes from his shirt pocket and offered one to his brother who had taken a box of matches from his pocket and thoughtlessly struck one on one of the cans between his legs before offering his brother a light. Deke had inhaled deeply then let out a satisfied sigh and observed, "Ahhh! Jus' like life itself…" and Zeke had said, "D'ya remember? That's jus' what Momma use't'say… Until the cancer took her off, a'course…"

Once the two of them had recovered their breath, Deke had suddenly exclaimed, "I know! You take one can o'gas n'go n'git the car n'I'll wait here'n'look after the rest o'the gas…" to which his brother had retorted, "Why me? You go n'git the car n'I'll stay here with the gas… After all, it wuz you as wanted t'bring all four cans. I said we cud make do wi' two…"

Just as Zeke had wheezed out encouragingly, "There she is… Nearly there… Not far now…", his brother had panted out breathlessly, "Car coming…" It had only been the second one they'd seen that morning. As Deke had looked round and seen the pick-up truck bearing down on them he'd said, "Shee-it!" and between gasps, "Unless I'm… very much mistaken… it's th'owneruv… this'ere gas… An' he looks mighty pissed…" The two overweight brothers had gratefully dropped their burdens and stood sheepishly, trying to catch their breaths, unable to flee even if their lives had depended on it, awaiting whatever wrath might descend upon them. Jack had pulled up sharply just beyond them, between them and their car and jumped out to confront them. With strong emphasis on the 'my', he'd snarled, "Where d'you think you're going with *my* gas?"

Deke had said lamely, "We wuz jus' burrowin' it, mister. Honest…" and his brother had added, "We need it t'git home…"

Jack cut in, "Well, so do I. So hand it over!"

As he'd advanced towards them, first one brother then the other had slowly sat themselves down on their cans and stared at him through bottle-bottom glasses as they'd reiterated, "We need this gas t'git home…"

Jack had pushed back his sleeves revealing his muscular forearms and said, "Well, I can see I'll just have to use a little persuasion…" but one of the boys had said, "Surely you wun't hit a person wearin' glasses, wud you?" and the other had echoed his brother in a slightly more accusatory tone, saying "No, surely you wun't hit someone wearin' glasses?"

Jack had suddenly been reminded of a drawing in Lewis Carroll's 'Through the Looking Glass', which he had read to the twins when they were little. And here were those two fictional characters, Tweedledum and Tweedledee, made very solid flesh right before his eyes. Struck by the absurdity of the image, Jack had let out an involuntary laugh.

One of them had protested indignantly, "T'ain't funny, mister…" and the other had added, "No! T'ain't no laffin' matter… Our Daddy'll kill us if we don't bring his car back. He on'y let uz burrer it t'visit our cuzins down in Vaginya afore the outbreak of hostilities an' we've bin stuck there since…"

Jack had said, "Well, I'm afraid you can't have the gas, I need it. You'll have to get your own…"

Deke had cut in, "We'll buy it from you, mister."

"It's not for sale…" and Zeke had added, "We on'y need a coupl'a cans. Ten gallons shud git uz back t'Geneva…"

"It's not for sale."

"Go on, mister. Ev'rythin's f'sale at the right price…"

"Not in this case…"

Looking a little deflated, Zeke had glared at his brother forlornly and conceded, "Well, we ain't got no money anyhow, ya dumb ass…"

Not wanting to simply abandon the hapless pair in the middle of nowhere to God knows what fate, Jack had said, "How about you ride with me? I could go through Geneva. I'll drop you off there…"

"But what about our Daddy's car?"

Irked by their seeming ingratitude, Jack had cut in testily, "I know, I know… He'll kill you if you don't take it back…" Suddenly, struck by an amusing thought, Jack had said, "I know. I'll buy it off you…"

"T'ain't f'sale…"

"As you said yourself, everything's for sale…"

"Besides, it not ours to sell…"

"…if the price is right… When did your daddy buy it and how much did he pay?"

Zeke had said, "He bought it sometime roun' ninety-four. I think he paid 'bout four thousand dollars f'rit…" but his brother had contradicted him, saying "Oh, I'm sure it was more like ninety-six an' he paid at least five thousand dollars…" until Zeke had finally nailed it down when he'd said conclusively, "No! It was definitely ninety-five… the year Momma went t'Jezus… But I think Deke's right. He did pay five thousand dollars for it."

Jack had said, "Well then, I tell you what I'll do. I'll return your father's original investment and buy it from you for five thousand dollars. He's bound to be impressed when you show him just what good businessmen you are. Now, I can't say fairer than that, can I?"

Zeke had looked at Jack gone out and said incredulously, "What? Five thousand dollars f'that heap'a crap. T'ain't worth more'n a shovelful'a chicken shit!" but his more financially astute sibling had smartly closed the sale by saying, "You jus' bought y'self a mighty fine vee-hickle, mister. So hand over the cash and we'll be off… Or d'ya need t'tow us t'the nearest bank?"

Both boys had been astonished when Jack had gone back to the pick-up and returned a few moments later with five thousand dollars cash in hand. And they'd been even more astounded when, instead of hitching it up to the truck, Jack had driven off and left the dilapidated old Dodge sitting at the side of the road.

Within twenty miles, Jack had had to stop the truck again. This time he'd climbed out and clambered underneath and had seen the problem right away: the bottom hose on the radiator had perished with age and, as a consequence of the increased water pressure developed by the new circulating pump, it had split. At Zeke's suggestion, Jack had tried effecting a temporary repair by wrapping some rags around the hose which he had tied on with the twins' bootlaces, which had stemmed the outflow a little but the benefit had been negated by the fact that the split had continued lengthening and the increasing ambient temperature of the hot summer's day had meant that the engine had overheated sooner, so that their progress had been made in shorter and shorter increments. As a result, Jack had pulled into Geneva in the early hours of Thursday morning. At one point, Deke had shown himself fairly astute at haggling, having bought a torch for one hundred dollars from an owner who had been reluctant to sell it at a house at which they'd stopped to ask for water the previous evening as the light had been fading, which had allowed them to continue on through the night. It had been during this intermission that Jack had thought to ring ahead and let his family know what progress he was making and discovered that he'd lost his mobile phone. When and where he had no idea but he suspected it must have been whilst he'd been scrambling in the ravine, trying to get out. He had cussed in a low voice, "Shee-it", having picked up the colorful expletive from Deke who'd used it at least a dozen times in Jack's hearing. The twins had invited Jack to take breakfast with them, none of them having eaten all day but Jack had declined, stopping just long enough to fill up the water container, down a large cup of strong, black coffee and call his father to let him know that he should be home by mid-morning at the very latest and that they should get off without delay as soon as everybody was ready.

As Jack had driven into Irondequoit along the Culver Road, named after his great grandfather in recognition of his substantial contribution in helping to establish the industry on which much of the prosperity of the thriving local community was based, he had reflected on the tortuous routes taken by many of his clan members to get to where they were today and thought that none could have had any stranger travelling companions than the one's he'd just left behind. There had been a sign stuck to the front door, 'Nicky. Key in usual place. Let yourself in'. Jack had retrieved the key and let himself in. There on the wall directly opposite the door had been another sign, 'Nicky. Go to basement'. Jack had followed the trail to the basement where he'd found a

282

large sign screwed to the wall that had been hand-painted in bold red letters on a sheet of plywood. 'Nicky. We have gone to CABIN. Your mom sister & brother are there. Your dad should be there Friday August 20 latest. If you read this, write your NICKNAME and date below, then make your way DIRECTLY there by our USUAL route. We will try to find you'. It was signed 'Grandpa John' and dated 'Thursday August 19 (06:35)'. Jack had examined the neatly-painted sign closely and noticed it had been carefully worded and laid out with precision before painting, just as he would have expected of his father who was nothing if not meticulous. He had lightly touched the paint of the closing bracket and found that it was still slightly tacky. Beneath the sign had been a pot of red paint, a paintbrush, freshly washed and still with a faint odour of white spirit and a couple of indelible, thick, black marker pens. He thought affectionately that his father had always been one for holding up his trousers with a belt and braces. As he'd stepped back from it again he had noticed the pale tracks down the walls and the tiny piles of concrete dust that had accumulated on the floor beneath the sign, debris from the holes that had been drilled for mounting the sign and had thought, 'He never does anything by halves, God bless him!'

Once the engine had cooled down, Jack set about repairing the leak. He searched the garage but his father had stripped it bare of anything remotely useful and taken it with him to the cabin. Every few minutes Jack popped to the garage door and scanned the drive which sloped gradually down to the lake shore road about quarter of a mile away for any sign of Nicky but there was none. He then went round to the back of the house and looked in all the outbuildings. After a brief inspection, Jack decided that his mother's potting shed held out very little hope of finding anything useful but when he entered the garden shed there, amongst various ride-on lawnmowers and miniature tractors with aerators and feeder attachments and a plethora of other accessories, were a jumble of bicycles festooned in cobwebs, which had once belonged to himself and his brother and sister when they still lived at home. His mother's brand new bicycle, bought seven years ago as part of a short-lived fitness regimen and intended for cycling into town and visiting friends, which had been used once and abandoned because she had been frightened by a passing truck, was still propped against the wall. As he stood sifting through the trove of overlooked gadgets piled high on the shelves an idea came to him. Jack tried the small, fat tires on his mother's bike and found they were flat, so he used his powerful hands to roll the front tire clean off its rim and found that it had an inner tube. Being a folding bike with a dismountable front wheel, he quickly removed it from the forks then undid the nut that retained the valve and stripped the tube off the rim in moments. Jack stretched it as far as he could but it felt as though it still had plenty of life left in it. He rummaged around a little more and found an unused puncture repair kit in the little saddle bag hanging from the stiff leather seat of his father's vintage bicycle.

Jack wriggled his way under the front of the truck. "Hallelujah!" The radiator hose was secured at both ends by Jubilee clips. He returned to the kitchen and took a pair of scissors and a table knife from the cutlery drawer then went back out to the truck and used the rounded tip of the blade like a screwdriver to undo the clips. Careful not to over-strain the hose and worsen the split, Jack removed it then removed from it the rag that was still wrapped round it. He cut the inner tube in half and tried sliding one cut end over the end of the hose but it was marginally too tight to go on. Again, "Hallelujah!" then, "Thank you, God, for granting me one small triumph." He examined the hose and found that the split was about quarter of an inch long. For half an hour Jack carefully dried the hose using a hairdryer he'd found in the guest bedroom. He prepared the surface by gently abrading it then stuck the largest patch from the repair kit over it. 'Will it hold? Or will the hot water soften the adhesive and cause it to fail? If it does, let's hope my second line of defense holds...' and Jack rolled up a length of inner tube approximately twice the length of the hose then unrolled it, condom-fashion, onto the semi-rigid hose. 'If Martha could see me now, I wonder what she'd say?' he thought, laughing to himself. It was the first light-hearted thought Jack had had in three weeks. Fully open there was still plenty of clearance to slip the Jubilee clips on over the ends of the hose so Jack went back to the shed and recovered the inner tube from the rear wheel and doubled the thickness of the outer sleeve. After a few more minutes of foraging he found a roll of duct tape in the greenhouse and spirally wound three overlapping layers round the hose, to prevent the sleeve from swelling under the pressure of the water if the patch gave up the ghost, by which time the Jubilee clips only just fitted. When he'd trimmed the loose ends of the tape flush with the ends of the hose Jack stood admiring his handiwork until he was suddenly jerked back to reality by a cold shudder that ran down his spine and made the hairs on the back of his neck bristle. Instinctively, he spun round and looked down the drive but there was no one there. Disturbed from his reverie he replaced the hose then filled the radiator with water but the sense of unease that had inexplicably come over him stayed with him for the rest of the afternoon and into the evening.

Having repaired the truck Jack started the engine and checked the water level again, which had held up, then emptied the last of the gas from the cans into the tank. He checked the fuel gauge which told him there was slightly more than two-thirds of a tank. He sat gnawing over the problem of whether there was sufficient fuel to get all the way to the cabin and decided there wasn't so he set about repairing the bicycles in the shed. His father's was beyond salvation, the tires and inner tubes having long since perished to the point where they'd lost most of their resilience and the chain being so rusty that the links had fused together but he managed to make something of his old bike and his brother's. He then spent another hour immersed in riding first one then the other up and down the drive, stopping every now and again to make small adjustments to brakes and gears and so on until he'd convinced himself they were both roadworthy. Each time he sailed down towards the gates Jack looked hopefully, willing his son's lanky frame to emerge from amongst the trees but it didn't. He heaved the container of water and both bicycles into the back of the truck then parked it in the garage and locked the door, on the off-chance that looters might come round during the night looking for anything useful they could readily lift.

His mother had thoughtfully left two airtight packs in the kitchen, one marked 'Jack' and the other 'Nicky', food clearly intended for the journey. Even though he'd eaten nothing for more than twenty-four hours Jack felt anything but hungry, being unable to think of food but he took his pack and sat in front of the television with it, to distract his mind away from the vague, indefinable dread that was nagging at the back of his mind. He switched on the TV using the remote control. There were no commercial programs, only a crude sign informing viewers that the next news would be at twenty hundred hours local time. Clearly, the military was still maintaining its iron grip over all public broadcasting. Jack quietly munched the snack, hardly registering what it was he was eating, until the screen flickered and jumped into life. As he watched, Dan Ackland appeared, quietly delivering the same cautious messages about S241 in the same calm, carpet-slippered tones. Irritated by the triteness of the vapid comments which still gave away nothing of the true horror to come, Jack impatiently snatched up the remote control and turned off the TV. He sat in silence for a while then picked up the handset of his parents' cordless house phone and dialled a cellphone number. After a few moments, a voice at the other end said, "Hello?"

"David, it's Jack. I'm just calling to find out how you're doing…"

"Jack! I thought you'd forgotten us. Where are you? Have you found Billy yet?"

Jack gave his erstwhile assistant a brief rundown then asked, "Where are you?"

"I'm still here… At the Observatory… There's a bunch of us. We're still manning the 'scope…"

"Who?"

"Arthur and Angela… And myself, of course…"

"Why, David?"

A little irritated, David replied, "Why not, Jack? Where else do I have to go? A flimsy little condo down on the ocean that'll be completely obliterated by the impact… Arthur's got no one to go home to since his wife died and his son left… And Angela's family's back east. There was no way she could get home…" Jack thought briefly of his attractive research student until David Johnson continued, "Dan's asked us to hold the fort for as long as we can. He's phoning in daily for updates but it's basically the same story. In fact, if anything, it's slightly worse because now the latest projections consistently show S241 coming down about six hundred miles west of San Diego, on roughly the same latitude as the island of Guadalupe…" The two talked for a little while longer, David Johnson confirming that they would all be staying up at the observatory, riding out the impact in the underground control room. "We might just survive the impact down there if the shock doesn't kill us and we don't take a direct hit from a large bomb…"

"And then what?"

With the first hint of fear that Jack had detected in his voice, David Johnson snapped back, "How should I know, Jack? You tell me what we can look forward to when we're interred under ten feet of ejecta…" and then, injecting his own typical brand of gallows humour, he said, "Anyway, one thing's for sure. We'll all be looking for new jobs when this is over because the blast'll blow the observatory clean off the mountain top…"

That night Jack slept fitfully. The following day he roamed restlessly round the house and its vast garden, regularly returning to the front of the house to gaze hopefully down the drive but each time his hopes went unfulfilled. As the Sun passed overhead Jack kept looking at his watch, willing Nicky to arrive before five o'clock which was the very latest time he thought he could delay departure until and still be certain of reaching the cabin safely. At six-twenty-five, feeling bleaker than he'd ever felt before, Jack locked the front door and put the key back in its usual place then climbed into the truck and started the engine. As the electric gates closed behind him, he pulled the truck forwards until its nose nudged out into the road and looked left and right along the lake shore road, half-expecting to see his son come striding into view. As the clock reached six-thirty exactly, with a heavy heart Jack pulled out of the driveway and headed east.

Shortly after passing through Childwold, the engine spluttered. Jack checked the fuel gauge for the thousandth time which confirmed he'd run out of fuel. He swung the steering wheel sharply from side-to-side making the truck weave wildly. The engine briefly picked up again as the last puddles of gasolene sloshed into the fuel outlet, which carried him another mile before it cut out altogether. Jack looked up and down the road but there was nobody about. In the darkness he could make out nothing beyond the pools of light cast by the headlamps; all lights had gone out at midnight as electrical generating capacity shut down, to avoid overloading the national grid as a consequence of the electro-magnetic disturbance that would be caused by S241.

Having cycled this route many times, the first time with his father and brother when he'd been fifteen, Jack knew there was still about forty-five miles to go; he also knew it would probably be futile waiting for someone to come along and offer him a lift because he'd never known the road be so deserted, so he hauled one of the bicycles out of the back of the truck and set off. Three-and-a-half hours later Jack dismounted where the metalled road ran out at the start of the track up to the cabin, his clothes wringing wet with persperation, his thigh muscles stinging with the exertion and the insides of his buttocks sore and aching where they'd pressed hard against the saddle. He checked his watch, the figures illuminated by the eerie blue glow of the back-light – two-forty-two a.m. – then removed the cycle lamp and propped the bicycle against a post and started walking as briskly as his stiff ankle would allow. It took Jack almost an hour to reach the cabin. He'd had to pick his way carefully over some of the rougher sections because the track had been in deep gloom, with the glow from the Moon only penetrating the dense tree cover occasionally and the feeble light from the bicycle lamp being virtually useless in the unremitting darkness.

As the track emerged from the trees Jack could see the cabin which stood out a slightly lighter shade of phosphorescent gray against its dark backdrop but the front door was open and through the small windows Jack could see the dull yellow glow of the oil lamps that lit up the interior. He stood for a minute, trying to imagine life before modern technology filled people's lives with instant heat and light, comfort and convenience, all thanks to fossil fuels and nuclear energy and electricity and cars and telephones and the Internet and microwave ovens and washing machines and dishwashers and... and... and... And he realised that they might just find out at first hand what it had been like in those pioneering days. As he stared, he thought he could make out a movement at one end of the porch, a faint, rhythmical change in the density of the dark shadows. He realised that someone was sitting on the swing seat, rocking backwards and forwards.

Claudette sat deep in thought, idly pushing herself backwards with the tips of her toes each time the seat swung back, to maintain her momentum, her sense of despair and deep sense of loss starting to take physical shape. The night was still and quiet, broken by the occasional hoot of an owl. Just then she heard a crunching sound from the darkness beyond the porch, a heavy footfall in the gravel outside the pool of weak yellow light cast from the open door. She halted the swing and sat stock still, not knowing what nature of creature might be watching her or, more probably, scenting her from the shadows and imagined the worst, most frightening sort. As it came closer

Claudette was about to scream when she thought she could make out the faint outline of someone tall coming towards the cabin, walking with a slight limp. At first she had the vague impression that it was her twin brother but then she realised it was her father. Claudette leaped up. She ran to the steps and jumped down onto the gravel and ran to meet her father screaming, "DADDY! DADDY! DADDY!"

As Jack entered the pool of light Claudette threw her arms around his neck, sobbing with delight. Jack hugged his precious daughter more tightly than he'd ever held her before. Within moments Martha appeared on the porch followed by his mother and father. They all swept down the steps to greet him with his grandfather slowly bringing up the rear. Jack unwrapped one arm from around his daughter and wrapped it tightly round his wife, drawing her to him and kissing the top of her head repeatedly. When he looked down momentarily, he saw his mother standing in front of him, head bowed, tears streaming down her drawn face. He let go of Martha and Claudette and put both arms round his mother and said in a soothing voice, "Hush, Mom. Don't cry. Everything will be alright..." but between sobs his mother said, "Don't say that, Son... How will they be? Things'll never be right again..."

Suddenly, Claudette said, "Where's Nicky, Dad?" and Jack said forlornly, "He never turned up, darling. I waited as long as I could... longer, in fact... but eventually I had to set off without him or I'd never have made it up here. I'm only just in time as it is..."

Hurt, Claudette burst into tears and scolded him accusingly, "How could you leave him? How could you?"

Before Jack could speak, Martha said quietly, "Don't be cross with your father, Claudette. It's my fault! I should never have let Nicky go off like that..." but Jack cut in firmly, "Stop it, Martha! It's no one's fault! Nicky's old enough to make his own decisions and stand by them..." but secretly he thought, 'I only hope he's old enough to look out for himself...' Suddenly realising there was someone missing, Jack looked round the group. "Where's Billy?"

After a moment's hush, Jack's father said, "He's gone up to the old watchtower..."

Jack exclaimed angrily, "What! Why didn't you stop him?" then, looking at his watch, "For Christ's sake, S241 comes down in... in fifty-seven minutes... The ejecta starts arriving twenty-five minutes later... It takes at least twenty minutes to get up there in broad daylight, never mind in pitch dark..."

Jack's grandfather cut in, "Billy's been going up there every night. He insisted on going tonight even though Martha told him not to. He knows the route like the back of his hand. He can do it in the dark in eighteen minutes or so he says, although he's puffing a bit by the time he gets back."

Jack quickly ushered everyone into the cabin and told his father to get them all down into the bear pit – a basement with thick concrete walls and a heavy door set in the floor above, put in as somewhere to hole up in the event of an attack by a black bear rather than having to shoot the dumb animal, although it had never been used for that purpose – whilst he picked up a torch and tested it for brightness. "I'm going up there to get him."

Winded and sweating profusely from the steady climb, Jack looked up at the silhouette of the old fire lookout tower set against the night sky. He briefly remembered back to when he'd first come here as a child, when the tower had been manned by solitary rangers watching for forest fires in what had seemed to Jack a very romantic job but it had since been abandoned as remote sensing technology had overtaken this simple human enterprise. The first two flights of stairs had been removed some time ago, to prevent access but someone had lashed a ladder to the support pylon so that it bridged the gap. Jack put his foot on the bottom rung then leaned back pulling heavily on the ladder but it felt as fast as a church so he began to climb. His ankle throbbed from its injury and from the night's exertions. He cleared the ladder and wearily climbed the stairs to the crow's nest about forty-five feet above ground level. As he entered the square, wooden cabin with its glass walls on all four sides, Jack could make out the small figure of his son standing at the window staring intently towards the west but before Jack could say anything a small, detached voice in the darkness quietly said, "Hello Dad".

–•–

His wristwatch beeped insistently. Graham Tandy slowly roused himself from his slumber and turned off the alarm, set for two-thirty a.m. Mountain time. His neck and back ached from having lain in an awkward position, even though he had arranged the musty old blankets as comfortably as he could in the bottom of the rowing boat. He gradually eased himself up until he was sitting on the seat then lit the hurricane lamp and shrugged on his battered, waxed cotton jacket which he'd been using as a blanket to keep out the cool night air. He poured himself a cup of coffee from the flask and took a sip. It still held some vestige of warmth, less than he'd have liked to drive the chill from his old bones but he reflected that it had been made for nearly twelve hours.

He'd set off from the landing stage at three-thirty the previous afternoon. He had motored out, the small outboard motor putt-putting quietly in the still afternoon, until the lakeshore village had almost disappearred from view, to where he knew the water was deep, deep and cold enough to harbour his arch enemy, *Salvelinus namaycush*, the Mackinaw, or lake trout, a close relative of the Arctic char and a non-native species that had been introduced to Yellowstone Lake by an environmetal saboteur in the early nineties that predated mercilessly on the smaller, native, cutthroat trout, *Oncorhynchus clarki bouvieri*. He had baited the hook then swung out his rod, the reel paying out about thirty yards of line before the weights plopped into the still water. He'd waited for it to sink before trawling it slowly back towards the boat. He had known that something big lurking in the depths had taken the bait when the rod jerked and twitched violently. He had tugged the line once to ensure he'd firmly hooked his prey before reeling it in. As the taut line had hung vertically from the end of his bouncing rod, bent under the load and the thrashing fish had broken the surface, its dark green skin mottled with bright silver spots, Graham Tandy had known that he'd apprehended the most serious villain in the lake and had taken comfort from this fact when he'd slipped his landing net under it and hauled it into the boat then dispatched it with a single sharp blow to the head before packing it in ice in his cool box. Having spent most of his leisure time pursuing this particularly treacherous repeat offender which could devour up to a hundred or more of his precious cutthroats per year and was gradually beginning to get the upper hand despite concerted efforts at managing it, Graham Tandy had developed an almost uncanny knack for finding and catching it and doing so gave him far greater satisfaction than any other pastime. He had continued fishing and caught half-a-dozen in fairly quick succession, killing the last two before throwing them back because he had no more room in his cool box.

As the afternoon sun had started to sink lower in the sky, Graham Tandy had packed up his gear and started the motor and headed off to his favorite fishing spot. When he'd arrived, the Sun gently warming his weathered face, he had shut off the motor, letting the boat drift slowly to a halt. He had looked over the side and, directly below him through the clear water, he had seen those streamlined silver shapes gliding effortlessly over a backdrop of delicate green fronds: his prized Yellowstone cutthroat trout. As he'd taken off his hat and removed a gaudily-colored fly from the hatband, one of hundreds that he'd tied himself on the dark winter's evenings when the lake had been frozen over making fishing impossible, he had heard the faint plopping sound characteristic of fish rising to take midges and mosquitoes from the surface and had seen the concentric rings radiating out from the tiny patches of bubbles and he'd known that this was his special place; almost a place of pilgrimage for this quiet, unassuming, modest man. He had deftly tied the fly to the line then worked it out over the lake, expertly casting in ever larger loops until he had positioned it exactly where he wanted it, then landed it softly on the water. With no perceptible current to move the fly, Graham Tandy had inched it towards the boat until there had been a sudden flurry at the surface and he'd briefly caught a glimpse of a silver back as the fish had taken the fly then dived again. Finding its progress rudely arrested the fish had jinked about, darting here and there. Graham Tandy had played out a little line so that it had gradually tired itself out. When he'd decided that it had lost some of its initial fight, he slowly wound in the line until the fish had come alongside the boat. Finding itself defeated, the fish had calmly allowed its captor to lift it into the boat where Graham Tandy had carefully removed the hook from its mouth then admired this beautiful silvery-yellow creature with the two red gashes on its lower jaw from which it took its name and a rash of large, dark spots which were concentrated on its dorsal fin and over its tail, before weighing and measuring it and recording the information in his notebook. He had then lowered it back over the side and held it lovingly whilst the life-giving water pumped through its gills. Once it had recovered sufficiently, it had swum lazily out of his hands and back into the yellow-green depths.

As the light changed he had sculled backwards and forwards over the dome, each time stopping at places where he thought the Sun's slanting rays provided the fish cruising amongst the weeds below with their best view of the flies on the surface. Eventually, as the Sun had sunk low over the horizon, he had laid his rods across the seats and taken out a pack of sandwiches and sat quietly eating, all the while staring at a faded photograph of a strikingly attractive girl in a large hat and flowery summer dress sitting demurely on the edge of a fountain with her bare feet in the water. When he'd finished eating, he had put the photograph carefully back into his wallet then taken a book from his backpack and begun reading. As the Sun had set he'd lit the lamp and continued reading, breaking off long enough to enjoy watching the twilight fade to night before resuming. He had been woken by the sound of the book dropping into the bottom of the boat. The gibbous Moon had been overhead with about seven-eighths of its visible disk illuminated, giving the lake's surface an almost luminous quality. He had calculated that there were about four hours to go before S241 collided with the Earth, so he'd set the alarm on his wristwatch, arranged the blankets that he'd brought along specially for the occasion and laid down on them, turned out the lamp and fallen asleep within minutes.

Now, as his watch told him it was two-forty-two a.m. on the morning of Saturday, August twenty-first, two-thousand-and-ten, Graham Tandy turned out the hurricane lamp again then wondered why he'd bothered doing so. 'It's hardly going to spoil my view of the lightshow to come…' and he sat calmly in the little wooden boat looking over the stern towards the south-west. He thought how serene the lake was, with not a breath of wind, the surface unruffled and smooth as ice. Suddenly, silently, the whole, immense panorama was illuminated by an intense light below the south-western horizon, burning more fiercely than fifty Suns, putting the Teton Range in sharp silhouette with Mount Moran slightly left of center and Grand Teton peeping over its left shoulder and behind them the looming bulk of the Rocky Mountains. As the fireball grew, the radiation steadily encroached on Graham Tandy who had involuntarily stood up in his boat as the awesome and dreadful spectacle revealed itself to the world, making dark night far brighter than the brightest day filled with the shadows of giants. As quickly as it had come on the brilliance dimmed as the airborne ejecta blocked some of the light.

Graham Tandy sat slowly back down on the plank seat and waited; he knew that events would now unfold very quickly and very decisively. The tranquility of his life lasted for just eight minutes more before it was shattered forever, never to be regained. As he watched, a wave raced across the lake towards him driven by the seismic disturbance of the Earth's crust that radiated out from the impact site, the water at its broad crest dancing wildly. As it passed beneath him, the flimsy little boat was tossed about violently, nearly pitching him out, leaving him sprawled helplessly on his back in the bottom of the boat as it did a wild jig. Whether the broadside of ejecta would have killed him or the air blast followed by the supersonic winds would have crushed him or capsized his little craft and drowned him is immaterial. Before the water had had chance to calm the crust beneath the lake bottom rumbled and rose up. With a mighty roar a solid jet of rocks and tephra propelled by superheated steam from the magma chamber three-and-a-half kilometers below the surface, blasted the charred fragments of Graham Tandy and his little boat and his beloved Yellowstone cutthroat trout thousands of feet up into the air to become part of the giant eruption column of the Yellowstone volcano.

—•—

Jack went over and stood by his son and leaned on the sill. "Hello Billy." Billy continued staring out of the window. Father and son stood in silence, Jack shoulder-to-shoulder with Billy. Eventually, Jack said, "When did you know for sure, Billy? About S241, I mean… And how could you be so certain you were right?"

"I've always known something big was going to happen for as long as I can remember. Not what exactly or when but something… All I could do was make sure I was ready for it, whatever it was…" then, after a brief pause, Billy continued, "I'd been following S241 round the Solar system since April thirtieth, which is when I first saw it… Of course, I didn't give it that name, you did. To me it was just another asteroid. I called it 'Titleist five-iron'. Titleist after your golf balls because it's round and five-iron because it was the fifth one of its kind I'd seen and it's made of iron. I tracked it for the next eighty-nine nights whenever I could see it… It wasn't until July twenty-ninth that I knew there was almost a hundred percent certainty of it hitting Earth. I just couldn't figure out where exactly. My measurements weren't good enough to work that out accurately… I knew I could stay and take more sightings but then I might not have got away in time…"

Jack said incredulously, "But that was two weeks before we knew for certain, Billy. What made you so sure it would actually hit the Earth? So sure it made you run away?"

"The dolphins… The dolphins confirmed it for me… When I heard the dolphins were leaving the Pacific, I knew I was right… They told me where it would come down…"

After a brief pause Jack said, "You say if you'd waited any longer before leaving, you might not have got away in time… In time for what, Billy?"

"To save us, of course." All the time, Billy continued staring resolutely into the west.

Jack let out a little laugh and shook his head in wonder. "Why didn't you tell me about Titleist five-iron, Billy?"

"I didn't need to. You already knew about it. I saw your file on S241 on the arm of your chair one evening when you went to pour yourself another drink. I recognised the coordinates at once."

Looking at his watch, Jack said, "Anyway, come on Billy. We'd better get back now whilst there's still plenty of time…" but Billy said adamantly, "No, Dad, I'm not going. I want to see this…"

"But…"

"This is what I've been waiting for all my life. I'm not going to miss it now. You go if you like. I'll come after…"

"Billy, you won't see very much. It's coming down three thousand miles away, well below the horizon…"

"I know! But whatever there is to see, I want to see it."

Knowing it would be well nigh impossible to coerce Billy into doing something he didn't want to do, Jack said, "You understand, Billy, we must go back to the cabin as soon as S241 comes down?" and Billy simply said, "Yes Dad, I know."

As they stood at the window, Jack noticed that the panes on this point of the compass were spotlessly clean inside and out – all the others were still coated with years of grime. He assumed Billy had done this in anticipation of tonight's viewing. Jack was distracted by a barely audible drone that broke the otherwise total silence. Billy was standing absolutely motionless gazing intently through the glass and Jack was watching his son's profile equally intently. Billy's lips moved constantly and, as Jack moved closer, he could hear his son muttering almost imperceptibly under his breath, "…two-five-six, two-o-four, nine-five-one…yes… two-five-six, two-o-four, nine-nine-seven… yes… two-five-six, two-o-five, o-o-nine… yes… two-five-six, two-o-five, o-three-nine… yes…"

Jack exclaimed, "Billy! What are you doing?"

Surprised by the sudden interruption, Billy mumbled, "What? Er… Oh… That. It's just a habit, something I do to pass the time…"

"You're counting in primes, aren't you? You must have counted over ten million by now…"

"Fourteen million, one hundred and seven… But I'm not just counting primes. I'm checking my proof of Riemann's Hypothesis… Checking that each one lies on Riemann's ley line, as he predicted…"

Flabbergasted by Billy's revelation, Jack asked, "And do they?"

"So far, yes."

"And how far will you go, Billy? Don't forget, there's an infinite number of primes…"

For the first time, Billy turned and looked at his father. After a few moments he said quizzically, "I don't know… I never asked myself that question, so I never thought of stopping…"

Jack took hold of Billy's shoulders firmly in his powerful hands and looked his son square in the face. He said gently, "Don't you think it's time to stop now, Billy?"

Billy stood gazing into his father's eyes. Jack could only guess at what might be going on in his son's mind. After a while, Billy said quietly, "Yes". Jack put his arms around the small boy and hugged Billy closely to him. Billy put his arms around his father's waist and buried his face deep in his chest and, for the first time in his life, Billy wept. Jack could feel his small body wracked with sobs, quivering from its very core, as the dam broke and the vast reservoir of pent-up tension and anxiety that had accumulated over the years spilled out. Jack hugged his son tightly to him. Once the flood had subsided and Billy had calmed he said, "I think I'm ready to go now, Dad." Jack looked at his watch. His own fatalistic curiosity having been stirred, he said, "There's only a couple of minutes to go and we're here now son. It'd be a shame to miss it. There's not likely to be another show like this in our lifetimes. In fact, probably not for another four billion years… Are you sure you don't want to wait and see it?"

"No, I don't think so."

Although he knew that Billy must have been up and down the ladder dozens of times, Jack insisted on going down first. Billy followed him. As he reached the bottom the alarm on his wristwatch went off and Billy reset it, saying, "Impact! We'll still have to run. We haven't got that much head start

294

on it…" Up above, in the crow's nest, the ghost of Billy's former self stood transfixed, watching the false dawn break in the west as the faint glow appeared over the southern flanks of Mount Marcy. Billy hurriedly keyed another time into his alarm then father and son set off, Jack shining the torch ahead of them and Billy panting out a constant stream of warnings as they ran in the dark. "Watch it! It's slippy here… Mind the rocks… Hands up! Overhanging branches…" Jack stumbled and slipped a couple of times and once he went down heavily, winding himself as he hit the ground but fortunately it was soft turf and he did no serious damage other than jarring his injured ankle. Billy helped him up and urged him on, "Come on, Dad, we mustn't fall behind" but the injury was hurting and it slowed Jack down a little.

As they entered the small clearing above the cabin, the alarm on Billy's watch went off again and Billy grabbed his father's arm and barked out a command, "Stop! Get down!" Jack could just make out a tiny yellow light in the distance. He gasped, "No! It's there, Billy… The cabin… Keep going!" but Billy tugged his father's arm so sharply it brought him down. Billy dropped down beside him. As Jack sprawled on the ground he gasped out, "What the hell…" but at that moment the very earth beneath them moved so violently that, had Jack been standing up, it would have taken his feet from under him. Instinctively, Jack grabbed Billy and dragged him underneath himself and the two of them remained like that, father shielding son, their ears filled with the shrill screams of terrified animals and the frenzied creaking and rustling of the trees, interspersed with loud reports as dead trunks and large limbs cracked and snapped, until the tremor passed.

Jack pushed himself up on his arms. Billy scrambled out from under his father. He jumped up and said urgently, "Come on, Dad. Only two more minutes from here…" and they got up and ran for their lives, Jack lagging behind his fleet son. Jack gasped out, "Run, Billy! Run!" As Jack reached the bottom of the path, he could just make out his son's outline as Billy reached the lamp which his father had thoughtfully left standing in front of the cabin a few yards from the stoop as a beacon to guide them home. Billy held it up and Jack could hear him shouting hoarsely, "Keep going Dad! Keep going!" Jack slowed down just long enough to put his arm round Billy's shoulder and steer him towards the cabin. As they mounted the steps, Jack noticed that someone had closed the shutters. They went inside and Billy held the lamp whilst Jack shut the heavy door then locked and barred it, bringing to a close forever the final chapter of their old lives.

Afterthought:

Kill every Christian, destroy every church, burn all copies of the Bible and expunge any reference to it and Christianity wouldn't exist; within a very short time – a few generations at most – it wouldn't even be a memory. Likewise, kill every Muslim, destroy every mosque, burn all copies of the Koran and expunge any reference to it and within a very short time Islam wouldn't exist either. The same holds true for any religion. Such is the fragility, the impermanence and, ultimately, the inconsequentiality of all religions. Strip away all of this and the only thing that remains – that stands immutable – is God.

Kill every human being and the Earth would still keep turning on its axis, spinning through space on its endless orbit round the Sun.

If you want a child to have any appreciation of God's power, don't give it a copy of the Bible or the Koran or any other religious book written by the hand of man. Give a child a telescope: let it witness the awesome might of God's creation for itself.

Anything that has been written down or is taught or propagated by men starts corrupt and becomes more corrupt with age and use or, more likely, misuse. Only by discovering God for itself does a child stand any chance of remaining pure in heart.

If, in your soul, you truly believe in God you don't need to subscribe to any particular brand of religion to witness your faith; if you don't, no amount of religion will change that.

And finally: A Deist's view on religion

When I sat down to write this story I started with two things: Firstly, the ending, which (not wanting to sound too dramatic) came to me in a dream. Immediately I began to put it down (from the beginning), the rest – the storyline, characters and everything else – flowed intuitively. I had a story to tell and I had no hesitation in telling it. In fact, the only section I struggled with was this last one and that was not *how* to write it, but *whether* to write it. And, secondly, a deep-seated unease about and distrust of revealed religions – that is, religions that claim at their inception to be based on revelations by God to man – their purpose, their influence on men now and throughout history, and the direction in which they're taking mankind. If, like a good meal, you've enjoyed this book and feel comfortably satiated, you might like to put it aside now and relax and reflect on the subtle piquancy of its underlying message. However, if you're still hungry for more, read on. The remainder is my view on religion, which you might like to think about in the context of this story. [Of course, religion isn't the only cause of conflict in this story but it certainly polarises the opposing sides. Consult any news media and, more often than not, the headline stories are about conflict: between Shi'ites and Sunnis; Muslims and Jews or Christians; Catholics and Protestants; Sikhs and Hindus… So the depressingly long list goes on. And every instinct tells you it isn't all going to end happily. The common factor that defines the opposing factions is religion.] If, when you're part-way through it, you find it a bit tough and indigestible, leave the rest; I won't be offended. And so to it!

When I was at (a Church of England) senior school in the early 1970s I was excluded from Religious Education classes (with my agreement, I might add) not because I was irreligious or disinterested but because, instead of simply copying out and learning verbatim passages and stories from the Bible, which is what passed for RE at that time, I wanted to know about the provenance of the Bible, its history, its authority and its relevance and, most significantly, what proof there was that the Bible was the *literal* Word of God as it is claimed to be by Christians. None of my questions were answered satisfactorily, if at all, the instruction to me being that I should take the Bible unquestioningly at face value and accept it as an act of faith, which I could not do. It now seems to me that most people who do so either do so out of habit, primarily because of their upbringing and education, or who do so out of fear of exclusion, or who come (or come back) to it in their introspective search for some meaning to their life and, having found (or 're-discovered') it, cling to it like a drowning man clings to a lifebelt in a fathomless ocean. And so be it if, having found your faith, your soul is at peace; you're entitled to your own beliefs. But what of those whose religion makes them intolerant, intent on denying others of different faiths their

297

beliefs, or fires their distrust and hatred of others whose beliefs are different? If Israelis and Palestinians, for instance, simply accepted God without polarising their respective camps by being Jews or Muslims, what would prevent them from agreeing to share the land and living together peacefully in homogeneous, mixed communities? Instead, what do they do? Israel erects a 400-mile-long barrier to segregate the two groups of human beings from each other, ostensibly to deny Palestinian suicide bombers access to Israel but also virtually guaranteeing that the two groups will never find sufficient common ground between themselves for reconciliation, at least whilst the barrier remains. The situation of Protestants and Catholics in Northern Ireland has strong parallels, although here there has been movement towards reconciliation in recent years. Thankfully! But at what cost? And so the depressingly long list goes on.

It was in thinking about the Bible and other holy books as the basis of revealed religions that the seeds of this book were sown. However, it was as a result of observing man's behaviour in the name of religion that those seeds germinated to produce my strong aversion to it.

My growing skepticism about religion has been driven by two things operating in parallel: Firstly, as science provides sound and substantial proof of the nature of the Universe and everything in it, based on minutely detailed observations of the physical World (proof that is constantly being challenged and exhaustively tested but which continues to hold up under rigorous scrutiny), the contrary position that the Church has taken over various issues by its insistence on clinging to a literal interpretation of scripture – that is, what it says in the Bible – has made it look increasingly out-of-touch and less relevant in the modern world. One example is the Catholic Church's treatment of Galileo Galilei who was tried for heresy by the Inqisition in 1633 and found guilty for his support of Copernican theory which stated that the Earth and other celestial planets revolve around the Sun, something that had been arrived at by Nicolaus Copernicus as early as 1514 (and by others before him) after observing the motions of the planets but which was not published until 1543 – the year of his death – for fear of the Church's retribution. On pain of torture and death, the Inquisition *persuaded* Galileo to recant his (correct) belief, arrived at scientifically after careful observation of what was actually happening in the Heavens (something that was there for any one to see, if they cared to look). Galileo's punishment was house arrest until his death in 1642. ["Well, of course the Earth orbits the Sun..." I hear you say. "Every child leaves elementary school armed with that basic knowledge". Yes! But no thanks to the Catholic Church. Had it been left to the Church Fathers, we would still be living in ignorance of that simple truth even now, believing in a very limited and geocentric Universe in which the Sun and local planets revolve around a fixed

298

Earth.] And if you don't believe that the Inquisitor's threats were real consider the fate of another Italian astronomer, Giordano Bruno, who was burned at the stake in February 1600 for heresy. Why? Because, amongst other things, Bruno's (correct) beliefs that the Earth orbits the Sun and that our solar system exists in an infinite (i.e. immeasurably large) Universe filled with 'a Plurality of Worlds' conflicted with the Church's own doctrine; he also argued (correctly) that the stars we see at night are just like our own Sun. Irrespective of their scientific merit and the quintessential truth contained in them, Galileo's and Bruno's works were put on the Church's *Index Librorum Prohibitorum* which prohibited their publication. It was only due to the determination of brave individuals intent on seeking for the truth – and not without very real risk to themselves – that these works were brought to our attention at all. ["So what?" you might say. "That's ancient history. Get a life, Grandad! My church is a real cool and funky place where young people sing along to guitar music and jive in the aisles."] So what is, or was, the Church's position on this? It wasn't until October 1992, three-hundred-and-fifty years after the death of Galileo (and long after the fact that the Earth orbits the Sun had been irrefutably proven and widely accepted) that Pope John Paul II admitted that the Catholic Church had been wrong about Copernicanism. WRONG! I doubt this was much comfort to Galileo (who, coincidentally, was a devout Catholic) and I'm fairly sure it offered none to Bruno. So, without overdoing it, let's consider a more contemporary example: There had been much heated debate in scientific circles about the age of the Earth (and the Universe) for hundreds of years. However, it wasn't until recently, as a result of the discovery of radioactivity and dating techniques based on the rate of decay of naturally-occurring isotopes, that the age of the Earth has been arrived at with any precision. The figure most commonly agreed upon by experts in the field for the age of the Earth, which has stood unchallenged since 1956 after the most painstaking scientific investigation, is 4.55 billion years plus or minus 70 million years, in a Universe that is between 10 and 20 billion years old, although the latest estimate (arrived at in February 2003 by a team from NASA and the Goddard Space Flight Center in Maryland, based on the results of an incredibly accurate and detailed survey of space carried out by a new satellite called the Wilkinson Microwave Anisotropy Probe) puts it more precisely at 13.7 billion years give or take 100 million years. So what is the Church's official take on this? I don't know... but what I do know is that there are factions in the church today which insist that the Earth is about *six thousand years old*. Why? Because in 1650, James Ussher, Archbishop of Armagh and Primate of All Ireland, counted the number of generations mentioned in the Old Testament going back to Adam and Eve (all that begatting!) and the creation of Heaven and Earth, allowing so many years for each generation. The net result was that Bishop Ussher pronounced that God created the Earth in the year 4004BC (on the evening preceding

October 23 to be precise, although the exact hour is in dispute). But why, you may ask, should I (or indeed anyone) get so het up about that? Because exactly as the Church's geocentric (and completely WRONG) view of the Universe was arrived at through a literal interpretation of two-thousand-year-old scripture, so too was an age for the Earth of six thousand years. [It's interesting to note that, even in 1650, there were Biblical scholars who argued (with good reason) that the Hebrew text of the Old Testament from which Ussher had worked was less reliable than the alternative Greek translation – the Septuagint – and the Samaritan Pentatuech which, using the same method, dated Creation differently. I mention this not to impress you with my diligence but simply to highlight the fact that there was widespread disagreement about the accuracy of the Bible even then and it isn't becoming more accurate with time. If anything, the passage of time further obscures the origins of the Bible, making it more difficult to properly determine its provenance because, unlike the background microwave radiation measured by NASA's probe to determine the age of the Universe, which still persists in pristine condition today, 13.7 billion years after the Big Bang in which it was created, any earthly evidence of the origin of the Bible has either already been lost to us forever or is turning to dust as you're reading this.] But what is really frightening about this, to the extent that it becomes sinister, is that far from treating the Bible stories as allegorical there are rigid factions in the church which insist that it is taken literally – that is to say, *as an absolute truth* – and furthermore insist that school children are taught that the Earth is actually six thousand years old to the exclusion of all other possibilities and that this is to be enforced by law. And all this is based solely on their narrow (and narrow-minded) interpretation of the Bible – a text which the Church has already acknowledged as being so spectacularly WRONG about something so fundamental as the arrangement of our solar system; something that is also so much more readily observable and so much easier to determine than the age of the Earth. In truth, if men had blindly accepted everything in the Bible unquestioningly, we would be as ignorant today of the Universe and its workings as people were two thousand years ago.

Secondly, there is the Bible itself, on which the Church and the whole of Christianity is founded. The notion that God would reveal Himself to man *at all* beggars my belief, let alone would choose to do so *through a book*. But for God to do so through such a disparate jumble of fabulous, fantastical, brutal, barbaric, squalid, monotonous, dismal, petty and pointless writings that has been cobbled together to make up much of the Bible stretches my imagination beyond breaking point. Moreover, the Bible in turn makes God look vengeful, vindictive, spiteful, malicious, cruel, petty and jealous – in other words, filled with human weakness – and, above all, the dupe of the Devil, none of which I can reconcile with the awesome reality and overwhelming beauty of Creation.

That there was a person called Jesus of Nazareth, son of Mary, and Joseph the carpenter, is highly likely. That Jesus was called 'messiah' which (I think) meant spiritual leader in ancient Hebrew, who preached in the name of one almighty God and spoke of freedom from oppression for the poor and down-trodden and was crucified for taking a contrary stance to the established church (compare the fate of Giordano Bruno) is also highly likely. However, that's where likelihood ends and conjecture, speculation and invention – in other words, fable – begins. The central tenets of the Christian faith are not just impossible to prove, which is why it's called a 'faith' (because you accept these things without proof) but in the main appear to have been manufactured by the Church for its own convenience. Moreover, in editing the Bible, the Church appears to have taken those writings it thought would best serve its purposes and, by applying the wildest interpretation, has attached to them meanings that the original may never have had. I am not sufficiently knowledgeable about the Bible to analyse every chapter and verse (then again, I doubt that very many Christians are either), so I will not embarrass myself here by trying to do so. But what evidence is there to support the Church's assertion that Jesus was the Son of God in the divine sense that they attach to it, as opposed to Jesus being the son of God in the same sense that we are all sons and daughters of God? What evidence is there of the virgin birth? Merely the dreams of an old man, that he had been visited by the Angel of the Lord telling him that his wife was with child by God. Consider this scenario which is far more likely if you imagine it in the context of the social and political conditions prevailing at the time: That instead of Mary being a virgin which (I think) simply meant young girl in ancient Hebrew, Mary had been the teenage whore of a Roman soldier, sold to him by her parents who were too poor to support their entire family, who kicked her out when she became pregnant and, being ignorant of her delicate condition, was then taken on by a lonely old man to be a comfort to him in his twilight years. If you were Joseph wouldn't you want your young bride to be pregnant by God, rather than by one of your enemies from the occupying force? And if you were Mary, wouldn't you go along with that for the sake of your own welfare and that of your child? And if the so-called "virgin birth" really happened in the way I've just postulated then every other fabulous claim made by the Christian Church about Jesus Christ has also been manufactured. But most significantly of all for me: Why would God need such an unambitious feat to convince man of His greatness when the whole of Creation bears witness to God's greatness? The reason the Church needs such a claim to stick is to give credibility to the rest of its fantastical story.

So why, if I believe in a live-and-let-live credo, do I have such a bug up my ass where religion is concerned. Why don't I just shut up and let others get on with their own lives as they see fit? Why bother saying anything against it? Because whilst ever man is burdened with religion, I cannot foresee a time when men will truly be free, or happy, or responsible for themselves and their actions; because, instead of looking outward to the Universe and everything in it to witness God's greatness, men are looking inward, poring over dusty, antiquated tomes trying in vain to find a truth that isn't there or, worse still, looking at their fellow men and wishing or even planning to visit harm on them because they have a different faith and are therefore considered to be heretics or infidels. Certainly, these are troubled times with people living in fear because of the distrust, hatred and violence engendered between people of different religions (or even between different sects of the same religion).

I believe God gave man free will, amongst other things, to choose what he believes in and reason to be applied before making that choice. And if you're a Christian or a Muslim then you believe in the Bible or the Koran as being the *literal* Word of God. You cannot pick-and-choose which bits to believe – you either believe the whole of it or you don't believe any of it for, if it is the Word of God, God isn't going to be honest with you over this matter but deceive you over that matter. However, neither you, nor I, nor the most fervent believer, nor the most ardent atheist, can prove or disprove that one or other holy book is or is not the Word of God; you can only accept that it is as an act of faith or not (although how both the Bible *and* the Koran can claim to be the Word of God when one contradicts the other over fundamental issues central to each religion God alone knows; only God could resolve that conundrum... And therein lies the reason why revealed religion is so pernicious: because each one claims to be the *only* truth, to the exclusion of all others, therefore every other religion *must be* a lie deliberately set out by men to deceive other men.) And how can someone who is a true believer, having nailed their colors to the mast of one particular religion or another, suddenly doubt it as a result of my ranting, however persuasive the arguments against it might seem to an uncommitted onlooker? [My guess is that, whether or not they applied any reason to their choice of it in the first place (and they probably didn't), having accepted their religion most believers would simply close their mind to any other point of view (probably telling themselves they were being tempted into infidelity by the Devil by even entertaining such thoughts), so they would never go so far as applying reason to question their beliefs. NB: At this point, it might be useful to remind yourself that all this ranting is about men's acceptance of and adherence to a particular brand of religion, NOT about the fundamental issue of their belief in God, which is an entirely different thing.] It is interesting to note that two of the three great monotheistic (i.e. one God) religions, Christianity and Islam, both believe in Satan or the Devil. [I cannot comment on the third monotheistic religion, Judaism, which stems from the same root because I know very little about it.] Personally, I think the Devil is a purely human invention, to explain or possibly even excuse the dark side of man's nature. But just suppose that if, instead of it being the word of God, the Bible actually turned out to be the work of the Devil, set out purposely to confound man's reason and rob him of his free will; in short, to bend men to the Devil's will. And having seen how effective this strategy was wouldn't it be even more ironical if, instead of the Angel Gabriel handing down the Word of God to the Prophet Mohammed, it had been the Devil whispering the text of the Koran in Mohammed's ear. What more cunning or effective ploy could the Devil have dreamed up for corrupting God's creature? And if that was the Devil's intention then it's certainly worked, considering the chasm that exists between different religions and the things men do to each other in the name of religion.

I can only guess that devout Jews and Muslims who profess to believe in God *actually do believe* in God. And I can only guess that when Israelis and Palestinians look at each other they see Jews and Muslims – adherents of Judaism and Islam. And I can only guess that each sees in the other an infidel; an unbeliever – someone who does not truly believe in God, in *the one true* God, in *their* God – because the other is of a different faith. But why? What do they think the One God would see if He looked down? [My guess is that a Jew would think God would see His chosen people, beset by devils, valiantly defending the one true faith, whilst a Muslim would think that God would see His true believers, beset by devils, valiantly defending the one true faith… which is impossible, because there can only be one true *anything*; everything else is false.] Stand an Israeli Jew and a Palestinian Muslim side-by-side, strip them naked, and it would be difficult to tell them apart. Strip away from them the clutter of religion and make them contemplate each other quietly and I suspect that each would simply see in the other a human being with the same physical, emotional and spiritual needs, who probably wouldn't mind being next-door neighbours. The same probably goes for Catholics and Protestants, too. And so the list goes on. [As an aside, it is interesting to note, for example, the position of the Catholic Church on the troubles in Northern Ireland. Even at the height of the sectarian killings, the Pope was strangely quiet on the subject. I certainly don't remember him damning the Catholic perpetrators to Hell (irrespective of what the other side was doing) and threatening to ex-communicate anyone who participated in violence. It would appear that the Church takes a very relaxed view of God's sixth commandment (and the most important one regarding men's relationship with their fellow men): "Thou shalt not kill".]

But all of this still doesn't get to the very heart of my antipathy towards revealed religions. So where to start? With the Bible and the other holy books, I suppose. Keith Moser described the Bible to me as "God's inspired message to

303

man". I haven't read the Bible from cover to cover but in none of the passages from either Old or New Testament that I have read did I feel any sense of divine inspiration, neither was I left with the impression of words attributable to God. What did come across very strongly was a sense of antiquity and of time and place, which could only have come from the hand of a human author, however inspired (strictly with a lower case 'i') that author may have been. Amongst the other things that strike me most forcibly are just how parochial events described in the Bible are and the severe limitations of its authors who were writing under the influence of local conditions and the level of knowledge at the time, whereas I would expect the Word of God to have the qualities of Worldliness (as opposed to 'worldiness'), timelessness and infallibility; the example of Galileo and the geocentric Universe being just one that exhibits none of these qualities. Furthermore, there is no way that I, personally, can reconcile the brutal, unjust and unloving monster that is the God portrayed in the Bible, particularly in the Old Testament, with the compassionate, loving God that Christianity so blatantly sports in contradiction to the image that the Biblical God conveys; neither is the repeated use of threat and coercion that God constantly resorts to compatible with my simplistic impression of the ultimate force behind Creation. Having asked a number of Christians whether they have actually read the Bible, sufficient have replied either, "No", or, "a little", to convince me that the view of the Bible (and by extension the view of God) held by many Christians was either formed at Sunday school, or in RE classes at school, or from highly selective readings from the Bible in church and inasmuch is one of a benign, loving and caring God. In fact, the church subtly dissuades Christians from reading the Bible themselves but encourages conformity by feeding its congregations plenty of passages promising eternal life for those who acquiesce and unquestioningly accept the message they want to put over, with just enough of the fire-and-brimstone passages promising eternal damnation to subdue those who don't – the classical carrot and stick approach. On the other hand, the Church probably doesn't want its members straying unaccompanied too deeply into the Bible, much of which is either completely impenetrable, or absurd, or confusing and contradictory, or an orgy of blood-letting and depravity, with a cruel, vicious, jealous God who sometimes gratuitously advocates (amongst other abuses) ritual human and animal sacrifice, rape, murder and slavery, and at other times demands them as a sign of man's total submission before Him. Which brings me to the Koran. Having had six hundred years to observe the growing influence and success of Jewish and Christian monotheism, [I understand, from reading the history of the Koran, that] a number of fundamentalist Arabic religious leaders (hanifs) had already become impressed by Jewish and Christian monotheism and rejected idolatry for a more ascetic religion of their own; Muhammad appears to have been influenced by these hanifs. And lo and behold along came Islam at just the propitious moment. And here is the beauty of Islam: Its holy book – the Koran – on which Islam is based not only *claims to be* the literal Word of God handed down to the Prophet Mohammed by the Angel Gabriel but much of it reads as though it really is. And who can dispute that claim? Not I. But, having read parts of the Koran, it seems to bear many of the same hallmarks that render the Bible implausible as God's work, notwithstanding the fact that it seems to be more elegantly and poetically written. But here is the pivotal issue for me: Why would God choose to reveal Himself selectively to certain men through one very narrow channel and, even stranger still, through two (or more) very disparate and conflicting narrow channels, whilst He neglects the spiritual welfare of the majority of His creatures? Why not, if God has a message for us all, reveal it to each one of us in exactly the same way down every generation so there can be no doubting His omnipotence? And for me (as for everyone whose eyes and heart are open to it and whose mind is not cluttered with the bric-a-brac of religion) He has done just that: through the miracle of Creation.

However skeptical I am about the authorship of the Bible and however much I believe it to be the work of men it is, at the end of the day, only a book and one, moreover, that is two thousand years old and stuck in antiquity. The essence of its message is simple: Love God (but also fear Him) and love thy fellow man, which could equally well have been written by man as by God. But my real antipathy towards religion stems from my distrust of organised, institutionalised religion, its practices and its motives, which works on many levels (and is not restricted to Christianity). Even now, in the twenty-first century, the Catholic Church is being rocked by numerous scandals ranging from sexual abuse of children by priests to alleged involvement in serious fraud and financial misdealing at the highest level of the Church, all of which it has attempted to deny, downplay or cover up, leaving the injured parties struggling for justice whilst the Church has remained a cold, unresponsive edifice. And these aren't isolated incidences on an otherwise unblemished record. Dipping into the history of the Catholic Church reveals that it is not the single, seamless, harmonious unity whose sole purpose is to represent God on Earth and whose sole intention is to save men's souls from damnation, which is the image the Church would like you to believe. From its inception, the Church has been riven with corruption, intrigue and worldly interests, which stem from its power, position and wealth, and maintaining and increasing them. But, unlike any other institution, the Church has had a unique power which is its influence over and control of men's thoughts and it is this that I think the Church has abused most shamelessly.

So what are the levels of my distrust? Firstly, the calculated deceit of the Christan Church which has always sought to attract and ensnare its followers with a promise it cannot possibly keep. But isn't it also extremely clever of the Church to bait its hook with the one promise it knows will be irresistible to vulnerable, susceptible people living difficult, often miserable lives in abject poverty and grinding hardship on Earth: the promise of a better life in the next world than the life they're living in this world. What an empty promise! If the Church is really doing God's work, why hasn't it used its wealth, power and influence to improve the lot of people in this life and encouraged them to respect God, rather than fear Him?

Secondly, that the Church constantly plays on the threat that anyone who does not accept its creed will be excluded from the better life they're touting, which helps to ensure that it keeps its converts but only by frightening them into doing so. [I remember the smug arrogance of a couple of members of the Christian Society at the university I attended (derisively known around campus as the 'God Squad'), who tried converting me to Christianity by telling me that they had been saved and that their passage to Heaven was assured because they had accepted Christ into their lives, telling me that none could go to the Father (God) except through the Son (Jesus Christ) and that unless I likewise accepted Christ into my life (and along with Christ the whole of the Christian faith) I would be damned to spend eternity in Hell. These 'henchmen of The Lord' clearly enjoyed their work because, after the briefest introduction to their faith, they were shamelessly extorting my soul. In Heaven and Hell the Church has created two extremely powerful marketing tools but also ones that are extremely manipulative; at the end of the day the Church's very existence is attributable to the former and its survival is attributable to the latter.]

Thirdly, far from the Church's position on God being steadfast and unwavering, which it would be if it was bearing witness to an absolute truth, it is constantly changing its stance to suit the mood of the moment. [Even the Bible was something of a moveable feast. To the best of my understanding of the history of the Catholic Church, the content of its Bible wasn't finally fixed until 1546 by the Council of Trent (sitting at Trento in what is now modern-day Italy). Until then it would appear that different factions of the Church continued to pick and choose those bits of holy scripture that best suited their needs, which undermines its claim to be an eternal truth.] Anyway, to return to the example I cited earlier of the age of the Earth: Based on the Old Testament account of Creation in Genesis, the Bible would have us believe it took God six days to create Heaven and Earth and everything in it (including man) which He did six thousand years ago and when He'd done He was so knackered by His labours that He had to give Himself a day off. However, the Church cannot now simply ignore the overwhelming mass of scientific evidence available today which finds that the Earth and Universe (i.e. Heaven) are considerably older than

Bishop Ussher would have us believe and that our planet and the life on it have evolved gradually over eons, in the Darwinian sense, interspersed with occasional cataclysmic events that have thrown everything back into the melting pot. As a consequence of this controversy, the Church has now shamelessly shifted its position to bring itself in line with modern scientific thinking but it has tried explaining away this discrepancy by quoting from scripture [2 Peter 3:8], "...that one day is with the Lord as a thousand years, and a thousand years as one day" and claiming that Genesis was not actually referring to a 23-hour-56-minute sidereal day, equivalent to one rotation of the Earth, but to a far longer period. Notwithstanding the fact that all the convoluted arguments the Church has employed to square this particular circle ultimately fail under close scrutiny, they also make it look ridiculous into the bargain. But in burdening the Creator with all the same human frailties as the rest of us the Bible severely restricts God's power. I cannot even begin to guess at the link between the physical reality of Creation and its metaphysical dimension – this is my one and only act of faith – but for me that God created the Universe in an instant is far more awe-inspiring than it taking Him a working week. And for me that the Earth is four-and-a-half billion years old – a venerable age in itself – in a Universe that is three times that age is far more majestic than it being six thousand years old.

Another consequence of the Old Testament version of Creation is that God created everything as it is today, including man's weakness and his susceptibility to temptation, as well as pain, suffering, loss, tragedy and everything else that we rail against God for when times are bad and thank Him for when times are good. But ditch the narrow view of Creation as presented in the Bible and along with it the idea of an interventionist God and it allows you to think of God more simply and clearly: as the force which inspired Creation, which brought the Universe into existence and then let it develop according to the laws of nature (or physics, if you prefer) and you can suddenly divest God of all responsibility for earthly tragedies such as natural disasters, terminally ill children and all the rest; they no longer become His doing.

Finally, there is the abject and immoral state of the Church itself which, I believe, serves itself rather than God. The (Catholic) Church (in particular) has created a system of religious beliefs enforced by exceedingly complex laws and rituals which can only be defined, interpreted and administered by its appointed ministers. All of this is extremely proscriptive and removes any freedom of thought and action from its followers who are in danger of going through the motions of their faith by rote – that is to say, robotically – without giving any real thought to God. If nothing else, I can only imagine that if God had been the author of the Bible and had established Christianity as the religion to represent

Him on Earth, He would have made it eminently simple, sensible, accessible and acceptable to all without the necessity of guardians. Even now, in an age of enlightenment when many people can read and the Bible has been translated into many languages, does the Church insist on complicating what should be a simple truth accessible to all. [For an example of how inaccessible the Church makes this, I have just read an interview with Rowan Williams, Archbishop of Canterbury, entitled 'Explaining God to the godless' in The Daily Telegraph of Saturday, August 20, 2005, which puts forward such arcane (and groundless) concepts and unsubstantiated ideas to explain God and man's relationship with Him that I for one cannot understand the Church's arguments (and, judging by the number of Letters to the Editor in the Monday 22nd edition about the interview, it would appear that many other readers, Christians included, cannot understand them either). However, the most telling points for me are when he states that, "...*the idea* of life after death isn't a function of something that survives *but something to do with our doctrine of God*" and a little later on admits [about the transition from life to death], "*And something has got to be* continuous between now [life] and then [death]. Unfortunately, we haven't got a clue how that works." All of this tells me that matters central to the Christian faith are simply men's invention (or possibly wishful thinking), rather than fact based on the word of God. The bald truth is that the Archbishop of Canterbury, who is head of the Church of England and whose role is the spiritual guidance of the Anglican Communion with 70 million members worldwide, has no greater take on God or on life-after-death than you or I. But, hitherto, before there was the degree of freedom of thought and speech that we enjoy today, the Church would have tried deluding or bullying you into believing unquestioningly that it is the only authority on all matters religious, speaking with the power of God. Why? To protect its own interests.] But why all this obfuscation? To bamboozle you and deter you from questioning matters that the Church would arrogantly say were exclusively its preserve and beyond your understanding; in reality, to prevent you from arriving at the realisation that the Church is (admittedly a strong structure) built on a weak foundation.

But far worse than the Church building on sand in creating the religion of Christianity from the Bible are the terrible and inhuman extremes it has resorted to to uphold it. Amongst other things, I cannot believe that any church which truly represented God on Earth would need to resort to the Inquisition which was to the Catholic Church what the Gestapo was to the National Socialist German Workers' (Nazi) Party – purposely to terrify its followers into conformity and to put down any dissent. If the Bible is God's truth that fact should shine through and be impervious to any questions about its veracity, whereas the Bible has been shown to be so spectacularly wrong over fundamental issues. On a superficial level, the Church's insistence that the

Bible is the absolute truth has made the Bible and the Church look ridiculous. But on a deeper, darker level, the Church's response to anyone who refused to accept its so-called "truth", or even questioned it, was, quite literally, diabolical. Coming back to the example of Galileo and the geocentric Universe, it is very illuminating to understand why the Church was so determined to suppress the truth: The charges of heresy were brought against Galileo by various priests because the Church asserted that dreadful consequences for Christian theology must follow if the Heavenly bodies were proved to revolve about the Sun and not about the Earth. The 'dreadful consequences' that so concerned Galileo's accusers included, "...his [Galileo's] pretended discovery vitiates the whole Christian plan of salvation"; "It casts suspicion on the doctrine of the incarnation"; and "It upsets the whole basis of theology. If the Earth is a planet, and only one among several planets, it cannot be that any such great things have been done specially for it as the Christian doctrine teaches. If there are other planets, since God makes nothing in vain, they must be inhabited; but how can their inhabitants be descended from Adam? How can they trace back their origin to Noah's Ark? How can they have been redeemed by the Saviour?" The Church was obviously terrified that Galileo's claim would totally discredit it by demonstrating that it was preaching a false doctrine. Working back from that, not only do their concerns suggest that the exceedingly implausible story of Jesus Christ had been woven by the Church to further its own ends (whether these particular priests knew it or not), but the Church realised that the whole carefully constructed deception would unravel if just one of the threads broke. It is also clear that the Church's sole concern at the time was to protect the status quo at any cost, rather than to arrive at the truth. It is very dangerous to claim divinity because that equates to infallability which the Church and the Bible on which it is founded clearly are not.

In the year 308, a member of the early Christian church, Lactantius, who stood for absolute freedom of religion, wrote in his Divine Institutes:
'Religion being a matter of the will, it cannot be forced on anyone; in this matter it is better to employ words than blows. Of what use is cruelty? What has the rack to do with piety? Surely there is no connection between truth and violence, between justice and cruelty. It is true that nothing is so important as religion, and one must defend it at any cost. It is true that it must be protected, but by dying for it, not by killing others; by long-suffering, not by violence; by faith, not by crime. If you attempt to defend religion by bloodshed and torture, what you do is not defense, but desecration and insult. For nothing is so intrinsically a matter of free will as religion.'
It is clear from this that, even then, the Church was either considering or actually resorting to torturing and killing anyone whose beliefs differed from those of the Church (even though at this time there were many factions within

the Christian community with widely differing beliefs). But it is absolutely appalling how the level of intolerance within the Church deteriorated so dramatically from the time of Lactantius that it produced the Inquisition which was responsible for a reign of terror that saw tens of thousands of innocent people murdered and hundreds of thousands tortured, imprisoned, dispossessed of their property, or otherwise punished by the Church or by the civil authorities doing the Church's dirty work. So what is, or was, the Church's position on this? In the year 2000, Pope John Paul II publicly apologised for "the unnecessary violence used", and later released a letter in which he wrote, 'The image of the Inquisition represents almost the symbol... of scandal'. This tepid and indifferent response is hardly a resounding condemnation of the Church's actions and a promise to put things right. For me, the *key* word in the Pope's limp apology is *'unnecessary'* (although I suspect the Pope meant that the degree of violence used was excessive, not that the Church had no right to persecute people for their beliefs in the first place). In my opinion, the fact that the Church and various popes down through history have sanctioned and encouraged systematic murder, torture, imprisonment and a gamut of other brutal punishments of *innocent* people simply because they would not bend to the Church's will is more than just a scandal; it is a crime against humanity and something God would never have sanctioned.

[And so you don't mistakenly think all this took place in medieval times before the Enlightenment, the last execution (called an 'auto da fé', or 'act of faith') due to the infamous Spanish Inquisition took place on July 26, 1826 and involved a schoolmaster by the name of Cayetano Ripoll who was tried on a charge of Deism and found guilty. He was hanged after repeating the words, "I die reconciled to God and to man". It is interesting to note that this innocent man was brutally murdered by the Catholic Church not for denying the existence of God – *he actually believed in God* – but for refusing to accept the Catholic Church's religion of Christianity. And had I lived in Spain or any other predominantly Catholic country two hundred years ago I would probably have enjoyed a similar fate for writing this piece and you may have done so too simply for reading it and expressing sympathy with its views.]

The focus of my comments so far has been on the Christian Church and other religious institutions. But what of their adherents? Whereas belief in God is simple, easy, and above all, unconditional – you either believe in God or you don't – acceptance of and adherence to a particular religion requires a certain degree of fanatacism, amongst other things to suspend credulity in order to believe its fantastical claims unquestioningly, in exactly the same way as believing in fairy tales would. [What is interesting but goes unsaid is that religion doesn't get its adherents any nearer to God than they would be without it.] Whilst conditions remain benign in that those religious beliefs go unchallenged and free from external pressures, that fanatacism remains in check. But when conditions become less favorable and adherents are forced to decide whether they are true believers, or not, they have two distinct but mutually-exclusive choices: either to abandon their religion, which raises the question, 'Why bother having it in the first place?', or to defend it, which raises the question, 'How far to go in defending it?'. And, for a true believer, the only answer must be 'As far as it takes, including going all the way, if necessary'. And recently we have seen the extremes that some individuals will go to in the name of their religion (whether their actions are to defend it, or to promote it), such as the attacks of 9/11, which includes the most fanatical believers killing others and, in some instances, themselves. [It was interesting to note that in the wake of the recent London bombings (July 7, 2005) by Muslim suicide bombers linked with al-Qaeda, the response of the moderate Muslim community (as well as some UK politicians and senior police officers) was to deny that these terrorists were true Muslims because their actions in killing others and themselves were against the laws of Islam. Notwithstanding the fact that this is a completely fatuous argument which was probably intended to distance the bombers from the Muslim community at large in the minds of outraged non-Muslims (Muslim leaders also declared that because the bombers could not be true Muslims, it was not for the Muslim community to deal with the problem) but, for all that, it doesn't change the fact that the bombers *believed* themselves to be true Muslims defending their faith and gave the ultimate sacrifice – their lives – to demonstrate their commitment to Islam. It is also interesting (and disturbing) to note that some young Muslims, interviewed shortly after the bombings, stated that it was their intention to turn Britain into an Islamic nation, which was rich coming from individuals who have lived here for only a very brief time, who have contributed very little, if anything, to the nation, who resist assimilation into British society and who live by and large in what could best be described as ghettos (although, in some cases, these ghettos extend to the whole, or greater part, of certain cities). In this declaration it is possible to see the seeds of religious fanaticism which can only cause widespread tension leading to inevitable confrontation once they germinate.]

It was in researching the age of the Earth on the Internet that I came across websites by Young-Earth Creationists who maintain that it is about six thousand years old, as proposed by Archbishop Ussher. [These generally employ the most arcane, unscientific and unsubstantiated arguments, so that when they fail to come up with anything convincing they usually resort to saying that, with God, everything is possible.] In these, the Noachian flood is heavily quoted to explain away geological features that are clearly ancient – and by that, I mean tens, hundreds, or even thousands of millions of years old –

many of which have evolved over eons, which set me about researching the story of Noah and his Ark. In all of this, I was most impressed (in a very dismal, negative sense) by the fanaticism displayed by the 'pseudo-scientific' YECs among the Christian community in trying to persuade a skeptical world (and themselves, I suspect) that these events really did happen as described in Genesis. I was also equally impressed (again, in a depressing sort of way) and occasionally amused by the alternative websites that used logical, scientific argument and widely accepted physical evidence to demonstrate that both claims are utter bunkum (one site putting forward rational arguments against it summed up the story of Noah's Ark as 'a load of old cobblers'). Whilst children may accept the story at face value, I suggest it would be impossible to convert to Christianity any right-minded adult that had been exposed to a modicum of science and natural history by telling them the utterly ridiculous and implausible story of six-hundred-year-old Noah and his Ark, with walk-on parts (or crawl-, slither-, hop-, skip-, jump- or fly-on parts) for (at least) one breeding pair of every land-based creature both living and extinct, and an all-consuming flood, none of which stands even the least probing scientific examination. So why, having been indoctrinated with this fairy story as a child, do so many Christians insist on clinging to it when they grow up? The answer can only be fanaticism. And how, if by the time they reach the age of reason they disbelieve it, can they still adhere to the Christian faith explicitly? Again, the only answer I can think of is fanaticism which allows them to suspend credulity, to believe that black is white solely because the Church tells them it is when the evidence of their own senses (if they stop long enough to exercise them) tells them that black is black.

As science uncovers more facts about the Earth and Universe, the Church, by its fanatical insistence that the Bible is the literal (and infallible) word of God (and therefore an absolute and incontrovertible truth), is making itself look increasingly ridiculous and less relevant in the modern age. In refusing to abandon its literal interpretation of two-thousand year old scripture written by men whose knowledge of the World was extremely limited compared with ours today (in favor, possibly, of an allegorical interpretation), the Church is asking modern people to abandon all current knowledge arrived at scientifically and instead accept things that confound their reason. Instead, why doesn't the Church do something really bold and abandon the Bible and simplify its creed to a belief in God as Creator – which must be the core of anyone's religious beliefs – and an acceptence of Christian principles which, surely, aren't that different from the principles of other religions because, at the end of the day, they are simply human values? And the same goes for Islam and the Koran, and for other religions and their holy books, too, then we might all live free from religious division. Why don't I expect religions to do this anytime soon?

Because the Bible, the Koran, and the holy books, belief systems and rituals that define all religions have nothing to do with God and everything to do with mortal men and their religious superstitions, that's why!

At the start of this book, I mentioned the Reverend David Sheppard, Anglican Bishop of Liverpool. One of the actions for which he is best remembered is walking together with his oppo', the Roman Catholic Archbishop of Liverpool, the late Derek Worlock, dressed in their robes of office, down the aptly named Hope Street (which, coincidentally, joins the city's two cathedrals) to sign a covenant of unity that helped to heal many rifts in the city. [At that time – 1985 – Liverpool was suffering from depression and widespread unemployment, leading to a dislocation of community life, and racial tension which culminated in the infamous Toxteth riots.] Sheppard (and no doubt Worlock, too) was reputed to be a great advocate of ecumenicalism – that is, the promotion of unity amongst different Christian churches – which suggests that he (they) thought the differences in their doctrines were of second-order importance and working together for peace and harmony was more important; the irony being that many of the rifts were down to the conflict between Catholics and Protestants, which can only have their roots in the superstitions of their religions even though such distinctions, however trivial, may long have been forgotten. Here were two men with so much in common – they were both white, English-speaking, with similar human (i.e. physical, emotional and spiritual) needs and [I assume] truly believed in one God. The only thing that divided them was religion and not fundamentally different religions either but versions of the same religion. Why? Because the two versions can't even agree on something so fatuous as how many angels can dance on the head of a pin! [By the way, I know the answer to this but I'm not going to tell you because there's bound to be some Bibled-up whack-job out there, drunk on holy spirit, who thinks they know differently and wants to dispute it!] How much simpler, more productive, influential and effective these men's lives and the lives of their parishoners would have been had there been no difference between their religions. And by extending this argument, how much simpler, more productive and more effective would men's lives be generally with only one, very simple religion – the religion of Deism – that only calls for a belief in God without all of the fantastical, divisive and ultimately pointless superstition that goes along with other, more complex religions that necessitate believing highly implausible or impossible things which are often the things that cause tension, division and conflict.

Where would that leave Atheists? Just as Deists and other believers cannot prove the existence of God, Atheists cannot disprove it. I have read various works by Atheists, which seem to argue against the existence of God either on

313

scientific grounds, stating that in their opinion it is extremely unlikely, or on the basis that the God of the Bible is cruel and brutal and undeserving of recognition which, to my mind, is denying God rather than denying God's existence. In fact, many Atheists seem to have given far more mature and considered thought to the existence (or, more precisely, the non-existence) of God and have put in more effort to arrive at their belief than many who profess to believe, although I think that both camps are equally (and infinitely) far away from knowing the truth. However, for an adult to declare themself an Atheist at least demonstrates they have given some thought to God which, in itself, is a form of devotion. So much for everyone else. What about myself?

It was in thinking about the Universe and the reality of existence that I became aware of God. I think it happened gradually, by a process of 'spiritual osmosis'. In my mind's eye, I would travel past the planets and out of our solar system, then past myriad stars out of our galaxy and across vast tracts of inter-galactic space toward the edge of the Universe. Every time, before I could arrive at the boundary between our existence and the void beyond, I always felt a presence watching me, which gave me the most unusual sensation as though there was a pressure on my chest preventing me from breathing. Although I couldn't actually see my watcher, I felt the presence all around me and realised it was God who was filling the void, *who was the void*, who was *seeing me* in His mind's eye. In the instant of recognition, I also sensed that our Universe is just one in an infinity of universes, continuously being brought into existence in the mind of God. And with infinity goes eternity. I can only believe that God is immortal, which suggests He also has infinite patience which He would need if He had to wait 13.7 billion years for a life form to emerge that has developed an awareness of Him [although here I differ from the Catholic Church in that I do not think we are alone in the Universe, or in believing in God, and I certainly do not accept their assertion that Creation was done specially for us. Notwithstanding the near-certainty, statistically, of there being other intelligent, thinking life forms on other benign planets orbiting life-giving stars in this vast Universe of ours (and irrespective of it), that would be far too profligate a waste of Creation]. But having waited so long for a creature to emerge that is capable of the abstract thought and articulate language necessary to express a belief in God, what must God think when, no sooner does it do so than it starts squabbling over who has first claim on God and killing each other to settle the dispute.

As I said at the outset, whilst I believe that nothing is or ever will be *known* of the existence or nature of God (the operative word here being 'known'), I *believe in* God. However, I also believe that had God wanted man to *know* of His existence and nature *explicitly* (as opposed to believing in God by inference

314

from the evidence of the Creator that we see all around us), I believe that God would have revealed Himself to all of us; that God chooses to remain mysterious is not for man to question or to speculate over. There is simply no explaining God.

It wasn't until I was part-way through writing this book that I discovered the works of Thomas Paine who was a Deist and a powerful advocate of human rights. On reading his book, 'The Age of Reason', and other essays such as, 'Of the Religion of Deism compared with the Christian Religion', I found that they so closely expressed my sentiments – and far more eloquently than I ever could – that I realised that all along what I am is a Deist; from that moment on, instead of feeling something of an outcast, I knew I had found my true spiritual home – one in which my soul is my church. I put my trust in God that, when my time comes to shrug off this mortal coil, He will deal with me mercifully.

Anyway, religion has been with man in one form or another for thousands of years and I don't expect my ranting will change that so, having said my piece, it's time to draw it to a close. If I've singled out Christianity generally and the Catholic Church in particular for scrutiny, it is only because the abuse of its power and position are most visible; I have no doubt other modern-day religions could be justifiably accused of similar abuses. I suspect that revealed religions have taken root, survived and spread more because they provide frightened men with some comfort in this world and some hope that they will not be alone in the void with no prospect when the light goes out in this life of it being rekindled in the next, than because they provide a personal link to God. But because of the power they have over men, revealed religions aren't going to relinquish their claim of divinity lightly.

The End, thank God!